CW00956355

Tom Cole was born in Engl
Australia as a seventeen-year-o.
bush, droving, horsebreaking and working as a stockman
in Queensland and the Northern Territory, as well as a brief
period as a linesman on the overland telegraph line. Then
he went buffalo shooting.

He described himself as the only buffalo hunter alive
who was an active horseback hunter, broke in his own
shooting horses, held five hundred square miles of country
and employed tribal Aborigines as his assistants. During
these years before the war, crocodiles were a sideline.

After the Second World War he earned a reputation as a
crocodile hunter in New Guinea. His experiences were the
inspiration for his collection of short stories, *Spear and
Smoke Signals*, published in 1986. He was awarded the
Medal of the Order of Australia in 1994 for his contribution to history. Tom Cole died in December 1995.

Hell West
and Crooked

TOM COLE

Angus&Robertson
An imprint of HarperCollins*Publishers*

Angus&Robertson

An imprint of HarperCollins*Publishers,* Australia

First published in Australia by Collins Publishers in 1988
Reprinted in 1988 (six times), 1989 (twice)
A&R Imprint edition 1990
Reprinted in 1990, 1991, 1992 (twice), 1993, 1994 (twice)
This A&R Classic edition 1995
Reprinted in 1997
by HarperCollins*Publishers* Pty Limited
ACN 009 913 517
A member of the HarperCollins*Publishers* (Australia) Pty Limited Group

Copyright © The estate of Tom Cole 1988

This book is copyright.
Apart from any fair dealing for the purposes of private study, research,
criticism or review, as permitted under the Copyright Act, no part may
be reproduced by any process without written permission.
Inquiries should be addressed to the publishers.

HarperCollins*Publishers*
25 Ryde Road, Pymble, Sydney, NSW 2073, Australia
31 View Road, Glenfield, Auckland 10, New Zealand
77-85 Fulham Palace Road, London W6 8JB, United Kingdom
Hazelton Lanes, 55 Avenue Road, Suite 2900, Toronto, Ontario M5R 3L2
and 1995 Markham Road, Scarborough, Ontario M1B 5M8, Canada
10 East 53rd Street, New York NY 10032, USA

National Library of Australia Cataloguing-in-Publication data:

Cole, Tom, 1906–1995.
Hell west and crooked.
ISBN 0 207 18984 6.
1. Cole, Tom, 1906– .
2. Stockmen–Northern Territory–Biography.
Hunters–Northern Territory–Biography.
4. Frontier and pioneer life–Northern Territory.
I. Title.
994.29'009'94

Cover photograph of Tom Cole
Typeset in Clearface by Love Computer Setting Pty Ltd, Sydney
Printed in Australia by Griffin Press, Adelaide

9 8 7 6 5 4 3 2   97 98 99

For my wife Kathleen,
who sadly will not see it now,
and my daughters Kathryn and Gabrielle
who will.

Hell west and crooked
A cattleman's expression meaning all over the place.
"The horses are hell west and crooked —
it'll take a week to muster them."

Contents

INTRODUCTION

I first saw the light of day in London, in 1906. It doesn't seem to have been an earth-shattering event — no bolts of lightning, no earthquakes, nothing whatever of a cataclysmic nature. Maybe just a muffled pop.

I have no recollection of that city as a child; we moved to the country in Kent a year or so later, which I loved. My memories are very vague. A big house, sweeping lawns, a magnificent wisteria smothering a large tree, orchards, glasshouses and a big dog, Jack, who went everywhere with me. My father was not a very good businessman, though I knew nothing of such things then. We left there and went to another place, also in Kent, to what I recall was a fairly large orchard that grew every kind of fruit. There are always memories that stay . . . there was a grove of huge walnut trees and my brother and I soon found we were able to dye our faces a marvellous dark colour with the skins, turning us into instant Indians. Our enthusiasm was not shared by our mother, the dye took a week to remove.

It was here that what I regarded as a serious interruption to my education occurred — I was compelled to go to school, one of the more undistinguished periods of my life. I have no doubt the relief I felt when I left was only exceeded by that of my teachers.

At the age of seventeen, I decided to leave England for what was then known as 'the colonies'. It was not a difficult decision to make. In a family of eight I was the eldest son, and though I believe I was of an amiable disposition, it was not sufficiently amiable to endear myself to my father — a feeling that was reciprocated. As events turned out, perhaps I should be grateful to him.

Like most lads of seventeen I was not unduly burdened with a wealth of worldly knowledge (and perhaps it was fortunate that the sum total of my beliefs were in inverse ratio to the facts); I have always been given to making lightning decisions and in 1923, when I saw posters beckoning young empire-builders, I had no doubt where my destiny lay.

The advertisements were for Canada, New Zealand and Australia. Those of Canada and New Zealand depicted scenes of emerald green pastures with a backdrop of breathtaking snow-capped mountains. I had no doubt what winter would be like there! I have always hated the cold and for several months of the year was miserable with cold feet and chilblains: most kids looked forward to presents at Christmas — I always knew I was going to get chilblains.

Although I regarded myself as having reached 'man's estate' (I have always believed that the year a person was born and the age he is are two different things), my next move had to be planned with a good deal of circumspection. Regardless of what I thought, I was still a minor by law and consequently my parents' permission was required; while my father had little affection for me, he would undoubtedly have vetoed my projected Australian adventure had he thought it was something I wanted to do.

My mother was a very patient and lovely lady and I now know that when I asked her to help me go to Australia, it was a heart-wrenching decision for her: but she believed it was for the best.

We enlisted the help of my Uncle George who, presumably, forged my father's signature on the relevant documents. I received my sailing instructions and set off for London on a rare and lovely August day. I stayed with my grandmother for a few days before joining an Orient line ship RMS Ormuz at Tilbury, on the Thames. My elder sister Peggy was the only one who came to farewell me.

August has always been an eventful month for me: it was the month I left England; it was the month when I started buffalo shooting for myself; the month in which I was married; my wife's birthday is also in August and it also marked the arrival of our firstborn, our daughter Kathryn.

I suppose the date of sailing should be imprinted indelibly on my memory, but I must admit that all I can recall is that it was about the middle of the month.

It's worth recording that, though my absence from the hearth and home must have been obvious, it would seem my father was determined not to notice it. A fortnight later, when presumably he couldn't stand it any longer, at breakfast one morning he asked: "Where's Tom?" My mother replied: "He's gone to Australia." He never mentioned my name again.

The voyage was almost uneventful. I saw Mount Vesuvius erupting and lighting up the Mediterranean. I had the depressing experience of seeing a man buried at sea and we fouled the anchor chain on a buoy in the Suez Canal.

My first sight of Australia was Fremantle. Then on to Adelaide and Melbourne. A few days later we sailed through Sydney Heads as the sun was rising; I thought it was the most beautiful sight I had ever seen. We promptly went in to dry dock for repairs to the propeller, which had been damaged in the Canal incident. We were there for ten days.

When the repairs were complete, the ship continued to Brisbane, my destination. The Department of Immigration had lots of jobs lined up and I unhesitatingly took one on a cattle property in the Maranoa District — because it was the furthest out. There was no competition.

I have no clear recollection of my first experience with horses or learning to ride, but looking back it seems that riding never presented any difficulties and I liked horses.

I trapped rabbits in my spare time. I bought a Winchester rifle

7

and shot kangaroos, making a little money from the skins. Then, with the approval of the manager of the property where I was working, I went to the Northern Territory.

In the 1920s this was another world where cattle stations were measured in thousands of square miles; where there were no fences; where herds were too big to be counted and calculations were done by multiplying the brandings by four.

The first cattle station I worked on was Lake Nash. The furthest sub-artesian bore from the homestead was a hundred miles, yet still inside the boundary. I quickly adapted to the routine of station life. I went droving with a thousand and more bullocks in one mob, over a hundred miles, sleeping on the ground every night, taking my turn riding round the cattle in the still and silent watches of the night.

My experiences were many and varied: the Overland Telegraph Line; the packhorse mails; the bush race meetings; horse-breaking; then buffalo and crocodile hunting.

In this book I recount not only my own experiences but also those of other men with whom I worked and respected — the pioneers, such as Nat Buchanan, whose names and exploits were still fresh in men's memories. This would not be complete without a tribute to the many Aborigines with whom I worked and got to know so well. Their amazing endurance in that harsh unforgiving environment, their bushmanship and incredible tracking and hunting abilities, their uncanny skill with their primitive spears and boomerangs, never ceased to amaze me.

I have been fortunate in that for many years I kept diaries and also that my mother, who died at the age of 101, kept all the letters I wrote from the day I left England. I am glad to say I was a fairly regular correspondent.

CHAPTER 1

FROM SUITCASE
TO SWAG

E ngland seemed a long, long way away in 1925. In fact, it
was only eighteen months behind me, and I was nineteen
years of age.

I was in the head office of the Queensland National Pastoral
Company, a subsidiary of the Queensland National Bank, one of
Australia's largest cattle companies, whose dominion en-
compassed some 30,000 square miles, from the centre of Queensland across to the Northern Territory. The office was spacious and
well appointed. On the walls were photographs of ribbon-
bedecked cattle, magnificent horses and station homesteads set
among gum trees. Behind a polished oak desk sat a benign
gentleman of sandy complexion, peering at me over the top of his
rimless spectacles. Another gentleman sprawled in an armchair to
his side. I stood before them, burning with empire-building zeal.
The gentleman with the spectacles addressed me.

"Well, Cole," he said, "you are the type of man we are always
looking for — unfortunately, all too rare." I swelled with pride. "I
am confident," he continued, "that not only will you make your
mark with this company [I swelled a little more] but if you identify
yourself with your work, in the Northern Territory generally."
The swelling process continued until it was getting positively
painful. The gentleman in the armchair was nodding affably. What
great chaps they must be to work for, I thought. What a wonderful
company I am joining!

I assumed I was supposed to say something in the brief silence
that followed, but being suddenly overcome with a mixture of the

9

great Australian pioneering spirit, and intense verbal inadequacy, all I could do was stutter "Thank you!" The taller of the two, who sat behind the desk, nodded to his colleague, who then cleared his throat and handed me an envelope.

"You will find there your railway tickets", he said. "You take the train from Brisbane to Townsville and change to a train for Cloncurry. From Cloncurry you take another train to Duchess, and from there you take the mail coach to Lake Nash. There is also twenty pounds for out-of-pocket expenses. We wish you every good fortune."

The generosity overwhelmed me. The shorter man continued: "When you arrive at Lake Nash you will report to the manager, Mr Sutton. He is expecting you." There was a pregnant pause. "Your wages will be one pound a week", he added, "with keep of course", as though it were a bonus of considerable magnitude.

There was a drumming noise in my ears. One pound — he can't be serious! A fellow of my calibre! The deflationary process was rapid, accompanied by a slight hissing noise, which appeared to go unnoticed. A few minutes later I was standing in Queen Street, Brisbane, clutching an envelope that contained 1500 miles of tickets and twenty pounds. The words "one pound a week" were still ringing in my ears.

Three days later I left the train at Cloncurry; I asked the station-master when was the next train to Duchess. "The next day," he said — "if it gets back!" He didn't say from where: I assumed from Duchess. I stood there for a while collecting my thoughts, then asked him where the nearest pub was. "Up the road a bit," he said. I set off in the direction he indicated, lugging my suitcase. It seemed several miles from the railway station to the hotel, but I suppose at the very most it was no more than a quarter of a mile. There couldn't be anywhere like this in the world, I thought. The heat was searing, and flies were clustering in their millions. There wasn't a soul in sight, nor a breath of wind; and the temperature, I had been informed at the railway station, was 112 in the shade. What it was in the sun was anyone's guess.

I arrived at the hotel. Three unsaddled horses were tied up in the shade of a gum, and their saddles lay at the foot of the tree. A subdued hum came from the direction of the bar as I pushed through the door. It took a while to become accustomed to the gloom. Five or six men at the bar turned and looked at me as I came in.

It was an unusual scene.

They were unusual men. One lay stretched out on a bench, snoring, flies hovering over him in a black cloud. From time to time the beat of his snoring changed slightly as a few flies disappeared into his mouth. Another held the floor reciting a classic and anonymous bush poem:

We was going down the Hamilton
With a mob of travellin' stock,
The days was fuckin' dusty,
The nights was fuckin' hot.
The cattle they was rushin',
The horses fuckin' poor,
The boss he was a bastard,
And the cook a fuckin' whore.

A round of applause greeted this masterpiece of elocution, and they refilled their glasses from a bottle of rum that stood on the counter.

One of the men, who appeared to be a stockman, called to me: "Come and join us, stranger." I left my suitcase in a corner and walked over. He held out his hand and said: "I'm Steve Johnson and this is Duncan Booth, commonly known as the Spotted Wonder." Booth laughed. "This is Harry Sloan, and this old death adder is George Smith. Over there is Dan Howard, that's George McHugh and that old bastard passed out over there is Bill Anderson, and what will you drink?" I introduced myself. "I'm Tom Cole," I said, "and I'll have a cold beer."

"Well, you'll be bloody lucky to get that," he replied. The barman went to a box-like contraption, covered in damp hessian, that swung from a wire from the ceiling and took out a bottle of

11

beer. Feeling it he said, "It's pretty cold." Steve laughed. "It's probably just off the boil if I know anything."

I poured a glass, and thought Steve wasn't far wrong. Before I'd drunk half, flies started to drop into the glass; and as fast as I fished them out, more dropped in. One of the men said: "You'll never get a drink that way, just strain it through your teeth!"

Another said: "You're better off drinking rum — they're not so keen on rum" and added as an afterthought, "It's not as if they were real bad this time of the year — if it wasn't for Bill over there [nodding toward the man on the bench] there'd be twice as many!"

Bill must have heard him. He gave an explosive cough and flies shot out of his mouth like tiny black cannonballs. I looked at him and asked Steve: "Is he all right?"

"Christ yes! You couldn't kill him with a dose of his own strychnine. He's in the skin and hair trade," he added by way of explanation, and then he enlarged on that with, "He's a dog stiffener!"

I had no idea what the skin and hair trade was, but didn't like to show my ignorance. I thought perhaps it was something to do with catching stray dogs around the town. Someone asked where I was heading, and I told them I was going to Lake Nash.

Dan Howard said: "Well, you could do worse" George HcHugh: "And you could do better, but not much, I s'pose." Duncan Booth: "It's not too bad. I've broken in there for the past couple of years, and I've got about forty colts to break as soon as it rains."

We drank for a while and I listened carefully. I was in another world. I soon gathered that Dan Howard was a drover and had just delivered a thousand bullocks to somewhere outside Brisbane; Duncan Booth was a horse breaker; Harry Sloan was a stockman who had been with Dan Howard, and George Smith was one of his men too — the cook. I still hadn't found out about Bill Anderson the "dog stiffener" who was in the "skin and hair trade". They talked of nothing but cattle, horses, the tremendous cattle runs.

12

Anything less than 5000 square miles hardly got a mention —
Alexandria Station was 10,000 square miles, Brunette Downs was
8000, Wave Hill 6000 — but the daddy of them all was Victoria
River Downs, referred to as "The Wickham" because, as I found
out later, the station homestead was on the bank of the Wickham
River. Victoria River Downs was 13,000 square miles — slightly
larger than Belgium!

They talked of Western Queensland, the Northern Territory
and the Kimberleys in Western Australia as though they were
their back yards. They knew every stock route from Derby in
Western Australia to Rockhampton on the Queensland coast;
from Delta Downs on the Gulf of Carpentaria in the north to
Wodonga in Victoria. They spoke of droving trips with a thousand
bullocks, 1500 miles from start to finish, six months "on the
road", bores broken down and water holes a caked claypan —
three and four days without water, and not losing a beast. They
talked of floods, raging bush fires, cattle stampeding at night and
horsemen falling in the lead of galloping bullocks . . . and surviving.

I listened to the stories of Tie Wire Edwards — the toughest
manager Kidman employed, and proud of it — who managed
Glengyle Station: you got treacle only on Sundays. And Jack
Clarke, who lost 600 bullocks on the Birdsville track on a 100-
mile dry stage, the day before he was to have reached water. Of
Jimmy Fowler, the only man who ever rode the famous Alexandria
outlaw The Murderer to a standstill; of Bullwaddy Jack, and Peter
the Dane. Of Tommy Mathews, one of their heroes, who had stolen
enough cattle to stock at least two stations — ("He'd pinch a
bridle off a nightmare!") — and had never broken the eleventh
commandment (Thou shalt not get caught.). In years to come I
was to have nearly all these experiences and get to know most of
these men, and many others of a similar calibre. Men who lived
hard, and rode hard; men who never deserted a friend, who never
forgot an enemy.

The afternoon drifted by, and then the blessed relief of night. Suddenly there were no flies. At some time or other we left the bar, and I found I was sharing a room with Steve in a corrugated iron cubicle with two beds. With a bottle of rum between us we talked into the early hours of morning, and I will always look back on it as a valuable contribution to my education. I was anxious to learn and eager to listen. He had grown up with cattle and horses — knew no other life and wanted no other life.

He asked me a few questions about my own background, and I told him how I had come out from England, gone straight to the bush and had had two jobs, both with cattle in the St George district a couple of hundred miles west of Brisbane.

Rutherglen, the first place I worked, was 30,000 acres. Later I moved to a nearby property Homeboin, 150,000 acres — big enough to be called a station. Steve referred to that area as "inside". "You've come from inside," he said, "and you'll find things a hell of a lot different where you're going. I've never been on Lake Nash, but there's not much difference between any of these places. If you've got a good boss, that's the best you can expect. I've heard Frankie Sutton isn't a bad bloke.

"You'd better dump that suitcase and get yourself a swag cover. It's all you want; you can't carry a suitcase on a pack horse. We'll go up the street tomorrow and get you a few yards of canvas. You'll want a quart pot and a saddle bag. Get a quart pot you can fasten to your saddle Ds. Have you got a pair of hooks?" he asked.

I nodded, and pulled my spurs from my suitcase. "They're all right," he approved. "You can see some bush lairs in any stock camp — long goosenecks that chop hell out of a horse, or those terrible Mexican hooks that bruise like buggery. Have you got a stockwhip?"

I shook my head. Rutherglen and Homeboin were both in an area of heavy mulga scrub, I explained. "You'd better get yourself one: about seven feet. Anything any longer is too awkward. And

14

you're sure to be asked if you ride. Tell 'em 'Yes — a quiet horse'. Anyone who goes on to one of these places and says he can ride needs to be in rodeo class or he's a mug. Don't get caught with that one!"

Eventually we went to sleep, and both woke before sunrise. For about an hour it was glorious — cool and with a gentle breeze. The flies hadn't built up to full strength. We went to the dining room for breakfast, and it was my first experience of a peculiar class distinction. There were actually two dining rooms, but one was known as the Coffee Room; it was where managers, perhaps overseers and probably commercial travellers and suchlike dined. Stockmen ("ringers", as they were known), drovers, and those lower down the social scale were definitely frowned on.

"That's silvertail country," Steve explained as he steered me toward the dining room proper. The meals were a shilling dearer in the Coffee Room, which was important. Bed and breakfast was seven and sixpence a day, the midday meal two shillings and the evening meal was two and six. The food was plain, but there was plenty of it. I hoped the train for Duchess wouldn't be late; my finances couldn't stand much of this.

That morning Steve came along while I did my shopping. When I had finished I had a canvas swag cover, two swag straps, a quart pot and a saddle bag. But my most prized purchase was a beautifully tapered, plaited kangaroo hide stockwhip, which I didn't know how to use.

Back at the hotel I repacked my belongings. Steve showed me the way to roll a swag so it would sit on a packsaddle properly. I sold the suitcase to the barman for five shillings.

The train arrived and was in for an hour and a half. The stationmaster grumbled that he had held it up half an hour for me; which I doubted, since I had left the bar at the same time as the fireman.

We wound our slow, laborious way through undulating hills of red ironstone covered with spinifex and stunted gums. Mostly the

15

track was level, but when we came to a hill it seemed we would never make it — yet though the train was down to walking pace, somehow it managed. Downhill it probably got up to thirty miles an hour . . . assisted by a tail wind. Soot and cinders blew into the only carriage, which hadn't been swept for a week. That night I was thankful for my swag, which I rolled out on a seat and made as comfortable as possible. It was better than a suitcase.

As I woke the sun was just rising. The train was stationary: I stuck my head out of the window and there was a scattering of houses not far away. I was at the Duchess. I rolled up my swag for the first time (an operation with which I was to become extremely familiar over the next twenty-five years) and made my way across to what proved to be a hotel where, although it was six o'clock in the morning, the bar was operating. I asked the barman if there was a mail coach leaving for Lake Nash. He pointed to one of the two men drinking. "There's the driver," he said. I went over and announced my name and destination. "Okay," he said. "We'll be leaving as sooon as I pick up the mail and some stores."

I had discovered that a lot of town names were prefixed by "the" and often abbreviated: Duchess was "the Duchess", Cloncurry was "the Curry", Charters Towers was "the Towers", Urandangie was "the Dangie", and so on. We left the Duchess about ten o'clock that morning. It was a relief to get moving and leave the flies behind: the utility was travelling a bit faster than they could — not much mind you, but enough. From the spinifex hills we came to limitless plains, occasionally crossing dry watercourses fringed with coolibahs, sometimes passing waterholes. The cattle watering there were gaunt and miserable. We passed bores with great windmills towering over them.

Always there were several hundred head of cattle standing around. And always there were a number of dead ones with crows in hundreds feasting on the carcasses; the stench was unbearable. Once, in the distance, we saw a great cloud of dust, which resolved itself into a mob of bullocks driven by five or six men. When we got

16

level with the mob we pulled up under a small solitary tree and one of the drovers came cantering over. After an exchange of greetings, the mailman went to the back of his utility and pulled out two bags, obviously something he had obtained for the drover in the Duchess.

I was taking in the scene. The horse was a big raw-boned bay, with a heavy stock saddle on its back; strapped to the saddle Ds were a saddle bag and a quart pot on the other. I noted with satisfaction that they were similar to those I had bought in Cloncurry. There was a canvas waterbag hanging from the horse's withers, and around its neck was a pair of hobbles. The drover wore an open-necked khaki shirt, moleskin trousers, concertina leggings and short gooseneck spurs. He took the two bags, tied them together, slung them over the horse's withers and rode back to the mob. The mailman told me the drover had a thousand head of bullocks from Lawn Hills Station, and was taking them to Dajarra railhead for trucking to a fattening property near the Towers.

Occasionally we came to a gate, but they were few and far, very far, between. We dropped mail at Carrandotta Station, and at Urandangie, one of the two westernmost towns in Queensland, we stopped at the hotel for half an hour after dropping the mail off at the Post Office.

We stopped again at Headingly Station, left some mail and had a meal in the kitchen with a boundary rider and a horse breaker. The sun was setting when we took to the road again, and soon it got dark. There was a half-moon. I was dozing fitfully when the driver gave me a nudge. "Gates," he called. I woke with a start. The utility had stopped in front of two large gates, on each side of which I could see in the faint moonlight a netting fence stretching north and south. The vehicle moved through and pulled up, waiting for me to close the ponderous gate.

As I got back into the utility the driver said laconically, "You're now in the Northern Territory." To me it had a dramatic ring.

17

CHAPTER 2

LAKE NASH, NORTHERN TERRITORY

I reached Lake Nash in the middle of the night, and in the middle of one of the worst droughts recorded. I was driven out to the stock camp that night by the manager, Frank Sutton, who appeared to be an irascible old bastard, but wasn't really. The vehicle was a modern T-model Ford, but modern or not, it certainly had its moments. The stock camp was fifty miles out and we had two gates to go through. The engine faithfully stopped at each gate, and it took fifteen minutes or so to get it started each time.

Frank Sutton was an admirable, accomplished and vitriolic swearer. For years I modelled myself on him until I developed a virtuosity of my own, and it was not so much the Ford stopping that seemed to bring forth such an accomplished stream of oaths but the delay in getting it started. I got a distinct impression that he thought in some way I was responsible for the motor's vagaries and obstinacy. Since I was doing all the cranking at the risk of a broken arm, however, this lacked validity.

In the back we had our swags, some rations and, most important of all, two four-gallon drums of water. About every five miles the radiator built up a head of steam that would drive a locomotive, and Frank would endeavour to stop on a slope to expedite starting. We would wait for a quarter of an hour to let it cool down, then top it up again. We refilled the four-gallon drums at a bore and got to the stock camp as day was breaking. It had taken sixteen gallons of water . . . and three gallons of petrol to get us there!

The camp was active when we arrived; there were six white men, including the cook, and four Aborigines. There were sixty or so

18

horses rounded up: some stockmen were busy catching horses and saddling them, while others were leading horses up to the pack saddles, throwing the packs on their backs and hooking the large pack bags to the hooks on the pack trees. Tommy Dodd, the head stockman, came over as the car pulled up. "G'day Tommy" Frank said, "I've got a ringer for you — Tom Cole, from Queensland."

He looked at me and nodded, and turned to Sutton. "I'm shifting camp to move the rest of the cattle from Argadargada; I put all the breeders on the Meta waterhole; there are only bullocks and dry cattle left; I'll put them on No 17 bore."

Sutton said, "Are we losing many cattle?" Dodd looked grave. "I would say, overall, about a hundred a day, and the rate must increase until it rains. The trouble is the surface water dries up and I've got nowhere much to move them. Sure I can put them on bores, but every bore is overstocked now.

"Well, Tommy," Sutton said, "there's nothing to do except wait for rain. When you've got Argadargada cleaned up you'll have to paddock your horses. How are they?"

Dodd pointed to them. "Have a look." They were gaunt, listless and miserable; some had saddle sores. Everything was depressing. In the distance a dust cloud hung over a stockyard full of bellowing cattle.

"How many cattle have you got there?" Sutton asked. "About a thousand," said Dodd. "I'll put them on to No 10 bore. It can't really take another thousand, but there's some spinifex and a bit of top feed that'll keep them alive for a while."

"I know what you're going through," Sutton told him. "I went through it when I was running a camp, and believe me I'm going through it now — if those miserable bastards sitting in their plush offices in Queen Street had given me the money when I asked for four or five more bores, we would be 5000 head of cattle better off."

Sutton walked over to the car. "So long, Tommy — nothing I can do staying here — all the best." He called to me: "Wind her

19

up, Tom!", and said to Tommy, "The best self-starter I've ever had; I think he'll be a good man."

I gave the handle one crank and to my astonishment it started. "See!" said Sutton gleefully, "I told you so."

I was still pondering the value of his accolade as he drove away. With a certain amount of trepidation I turned to the head stockman. Suddenly I felt very lonely. I'd always wanted to get to the Northern Territory and here I was. This country of vast distances with cattle stations of almost unbelievable dimensions became very real.

Tommy Dodd was a hundred per cent man, with a tremendous weight on his shoulders trying to keep cattle alive (or as many as possible, anyway). He had a combination of toughness and humanity that is very rare. Tall, blond and slender, but all whipcord and wire. He sensed my loneliness and guessed my inexperience, which wouldn't have been difficult. He asked me where I came from, and I told him southwest Queensland. As I'd been on Homeboin Station for the past year and had learned to handle cattle fairly well I regarded myself as a fair horseman. I had done a lot of scrub riding in the mulga.

He named the stockmen to me as they were saddling their horses: Fred Stevens from "the Curry" and Jim Groom, a magnificent horseman who came to Lake Nash from Dalgonally, a station famous for its buckjumpers. Then there was Bob Roberts and Joe Brown and four Aborigines.

Dodd pointed to a heavy stock saddle lying at the foot of a gidgee tree with a bridle and a saddlecloth. "That's your gear; come over here and I'll show you your horses."

"Can you ride?" he asked, as we walked towards the saddle, and I remembered Steve Johnson's words of wisdom and said: "Yes, a quiet horse."

"Well, if any of these poor bastards tried to buck they'd fall over, but later on when they're fresh I'll find something that will try you out."

On every station in that country there's an outlaw out in a back paddock somewhere, and on the odd occasion he would be yarded for some exuberant stockman or a bet or two. There's a well-known saying in the northwest. "There's never a horse that can't be ridden, and there's never a man that can't be thrown!" But you don't see those horses in the stock camp. Head stockmen have enough trouble when the horses are fresh — a man thrown, chasing the galloping horse, mending a broken bridle, time lost — without having an outlaw in the camp. Most cattlemen's reaction would be "I'm running a cattle camp, not a bloody circus."

We walked over to the mob. "That grey there: Rainmaker's his name. The chestnut with hobbles on with two white hind feet, Sox. He's a bit hard to catch. And the chestnut mare with the silver mane and tail, Turtle's her name." I was carrying my bridle, and slipped it on Rainmaker and saddled him. The camp was pretty well packed up, the horse tailers and the cook were putting the packs on the last two horses. Six had already been packed up, and the bulging packbags held the camp rations and gear, greenhide ropes, spare hobbles, horseshoes and shoeing gear. Our swags were strapped on top of the pack saddles.

Most of the stockmen were over at the yard letting the cattle stream out in a cloud of dust, and the head stockman was sitting on his horse waiting for the last of the mob to leave. When they were clear he called to one of the stockmen — "Jim, there are five cows down in the yard; get the rifle and shoot them. I think there are three calves; kill them too."

I looked over and saw the five cows, two on their sides. It was obvious they would never stand again. A flock of crows — some on the rails, others flapping around. As we moved away from the yard I heard five shots. The calves were killed with a billet of wood.

Two men rode on each side of the milling mob of cattle, which gradually began to take some sort of form, two men on each wing keeping the sides straight. The stronger cattle took the lead but

21

the main bulk of the herd, cows with their calves, straggled along behind. The head stockman was up with the leaders, which by now had strung out and were more than a quarter of a mile from the tail. Bob Roberts and Fred Stevens were on the tail with me. Tommy Dodd rode back and when he reached us said: "I'm going to let them walk for an hour or so while it's cool, then I'll steady the lead and they can graze. There's a bit of rough feed about three miles away."

As we slowly moved along, the leaders got further and further away, the stronger cattle, bullocks, steers and dry cows (cows without calves) striding out. A stockman learns early — the speed of a mob is the speed of the slowest beast; you don't drive the tail to catch the lead. Tommy Dodd called to Stevens, "Fred, get up there and steady the lead!" Stevens cantered away and when he got to the leaders held them until the mob resumed a more compact shape, then let them go again.

The sun got higher; the heat increased. The leaders were steadied, and instead of the cattle being a long narrow mob they were spread widely across the plain, feeding fitfully on Mitchell grass stubble. We came to a patch of scattered gidgee timber, the spidery limbs and narrow leaves providing a sparse shade. This was our dinner camp. The cattle, needing little guidance, moved in gratefully to rest in the shade.

A pack horse that had been ambling along with the cattle was led up to a fire, quart pots were filled from water canteens and soon we were squatting on our haunches swallowing scalding black tea and tearing off hunks of corned meat and damper. Two stock horses were kept saddled; the rest were unsaddled and hobbled out. I went over to the best shade I could find, turned my saddle upside down for a pillow and passed out. But it seemed as though I'd only been asleep for seconds when a stockwhip cracked in my ear. Tommy Dodd was sitting on his horse grinning down at me. "Sorry to have to wake you, but we're moving off." The sun had moved around while I was asleep. I was no longer in the shade and in a lather of sweat. Somebody had bridled Rainmaker and tied him to a tree and I saddled him. The cattle were starting to move, and as we left the timber and topped a ridge I could see a windmill about five miles away. I guessed it would take us about four hours to get there. Two stockmen were on each wing up with the lead, and Dodd told them to let the leaders string out. "Don't steady the lead, I'll be up with you when we get close to the water."

About five o'clock he called to me: "Tom, come up to the lead with me and give us a hand with the watering," telling the men at the tail, "don't push them, it'll take at least two hours to get them all watered. I don't want too many hitting the trough at once."

As we rode away he said: "Have you had any experience watering cattle at windmills?"

"No, not really."

"We've got about a thousand head here," he said. "The trough is forty or fifty yards long and we'll let them in to the water in lots of 100 or so. It'll take about two hours to water them. We'll yard them tonight and tail them out tomorrow. By then they'll be settled enough to leave. A few are bound to go back, but they won't come to any harm."

We came up with the leading beasts about two miles from the tail; the windmill wasn't far away. Contrary to what a lot of people think, cattle can not smell water unless it is in contact with the ground: they can't smell water in a trough. Tommy called to Fred Stevens on the opposite wing — "Fred, canter up to the trough and throw a few quarts on the ground so they can smell it."

We were within a quarter of a mile of the mill, the cattle striding out, the wind was blowing off the trough and I could see Stevens bailing water on to the ground. As soon as the cattle smelt it they started to trot. "Tom," called Dodd, "get up with the lead and keep them steadied as much as you can. I'll cut off about 100 and we'll hold the main mob here, then they can go in 100 at a time. When they've had a drink, get them away from the trough; push them out on to the plain."

I trotted up to the lead and kept them steady until we were up to the trough. Then there was no stopping them; they were thirsty and buried their noses in the water. Soon their bellies were at bursting point, and I worked them away from the trough for another mob to trot in. They came in mob after mob. It got dark and still they came. The mob out on the plain grew larger and was being held by three men. Eventually we were finished.

In the dark the cattle were bellowing and surging over half a mile of plain. The head stockman and three others kept them together while the rest of us rode over to the camp. A fire was going, two camp ovens were sitting on the fire sizzling and a large billy of tea stood nearby. All the pack saddles were lined up in a row, everyone's swag lying beside the pack that had carried it. Four horses — the night horses — were tied up.

Each man took his swag, picked a place to sleep and unrolled it. After a hasty wash we gathered round the fire. The head stockman came in and cut the night into watches of an hour and a half. I was put on first watch with the horse tailer. We squatted down on our hunkers to gulp a plateful of corned beef curry and after a pannikin of black tea, saddled a night horse.

The stockmen holding the cattle had them rounded up into a more compact mob. We rode out and took over, and they went back to camp, unsaddled, and had supper. In a few moments the camp was silent. Only the flickering campfire marked its position.

We had taken over at nine o'clock and rode continuously all through our watch. The night horses knew their work, needing little guidance. When our watch was over, it was our job to wake our relief — they had no chance of sleeping over their time. We were thankful when the time came to hand over. Apart from the brief sleep on the dinner camp, I had been up for about thirty-eight hours: When I got into my swag the hard ground could have been a feather bed.

The cook called us before daybreak and as the first light of dawn appeared, the horse tailer brought the horses into the camp.

Soon we were all in the saddle. We watered the cattle again as the sun rose, a lot easier than the night before.

In the distance there were some low ridges and we took the mob over to what appeared to be good feeding ground, but in reality it was light timber and spinifex. Not as good as it looked, but the cattle were starving and began grazing hungrily.

The long, weary days of moving cattle from the failing waterholes to bores went on and on. The sun blazed relentlessly from a completely cloudless sky day after day. Looking into that sky it seemed as though it would never rain again. Eventually the cattle moving came to an end. There was nowhere else to put them. All the bores were overstocked, and from then on it was a matter of how many would survive. The plains were bare for a radius of ten miles and only the strongest cattle could reach the feed. As they became weaker they died: it was pitiful to see, and the smell of death was everywhere.

All the bores were carrying their limit, so the head stockman gradually cut his camp down, sending a lot of the horses to the paddock. Some of the stockmen were put out on bores to pump water. One day Frank Sutton picked me up from the stock camp. "You're going to No 17 bore to help old Dinny Downes out," he told me. "He's got 3000 head of cattle to water, and is complaining that he's got to pump twenty hours a day. The old bastard's getting soft!" No 17 bore was on the edge of a plain close to the western boundary, ninety-eight miles from the station homestead.

For a month I saw no one except Dinny. We worked ten-hour shifts, cutting up the tough gidgee to feed the boiler furnace, which kept the steam engine going to drive the pump. There was nothing soft about Dinny Downes. He swung that four-pound axe in the blazing sun day after day like a machine. I tried to keep up with him, but couldn't. I cut enough firewood for my shift . . . but only just.

One day he got toothache. He didn't say much, but I saw him rummage about in our tool box and take out a pair of fencing pliers. I looked at him in silent astonishment as he made himself comfortable on the ground with his back to a tree, and pulled his own tooth out! Jesus, I thought, that old bastard's tough! He spat a mouthful of blood out, shook his head a couple of times and looked at me with a grin. "Christ!" he said, "that 'urt. I'm glad there was only one!"

One day, just before sundown, I saw a cloud of dust approaching: a mob of horses, some carrying packs. Two men were riding in the lead.

They rode up to the trough and watered their horses. One called to Dinny with a wave, "How are you, you old death adder?" It was George Isaacson, a well-known drover; the other man was Byron Nathan, a half-caste widely respected as a legendary horseman and a tracker who had no peer. Also, I was told later — though not by Byron — he had Vice-Regal connections. His father was a brother of a Queensland Governor.

After they had unpacked and seen to their horses, they came over to our camp. We were curious to know what they were doing so far out; we had never had any visitors before. It was not customary to ask questions but, as in most cases, it wasn't necessary. They told us they were heading for the Sandover River, which was vacant Crown Land country. If they were satisfied after a good inspection they hoped to take it and stock it up in partnership.

Some years before, Byron had worked on Lake Nash and been involved in tracking a mob of stolen cattle. Around the campfire that night, he told the story.

Two men named Wickham and Fitzpatrick had helped themselves to 100 Lake Nash bullocks — which, no doubt, they would have got away with had it not been for an alert boundary rider who came across their tracks. The police were immediately notified and, being well aware of Byron's tracking abilities, asked him to accompany them. The tracks, which by then were over a week old,

26

left Argadargada waterhole (not far from where we were then camped) and travelled out into the desert in a northwesterly direction . . . to where there was no water. As they tracked the cattle further and further into the desert, Nathan told us the mounted constable started to panic and wanted to turn back. "We'll all die of thirst," he said, but Byron refused to give up. "If they can get through driving cattle," he said, "we've got a much better chance with horses — we can travel three times as fast."

So they continued and came to Hatches Creek, a mining field, with their water canteens dry. A couple of bullocks were being yarded for slaughtering and not far away a mob was being tailed out on grass. Everyone bore the Lake Nash brand — LNT.

It seemed that Messrs Wickham and Fitzpatrick had come earlier to a mutual arrangement to cover such a contingency as now overtook them. In the event of what Jim Wickham described as a "miscarriage of justice", he would shoulder the blame. This would leave Fitzpatrick free to look after their interests, which consisted of a couple of thousand square miles of country and a few hundred head of cattle. When the legal dust had settled, Jim Wickham reluctantly accepted the unavoidable hospitality of the Government for twelve months, less one third for good behaviour.

The four of us talked well into the night and the following morning they packed up and left for the Sandover. A week later we saw them again on their way back, full of enthusiasm for the future of Sandover River Station. Dinny and I went back to cutting gidgee.

Then it rained. It poured. It came down in torrents. The blessed rain had come at last, and overnight the country was transformed. The plains became a waving sea of Mitchell grass. Green was the most marvellous colour in the world. Water filled the billabongs, the dry watercourses, flowed into the parched, cracked earth. All the cattle watering at our bore disappeared, ranging far and wide. Never was the expression "looking for green fields and pastures new" more apt. I saddled one of the two horses left with us, took the rifle and rode out to a billabong not far away to shoot a few ducks.

After a while the country dried out enough for vehicles to move over the blacksoil plains and, inevitably, the manager arrived to put an end to our idyllic existence. He announced to me with what I thought was a leer: "I'm going to introduce you to some work — real work." I waited. "You can go and cut cordwood with Bob Roberts." He waited for it to sink in. I thought "what's the old bastard springing on me now?" I knew what cordwood was, the gidgee logs we used to fire the boiler of our steam engine.

I had an uneasy feeling there was a trap somewhere. He continued: "There'll be no stock work for a while, so I thought we'd better get ahead with firewood for next season." He took a breather, then "You can go to Meta" (which I knew to be a waterhole). "Bob Roberts is there now; you can join him. I'm giving you a contract, I'm going to pay you one pound a cord!"

A contract! It had a commercial ring. I wondered what a cord was; I didn't ask, but I thought if I couldn't make more than a pound a week there was something wrong. Well, I did make more than a pound a week . . . but not much.

The heavy gidgee hardwood was scattered and tough, we had to carry each piece separately and stack it, it was so heavy and twisted it wasn't possible to carry more than one piece at a time. I longed to be back on a horse, where at least I could work sitting down. When we had just about cut the area out, Sutton appeared again and as I anticipated, didn't shower us with congratulations on our ability to cut cordwood. He measured it all up and calculated how much we would get for our sweat and blood. After the cost of the rations was deducted, there was precious little . . . and it was certainly precious.

He moved us to a stockyard that needed repairing, which was a bit better but not much. It would be a long time before the stock camp started up again; a long time to be using axes, crowbars, and shovels — tools to which I was temperamentally unsuited.

CHAPTER 3

LIFE ON
A CATTLE STATION

I found that life on a big cattle station was unquestionably tough, and it gave me an insight into a breed of men who were in a class of their own. Looking back over a long span of years, I am compelled to come to the conclusion that at one pound a week I was well paid. I was incredibly green. I know now that I was accepted by these men after what might be termed "making the grade" in a comparatively short time. At first I did consider that anything from ten to eighteen hours a day in the saddle, six days a week normally (seven during a bullock muster) for one pound a week was a bit on the low side.

Wages ranged from five shillings a week for the black stockmen to a pound (me), three pounds for an experienced stockman, three pounds ten for a cook (more than those bastards were worth, but never mentioned in their hearing because they were inclined to be a bit sensitive), and the head stockman four pounds.

We got what was loosely referred to as "full keep"; board and lodgings, I suppose. The board part was mainly corned beef and damper, a tin of treacle a week, known through the west as "Kidman's blood mixture" for its presumed health-giving qualities, a bottle of tomato sauce and a bottle of Worcestershire sauce — which, we were reminded, was "made from a recipe of a nobleman of the country". The lodging was Mother Earth, plus a shady tree. Some stations did a bit better; Rocklands was well thought of because they used to throw in a few tins of apricots and peaches, a tin of custard powder and a tin of butter — usually half rancid but all right for cooking. The lubras were better on

29

Rocklands too, so everyone wanted to work there. There was never any shortage of beef; a fat cow was killed about once a week. Then we were able to gorge ourselves with fresh meat, but only for a day or perhaps a couple of days in the cold weather — it wouldn't keep any longer. The rest was salted down and, if we were in camp, stacked on a table made of saplings and a fire lit beneath to keep the blowflies away. That was the theory, anyway. The fire would flare up and die down: when it subsided, the flies would return with renewed frenzy and when the fire flared up it would smoke and dry the maggots. The cook would brush most of them off when he cooked the meat.

After a couple of days "shit beetles" appeared. Normally they lived in the cattle dung, but they found corned meat a much more desirable area for their activities. They burrowed and made themselves at home in large numbers. The cook dealt with these by soaking the beef in water an hour before cooking. Most of them would float to the surface and could easily be skimmed off. A really dedicated cook would change the water, but there weren't many who were that dedicated.

On the big western Queensland and Northern Territory stations, such as Lake Nash, we'd get our rations every six months. Two tons of flour would arrive at a time, to be stacked in corrugated iron sheds. Before long the weevils would invade it and breed with incredible rapidity, though this was never a matter of concern until they left the flour. A fifty-pound bag of flour that has gone through the bowels of fifty million weevils has no food value whatsoever.

There is a lot of literature available on the subject of losing weight, but all those dieticians have overlooked a programme of twelve hours in the saddle in a temperature of over 100 degrees, an irregular diet of weevil-infested damper and corned beef liberally impregnated with shit beetles.

Epsom salts was an important part of the first aid kit. Constipation was almost a way of life: three or four days was considered a reasonable time lapse, but five and over called for an ounce of

Epsom salts. An ounce of salts was equal to about a quarter plug of dynamite!

When the stock camps came into the head station every few months for a change of horses, it would mean three or four days spent mustering the fresh ones and shoeing them. We were then able to luxuriate on broken spring iron beds in the men's quarters that were an igloo in the winter and a pressure cooker in summer. When we were out on the run mustering, nature did a much better job, our swags rolled out under trees beside creeks.

Lake Nash was about 6000 square miles. The herd of shorthorn cattle varied from 20,000 to 25,000 head, depending on the season. During a drought the losses would be very heavy, mostly old cows with young calves at foot; as the feed around the water got eaten out, they had to walk further and further for feed until it became too far and their milk dried up. They would stagger into water because of the intense heat, and often get hopelessly bogged; the calves standing by bellowing plaintively.

The crows were always there in flocks, and would pick the eyes from the bogged cattle. After that it was the calves' turn. How you get to hate crows! Overhead the kite hawks would be wheeling— at least they had the decency to wait for death.

The hours were long and arduous, more so in times of drought; sixteen hours in the saddle was by no means unusual. The routine started at four or five in the morning. Out of the swag, a quick wash if there was sufficient water, swags rolled and laid beside the pack saddles. Breakfast was rough and ready — more rough than ready — sometimes curried corned beef, sometimes stewed corned beef, sometimes corned beef dipped in a batter and fried (called, for some reason, 'Burdekin duck') but always corned beef, except for a couple of days after we killed.

That stockmen were lean and wiry was due to their diet. That most were healthy, was a miracle.

Each man was allotted three saddle horses. Each horse was worked one day and had two days' spell. The station supplied the saddles and bridles, mostly heavy and uncomfortable. The older hands usually had their own saddles. Everyone looked after their gear and horses, especially their horses. All of them, with few exceptions, were genuine horse lovers.

Mainly because of drought, the horses had to put up with hard times, but they were never deliberately ill-treated. If there were an occasional stockman who knocked his horses about unnecessarily, he would be referred to contemptuously as a horse-killing bastard. He was reckoned guilty of one of the worst crimes in a cattleman's calendar.

Before all else, before we went to the campfire after a day's work, we saw that the horses got a drink whenever water was available. Their backs would be given a rubbing down, if only with a saddle cloth, and they were handed over to the horse tailer with a friendly pat on the rump. He would hobble them out on the best grass he could find; in a bad time, as often as not it would be some miserable stubble.

We soon got to know our horses . . . and they got to know us. Like people, they all had different temperaments. Some were highly strung, some were placid, some were difficult to catch, others were bad-tempered. There were hard-mouthed horses, there were obstinate horses and there was just as wide a difference in them as hacks. Some were a pleasure to ride with a smooth easy gait whether walking, cantering or galloping, but you wouldn't walk behind the bad-tempered ones in case they lashed out with a violence that would break a leg. The best horses, naturally, were always in the head stockman's string, one of the few perquisites of the job.

The general run of horses on Lake Nash was good. The thoroughbred stallions used for breeding may have had their day as racehorses, but they had many virile years of stud duty left. Consequently, many of the stock horses were half and three-quarter thoroughbred. Unless they were very well grown and developed they were not broken in until they were four years old. One sees hundreds of racehorses racing at two years old — a simple explanation for the high percentage that break down.

The horsebreaker was about the best paid man on a station. In addition to the ordinary stockman's wage of three pounds a week, he received twenty-five shillings a head for every horse he broke. Sometimes a manager would limit his breaker to four a week, maintaining that any more than that could not be given proper attention, but not very often.

When a breaker came on to a station to break in he might ask, "What's the limit?" and normally the manager would say, "That's up to you". When broken in, the horses were delivered to the head stockman who, if not satisfied with any horse's performance, would give him back and tell the breaker why. Six colts a week was a fair thing. The breaker was always given one of the Aboriginal stockmen as an offsider.

Breaking in was rough and ready. Horses were branded when no more than a few months old, then turned out for the next three or four years. When the breaker got them they were pretty wild.

CHAPTER 4

THE LAWS OF DROVING

Finally I got away from the drudgery of wood cutting, digging postholes and yard-building. The stock camp was swinging into action.

Our first job was getting horses ready, mustering the horse paddock, drafting off the working horses, stock horses, night horses; fifty-odd altogether. Then the breeding paddock, where about fifty mares ran with two stallions. They were brought in and the youngsters branded with the station brand LNT consecutively numbered with a separate branding iron and entered meticulously in the horse book.

Each man was allotted his three horses and the next job was shoeing. We shod our own. I learned to shoe; how to make a shoe fit, shaping it on an anvil, rasping the hoof down. The shoes were malleable, but it was hard work just the same; most of the horses didn't take too kindly to the operation. The nails had to be driven in the right way, bevelled at the tip so that they came out of the hoof at the right place. If the nail was driven in the wrong way it would turn into the hoof and prick the horse — you'd soon know, because he'd do his best to kick your head off. It could be quite entertaining: half a dozen stockmen shoeing up horses that had been out in the spelling paddock for five or six months and determined not be be shod. I've listened to a few of them, a hind leg of a powerful young horse under their arm, a shoeing hammer in one hand and a horseshoe in the other, a mouthful of nails, trying to give a rundown on the horse, its ancestry, its future, shoeing as a form of occupation. Even the owners get a colourful passing mention.

Among my three was a powerful bay called Fox, which the head stockman told me might buck. I had ridden a few mild buckjumpers in my time, but this fellow looked like the real thing, as though he'd throw me clean out of the yard. But when I got on him he wasn't much trouble and soon settled down. Some of the other fellows weren't so lucky. Jim Broadbridge, who hadn't been with us long, got thrown and badly shaken, and the head stockman got a bitch of a mare that bucked badly; but he rode her well.

When the horses were fresh it was always a challenge and even the best horsemen could be tested. A stranger seeing their casual seat in a saddle under ordinary circumstances could be forgiven for thinking they were indifferent horsemen until that moment — a fresh colt saddled, ears pricked, nostrils distended, tensed and waiting, the near rein tightly held, a foot in the stirrup, a graceful easy swing into the saddle . . . then a cyclone unleashed.

There have been numerous descriptions of bucking horses and I think I have heard them all. In bars and around campfires there have been some graphic stories of epic rides, some of which test one's credulity. But anyone would agree that the hardest horse to ride is one which, when well off the ground, twists and kicks up. When that happens you know — by God you know — one stirrup iron gone, a second later flying through the air.

While all this was going on, the cook was busy drawing rations from the store and when we rode out from the station with pack bags bulging, riding fresh horses that were reefing at the bit, their muscles rippling under their satin coats, there was a different feeling. The creeks and waterholes purged of the rotten carcasses were sweet and clean. Waving Mitchell and Flinders grass grew to the water's edge. Wildfowl were everywhere; on the plains, stalking turkeys gorged themselves on the swarms of insects, wild ducks were on every billabong. All of this was very tempting.

But this was no time to indulge our sporting instincts: a bullock muster was a serious business. We made camp on Kelly's Creek, unpacked and hobbled the horses. Now there was an autumn feeling; the nights were starting to get cold, the mornings were crisp and clear. We were called before daylight and squatted around the campfire, shovelling some sort of stew into ourselves and swallowing a quart pot of black tea.

The horse tailers had left to muster the horses before the first glimmer of light and were rounding them up in front of the camp. We saddled up and as dawn swept acrosss the plains, rode out behind the head stockman.

The country was mustered in segments radiating from our camp, and as we rode along two men at a time were dropped off to make a sweep around — about four or five miles, depending on how much we had to cover that day. When we all finally met at the camp we would probably have more than 1000 head of cattle in hand.

In the afternoon, the bullocks were drafted off by the head stockman on a camp horse; the most highly trained and intelligent horse in the whole mob. I believe it is difficult for anyone who has not seen a camp horse in action to appreciate not only the horsemanship, but the poetry of motion.

There are camp-drafting competitions to be seen at most agricultural shows in Australia, but there is no comparison between this type of competitive horse work and a station camp draft.

The cattle are held in a compact mob by the stockman. The man (usually the head stockman) on the camp horse rides into the mob and selects the beast with a flick of his stockwhip. Then the horse takes over.

Doubling and turning, twisting and propping, the bullock is determined not to be taken from the mob. But the horse is complete master, one moment blocking it, the next shouldering it until it is forced to the edge of the mob, known as the face of the camp. Here another rider sweeps in and takes the beast from the

36

camp drafter. With a crack of his whip he takes it over to the "cut" where the selected bullocks are held.

When the drafting was finished 100 to 150 sleek, fat bullocks would be in hand. This was pretty well the pattern on all the big stations. The stock camps were about the same size; eight or nine men including the cook, between fifty and sixty horses. The mustering procedure and the number of cattle handled in a morning's muster would not vary very much. Not much more than 1000 head could be comfortably or efficiently handled. The afternoons had to be set aside for the drafting off of the "fats". When that was done, the mob was let go to wander back to where it had come from and the bullocks yarded for the night. Later, as the number of bullocks increased, they would be watched instead of yarded. The target would rarely be less than 1000, usually 1250; a standard mob for a drover.

It was arduous work, seven days a week and nothing less than twelve hours a day in the saddle — fourteen to sixteen when night watching started. Most of us preferred the bullock musters. It was straightforward work and, of course, the best time of the year. Grass and water were plentiful and the horses in good condition.

After about ten days' mustering, we had some 1400 bullocks in hand. Another day was taken up cleaning them out, drafting off anything a bit doubtful. The number required for the drover was 1250 plus killers for his meat supply. This was calculated at a beast a week for the length of time it would take him to reach his destination, though drovers would go to a lot of trouble to avoid killing one of these.

The contract price for droving in 1926 was two shillings per head per hundred miles. It seemed a long way to drive a bullock for two shillings, but that was the going rate. When the drover delivered them there would always be shortages for various reasons — lameness, sickness or perhaps losses at night — but every beast was precious, and no one enquired too closely as to how he managed to keep his killer allowance reasonably intact. No one, that is, except perhaps the cattlemen whose country he passed through. They may have had grounds for suspicion but, as they used to say, an old dog for a hard road; and a hard road it was indeed.

Before our cattle were counted over to the drover there was one last task. They had to be dipped under the supervision of the local mounted policeman who, in addition to his other numerous duties, was Inspector of Stock. This job entailed putting them through an evil-looking arsenical brew to kill off whatever ticks they carried. They were forced up a race into a concrete plunge bath about six feet deep and fifty feet long, stockmen on each side, armed with long poles to push the poor creatures under as they swam through to ensure they were thoroughly immersed.

We delivered one more mob of bullocks, making 2500 head altogether, then after a couple of days' spell pulled the shoes off our horses, mustered and shod a fresh lot and set off again to start branding.

This was a lot different. This time, when we brought the day's muster together, the cows with cleanskin calves were cut out and yarded and the branding started the following morning.

Nearly all the branding was done in a bronco yard; a holding yard with a bronco panel in one corner. The cleanskin calves were lassoed from a horse — the bronco horse with a heavy leather breastplate strapped over the saddle, to which a greenhide rope was buckled. The horseman rides into the mob, the rope coiled over his arm. The rope snakes out and drops round the neck of an unsuspecting calf. The struggling, bellowing youngster is then dragged to the bronco panel, speedily leg-roped, dropped on to its side, hit with a branding iron by one man, earmarked by another — if a bull, castrated by a third — the whole operation over in a matter of seconds. The Aboriginal stockmen pounce on the testicles and throw them on the branding fire — delectable morsels!

The branding went on day after day as we moved from waterhole to waterhole, staying from a week to ten days at each camp. The tally gradually crept up — 1000, 2000, 3000.

At night that stockman's forum, the campfire, was always good for some spirited and humorous discussion. There was never any lack of wit or imagination, especially when support was required for some hair-raising and dubious story.

Shortly after passing the 3000 mark, Stevens casually asked how many testicles had been eaten in the past two months by our four Aboriginal stockmen. It was immediately taken up with hilarious enthusiasm and some heavy calculating took place. Three thousand branders, half of them heifers, some too small — their testicles would shrivel quickly to nothing in the fierce heat of the branding fire — 2000 they'd eaten in eight weeks. What did that come to? I was called on to supply the answer.

"That," I announced solemnly, "is 250 a week between you fellows." Our black stockmen, gathered round the fire with us, were not able to quite follow what we were talking about. Jack-knife Billy said rather apprehensively. "What you all about fella talking about?" The lanky Jabiru said: "They talking about how many balls we fella eaten; Tom says two hundret fifty one week!" "Ho!" shouted little Jacky. "You talk about me fella — I see you fella eatem plenty, I lookim Tom eatem some fella, Freddy eatem some fella, Jim too." We all roared with laughter. Little Jacky said, "I think you fella beatem me fella."

The talk then switched to the food value, and not only muscle building. It seemed that Jabiru, in addition to a couple of wives, also had a girlfriend or two.

"That Jabiru properly greedy bugger," said little Jacky, "he like eatem plenty ball, try make 'im strong long girl friend." Everybody laughed, enjoying Jabiru's discomfiture. He said, "Me tink you fella jealous." I thought maybe he wasn't far out there.

It's the same old thing wherever you are.

A few weeks later I left Lake Nash. There was no particular reason, except that there was so much to see. We had come into the station to get fresh horses for the next muster and I heard that a drover named Christie Newton, who was camped on the lake wanted someone to help him take his sixty-odd head of horses to Cloncurry, where he lived between droving. I took the job.

A week later in Cloncurry, I called at one of the pastoral houses and immediately got a job on Strathfield Station. Two days later I was in the saddle again.

Strathfield was in the middle of a devastating drought, and all the breeders were being mustered and moved to another of the company's properties, Glenormiston, where they were fortunate enough to have a surplus of feed. Two mobs had already gone and a drover was waiting for another two, which would be the last. They would be mostly breeders with young calves, some young males; about 3000 head altogether, give or take 100 or so.

The drover was Jack Clark, a grizzled veteran of many a dry stage, known throughout Western Queensland and South Australia.

It was he who had the misfortune to lose 500 Kidman bullocks on the Birdsville Track. I had heard it talked of around various campfires from time to time, and one night during a muster — I think we were changing horses — he came to our camp for a yarn and told us the story.

Glengyle, on the Georgina River, one of Kidman's properties, was managed by Jim Ronan. Clark was one of Kidman's most respected drovers. He took delivery of 500 fats; their destination was Farina railhead in South Australia. From there they were to be trucked to Adelaide.

When they left Glengyle early in June, the stock route was in fairly good shape. Some of the watering places were bores, some were waterholes. They passed Birdsville, and crossed the border into South Australia, and shortly afterwards, started to get into difficulties.

Several days after leaving Birdsville they were approaching a bore that had a windmill on it and, as Clark had been previously advised, was broken down. There was water in the two tanks, but only horse water; nowhere near enough for 500 bullocks. He planned his stages so most of the travelling was done at night for the next couple of days. By that time he expected to be out of trouble.

They would get water in the Warburton, a tributary of Cooper Creek. A man was sent ahead to have a look, and returned with the bad news that it was nearly dry and they'd be lucky to get water for their horses. Now it was really starting to look serious. There was another bore twenty miles further on from the Warburton. To avoid dehydration as much as possible, the cattle were rested as soon as the heat started to build up. By the time they reached the next bore they'd walked eighty miles without a drink. And it, too, was broken down.

There was no water.

The bullocks now were dangerously thirsty, and the horses were in a bad way, too. The next bore was twenty miles. There was only one way they could go — on. Jack said, "It was the only time in my life I ever prayed — I s'pose I'd left it a bit late."

"We walked them for a couple of hours and when the sun got up a bit I turned them into some shade. Late in the afternoon . . ." [he paused to roll another smoke] ". . . we moved off again. They were really striding out; they always do when they're thirsty. There was a good moon, I let them walk till about three in the morning and then steadied them down and tried to camp them. Some of us had to get a bit of sleep — we'd had practically none for thirty hours. Our horses were nearly done in too. The cattle were milling and surging badly. I was watching them with two other men. About four o'clock a sandstorm came up."

We were all silent, reliving those moments with him as he paused for a while, the flickering campfire reflecting the quiet faces of the stockmen.

He drew on his cigarette before he continued: "I've seen some sandstorms in my time, mostly on the Birdsville Track, but I've never seen one like this before, and never want to again. The wind tore at us, the sand slashed our faces like stockwhips, we couldn't open our eyes, we were blinded, our horses were blinded. Our horses backed into the wind and wouldn't move. When there was a lull I tried to find cattle, but I could only hear them. I called out to the other men, but they couldn't hear me.

"When daylight broke there were no bullocks. They'd all gone, back the way they had come, of course; the only way they knew there was water. Our horses were too bad to follow them. Every bullock died."

CHAPTER 5

DROVING FROM STRATHFIELD TO GLENORMISTON

We mustered for another fortnight into a holding paddock of about a hundred square miles. We had something over 3000 head in hand, but a lot weren't fit to travel. The drover wouldn't accept any he thought wouldn't get there . . . which, on appearances, was just about all of them.

It finally got down to 1700, and Clark decided to take them as one mob rather than two. A bit unwieldy but, as he pointed out, "They'll soon fine down." He wasn't far out there, either.

When Clark left, Strathfield would just about be shut down until it rained, and that looked a long way off. What was left was mainly bullocks that would probably see the drought out or breeders that were too weak to travel, and certainly wouldn't. In any case I would have been out of work. Clark was a couple of men short, so I took a job with him.

Anticipating two mobs of cattle, he had more than eighty horses, a waggonette and six pack saddles. I got the job of offsider to the horse tailer; normally a one-man job, but this was two droving plants in one.

The cook was Jack Cassidy, not suprisingly known as Hopalong. There was a Black, a Brown and a White, and everybody got them mixed up. I could identify Black because he had black hair. Another man was named Dutchy. I never did hear his right name — it might have been Dutchy. The horse tailer was Percy Norris, who'd been with Jack Clark for years on and off.

We left Strathfield boundary early one morning. The head stockman, Ernie Hamilton, rode over to say goodbye and said he'd probably see me at Glenormiston.

We headed the cattle for the stock route about a mile from the Strathfield boundary. It was a mile wide and fenced each side. This was my first experience of droving, though I had a fairly good idea of how it was carried out. There was very little grass except outside the stock route, and that was jealously guarded by the owners, their stockmen and overseers. Getting a feed for the horses was a continual battle of wits. At night we would open fences and put them into someone's precious grass. Sometimes we'd take a swag and camp with them in order to get an early start before we were discovered. There were some bitter rows; most of the station men had some sympathy for us, but they too had a job to do.

Each man had his three horses and our first task was to get the mounts that were due to be ridden that day. It would be dark when we went out to muster them in the mornings and bitterly cold, and they would be scattered hell west and crooked. Bells were put on those we wanted, but when we went out to find them, as often as not it was when they decided to have a doze — they had no intention of allowing their rest to be disturbed by a clanging bell.

It was important to get them back early to get the cattle moving in the cool of the morning. After a quick breakfast the rest of the horses would have to be mustered. Then we would help the cook pack up, drive them to the next camp, unpack, get a load of firewood (one of the horse tailer's less popular jobs), water the horses, take them out to the best feed we could find, hobble them, at sundown bring the night horses in for the watches and when the cattle got to the camp, take the stockmen's horses out and hobble them with the others. On top of this, we all did our watch.

Sometimes we would help in watering the cattle, too. The waterholes were mostly a stinking, boggy morass, and the cattle would have to be strung in a few at a time to avoid overcrowding.

When they were thirsty they would knock each other down if too many were let in at once. At nearly all the watering places there were dead cattle, most left by previous drovers but some no doubt from surrounding stations. Wild pigs tore at the carcasses; the stench was appalling, and always there were the crows. Sometimes there was an unfortunate beast, its eyes gone, swinging its head in sightless agony, begging to be put out of its misery. We always despatched them.

When we watered our cattle there would nearly always be one or two, bloated with water, that didn't have the strength to drag their emaciated frames from the gluey bog. We shot them where they were; if there were calves they would have to be killed, too.

The cook got our camp water from these waterholes. There was no other water, except when we came to a bore, and bores were few and far between. He always filled the canteens at a place where there weren't too many dead cattle. The water was boiled but that did nothing for the flavour. This was drought.

The popular bush poet, Banjo Paterson, wrote:

> *In my wild erratic fancy visions come to me*
> *of Clancy*
> *Gone a droving down the Cooper where the Western*
> *drovers go;*
> *As the stock are slowly stringing Clancy rides behind*
> *them singing,*
> *For the drover's life has pleasures that the townsfolk*
> *never know.*

Well, wild erratic fancy was right, we thought, but for the rest of it we reckoned he carried this poet's licence business a bit far.

Getting beef for the camp was always a worry, because there was nothing among ours fit to eat. The boss knew the manager of Toolebuc, a sheep station, and he filled our packs with mutton, but that didn't happen very often. Sometimes providence gave a helping hand, and sometimes we helped providence.

One of the laws of droving was that the properties through which the drover passed had to receive notice of his approach twenty-four hours before he got to the boundary. A stockman would then come along, meet him and "see him through the run". The idea was, of course, to keep him honest. If the stock route were fenced they didn't always bother, an omission for which we were sometimes very grateful.

A week after we passed Toolebuc some cattle walked in for a drink where we were watering. Among them was a young bullock in good condition: it committed suicide before our very eyes, deliberately running into a bullet from Jack Clark's Winchester. The meat wasn't wasted.

Some time later (we were well down the Hamilton) Jack and I came across half a dozen cattle under the shade of a gum tree. Jack had a rifle with him, and waved it about so carelessly that it went off and a fat cow became mortally wounded. Telling the story later to a few very select friends, Jack said, "It was so mortally wounded it dropped dead on the spot!"

This time the situation nearly got serious. Dutchy, Black or White — I forget which — and I were butchering it, the boss sitting on his horse rolling a smoke, watching us and giving lots of free advice, when suddenly he spotted a couple of horsemen riding towards us. We rightly assumed them to be men from Warenda, the station we were passing through. At that particular moment we didn't need company, especially Warenda company. They were right at the bottom of the list.

They had started to canter their horses and were getting perilously close. I wondered how the hell we were going to get out of this one. Jack said: "Tom, whip those ears off, Dutchy, cut that bloody brand out, quick and lively now!" A few quick slashes and it was done. "Righto," the boss said, "shove it all up his arse, hurry up!"

The two men reined their horses, giving the carcass a close inspection before they spoke. They were well mounted: the man

46

on a fine chestnut clearly in a position of authority (the head stockman, as I learned later). The other on a bay mare had the look of a jackeroo about him; smartly dressed, shiny riding boots, bright jangling spurs.

The boss was having trouble with his smoke and we were waiting to see what was going to happen next.

The head stockman knew the boss, as I would have expected. "Day Jack, killing, eh? One of yours?" he asked.

"Course it's one of mine," very indignantly, "you don't think I'd be stupid enough to knock one of yours over do you?"

He didn't answer but said: "Well, you wouldn't mind if I had a look at the brand and earmark would you?"

"No," says Jack, "go right ahead, it's a bit hacked about but they'll be there somewhere."

The two men got off their horses and pulled the hide away from the carcass. They held it up, they laid it down, they turned it over, the jackeroo got down on his knees, then they looked for the earmark, again without success. They never thought of looking up its arse.

When they got back on their horses, I saw the head stockman look across at our poverty-stricken cattle grazing nearby and then down at the well-nourished carcass on the ground. Just as he turned to go he said "Okay Jack — you win."

We left the Hamilton River and crossed over to the Burke, following it down to the Georgina. At last we had got to good feed. The river had run and spread through its numerous channels and there was an abundance of lush herbage and plenty of water. We had two days' spell and turned up the Georgina. We were on Marion Downs country, which adjoined Glenormiston, and in another week would reach our destination.

The day before we were due to arrive, the boss sent one of the men on to advise the manager. At the boundary gate we were met by Ernie Hamilton. I remembered him saying that he would see me at Glenormiston, but I hadn't given it any more thought. He had

47

been appointed manager. After the cattle were counted he came over to me, shook hands, and asked if I would take a job in the stock camp. This suited me fine, so I went straight on to the Glenormiston payroll.

The Glenormiston camp was a good one. Mick Nulty was the head stockman, there were four white stockmen including me, four black stockmen and a cook who had a very good voice and who used to entertain us around the camp fire at night with old bush songs.

The work was routine; branding was in full swing. A couple of times we attended a boundary muster on the northern boundary that adjoined Roxborough Downs, a station belonging to the same company as Lake Nash. It was always something we looked forward to, swapping yarns, genuine and otherwise, around the camp fire.

I had a bad fall. A dirty little chestnut horse threw me in some rough country and I was badly cut about the face. The flies attacked the cuts in swarms. Mick Nulty swabbed them liberally with iodine, which was very savage treatment and when I got my breath back I told him so.

Not long after, I was unlucky enough to get a bad attack of sandy blight. I went through agony. It felt as though someone was rubbing sand into my eyes with the heel of a boot. They stuck together with a horrible yellow discharge and I was sure I was going blind. I bathed them continually but they got worse. After a few days Hamilton took me to Boulia Hospital. There wasn't much in the way of treatment. It seemed it had to run its course, but gradually I got better and after a week took a room at the only hotel, Ma Howard's, giving some not very serious thought about what to do next. I could have gone back to Glenormiston but had itchy feet.

After a couple of days someone asked me if I wanted work. I said yes, which wasn't strictly accurate, but I realised I'd have to get on to someone's payroll fairly soon.

A drover was in town looking for men and had dropped word at the pub that he had 1000 bullocks to lift from Chatsworth. I asked, "Where to?" Someone else said he thought it was Wodonga. Where the hell was that? I had never heard of it. The barman yelled through to the billiard room, "Harry, where's Wodonga?" Some geographical wizard yelled back, "Wodonga! Christ! That's halfway to the bloody South Pole!"

The next day I joined Bill McEwen — my destination "Halfway to the bloody South Pole!" [actually in Victoria].

Bill McEwen was one of the best cattlemen I've ridden with. He "carried the whip" on Dalgonally for some years before he took up droving, and anyone who could claim to have been head stockman there was above average. I knew I was going to get on well with him.

We had to get stores and supplies, which would take the best part of a day. His camp was thirty-odd miles down the river and Bill had engaged the only truck in town to cart everything back. While he was busy at the store he asked me to try to pick up a couple of men and, if possible, a cook. I was able to muster a couple of stockmen but no cooks were around, they weren't very plentiful anywhere. I bought myself a good riding saddle with my remaining few pounds; a pig's ear poley, so called because of the shape of the kneepads. It was very comfortable, made by McDonald, a well-known Cloncurry saddler. I was sick of riding in the usual run-of-the-mill stock saddle supplied in camps, and even though it took all my money I didn't regret it. After all, I lived in it for anything up to fifteen hours a day, seven days a week.

Late that afternoon we packed everything into the truck, which was parked ouside the store. Bill asked me to find the driver, whose name was Ted and who was sure to be at the pub. I went to the pub and asked for Ted. Someone pointed out an aggressive-looking character who looked a lot the worse for wear, at least half-drunk and engaged in what was without doubt a very serious argument with another man. I approached him a bit cautiously and said, "Ted, Bill's ready to go." He turned on me and said: "You keep out of this or I'll flatten you too!" The other fellow said: "No you bloody well won't, if there's any flattening to be done here I'll do it!" and with that he swung a punch and fell over. As he scrambled to his feet the barman jumped over the bar, got between them and copped a beauty from Ted. That was a very grave mistake on Ted's part; as it turned out, the barman was a very capable pugilist. He took one step back, carefully measured the distance, and laid Ted out cold. I looked down at him stretched out on the bar-room floor and thought it was unlikely he'd be driving us that night.

I went back to Bill McEwen and told him the bad news. He was fairly philosophical about it and said that it would be a bloody miracle if he ever came to town and got out again without something going wrong. We both settled in at the pub for the night. The next morning a friend of Ted's turned up and said he would drive us out, explaining that Ted was "a bit crook". We picked up the two men I'd recruited and left.

Bill's camp was at Yellow Waterhole, just below the junction of the Burke on the Georgina; he'd put on two men just before he went to Boulia for his stores. There were now six of us; nearly a full camp, but without a cook.

We mustered the horses, shod them and left for Chatsworth, nearly 100 miles away. As the delivery date wasn't for another week we took it in easy stages and got to the boundary five days later.

We took delivery of the cattle and headed them for the stock route, the Chatsworth head stockman and his camp staying with us for a couple of days until the cattle settled down. When they left we could hold them at night with two men on watch. A couple of days later we were down one.

I was doing the horse tailing and some cooking. The boss helped out now and then; it was rough, but no one complained — not too loudly anyway. I had four saddle horses (one more than the usual quota): Vanity, a grey; a chestnut mare called Music; a black horse, Friday; and a big bay horse called Clown. I didn't think he was well named, he stood about sixteen hands with as evil an eye as I'd seen. Earlier Bill had said: "You'd better take that bay horse, Tom; I think he might be a bit too much for any of these other fellows." And as an afterthought, "He might buck a bit."

"Might buck a bit, eh?" I looked him over — when Bill McEwen said that, he was sure to be rough. "What kind of a bit, Bill?" I asked him. "A big bit or a little bit?"

He laughed and said, "Well, sort of in between."

"Yes," I said "I think you're right, Bill, but it might be me that's in between — in between the saddle and the blue sky." Whenever I went to unhobble him or hobble him he always stood tense and laid his ears back; the milk of equine kindness ran very thinly in his veins.

It was several days later and I hadn't put a saddle on him. It wasn't because I was scared, I told myself, but there was always some reason to put it off. One morning, just before daylight, over the campfire Bill said, "When are you going to ride that bay horse, Tom?" I said, as casually as I could: "As a matter of fact, Bill, I was going to put a saddle on him this morning." Which was a blatant lie. It wasn't the kind of morning anyone would pick to ride a rough horse. It was dark, it was quite cold, it was drizzling rain. But now there didn't seem to be any getting out of it and I decided the sooner I got it over the better.

I caught and saddled him, and as I girthed him up he laid his ears back and snapped at me. Frankly I had the shit scared out of me. I reined him up, keeping the near side rein tighter pulling his head towards me. I put a foot in the stirrup, pressing my knee into his shoulder, and swung into the saddle. For a fraction of a second he stood still, then reared straight up on his hind legs. I thought for a moment he was going to rear over backwards, which is a nasty one, but he came back on to all fours and started to buck. He spun, he twisted and he reared up again, he came back and bucked and

51

twisted. I nearly went that time and thought it wouldn't be long now. Then I could feel him easing up, but only a little. I thought I might make it, but I was nearly done. A few more bucks and I knew I had him, but it was touch and go. I thought, I'm going to make it. Suddenly he stopped, I could feel him trembling all over. I patted him and rubbed him along his neck and spoke to him, putting as much affection into my voice as I could — certainly a lot more than I felt. He gave a few more half-hearted bucks, then stopped. He was really done in — and so was I. If I had seen him bucking beforehand I would never have believed I could have ridden him.

All the camp had been watching silently. I got off and led him back to the camp fire. Bill McEwen said: "That was as good a ride as I've seen, Tom." It was a good moment for me. I knew then that I could ride. Bill would have been a good horseman in his day — Dalgonally was a place of which it was said, "where the man that holds his own is good enough".

I coughed up a couple of spots of blood, had a pannikin of hot tea and went out and mustered the horses.

A week later we came to Bedourie, a little town on the Georgina, which at this stage had now become Eyre's Creek. There was a combined pub and store, a police station and an empty house Bill said was some drover's home when he wasn't on the road with cattle. A few blacks were wandering around and the usual mob of goats.

Our rations were replenished from the store and a cook joined us, which was a godsend. As it turned out he wasn't much of a cook, but the men were no worse off than when Bill and I were doing it; not much better, either, but at any rate it let me off the hook.

We went on and when we were close to Cluny Station the head stockman came out to meet us. Billy Mackie had worked in a circus and consequently had got the name of Circus Billy. He had a reputation as a trick horseman, and was something of a legend in the west.

He was mounted on a fine-looking grey when he rode into our camp. We had been looking forward to meeting him, but he was in no mood to demonstrate any of his skills. He'd just given his cook a hiding and sacked him after catching him *in flagrante delicto* with a pack mare.

It shook me somewhat, I'd heard of this sort of thing before, but never really believed it happened. Everyone thought it was a marvellous story, and it was going to do the rounds of the campfires for a long time.

As Mackie told the story, the camp had been out mustering and, being shorthanded, he had left the cook to bring the plant to the next camp. He was such a long time arriving that the head stockman rode back, thinking that perhaps something had gone wrong. I suppose it had in a way. He was caught in the act.

Mackie stayed with us until we got to the Monkira boundary, no doubt thinking we would have killed a Cluny bullock, which was reasonable thinking.

When he left us, still carrying on about his ex-cook. His last words were: "It wasn't even a good-looking mare!"

When we got to Monkira we had done forty miles without a drink for the bullocks. We'd got horse water at a bore ten miles off the stock route, which was too far to take the bullocks. We were now on the Diamantina River. There was good water but nothing in the way of feed — the stock route was eaten out. After the forty-mile stage we would have liked to have had a day or two's spell but there was no point in it. The Monkira manager told McEwen there was good feed on Farrar's Creek: nearly seventy miles away with one waterhole, Toonka, in between.

The day before we got to Toonka was December 25. The cook was developing sandy blight; I had every reason to be sorry for him, not the least being that it looked as though I'd have to do the cooking again. It was not a Merry Christmas.

We got to the low and boggy waterhole late in the afternoon. Bill had let the leaders stride out two or three miles back so that they got to the water a few at a time. Two got bogged; we couldn't

53

get them out, and they had to be shot. Before we got to Currawilla on Farrar's Creek we dropped a few more along the track. They were starting to feel the effects of the dry stages and shortage of feed.

When we got to Farrar's Creek it was like riding into Paradise, just to see green grass again — and in such profusion. It was a marvellous experience. It was belly deep and I almost felt as though I could get off my horse and have a feed myself.

That night there was no need to watch the cattle; they wouldn't stray far in that kind of feed. The creek was wide, a series of channels and there was plenty of water.

After a couple of days we got the cattle together very reluctantly and went on. We would have liked to have stayed longer but at two shillings a head, a hundred miles, McEwen couldn't afford to dawdle. He was paid for what cattle he delivered and the losses were already starting to mount.

Two days later we got to Mooraberrie Station, owned and run by Mrs Duncan-Kemp, a widow of oustanding ability and character, who carried on after her husband died. She had two younger sisters with her, also very competent horsewomen. One was Laura (called Sandy); the other one I think was Beatrice, but was always called Trixie.

Mrs Duncan-Kemp wrote several books. I recall *Where Strange Paths Go Down, Where Strange Gods Call* and *Our Channel Country,* describing five terrible years of drought. Bill McEwen knew her and we got our packbags filled with good meat. Bill said later, "I expect it was one of Sid's bullocks," referring to Sir Sidney Kidman, who owned most of the country in those parts.

After Farrar's Creek there was no more green grass and not much of any other kind. We got to Windorah, the first town we'd seen since leaving Bedourie. We camped a couple of miles out and the boss rode in to get rations and what news he could glean regarding what was ahead in the way of water and grass.

The news wasn't good, he told us. There was no grass and the local stock inspector had told him that there was a 100-mile dry stage ahead. There was no way we could have got over that so he sent a telegram to the owners, telling them the situation and advising them to paddock the cattle.

A reply came back instructing him to find a suitable paddock and he got the job of looking after them, which amounted to riding the fences.

So that was that. We got our cheques in Windorah and two days later I got a job on one of Kidman's stations, Durrie, about halfway between Windorah and Birdsville.

CHAPTER 6

MUSTERING ON A KIDMAN STATION

The manager, Barbed Wire Edwards (his brother, Tie Wire, managed Glengyle), had come to Windorah on business and was looking for a stockman. After talking to Bill McEwen, he asked me if I'd take a job: he only needed one man, and I think Bill had told him I was all right and could ride a bit.

The next morning, before daylight, I threw my swag, saddle and bridle into the back of his utility and we left. It was about 140 miles to Durrie and as we travelled along the dusty road the manager told me they had been through a bad drought and hadn't been able to brand for two years, but now there had been rain and the cattle were in good condition. The losses had been heavy but the younger cattle had survived, mainly on spinifex, a spiky plant which could stand any amount of drought.

In the afternoon as we drove along I saw in the distance a cloud of dust from a stockyard. Edwards turned off the road and drove across to the yard, pulled up, got out and walked over. There seemed to be about 150 head of cattle yarded up, I could see a lot of big unmothered cleanskins among them. I stayed in the car. A man with a branding iron in his hand put it back in the fire and came to the rails.

I watched the Durrie manager as he talked to the stockman through the rails, and they weren't exchanging pleasantries. From the odd word I could catch it seemed quite heated.

After a while Edwards came back to the car looking far from happy and as we drove off he told me what had upset him.

The man he spoke to was Monty James, the Mooraberrie head stockman, and the cattle in the yard had been mustered from country that was close enough to the Durrie boundary for Edwards to have been notified of the muster so his stock camp could attend, collect what cattle of theirs turned up — there were sure to have been some — and split the cleanskins, which was an unwritten law. James had slipped in and mustered the country without giving notice: a dirty trick though, as I well knew, practised fairly frequently, especially when the neighbour was someone like Kidman, who owned half Queensland and would come under the heading of legitimate prey.

As I learnt afterwards, and would have expected, Mrs Duncan-Kemp, a widow with daughters, running a cattle station in far Western Queensland — one of the harshest environments in the world — would have plenty of sympathetic admirers among the cattlemen, and picking up a few of Kidman's cleanskins wouldn't be regarded as serious by anyone . . . with the possible exception of Kidman's managers. The men of the west, rough diamonds though they were, were undoubtedly very chivalrous toward women — but would be the last to admit it. The Mooraberrie head stockman would be expected to keep within reasonable bounds — fairly reasonable, anyway.

We got to Durrie at sundown and Edwards handed me over to the head stockman, Jack Lee. The other men were Norman Hagen, Greenhide Joe — I don't think I ever heard his other name — a half-caste named Bill Gorringe and an Aborigine, Tommy Scarlett. They were all good men; I liked Bill Gorringe very much. He was a superb horseman, as was Tommy Scarlett, a most likeable bloke. It was a happy camp.

The next day I was right among the action. Horses were brought in and drafted through the yard in preparation for mustering. The next two days we were all busy shoeing.

The head stockman pointed out four horses that were to be mine for this muster. Among them were a bay called Bengal, which he said would buck, and a brown horse, Bobs, which he described as a "dirty bastard". He didn't have to tell me he was going to be a handful; I could see that. Also, his name was some indication. "Bobs" was the name of one of Queensland's most famous outlaws, and I expect he had been named after that outlaw for a very good reason.

The day we left I saddled Bengal in the round yard, the breaking-in yard, and he bucked a bit, though not too badly. I rode him fairly comfortably. Someone opened the gate for me and as we went through he bucked fairly high and I hit the side of my head on the gate cap, a heavy log across the top of the gate posts. I suppose I turned my head instinctively as he bucked under the cap: anyway, it knocked me out of the saddle half-stunned. I got up and walked straight into the stockyard rails, which flattened me. I remembered none of this. I was led back to the quarters and, I think, laid down. Someone poured cold water over me and I started to come to. The manager arrived with a bottle of rum and gave me a good one. I was nearly right but not quite; it took another rum to do that. It delayed our departure for a while, but I seemed to recover fairly quickly. I changed to a quiet horse and we all rode off.

We mustered down the Diamantina River. The cattle, not having been handled for a couple of years, were wild, but we had good horses. I saddled up the brown horse, Bobs, and took him down into the river bed where there was loose sand fetlock deep, which made it harder for the horse and softer for me if I was going to take a fall. Jack Lee suggested I didn't wear spurs on him — superfluous advice. I had no intention of doing that. He gave me a hard time, but I rode him out.

The waterholes were brimming and there was an abundance of wild duck. The head stockman dug an old shotgun out of one of the pack bags, put it together and gave it to one of the Aboriginal stockmen with a couple of cartridges. It was a genuine museum piece: the stock had been broken at some time and repaired with greenhide lacing and the barrel was bound with copper wire. It looked equally lethal at both ends. The man took it with a lot more confidence than I could have mustered; and came back in one piece and with half a dozen ducks.

We worked our way down the river until we got close to the boundary of our western neighbour, Roseberth Station. Their camp joined us for a couple of days along the boundary.

Our last camp for that muster was close to Birdsville and as we'd been working for nearly two weeks without a break, we all rode into the town. We made a beeline for the hotel where there seemed to be some action. Two stockmen, drover's hands as it turned out, were having a fight outside. It didn't seem very serious. We watched them for a while but it wasn't very interesting. Bronco Smith, a drover, had just come back from Marree after delivering a mob of Kidman's bullocks to the railhead. As I found out, Kidman dominated everything and seemed to own pretty well all the cattle and most of the country. The two men who had been fighting came into the bar, had a few drinks, went out again and took up where they left off. No one was taking much notice of them and after a while they gave up. It was very hot, too hot for that sort of thing, and they didn't seem to be bad friends — not too bad anyway.

After a couple of days in Birdsville we made our way back to Durrie. Our next muster took us over to Mt Leonard Station and it was here, camped on a waterhole called Milkerie, that I had my twenty-first birthday. It didn't seem worth mentioning to anyone, and of course it was no different from any other day.

I worked on Durrie for nearly six months but never really liked the country. I think that would be impossible, and it has always amazed me that anyone would want to live there. But there were plenty of people, bred and born there, who lived their life out in that harsh environment hundreds of miles from any township, suffering heartbreaking droughts of years' duration, savage floods, and sandstorms of unbelievable ferocity. Their only lifeline for many years was the strings of camels plodding wearily over several hundred miles of what must have seemed interminable sandhills from the railhead in South Australia to Birdsville. When they departed their vale of tears they may not have always been unwept, but they were certainly unhonoured and unsung.

And though it was an experience that I did not regret, it was with some relief that I threw my saddle and bridle on to the back of a truck and headed north. I got to Boulia once again and the first man I ran into was Jack Clark, who was about to leave for Mt Merlin Station to lift a mob of bullocks for trucking at Dajarra. I wasn't particularly anxious to go droving again, but he was going in the right direction and I would be paid.

A few days after the bullocks were trucked I reached Camooweal, I was in sight of the Territory border.

I was, by my standards, fairly flush with money. I had nearly forty pounds so I stayed at Reilly's Hotel, the Top Pub. This was not so much dictated by my opulence but because old man Reilly had two attractive daughters, Kathleen and Dooley, with whom I had a previous passing acquaintance I was hoping to renew.

The Queensland and Northern Territory Aerial Service was coming into Camooweal. One of the pilots, Norman Evans, was also staying at the hotel and he and I became good friends. He used to tell fascinating stories of his experiences in the Royal Flying Corp as a fighter pilot in the First World War. He had been flying for this company, which he called "Qantas", for about twelve months. He didn't think they could last much longer — they had recently had a bad crash near Longreach in which everyone had been killed, and since then they were having difficulty attracting passengers.

Evans was taking one of the girls out and I helped out with the other one. We used to go for picnics on the river. One day we went to Rocklands Station with a few others to say goodbye to Mrs Donaldson. It was very sad. Her husband, who was the manager of Rocklands, was one of the passengers in the aeroplane that had crashed.

Then there was the annual race meeting which, although not financially rewarding, was great fun. It was the first race meeting I had ever been to in my life. People came from hundreds of miles, the two hotels were full, and tents were strung along the bank of the river.

A couple of days after the races I made a rapid calculation of my resources, a by no means complicated exercise. The result was that I would have to give serious consideration to getting a job; and not waste too much time about it, either. My unrewarding investments on horses, plus a few other extravagances, had left me with barely enough to pay my hotel account. Needs must when the devil drives and I could feel His Eminence's hot breath uncomfortably close to the back of my neck.

I reluctantly made my farewells, Norman Evans and I swearing to be at the next Camooweal Race Meeting. This of course, never eventuated and it was with great sadness that I learned, some years later, he disappeared on a flight between Melbourne and Tasmania. There were no survivors and I don't think any part of the aeroplane was recovered.

CHAPTER 7

STOCK CAMP COOK AT BRUNETTE DOWNS

O nce again I was on a truck heading west, and when we crossed the border into the Northern Territory I had a feeling of great content.

The truck on which I'd hitched a ride was driven by a genial Irishman named Monty Montague. Apparently it was his first command. He told me that when he took the job with Noel Healy, a well-known character who was revolutionising transport in the Territory, he had never driven a vehicle before in his life. I asked him how he managed to get the job, "Good old Irish blarney," he said, which was easy to believe. Anyway, anyone with any sort of mechanical knowledge was very rare. Horse teams were the principal means of transport.

The various trucks I'd been in until then had all been Fords. Their mechanism seemed a whole lot simpler than this one, with its great variety of clocks, levers and pedals. It was the biggest I'd ever seen. It had an enormous engine, the tyres were solid and, Monty told me, it was designed to carry two tons. But he said: "We never put less than three tons on any of the trucks. Sometimes I get to three and a half, but I try to keep it down to three."

I asked him about the clocks with their quivering needles and he said one indicated the temperature of the water in the radiator, another one was something to do with the battery, and he didn't know what the third one was for — the needle had fallen off and was jumping around at the bottom.

He said, "Anyway, they're not important; none of them work."
"But the needles are moving about," I said. "Yes," he replied,
"that's the rough ground."

We passed Avon Downs, dropped some loading at a lonely store
on the bank of the Rankine River at midday and went on. The next
stop was Alexandria Station, the second biggest cattle property in
the world — probably the second biggest property of any sort, I
thought. It was about 10,000 square miles. I'd heard of Victoria
River Downs, the biggest, which was 12,000 or so square miles.

We unloaded about half the cargo. Monty said we would camp
here, mainly because his lights didn't work. I heard a familiar noise
— someone was rattling a horse bell, heralding the evening meal.
We had a shower and went to the men's kitchen, where enormous
dishes of food were laid out on a side table. Tremendous juicy
steaks, oxtail and kidney stew, steaming potatoes and baked
pumpkin.

Two or three men strung in, and later the Chinese cook joined
us. The stock camps were out on the run, and the men who were at
dinner were fencers, a blacksmith, a wheelwright. Most of them
knew Monty.

At the first crack of dawn we were thundering along the road
again. We passed a few drovers, their bullocks spread over half a
mile of country feeding their way to Queensland. Monty suggested
I try for a job, because most of them were sure to be shorthanded,
but I firmly said no. For one thing I'd had enough of droving to last
me for a long, long time; and they were going in the wrong
direction.

Brunette Downs, the next station, was as far as Monty was
going so I'd have to get a job there. If I didn't I had no idea what I
would do, but I wasn't giving it too much thought. Hurtling over
the plains in the cool morning at thirty or forty miles an hour was
very pleasant. It seemed a lot faster, but that's what Monty said we
were doing. Sometimes the speedo, as he called it, would leap

round to sixty, which was as far as it would go, but only over rough ground.

Brunette Downs hove in sight at midday. We could see the cluster of buildings shimmering in the mirage a long time before we got there, looking as though they were sitting up on high stilts. As we got closer they gradually came back to earth.

We pulled into the store, I helped unload, and then I asked the storekeeper if there were any work. He said, "See Doug; he's in the office."

Doug Cotton was the manager, I knew him, having met him at Camooweal races. Also, I recalled, he was among the party that said goodbye to Mrs Donaldson at Rocklands. I walked over to the office. He remembered me very well and when I asked him if there was any work he said: "Well, nothing that would suit you, Tom."

I replied: "Any clothes will fit a naked man, Doug." He smiled and said, "Oh well, if you care to take it on, Jack Everett wants a cook. I don't think you'd have to be a culinary genius. In fact, I know he's bloody desperate."

Hell, I thought; a bloody cook. Then the manager said: "If you took it on it mightn't be for long. Something would be sure to come up on one of the stock camps." There were two camps on Brunette. That definitely swung it.

"He's getting ready to go out mustering right now. He's over at the stockyard," Doug said.

I made my way to the yard, where Everett was struggling with a horse that didn't want to be shod. "Tom Cole's the name. Doug Cotton sent me over. He said you wanted a cook. Will I do?" He only asked me one question, and it wasn't anything to do with cooking. "Can you drive a four-in-hand?"

I said sure, and though my experience was limited to driving Jack Clark's team a few times, there wasn't anything difficult about that. Well, as I've been finding out all my life, you can always learn something.

I said goodbye to Monty, carried my gear to Jack Everett's camp and settled in. There were eight stockmen, all Aborigines, a jackeroo, and of course the head stockman. Everett's camp was the number two camp and mustered the western half of the run. The next muster was to be Corella Lakes, and we were to leave in a couple of days.

The morning of our departure started at four o'clock, once breakfast was out of the way. The waggonette was packed up with the rations and gear, the horses were rounded up at the camp, and they started to catch the harness horses.

It soon dawned on me why a four-in-hand driver was more important than a cook. It seemed that on Brunette anything that was uncontrollable, anything that couldn't be ridden, anything that savaged — there was only one place for it: "Put the bastard in the waggonette!"

I climbed up into the driver's seat and made myself comfortable, one foot firmly on the brake. A couple of boys were dragging over a black horse that didn't want to be dragged anywhere. It didn't have much option, because a greenhide rope around its neck was slowly strangling it, and eventually they got it harnessed into the nearside pole. The offside poler, which was blindfolded, came a bit quieter. The leaders were then hooked up, one reasonably quiet, the other blindfolded too and lashing out with both feet. Everett called to me, "Are you right, Tom?"

I took a firm grip of the ribbons and nodded. "Let 'em go," he yelled.

The boys who were hanging on to the head sprang clear. The two horses that had been blindfolded with bags over their heads looked startled for a moment, but only a moment. As I eased the brake off they gave a powerful plunge forward — I thought they were going to pull the waggonette in half — and we went at a half gallop.

I headed them along a road towards a gate in the fence around the station buildings. Someone was supposed to have opened the gate for me, everybody thought of it at once, but it was too late. The head stockman was shouting, "The gate! The bloody gate!"

Two or three stockmen galloped alongside the waggonette trying to reach it first, but they had no hope and all they did was stimulate my team to greater efforts. For a brief moment I felt like a Roman charioteer. A very brief moment. Suddenly I discovered that someone had omitted to buckle the reins to the offside leader's bit; I had some sort of control over the horses in the pole, a little over the nearside leader, but none whatever over the offside horse.

We were getting perilously close to the gate, I thought, "Christ! What do I do now!" I had the brake partly on, but couldn't apply too much pressure or I'd have turned the whole outfit over. With some little control over the nearside leader I managed to turn them, the waggonette swaying dangerously from side to side. We were following the fence, which ran down to a big lagoon fed by Brunette Creek. Everett was galloping behind me shouting instructions, or maybe encouragement. I tried to ease the team around, and gradually got them turned. We were now galloping along the edge of the lagoon, and came to a log that had been deposited by the last flood. To avoid it the horses had to veer toward the water: the wheels sank in the mud and the whole outfit turned over.

I was catapulted from the driving seat into deep water, still holding the reins, surrounded by swags, billycans and miscellaneous paraphernalia. The horses were terrified. Two had fallen and the other two were frantically kicking their way out of the harness, which didn't take very long. As I clambered out I saw one disappearing through the gate (which by this time someone had carefully opened) still with his blinkers and collar on.

The head stockman was sitting on his horse laughing. I couldn't see what he was laughing at. Doug Cotton drove up in a utility truck and Everett stopped laughing. The rest of the camp arrived and started a rescue operation. The waggonette had a broken pole, everything was soaking wet, all the rations were ruined.

So we started all over again, we dried our swags out, fresh rations were drawn from the store, two stockmen rode out to the horse paddock, presumably to find another bloody outlaw to replace the horse that had galloped through the open gate — and which wasn't found for three weeks.

Their best efforts were unsuccessful and they returned with a big black horse whose only fault was that he bit. After savaging a couple of stockmen he'd been promoted to the waggonette. I consoled myself with the thought that he'd have to be bloody smart to reach me in the driver's seat.

Surprisingly, Jack Everett told me I'd handled the team well and although I'd been in the driving seat for about five minutes I felt I'd packed a fair bit of experience into that amount of time. The station blacksmith fitted a new pole and once again I was up in the driver's seat wondering what was going to happen next.

This time we got away quite uneventfully, the gate was open and I went through at a half gallop. After a few miles the team settled down, trotting along peaceably.

We got to Corella Lakes and settled in. Arrangements had been made to meet a stock camp from Alroy, a neighbouring station to the south, which had cattle mixed with ours along the boundary. They were already there, four Aboriginal stockmen in charge of a jackeroo named Marcel Verbruggen. Verbruggen's father was the conductor of a Sydney symphony orchestra and a friend of the owner of Alroy Downs. Apparently young Verbruggen was a bit of a handful and the conductor asked old man Schmidt to take his son out to the most remote of his several stations and keep him there for a couple of years.

I liked Marcel from the start; he had adapted himself to the bush extremely well, but my most enduring memory of him is that he taught me to make yeast and bake bread, which was no mean accomplishment. Counting the Alroy camp I had fourteen hungry stockmen to feed, and keeping bread up to them was the biggest job.

Up to that time I had been making dampers of varying quality and colours. A damper is flour with cream of tartar and bi-carbonate of soda — the basic ingredients of baking powder — mixed with it. Real bread had been far beyond my limited talents.

Marcel's father mightn't have thought much of his son, but when he showed me how to make bread I thought he was a bloody genius. It wasn't too good for a start and I'd dug a few holes to bury the first two or three efforts, but after a while I was turning out very creditable products. In an expansive mood, Jack Everett told me I might make a cook one day. Not if I had anything to do with it, I thought.

We finished the Corella Lakes muster. Alroy got about two hundred head of its cattle, and after the cleanskins were split, had nearly three hundred altogether. They went back to Alroy, we moved to another area and mustered for a few more weeks. Jack Everett said we had branded more than 1000 head: the camp was packed up once again and we went back to the station, the shoes were pulled off the horses and they were turned out. My career as a cook came to an end and, though I didn't exactly go out in a blaze of glory, no one died of food poisoning either.

The year was galloping past, the waterholes were getting low and most of the cattle were now on bores. I was packed off to Anthony's Lagoon, an outstation seventy miles to the west, and handed over to the head stockman, Jimmy Wilson. I was to go to a bore and run an engine that in turn worked a pump. I was on my own, seeing Jimmy only occasionally when he came to my camp with a pack horse with rations for me. It was pretty deadly. I tried talking to the cattle but they took no notice, except to look at me in a peculiar sort of way. I was sure I knew how they felt. The odd drover passed and sometimes a travelling stockman. Once a car went past but didn't stop; but otherwise they all called in and camped the night. I think most men looked forward to some fresh conversation.

After a few weeks I realised Wilson knew I was getting restless, and could see I wasn't going to stay much longer. If I went and he couldn't get hold of a replacement he might be stuck with the pumping himself; and he wasn't keen on that. But, as is usual in such situations, everything worked itself out. Some young fellow turned up at Anthony's Lagoon looking for work and the next day Wilson rode into my camp and stayed the night.

Talking over the campfire he got around to my immediate future, and had it all worked out. "Tom," he said, "I think you're getting itchy feet and don't quite know what to do about it."

We both looked at my riding saddle; as a means of transport, it wasn't much good without a horse or horses. "Yes, you're right Jim; I must admit you've hit the nail on the head." I was silent for a while and went on, "I've got enough money to buy a horse, perhaps two, and a pack saddle, but that's not good enough."

Then Wilson produced his trump card. "Look Tom," he said, "I can fix you up. There are four fresh horses running in my horse paddock, they belong to Bill Crowson, the drover. He lost them when he passed through on his way back to Wave Hill a couple of months ago. You take them, you'll find Bill at Wave Hill, and he'll be glad to see them, I know that. He's got a mob of bullocks to lift in early March, and by the time you get there there'll be plenty of stock work available."

I thought it was a good idea and a couple of days later I handed the pumping over to the new man — who was as anxious to get the job as I was to get out of it.

CHAPTER 8

BANKA BANKA AND BARROW CREEK RACES

Once I was back in a saddle and moving, life seemed a lot better. I headed west following the stock route, the only outlet for cattle going to Queensland: In the droving season, tens of thousands of bullocks from as far away as the Kimberleys in Western Australia walked to properties where they would be spelled and fattened or to trucking yards like Dajarra. Depending on their destination, they could be up to five or six months on the road.

From Anthony's Lagoon to Newcastle Waters was 170 miles. There was nothing in between, not a homestead, not a fence, and what few waterholes there were had long since dried up and would not fill again until the next wet season, several months away. Every thirty miles or so were sub-artesian bores. On each bore was a windmill with a wingspan of thirty feet, sitting on top of a steel tower about sixty feet in height. The water was lifted from several hundred feet and pumped into huge earth tanks that held 500,000 gallons. It was then piped into a long trough; the flow was controlled by a float valve that automatically shut the water off when the trough was full.

Although unstocked it was all wonderful grazing country — rolling Mitchell and Flinders grass downs, most of it belonging to the owners of Brunette Downs. The grass within a few miles of the bores had been eaten out by travelling stock, and for that reason I watered my horses in the late afternoon and went on until I came to good grass before I made camp.

Six days after leaving Anthony's Lagoon I rode into Newcastle Waters and over that lonely track I had not passed a single homestead or building or seen a single person.

Newcastle Waters was a fairly big property. Something in excess of 4000 square miles. The homestead sat up on a ridge overlooking the waterhole, which was about half a mile long and a very welcome sight.

There didn't seem much grass for my horses, but then I wasn't expecting any. I unpacked about fifty yards from the edge of the lagoon. I could see a camp further up the creek — a drovers' camp by the look of the gear and the number of pack saddles and riding saddles.

I walked over and made myself known to a couple of men at the camp. One was Charlie Swan, a western drover, and the other was working with him. They told me I would have to take my horses four or five miles to get them a decent feed, which was pretty well what I expected. Swan said he was waiting for a telegram that would tell him where to go for his next mob of cattle. I realised then that I was on the Overland Telegraph Line. Newcastle Waters Station acted as an unofficial post office; there was also a store from which drovers and travellers could stock up with rations.

I took my horses out about four miles and hobbled them: the feed wasn't too bad, but I wasn't going to be staying very long. I had to give some thought to Bill Crowson's horses. It was November, the droving season didn't start until March — four months away — and there was no great hurry. Crowson wouldn't be worrying; he didn't even know I had them. I decided to let nature take its course.

The next morning I mustered my horses early, went to the station store and filled up with rations. Among my purchases was a bottle of strychnine, sold freely in all stores in the back country despite being one of the deadliest poisons. Buying the poison was a last-minute decision. Chatting to the storekeeper, who was also the station manager, the subject of the scarcity of work came up. He said "Why don't you do a bit of dog stiffening?" — the bush term for dingo poisoning — "They're giving my cattle bloody hell, there's packs of 'em down Newcastle Creek."

So I turned south following Newcastle Creek. I didn't expect to make much but I thought I might as well be idle as doing nothing. At the best I might keep my tucker bags full. Dingo scalps were worth a bounty of five shillings each, with payment made through police stations. There wasn't a police station within 200 miles, but any storekeeper would take them. They were good currency. I was in "the skin and hair trade" at last!

The station manager was right: there were packs of dingoes. I rarely saw one in the daytime, but at night they howled and snarled and fought — over the baits I had laid, I hoped — but they weren't keen on getting poisoned. I usually got one each night; twice I got two. I scalped them and dried them in the sun. My rations took on the peculiar odour of dry and half-dry dog scalps.

I followed the Overland Telegraph Line and sixty miles from Newcastle Waters I came to Powell's Creek Telegraph Station, manned by two white men and a number of Aborigines. Bill Phillips was the operator and in charge of the station. Jim Andrews was the linesman.

The working of the Overland Telegraph Line was a smooth operation. Between Darwin and the South Australian border were six telegraph stations, roughly 200 miles apart; Daly Waters, Powell's Creek, Tennant Creek, Barrow Creek, Alice Springs and Charlotte Waters. These were repeater stations that boosted the power conveying the traffic.

Each station with an operator and a linesman, was completely self-contained. Each had twenty or thirty horses for transport, and a herd of around 200 head of cattle to supply beef and milk. The linesman's job was to look after the stock, brand and break in the young horses, and kill a bullock for meat when required.

Should a break occur in the line he would have to ride out, find it and make repairs. When this happened — which it seemed was not very often — he would take pack horses to carry at least a week's supplies, saddle horses and Aboriginal assistants. Locating the fault would sometimes take days.

The Overland Telegraph Line is steeped in history, adventure and romance and must rank as one of the greatest accomplishments in Australia's pioneering history. Before the line was built, the only form of communication Australia had with the outside world was by ship and even with the advent of steam, mail took a minimum of six weeks between England and Australia.

There was already a line between Java and Europe and the British Australian Telegraph Company was established with the object of closing the gap with an underwater cable and an overland telegraph line. The South Australian Government pledged to build the line from Port Augusta to Darwin, the BAT would finance it: the distance was 2000 miles and it was to be completed and open for traffic by January 1, 1872.

All that was known of the terrain were the records of John McDowell Stuart, the explorer who had ridden from the south to the north and back eight years previously. The little that could be gleaned from his records was daunting, to say the least. During the dry period there were stretches of 200 miles and more without water, there were hostile blacks and little chance of the land yielding any sustenance.

Eighteen months to construct 2000 miles of telegraph line through what was virtually an unknown wilderness with bullock waggons, pack horses and camels, and a penalty clause of seventy pounds sterling a day after January 1, 1872: the British Australian Telegraph Company had no intention of encouraging idlers!

Charles Todd was an astronomer, but he was no stargazer. He came to Australia from Greenwich Observatory to develop the infant science of telegraphy and by an unusual stroke of genius and foresight — qualities to which governments are not usually

73

given — the South Australian Government elevated Todd to the position of Postmaster General and dropped the embryo telegraph line in his lap.

Men were recruited at a wage of twenty-five shillings a week and keep, and there was no shortage of applicants. Miracles of organisation and logistics were performed and though the line took six months longer than the specified time, the penalty clause was not invoked; the British Australian Telegraph Company had its own problems, which caused several delays.

In one year and eleven months Todd and his men built a line through 2000 miles of country that for the greater part, had been crossed only once before by Europeans. In that time they had also built a twenty-two-room stone building at Darwin and a number of buildings, also of stone, at several other stations, of which Powell's Creek was one.

The cost was £479,174.18.3d. The people who built the Sydney Opera House couldn't have done it!

I stayed at Powell's Creek for three days. When I rode on, my pack bags were well replenished by the generosity of Bill Phillips and Jim Andrews.

Three days and four dog scalps later I rode up to Banka Banka Homestead, a cattle station owned by Paddy and Jim Ambrose, who gave me a hearty welcome. Banka Banka was a nice property of about 2000 square miles, running a herd of 20,000 or so Herefords. The horses were good quality, probably three-quarter thoroughbred.The homestead was at the foot of a low range, alongside a beautiful clear spring. It was built of mud bricks made of antbed. The first time I had seen this kind of construction.

After a couple of days I mentioned moving on, but the Ambroses pressed me to stay, not because of the odd jobs — making greenhide ropes, helping to put a few rails in the stockyard — but because they genuinely liked company.

Eventually it was suggested that I break in some horses, to which I agreed readily. I hadn't done any horse breaking before, although I had given a hand a few times, but I was confident I could do the job and I was anxious to get the experience.

Paddy explained they couldn't afford to pay wages, but if I'd like to break in some colts I could have one for every four I broke in. I thought this a good idea, since I didn't own the horses I was using.

He gave me a good offsider and the next day we got greenhide ropes and breaking tackle from the harness room and started work.

The arrangement was very fair. The first four horses I broke in were inspected by Paddy and passed; and he let me have first pick. From the next batch Paddy had first pick, and so on. The standard of horse flesh was pretty good and after a few weeks I had five good horses: a nice bay, a beautiful chestnut, a well-built chunky mare, ideal for a pack horse, and a couple of others.

It was early December and I had to give some thought to making back north and going across to Wave Hill, so I could return the four horses Jim Wilson had given me to their rightful owner, who was blissfully unaware of their peregrinations.

But I got side tracked again. There was going to be a race meeting at Barrow Creek, 200 miles to the south. The Ambroses intended to go and I was soon infected with their enthusiasm.

Something like forty head of horses were mustered up and drafted through the stockyard. The quality was very good: like most cattlemen, the Ambroses were horse lovers and from time to time imported thoroughbred stallions; but a good stock horse and a racehorse were, you might say, horses of a different colour.

For two days we galloped horses over a plain nearby and in the end two came up with fairly good credentials, one a big black called Black Watch and the other a nice bay colt, Curio. And I got the job (honorary, of course) of taking the pride of Banka Banka to Barrow Creek. I became chief transport officer, trainer and, as it turned out, jockey.

Reflecting on it all now, it seems like some sort of insanity to take horses 200 miles to a race meeting — a few weeks *before* the meeting — with water anything up to forty miles apart. At least they'd have to have stamina.

Accompanied by two Aboriginal stockmen I set off full of confidence. With saddle horses and pack horses — and, of course the racehorses — I had eighteen head. The first water, Attack Creek, was twenty miles and from there it was forty miles to Tennant Creek Telegraph Station. Then on to Kelly Well, thirty-two miles further. It had been a stinking hot day and we arrived hot, tired and thirsty. The two stockmen manned the windlass and wound up the heavy bucket: and floating on top of that precious water was a dead snake, putrid and foul.

Three days later we arrived at Barrow Creek, also a Telegraph Station, chiefly famous for an attack by blacks many years earlier when the telegraph operator, the linesman and another man were speared.

It was without doubt the wildest of all the wild bush race meetings I have been to.

The first day's racing was on Christmas Eve. Paddy and Jim Ambrose arrived in their car the day before and came to my camp on the creek. There must have been fifty camps strung along the bank.

There was no hotel, but it would have been unthinkable to have a race meeting without liquor. One public-spirited gentleman brought a two-ton truck loaded with a large assortment of grog on which he confidently expected a 300 per cent profit. Paddy and Jim Ambrose deciding to put in a short cut, went to the would-be publican's camp and made him a generous offer for the entire outfit — lock, stock, barrel and bottle. The Banka Banka camp then became host for the rest of the meeting and everyone agreed that the Ambroses were "terrible good fellows". When the meeting was over they were still good fellows; and they both looked terrible.

I rode in three races and managed a second and a third. Though we didn't win a race, it seemed unimportant: as Jim Ambrose said, "It's the booze and the company that counts."

76

I then got the job of driving the newly acquired truck back to Banka. The stockmen brought the horses along a few days later. It was mid-January and Banka Banka was beginning to feel like home, but as pleasant as the companionship was, I had to make a break soon. There had been much-needed rain and Jim said, "You'd better wait until the country dries out a bit", and another week went by. Then we decided that I would make north about the time Jim and Paddy went to Alice Springs to replenish their stores — about another week, Paddy said. I went out with some of the stockmen and mustered twenty-odd brood mares and branded the foals.

Banka Banka was of course hooked into the telephone line and at fairly regular intervals we would get a call from along the line, keeping up with the Territory gossip, cattle markets, rainfall and so forth. Then one morning, some really startling news came in from Katherine, a small township on the bank of the Katherine River.

It seemed from what we could gather from the rather garbled story passed from one station to the next, that there had been a large mob of cleanskin cattle stolen from Victoria River Downs and the poddy dodgers had been caught red-handed.

It was some days before we were able to get any details, but bit by bit we managed to put the story together. A station owner named Stan Brown had been arrested together with some other men. The Ambroses seemed to know him casually, I gathered. He had a station on the Daly River called Dorisvale.

The trial was to take place at Katherine in about a week, and the Ambroses decided that they would go to Katherine for their stores instead of Alice Springs. Would I like to come with them? There was only one answer to that.

We all thought it a magnificent story, an epic of considerable proportions. It seemed that three men had been arrested: Stan Brown, a half-caste cattleman named Fred Martin and Jack Gordon, a tin miner. No one was sure how a tin miner had got involved in it.

The real "hero" was Jim Webb, but he had "gone into smoke".

Jim Webb had come from Queensland a couple of years previously, leaving that State in a hurry due to a misunderstanding over some cattle branding. In order to avoid a "miscarriage of justice", he had slipped across the border into the Northern Territory only a few miles ahead of a Queensland mounted policeman and two of the best black trackers in the north.

The authorities were reasonably philosophical about it and though they could have got warrants extending their authority across the border, they decided first that it was good riddance, and second that he wouldn't be likely to return to Queensland and disturb the even tenor of their lives while there was a warrant hanging over him.

When he crossed the border he assumed, for reasons of expediency, the name of Jim Webb. Travelling with the caution the circumstances dictated, keeping off the stock routes and better-known tracks, he rode from creek to river, from waterhole to billabong; he was an excellent bushman and if he did chance across the odd stockman or drover he certainly wouldn't have been asked any questions. It was an inflexible unwritten law: if a man cared to tell you something about himself, well and good; if he didn't, that was his privilege — a respected one.

After travelling 400 miles he quietly and unostentatiously rode into Katherine. He had three mules and three horses. The railway line was being extended another 100 miles south, and Webb got work carting water for the fettling gangs. He bought a waggon and acquired some more mules, made up a team and carted water for six months until the railway was finished.

It was December 1927, and by this time there was very little work. A lot of men from the railway line were now idle. Webb pulled his waggon over to the Katherine River and made camp. It was a popular camping spot frequented by cattlemen. One of them, Matt Hart, owned a cattle station called Lewin Springs, about 1200 square miles, which ran across to the Daly River. Jimmy Webb and Matt Hart first met shortly after the railway line was completed and Webb's fertile imagination combined with Hart's cupidity resulted in a "gentleman's" agreement that would have been of considerable benefit to both had things gone according to plan.

The whole arrangement was absurdly simple. Webb was to deliver to Hart an unspecified number of cleanskin cattle, for which he would be paid one pound a head. A round figure of 200 was suggested, because anything less was not much of a proposition and anything more would be too unwieldy for the few trustworthy and competent men who would be recruited. The deal was made and sealed over a bottle of rum and a handshake.

Matt Hart went back to Lewin Springs and Jimmy Webb selected Fred Martin and Jack Gordon as his assistants. It was decided to go to Victoria River Downs. Jim Webb had ridden through the eastern side of the run on his previous trip from Queensland and over a span of thirty or forty miles he estimated, as he told me some years later, he saw 2000 head of cleanskins as he passed 6000 or 7000 cattle. From my own experience and observations, that figure was a fair estimate.

Apart from Victoria River Downs being the biggest station in the world, its second claim to fame was the number of cleanskins. Six stock camps did their best to keep the place mustered and branded but, because of the tremendous area, the inaccessibility of some of the country and the time factor, it was impossible. The combined annual branding was about 45,000 head of calves a year, but it wasn't enough to keep the place properly branded up.

The bullock muster usually started early March and the last mob was delivered to the drover about mid April. From then on they would muster and brand, muster and brand, day after day until it became too dry, water and grass too scarce and the cattle too low in condition. The weary stock horses were turned out and

79

the camps turned to yard repairing, making greenhide ropes and catching up on various odd jobs.

After the wet season — about March, as soon as the plains were dry enough — the bullock muster would start again. They would be lucky to get five months out of twelve for branding; it was nowhere near enough.

Shortly after the Hart meeting, Webb, Martin and Gordon rode out of Katherine. It was sundown and for such an expedition they suffered a couple of serious deficiencies that could be remedied only at night.

Manbulloo Station homestead was on the bank of the Katherine River seven miles below the township. The 4000-square-mile property was owned by Vesteys and was managed by Johnny Newmarch. Naturally, as manager, he rode horses that were the pick of the station. His pack saddles and gear were the best. But he was not given to riding the range himself to any extent — if it couldn't be done by car then the job, whatever it may have been, would be delegated or not done at all.

Webb and Martin knew this and that night they rode boldly into the paddock where the horses were running, mustered them into the yard, drafted off ten of the best stock horses, and then went to the saddle room and took two pack saddles. Fred Martin was able to replace his own rather battered saddle for one nearly new.

The trio camped that night on the King River. They passed Delamere Station and skirted Willeroo, both properties owned by Vesteys, and several days later, having travelled more than 200 miles, made camp not far from Victoria River Downs Station homestead . . . where another nocturnal exercise took place.

These vast areas were almost completely unfenced but of necessity there were paddocks in which the stock horses were kept, and which were usually of considerable proportions. VRD homestead was surrounded by two or three, the largest being the Camel Paddock.

The three men worked hard that night, and before daylight had a bottom wire out of the Camel Paddock fence, rolled up and on pack horses. They didn't think the loss of a mile of fencing wire would be noticed for while, and it wasn't. They then rode east to an area known as Killarney: Jim Webb had ridden through it on his way to Katherine and Fred Martin was familiar with it.

They picked a place to camp at the mouth of a narrow gorge and at the opening they strung a couple of wires from tree to tree. Although it wasn't a very high standard of fencing, it was reasonably secure and they started to muster cattle for Matt Hart.

The cattle were semi-wild and it was hard riding, but Webb and Martin were experienced cattlemen and they had good horses. Cattle bearing the VRD bull's head brand were galloped off.

The cleanskins were put up the gorge at night and the fence plus a campfire kept them in. During the day they were brought and tailed by Jack Gordon, and the mob gradually increased in size.

One morning they let the cattle out of the paddock, steadied them down and left them with Gordon as usual. Webb told me some years later that they had about 170 head of cattle in hand and hoped that day would be the last. He intended to move off, and if they were short of the target of 200 they could easily pick up a few extra between there and Lewin Springs. They got back to their camp that evening with about eighteen head of cleanskins — they were getting harder to find now — and to their astonishment found Gordon disconsolately watching ten head of cattle.

What had happened was fairly predictable. As Gordon told the story, the cattle were feeding quietly until they heard other cattle bellowing from the other side of a ridge, probably about a mile away and, as could be expected, started to move toward them. Gordon tried to stop them but they were fairly well spread out and he couldn't get them together. Before long they started to trot; the whole mob panicked and broke into a gallop . . . and that was the end.

The trio started to muster again, and it was another week before they got near the hoped-for number. They were getting edgy. They'd been there more than a fortnight and they were riding far

81

afield. Some stockman could pick up their tracks any day, and he wouldn't have to be very smart to read the story.

After obliterating traces of their camp as best they could, they started for Lewin Springs, more than 100 miles away, crossing the boundary between Victoria River Downs and Delamere. At night they put the cattle in the various stockyards that dotted the country. They came to a yard called Cueing Pen Springs on Delamere country and yarded the cattle.

A hundred yards or so up the creek, Webb noticed a wisp of smoke rising and rode over to investigate. It was two old nomad Aborigines cooking a goanna. They could hardly speak English.

The following day they pressed on, eventually reaching Flora River and camping at the foot of the Flora Range. The country was stony basalt and the cattle were getting sore-footed. Obviously they would be unable to travel much further unless they were rested. Stan Brown's Dorisvale Station was on the other side of the Flora Range, and Jim Webb thought he might be interested in buying the cattle. None of the men cared who bought them; Stan Brown's money was as good as Matt Hart's. So Webb saddled a fresh horse, left the cattle with Martin and Gordon, and rode to Dorisvale. He returned with good news, and the following day they breathed a sigh of relief as they turned the cattle into Brown's paddock. Stan wrote three cheques; £100 went to Webb and £50 each to Martin and Gordon, then the trio rode off for Katherine.

Along the track they dropped the Manbulloo horses; the packs were too good to throw away.

In the meantime something quite unexpected had happened. The old Aborigine and his lubra turned up at Delamere homestead: Delamere was an outstation and managed from Willeroo. When the old couple arrived, Paddy Griffin, the cook, was at the homestead by himself. The head stockman, Jim Bennett, was away mustering horses. The old blackfellow got into conversation with Griffin and said he'd seen the stock camp at Cueing Pen Spring. The cook knew there was no camp there, but casually mentioned the conversation when Bennett came back with his horses.

The more Bennett thought about the matter, the less he liked it. He called the Aborigine up and questioned him closely, then saddled a fresh horse and rode across to the yard. There the tale was written clearly — the ashes of a campfire and in the dust of the yard and on the blacksoil plain, the tracks of 200 cattle being driven by shod horses. Bennett wasted no time, cranked up an old car and tore off to Willeroo to give the manager the shattering news. Together they went to Katherine and got the police.

They came back to Delamere; Sergeant Woods, Bennett and two black trackers. As a precaution they armed themselves with Winchesters, and Bennett supplied horses. A mob of that size together with the horses could be tracked at a trot, and as they rode the tracks became clearer and, of course, fresher. Picking up a bruised leaf here, a broken branch there, they knew they weren't far behind. They pushed their horses hard.

Both Bennett and the Sergeant knew that if the stolen cattle were cleanskins (and that seemed certain), they would have to catch up with them before they were branded and turned out among other cattle, otherwise it would be impossible to establish that they were stolen.

A day later the tracks led them to a paddock gate on Dorisvale. Stan Brown was letting the last few cattle out of the yard to join those branded the previous day.

Woods told his trackers to round up all the cattle in the paddock. All were freshly branded with the Dorisvale brand. Woods asked Brown: "Do you claim these cattle?" He answered: "I claim every beast with my brand on!"

"Very well," Woods said, "I am arresting you and charging you with having stolen cattle in your possession!"

In the meantime the trackers had picked up the tracks of Webb, Gordon and Martin and informed the Sergeant. They had no idea as to their identity and Brown wasn't saying. With Stan Brown for company they left Dorisvale following the tracks. They were heading towards Katherine, and on the way they picked up three of the Manbulloo horses that had been dropped.

Blissfully unaware of developments, Webb and his mates made camp on the bank of the Katherine River close to the township. The horses were unpacked and hobbled out, a fire was started and Jim Webb took two billy cans down to the river 100 yards away. He got to the water's edge and as he did so, happened to glance back. To his astonishment, he saw Sergeant Woods riding into the camp with the two trackers.

For a fraction of a second he stood paralysed, but only for a moment. He dropped the billy cans, dived into the river and swam to the other side.

Martin and Gordon were arrested on the spot, and a search of their belongings soon revealed the three cheques signed by Stan Brown a few days previously. Webb was more fortunate. He was soaking wet but the hot sun dried his clothes. They were all he had in the world but he was a man of considerable fortitude and determination and as soon as it was dark he set out to walk to Marramboy.

Not far from the small township was a cattle station, The Veldt, which was being built up, mainly at the expense of neighbouring herds, by an enterprising cattleman, Jack Guild. He also came from Queensland, but not under such dramatic conditions as Webb, which was probably sheer luck (I should know, Jack Guild and I were partners ten years later). Anyway, Guild had a midnight visitor who arrived completely exhausted. Jack Guild could hardly be described as an oustanding Christian gentleman, and had no aspirations to be such, but he did have a charitable feeling towards anyone in trouble.

Two days later, Jim Webb shook hands with Guild and left The Veldt. He had a good horse under him and was driving three others, one of which carried a pack filled with rations. The horses were in good condition and his supplies would last a month.

Webb travelled west and again forsook the beaten tracks, crossing the West Australian border where it intersected the Sturt River and a few days later turning up at Hall's Creek. He dropped into the hotel one evening and a young stockman at the bar said "I think we've met before, haven't we?" "Maybe we have, maybe we haven't," was the reply. "But the name is Ted Whelan!" There was no more to be said.

Weeks later news filtered through from the west. Drovers spoke casually of a new head stockman at Lissadell Station named Ted Whelan. But this was by no means the end of the Webb/Whelan saga. It was to be continued some years later.

In the meantime Stan Brown, Jack Gordon and Fred Martin had been doing their best to convince a judge of their complete innocence. The difficulties, though, were too numerous and complex — the three cheques were very awkward indeed. Brown won first prize, which was two and a half years, Martin came second — one year — and Jack Gordon must have heaved a sigh of relief when he was advised he would be retired for three months. It appeared the judge had got the priorities right.

We stayed in Katherine for a few days after the court case. Paddy Ambrose and I went round to the lockup to say goodbye to Brown, Martin and Gordon, mumbling words of good cheer that didn't have much effect. Stan deplored the fact that cattle stealing cases were tried by a judge only. In the cattle country of Queensland, juries were abolished some years ago and the Northern Territory followed suit soon after.

It was found that it was impossible to empanel a jury to try cattle cases which did not contain a large percentage of sympathisers towards cattle duffers — it was a fraternity with strong bonds: even the landed gentry's history of development and cattle acquisition would not bear too close a scrutiny. After the abolition of juries the percentage of convictions was, of course, much higher.

A few days later the three men went to Darwin to serve their time at Fanny Bay gaol, which was renowned for its benevolence and flexibility. A certain Mr Dempsey was the supreme being, and he discharged his duties with common sense and compassion. His tenants were mainly Aborigines, mostly murderers according to the criminal code forced upon them, but in no way could they be classified as criminals. They acted according to tribal law, which could not protect them. They accepted their fate with remarkable resignation.

The three men arrived at Fanny Bay in July 1928. They were the first white men Dempsey had had under his care for some time and his welcome would unquestionably have been genuine. He explained the rules: there was no limit to the number of visitors; there was no limit to the amount of liquor allowed in the gaol; but, and he was emphatic about this, not one drop was to be supplied to any Aborigine.

They were allowed out every day but were asked to stay within a mile of the gaol. They were not to frequent hotels under any circumstances and, most important of all, if they were not back by six o'clock they would be locked out! It is a matter of history that one Jack Buscall failed to observe this last injunction and fearing the wrath of Dempsey, scaled the walls in a foolhardy attempt to return. Dropping to the other side he injured his back so badly that he spent the rest of his life in a wheelchair. He was discharged fom gaol immediately and until he died ran a shop in Darwin from where he sold picture postcards and bric-a-brac. It was known as the Curio Shop.

CHAPTER 9

HEAD STOCKMAN AT WAVE HILL FOR VESTEYS

The Ambroses were busy getting the stores and supplies needed for Banka Banka, while I filled in my time at O'Shea's pub. Tim O'Shea had four attractive daughters and I was completely infatuated with two of them. I was beginning to find out that I had some hitherto unsuspected talent for getting into difficulties without realising it. This was an area which, over a wide span of years, was to sidetrack and divert me to a considerable extent. However, looking back and recalling some of the alarming situations in which I found myself it appeared I was twice blessed — my talent for getting into difficulties was shaded, but only just, by a flash of genius which got me out. In this case it might be said I was saved by the bell.

One day I was approached by an elderly gent who introduced himself as Alec Moray. I knew instantly who he was, pastoral inspector for Vesteys, controlling all the firm's cattle stations. He came straight to the point; he wanted a head stockman for Wave Hill, one of Vesteys' larger properties. He had been talking to the Ambroses and they had recommended me, for which I was grateful.

I accepted with alacrity. Paddy and Jim were quite happy to look after my horses until I could make arrangements to get them; they also said that they would see that Bill Crowson, whose horses I had brought from Anthony's Lagoon, would get them back.

Everything fell into place nicely and two days later I was on Bob McLennan's mail truck heading for Wave Hill, 300 miles to the west. McLennan, the mail contractor, was a Gallipoli veteran and a seasoned warrior in many other fields. In the dry season he battled his way over what was not much more than a bridle track in an old truck that testified clearly to the rugged conditions. Dropping mail at Willeroo, the first stop, 100 miles from Katherine, then another thirty to Delamere, then seventy miles to Victoria River Downs completed the first day.

Pigeon Hole, an outstation of VRD, was next and finally Wave Hill. The round trip was 600 miles. There were other stations — Inverway, Limbunya, — further out whose mail he carried, but they had to make their own arrangements: there was only a bridle track. A native stockman and a couple of pack horses had to ride to Wave Hill: for them it was a couple of hundred miles there and back.

In the wet season, roughly from November until March, the roads were impassable for any kind of vehicle. McLennan would then muster up his horses and ten or fifteen pack horses and half a dozen saddle horses for himself and his two horse tailers; perhaps a couple extra if he had a passenger. Sometimes he did; there was no charge, but whoever it may have been certainly earned the ride.

Of the pack horses, two especially selected for their tranquillity carried a few dozen bottles of rum, the sales of which supplemented his income.

The principal rivers, such as the King, Battle Creek, Victoria River, perhaps one or two others, would often have to be swum, and at this he was an expert.

The crossing place would be carefully selected according to the force of the current, the most important feature being a gently shelving bank on the other side, enabling the horses to get out easily. Having decided on that, the water would be entered about half a mile upstream. If they missed the landing place they could be carried for miles downstream before they found another place suitable to leave the water, and sometimes they would find their way back to the side from which they had started.

The mail, rations, swags and gear would be packed into an enormous tarpaulin and tied at the top like a huge plum pudding. It was dragged into the water and floated with surprising buoyancy, pushed to the other side by two men swimming beside it, keeping it upright. A couple of trips were usually enough to get everything across.

At night the tarpaulin was slung between two trees and served as a shelter. In those latitudes, it rained more at night. The mail, the packs and saddles, McLennan, his horse tailers and any passenger slept under it. The mail was always kept dry, the men were nearly always wet and the mail was never late.

Bob told me that in all the years he had carried the mail to Wave Hill he had had only one serious mishap, when a crocodile took one of his horses crossing the King River. He was paid £400 a year and, as Bob explained to me, the rum sales were "fruit for the sideboard".

And so I came to Wave Hill.

Vesteys owned seventeen cattle stations, from Western Australia in an almost unbroken chain to the Overland Telegraph Line. Totalling something in excess of 40,000 square miles, they were but a fraction of this multinational company's interests.

Headed by Lord Vestey, the firm had substantial interests in Africa, Latin America, meatworks scattered around the world like confetti; and the Blue Star Line, one of the world's largest shipping companies, flew the Vestey house flag.

This vast empire was one of the most successful in the world, judging by the publicity given to what must have been one of the most ingenious accounting systems ever devised. It enabled Vesteys, while accumulating massive profits, to completely escape the demands of the British taxation authorities.

Among the tongue-in-cheek criticisms of this legal villainy one could detect a distinct note of jealousy, not unmixed with admiration and, if the press reports of the day are to be believed, it caused a serious fracture in a friendship between the polo-playing young Lord Vestey and a prominent member of the British Royal

House (which, I suppose, is understandable, the latter being the recipient of substantial largesse garnered from such sources).

Wave Hill Station was the jewel in the crown of the Australian pastoral division. Being head stockman there carried a certain amount of prestige; it gave me a lot of satisfaction to take over the camp of such a famous station.

It was first taken up by the incomparable Nat "Bluey" Buchanan in 1885. I have always thought of Bluey Buchanan as one of the finest and most courageous bushmen Australia has known, and it is unfortunate that more of his exploits have not been recorded. He rode with Landsborough in one of the earlier searches for Burke and Wills. He was with Cornish exploring the Diamantina River in 1861. He formed Mt Cornish Station, then the largest cattle station in the world, for the Landsborough Pastoral Company.

In 1887 he piloted 1200 head of cattle through country that was then unknown to Europeans, from Aramac in Queensland to a station called Glencoe, 100 or so miles south of Darwin. This property had been taken up by two partners, Travers and Gibson, who had a station called Punjab at Aramac. Travers came with the cattle but unfortunately was speared by the blacks on the Limmen River, a little more than halfway to their destination. Bluey buried him there and continued — there was nothing else he could do.

Shortly after this the surviving partner, Gibson, was discouraged enough to sell Glencoe to Fisher and Lyons, who had formed the North Australian Pastoral Company. They had already taken up the mighty Victoria River Downs. However, they were sufficiently impressed with Glencoe to commission Bluey Buchanan to oversee the buying and moving of 20,000 cattle from Queensland to Glencoe.

This must surely stand today as one of the greatest droving feats of all time: the number of cattle, the distance, the unknown terrain. It took nearly four years from the time they started and there are several astonishing features to this tremendous movement of cattle.

Fisher and Lyons, like Travers and Gibson, must have been deceived by the apparent potential of the country; one can only assume that they saw it after the first storms, when a lush growth of grass appears. They could not have been aware of what it was like a few weeks later when torrential rains were flooding the country, the gentle creeks turned to raging torrents and spear grass an impenetrable ten feet high. Twenty thousand head of cattle!

Even allowing for their lack of knowledge of the country, and endeavouring to see it through their eyes at that time, it is still difficult to believe that it was carried through with such determination. We are all experts in hindsight, especially in the area of other people's failures, but it has always seemed to me that a strong streak of sheer insanity ran through the operation. Victoria River Downs, with its beautiful Mitchell and Flinders grass downs, lay empty. And to cap it all, ticks reared their bloodshot heads and the dreadful redwater fever added to the decimation of those 20,000 cattle.

Forlornly they gathered up what was left of their herd and took them to Victoria River Downs. Meanwhile, Bluey Buchanan had taken up Wave Hill.

The Buchanan clan was then strong in the Territory and the Kimberleys. Among them were Bluey's wife's brothers, the Gordons: his nephews the Farquharsons, who had helped him blaze the trail with the Glencoe cattle, had stayed and pressed on further west. Hughie, Harry and Archie Farquharson had taken up a couple of thousand square miles on the headwaters of the Victoria River and Sturt's Creek and called it Inverway. Then there was Gordon Downs, Flora Valley, Birrandudu; they were all associated one way or another. It was a mighty saga.

Vesteys swept through the country in 1913 like a ravenous lion and the owners, all with empty pockets and open arms, welcomed them — the pot of gold at the end of the rainbow had, for them, materialised at last.

A meatworks was built in Darwin and in 1914 they were all

ready to go when war broke out. The Blue Star Line came into Darwin regularly and took meat away. Its ships were sometimes torpedoed, of course, but the British Government looked after that for them. Their contribution to the war effort was considerable; their profits massive.

After the war, things went badly for Vesteys; industrial troubles piled up in Darwin and eventually the meatworks closed altogether. The bullocks that used to go north were then turned eastward, 70,000 of them every year, starting in March.

This was when Wave Hill really came into its own. Beautiful land and ideally situated, it became an important link in the chain. All the bullocks from their properties to the west — Margaret River, Lower Sturt, Flora Valley, Gordon Downs, The Turner, Ord River, Mistake Creek, Waterloo, Limbunya and more. They all came to Wave Hill where they were rested for a year. It was a tremendous operation. After a year's spell they were walked to Queensland, and the drovers who brought the cattle from the west carried on with a fresh mob.

I introduced myself to the manager, Alec McGugan, a man of few words. He pointed out my quarters with the remark that he didn't think I'd be seeing much of them, which I took as a hint that he didn't expect to see much of me around the station area. After saying that he'd see me first thing in the morning to take me out to the stock camp, he left me to my own devices.

I made the acquaintance of the storekeeper, the saddler, the blacksmith-cum-mechanic and a well borer. I was trying to get as much information about Wave Hill as possible. One thing they all agreed on was that McGugan was "an odd sort of a bastard", and apparently he'd had quite a few men through his hands in a fairly short space of time. I was the third head stockman he'd had for the Number One Camp that year . . . and it was only July!

There were three stock camps; Number One, Number Two and Catfish. Number Two and Catfish were outstations and consequently didn't come into contact with the manager much which, it would seem, made for a better relationship.

As I was well aware, the storekeeper was the most important individual on stations owned by companies whose headquarters were in some distant city. He did all the ordering of supplies, calculating the quantity of rations required, the numerous items that kept the wheels of industry revolving. With the nearest source of supplies 300 miles away, the calculations had to be correct to the last ball of hemp for the saddler, the last handful of horseshoe nails for the stock camps. It was he who knew exactly how many calves were branded three years ago and who, after figuring the number of females to be deducted less the accepted mortality rate, would come up with a figure for the number of bullocks the stock camp would be expected to muster. They were never far out. And it was he who advised the distant general manager of a lot of other details. He was frequently known — not always affectionately — as a "company man".

Vesteys was very much the big company organisation and figures were its life blood; always a mystery to, and usually detested by lowly ringers and stockmen. When calves were branded the tally was cut into a stick, one by one with a castrating knife, at the branding fire. After adding them up and dividing by two — half females, half males — they were entered into a book most meticulously with what appeared to be, to quote Banjo Paterson, "a thumbnail dipped in tar". Sydney managers frequently developed apoplexy from such minor matters.

I wandered down to the blacksmith's shop and made the acquaintance of a genial old fellow who was busy repairing a pump rod. In between drilling and bolting he explained to me that he was "a bit of bloody everything".

"I'm the windmill expert," indicating the pump rod; "I'm supposed to know all about that bloody contraption", pointing to a truck (the inevitable Model T Ford), "not to mention blacksmith," nodding to a sheet of iron swinging from a rafter, on which was painted in letters of black:

Toiling rejoicing sorrowing
Onward through life he goes

93

Each morning sees some task begun
Each evening sees its close.

Unless a bloody bore breaks down
And water's running low
No matter whether night or day
This bastard's gotta go.

I laughed and asked him where the second verse came from, and he modestly said, "Me."

"Last time old Moray was here he took a photograph of it and said he was going to send it to the big wheel in London — Lord Vestey I 'spose."

Another fine character was an old Aborigine named Charcoal, who was just about pensioned off. He looked after the manager's horses, which wouldn't have put any great strain on him: managers never rode anywhere they could get their utility to go.

Charcoal told me he came from Newcastle Waters. He was just a piccaninny when Bluey Buchanan came through with a mob of cattle, giving his horse a drink at the big waterhole where the Newcastle Waters homestead is now.

Charcoal said: "I was sitting under a tree crying. My father had just given me a belting, I bin playing 'round with a quee-i [young lubra]." He laughed at the recollection, "She was the wrong skin [totem], I was playing wrong side, wrong kind play too." He chuckled at the memory: "Old Man Bluey said, 'You like come long me?' I said, 'Ui, me like', so he picked me up and carried me in front of him on his horse."

Charcoal was quiet for a while, enjoying the memories. Then he said: "I never bin on a horse before, first I liked it, then I got big fright and cried — he was taking me away from my momma and my poppa and my country. But old man Bluey was good to me: gave me plenty tucker, then we come up long Wave Hill and I saw the big river, plenty fish, plenty turtle, plenty duck, full up bush tucker — more better than Newcastle Waters, and I played with quee-is and no one belted me."

He told me Buchanan became a father to him; he accompanied Bluey wherever he went "Bluey learn me everything," he said, "show me how to shoot a gun, the Myall blackfellas used to spear plenty cattle, got plenty cheeky."

He told me they were attacked once by the Myall blacks. He said a friend had warned him they were planning to spear them and loot the store, but when he told Bluey he laughed and said: "They all talk-talk 'bout spearem me fella, all gammon."

Charcoal said, "I told him, 'I dunno, they talk-talk plenty, me tink-tink plenty.' "

He said Sam Croker was working with them at the time and they were about to start a horse muster. He got the saddle horses in from the paddock and Bluey, Sam and Charcoal rode down the river together, "We took Winchesters with us, we nearly always took our guns, we were way down the river. Bluey and Sam were riding in the lead, my horse was a bit lazy, I'd dropped back a bit. We came to a clump of paperbark saplings 'an my horse shied real bad, I look round 'an four Myalls had jumped out of the saplings 'an they all had long shovel spears.

"I sing out, 'look out Bluey, Sam look out, Myall blackfella here 'an I galloped into the scrub 'an got my gun out, it was under my saddle flap, there were some more Myalls in the scrub 'an they ran away, they all had spears but got fright, some ran into the river, some fella run all about. I heard some shots, one fella climbed up a tree 'an I got off my horse, he didn't know I'd seen him 'an I shot him dead. Then me an' Bluey an' Sam got together again an' I asked them how they got on an' Bluey said 'we give 'em the biggest fright they ever had in their life before, they won't come back'.

"Then I said: 'Well I gave one a fright that won't come back because I shot him dead!' Then Bluey got real cross with me, I thought he was going to belt me, I never seen him that cross before. He said: 'You shot one of those poor bastards dead? Jesus Christ! You shouldn't have done that!' He was real mad at me, he said we'd better go and have a look at the poor bastard, he mightn't be dead." So I took them to where I'd shot him. He was real dead, no gammon; my bullet had gone through his head. Bluey told I'd have to bury him but the ground was terrible hard an' I got some friends and we made a big fire an' cooked him up to nothing."

I could well believe Charcoal's story; Buchanan was known as a very humane man and treated the blacks, whether they worked for him or not, extremely well — a lot better than most.

Some time later Charcoal showed me the tree the Myall had climbed. If it hadn't changed much since then he wouldn't have had much chance of escaping.

McGugan took me out to my new command, which was camped on the Camfield River about twenty-five miles from the station. On the way he gave me a rundown on my duties. Number One Camp was the bullock camp and didn't have much branding to do, except towards the end of the year on the Camfield, sometimes meeting Pigeon Hole, an outstation of Victoria River Downs, for a boundary muster. The Wave Hill herd was about 30,000; the mustering and branding of these was taken care of by Number Two and Catfish camps. Wave Hill was a depot for bullocks coming from the western stations and Number One received them from the drovers, turned them out into the paddock where they would be rested for a year, and the drovers would be given a fresh mob — always 1350 — which they would take to a company station in Queensland, a walk of 800 miles.

The camp usually handled about 30,000 to 40,000 bullocks in a season. This sounds a very formidable figure, but not as daunting as it appears. The head stockman would know exactly when a drover was due. He would take delivery of the drover's bullocks, count them, turn them into a paddock, count a fresh mob over to him, all in one day. In some cases the drover might ask for a day's spell, but the schedule was a fairly tight one with mobs arriving four or five days apart.

We got to the stock camp at midday and after a brief exchange McGugan left. Whatever bonds of friendship there may have been once were now conspicuously absent.

I thought Gordon Smith, the outgoing head stockman, was a good type and though I was taking his job, I knew nothing of the circumstances of his departure. He greeted me warmly and together we went over details of the camp. He had the working horses rounded up, and we looked through the horse book. It seemed there were about 150 working horses; fifty to sixty were in work at a time, roughly five or six weeks between changes. They were very good horses and had been well looked after; they were all well shod and their backs were good. (In a badly run camp, saddle sores were frequently prominent.) All the saddlery was in good condition and everything was nice and tidy.

There were nine Aboriginal stockmen, a young jackeroo and a Chinese cook. Smith said all the stockmen were good, the jackeroo was a nice lad, he said "but don't let him out of your sight, don't let him get away on his own in the bush". He went on to say that he'd sent him out on his own once to look at a waterhole and it took almost the entire camp a day and a half to find him. "If you put him in a shithouse, turned him 'round three times and closed the door he'd never find his way out!" I made a mental note of this disability.

He said old Ah Ping was a good cook but hated getting on a horse, which of course he had to do when the camp was moved. "Make sure he's always got a quiet horse, one that'll wait for him when he falls off." "One thing about Chinese cooks," he went on to say, "they never complain — you can fuck them about, pack up

97

in the middle of the night, they'll never say a word. A white man would never stand it."

Gordon Smith stayed another day. I found him a very likeable bloke, he didn't say much but clearly he hadn't got on with the manager.

I ran the Wave Hill camp for the rest of that year and found McGugan a very difficult man to work for. In November I brought my camp into the station for a change of horses. We were busy pulling the shoes off before turning them out, it was stinking hot, I was struggling with a mare who was being twice as obstinate getting her shoes pulled off as she was when they were being put on: McGugan didn't choose an ideal time to come over to the horse yard and criticise.

I hadn't seen him coming and had just torn my hand on a bent horseshoe nail. I suddenly heard his voice: "What are you doing in at the station, Cole? You're s'posed to be mustering Cattle Creek."

"Well I'm not mustering Cattle fucking Creek because it's dry from one end to the other. Consequently there are no cattle there to muster, the reason for that being because they like to be somewhere they can get a drink now and then."

But he wasn't going to be beaten as easily as that. "Well, that may be, but I don't think you need a change of horses. Your horses are in very good condition — they're good for another couple of weeks."

At this stage I knew it was all over for me at Wave Hill. I climbed up and sat on the top rail, looking down at him from what I thought was a position of advantage. "I am head stockman of this camp," I said. "I am not going to work the horses into the ground, and if I'm not capable of deciding when they need a change then I'm not capable of running a camp . . . and you can stick the whole lot, one horse at a time, up your fundamental orifice!" Which I thought was a very good expression.

He turned and walked away. As he did so I heard him mutter, "Jesus Christ, I've got a line of fence and number seven bore up there now!" Apparently a fencer and another man who was pumping at number seven bore had pulled out and told him something similar. It was the first flash of humour I'd ever heard from him. I don't know whether it was intentional.

CHAPTER 10

TELEGRAPH LINES AND CAMELS

I left Wave Hill with some regret. I'd had a good camp to run, the stockmen were very good, it was beautiful country and fairly easy to work and the horses about three-quarter thoroughbred, some of the best I've ever ridden. But there was too much friction with McGugan.

I headed straight back to Banka Banka where I'd left my horses and gear. There had been some early storms and Paddy and Jim were about to start a horse muster, which I joined. After a week we'd got more than 100 together, including mine. Brood mares were drafted off, foals branded and some young colts that were ready for breaking.

With the wet season approaching I knew it would be a few months before there was any work. It was December; none of the stock camps would be starting up until the end of February or early March. I told Paddy I'd be more than happy to break the colts for him; a couple of days later I had some youngsters in the yard and the gear laid out ready to make a start when Jim walked over and asked how I'd feel about taking a job as linesman at Tennant Creek Telegraph station. This was something of a bombshell in a way. Linesman at Tennant Creek? That was another world to me!

I knew that Woodie Woodroffe was the operator in charge of Tennant Creek; I also knew his linesman was a man named Charlie Windley. Jim explained that Windley, a mad prospector, had found what he believed was a big copper deposit and had told Woodie he wanted to leave and work his mine.

"Woodie rang up this morning and wanted to know if you'd be interested in the job?" Jim said.

"What would I have to do as linesman?" I asked. "I don't know anything about telegraph lines."

"Well, you don't really have to know anything." Jim said. "If there's a break you have to go out and fix it, but that's the same as mending a broken fence wire: anyway, the line never breaks. I haven't heard of a break for years."

It started to sound a bit better, Jim went on: "What I know about the job isn't much. As I see it the main work is looking after the cattle and horses. They've got 100 or so head of cattle, thirty or forty horses, and I believe two or three camels."

We sat on the horse yard rail talking about it for a while and eventually came to the conclusion there was nothing to lose and four pounds a week to gain. We walked back to the house and I rang Tennant Creek. Woodie came on and I told him I'd take the job, when did he want me to start? "As soon as you like, I can't stand this bloody Windley much longer, all he talks about is copper porphyry, iron bloody priorities or something — all bloody Greek to me."

Two days later I rode up to the telegraph station, unpacked and handed my horses over to one of the stockmen. Woodie greeted me with enthusiasm and showed me my quarters. I was acquainted with the station, having camped there on my way to the Barrow Creek races with the Banka horses.

The next day I started to familiarise myself with the place, finding out what my work was, but carefully avoiding any mention of telegraph lines and how to repair them.

He gave me the stock book. There were 200-odd cattle and thirty-five horses, of which twenty-one were broken in. The rest were brood mares and youngsters.

I remembered Jim Ambrose had mentioned camels, but there were none recorded. I asked Woodroffe about them and he said: "Well, to be candid I'm not sure that they really belong to us. They

101

were here when I came here a couple of years ago. I was told that they had come from Crown Point Station."

"But what about their brand, they must have somebody's brand on them?"

"I don't know, I suppose so; I've never looked. I don't like them, stinking bloody things. Windley never used them, I think he was frightened of them — they're noisy bastards," Woodroffe said.

I asked him if anyone ever worked them and he told me one of the stockmen rode one occasionally. "Joe knows all about them; he's the best lad you've got. I think he likes them."

It seemed the camels were a bit of a mystery. They didn't appear to have many friends either. I had them yarded up and tried without success to find a brand. Woodie was right about them being noisy bastards.

All the telegraph stations branded their stock with a broad arrow, the same as the police. Joe was quite clear about their origin as far as Tennant Creek was concerned; he said they came from Crown Point. I didn't see any point in worrying about it further.

Including Joe (by far the most useful member of the team), there were four Aboriginal stockmen. Their wives worked in a very limited way in a garden that never seemed to produce anything in the way of vegetables; our cook was a half-caste girl, there were a couple of others who looked after the house, the office and my quarters.

There was the usual Aboriginal camp a short distance up the creek; nomads who came and went as fancy took them. When I killed a bullock they would always get some of the meat.

Woodroffe's duties consisted of sending a daily weather report — which never varied while I was there; the sky was always cloudless, the direction and velocity of the wind remained the same and it never rained. The only time I can recall Woodie's workload increasing was when a traveller called and lodged a telegram, which was dispatched immediately.

Nor could my work be described as exacting. Apart from the stock work I was there to repair the line in the event of a break, which seemed a very remote chance.

The camels interested me. Though I had never previously had anything to do with them, I had seen them from time to time passing through Lake Nash; usually a string of about thirty came through on their way from the Hatches Creek wolfram mines. They were always in the charge of Afghans, who apparently owned them. Being familiar with pack horse loads, what a camel could carry never ceased to amaze me. Bulls could comfortably carry half a ton and go a week without water.

They had made an invaluable contribution to the development of the Australian interior and had been used extensively in the construction of the Overland Telegraph Line. I am sure it would never have been completed in the time had camels not been available.

Sir Thomas Elder, who possessed that rare combination of wealth and foresight, was the first to recognise their potential, having tremendous holdings in the more arid parts of South Australia. In January 1866 Sir Thomas imported 124 camels, which were unloaded at Port Augusta. And though it is generally believed he was the first person to introduce them there is a curious story of the very first camel to reach our shores.

This first fleeter of the camel world arrived at Port Adelaide in October 1840, and was the sole survivor of several that came from, of all places, the Canary Islands. One wonders what purpose camels had in the scheme of things on that remote subtropical island. However, in the fullness of time it came to a sheep station called Penwortham, near Clare, owned by two brothers named Horrocks.

The Horrocks were interested in some largely unknown country that lay to the west of Lake Torrens, and an expedition led by John Horrocks left in July 1846. The party consisted of six men, a number of horses and the camel.

103

One day Horrocks decided to shoot a bird, probably for the pot, and taking the gun from the pack of the kneeling camel was in the process of loading it when the animal started to rise, causing the gun to discharge. It blew off two of Horrocks' fingers and knocked out some teeth, presumably from the recoil.

The wounded man was taken back to Penwortham. Septicaemia probably set in, because a few weeks later he died. Before passing away he instructed that the unfortunate camel be shot. It is not recorded if the two of them were burned together in a form of suttee but I often thought it would be an appropriate end to the story.

Though the Tennant Creek camels hadn't been worked much, they were quite tractable. I got them yarded, mainly from curiosity. Joe was undoubtedly the expert. We dragged the saddles from the saddle room — primitive-looking contraptions, something like a huge mattress with a hole in the middle through which the hump protruded. Sticks were lashed to the outside to keep it firm. The frame, called a tree, was of steel with three arches. On the front two were hooks on which pack bags were hung. From the centre arch to the one at the back a square of leather was attached by lacing. This was the saddle, from which stirrups hung. A crupper went under the tail and a broad leather strap acted as a breastplate.

The rider was seated behind the hump, and controlled the beast with reins fastened to the nose line — which in turn was fastened to the nose peg. The nose peg was put in when the camel was broken in and was a permanent fixture, as was about a foot of nose line.

There was one word of command: "Hooshta"! If you wanted it to kneel you said, "Hooshta"; if you wanted it to rise you said, "Hooshta"! As simple as that.

They fed mainly on a wide range of bushes, many of which cattle or horses wouldn't touch — a variety that added considerably to the camels' value, especially in times of drought.

Two of the camels were good riding beasts. I soon got used to the gait, which was entirely different from a horse; a kind of swaying motion though after the first couple of rides I was quite sore for a day or so. I thought they would be good travellers on long journeys and was sure they would beat a horse.

We were now well into December. The heat was building up but there was no sign of rain and nothing for me to do. I was getting bored; every couple of days I would get a camel brought in and ride out to the only really permanent water we had, a small spring that was struggling to produce enough water for our cattle. The horses watered at the station well.

Once a fortnight, Sam Irvine arrived with the mail. He also carried a stock of whisky and rum, which was more important than the mail. The deadly monotony was broken for a little while.

Tennant Creek was Irvine's last stop: from here he returned to Alice Springs. On his last trip for the year, a week before Christmas, he camped the night as he sometimes did. He drove away early in the morning and was barely out of sight when Woodie had started on his weather report. To our astonishment it had happened: there was a break in the line.

There were two strands, one copper and one iron, and both were out. There was no communication whatever with the south. This was serious; Woodie said he couldn't remember both lines being out before. To the north the blacks sometimes cut lengths from the line to make fish spears but the desert blacks never made that kind of spear. No fish!

Anyway, it was my problem, and to me it seemed of considerable magnitude; 150 miles of telephone line stretching away through semi-desert and both lines out. The operators to the north chattering away to Woodie. I could almost see lightning coming from his set — Bill Phillips from Powell's Creek, Wallaby Holtze, the operator at Daley Waters, someone else from further north butting in with, "What's wrong?"

Woodie was losing his temper. "How the bloody hell do I know what's wrong? Just leave us alone. I've got a good man here, he'll soon have it fixed."

Little did he know. I was almost in a state of mortal terror, imagining financiers throwing themselves from the top of the Empire State Building in New York, suicides in Wall Street, Threadneedle Street in an uproar while I was getting camels ready to set out and fix it.

It was late afternoon when I got the camels yarded, filled water canteens, drew a week's rations from the store, camp oven, billy cans, spare hobbles, a few other odds and ends. Woodie produced a field telephone from his office and pronounced it in working order. I'd never seen one before in my life! It was well after sundown before I had everything to my satisfaction. Woodie was well into a bottle of rum, wandering back and forth from the office to the saddle room muttering to himself, "Both bloody lines out, never heard of it before!"

I was going to get an early start in the morning and cover as much ground as possible before it got hot.

For the past week the temperature had passed 110 in the shade. Not that I would be luxuriating in the shade: where I was going was well and truly in the sun — where the temperature, if not up to four figures, would seem like it.

At four o'clock next morning we padded quietly out of the station; it was beautiful, cool and peaceful. To the east the morning star shone brilliantly, the Milky Way stretched across the entire heavens, the Southern Cross lay at an angle. Birds were twittering the sleep from their eyes and, a large owl swooped silently in front of me.

Without pushing the camels, I calculated I could travel a little better than five miles an hour. I wasn't worried about passing the break before daylight broke; I had previously sent one of my stockmen to ride the line for ten or fifteen miles as a precaution.

Daylight came, and it wasn't very long before the heat started to build up. The sun was nearly overhead when Joe and I got to

Kelly's Well, some water left in the trough by a traveller. The camels smelt the water but drank very little; I went on for another half an hour and pulled in to a group of shade trees then tied them to a mulga tree, on which they fed.

Joe hooked the telephone to the line and I wound the handle furiously trying to contact Tennant Creek, without result. Just as I thought I must have passed the break, Powell's Creek came on so it was still ahead of me. I boiled the billy, we had a feed of corned beef and damper and rode on.

Though we were both watching for the break, every hour or so I stopped and Joe shinned up the pole and hooked the phone on. I couldn't raise Tennant Creek but was able to get the Powell: once I got Wallaby Holtze at Daly Waters. I asked about Woodie but neither Bill Phillips or Holtze had heard from him. Bill Phillips said, "He's probably on the rum," which turned out to be right.

I rode to the next well on McLaren Creek where the camels had a good drink. I went on and camped at The Devil's Marbles. The break still ahead.

Next morning I was packed and ready before daylight broke. Standing beside the sitting camels, waiting for the first glimmer of dawn, I wondered what the real effect of the fault was on the outside world. I had some idea of the volume of traffic when I sometimes listened to the constant chattering of the instruments in Woodie's office. Day or night it never stopped. I had no idea of its importance, but a complete break would have to be serious. The restoration of communications was now dependent on myself, Joe and two patient camels, who at this moment were placidly chewing their cud. I thought of the saying "the strength of a chain is the strength of its weakest link". I suppose in a way we were the weakest link.

Soon I could see the two lines. We mounted and the camels were on their feet as soon as I said "Hooshta!". We passed the next well, but didn't stop. A few miles further on Joe suddenly gave a yell. "Look!" he shouted excitedly, "one fella bird!" A large bird,

107

probably an owl, had flown into the line; it must have had some pace up, as when it hit the line it had twisted the two together.

There it was swaying gently in the breeze, a few feathers blowing from the dried and decaying body. A few more days and it would have disintegrated completely. Sitting there on my camel in the middle of the continent, I pondered the little things in life and their far-reaching effects. In the meantime Joe had taken an axe from a pack bag and cut a long stick. He got on his camel, rode over to the trapped bird and gave it a whack. It flew to pieces and communications were restored between Australia and the outside world. Joe and I laughed our heads off.

At the next pole I hooked the telephone on and gave a few winds. Immediately it seemed everyone was on the line at once, even Woodie. From up and down the line congratulations were showered on me. Someone asked what had happened; what had been wrong? I modestly said: "It would take too long to explain, and probably you wouldn't understand." Which was greeted by hoots of laughter. Then someone said, "Well, have a Happy Christmas." I realised then it was Christmas Eve.

At my previous Christmas at Barrow Creek races I had made the acquaintance of almost the entire population of Central Australia. In the morning I headed the camels along a track leading to Singleton Station, owned by Bill Crooks. The range of festivities available in the middle of Australia was very limited; I intended to make the best of what there was.

The homestead, about fifteen miles from the telegraph line, was similar to most station homes: bush timber, corrugated iron roof and walls, floor of tamped antbed, a wife and two daughters struggling to make ends meet. One of many sagas of survival.

I rode up to the homestead and it didn't really surprise me to find they knew almost as much as I did about the circumstances that had brought me there. Bush telegraph, premonition, second sight may work for all I know, but mostly it's commonsense deduction. They knew about the fault in the line, they knew someone would be along to fix it, they knew I was linesman at Tennant Creek.

I enjoyed a very happy Christmas at Singleton Station with the Crooks family. Another cattleman, Bill Braitling, was there. I had met him when he passed through Banka Banka with 700 or 800 head of cattle, on his way to establish a station in one of the most remote parts of Australia.

He had come from a small holding of a few hundred square miles that he had taken up on his return from the First World War. He called it Passchendaele. It adjoined Victoria River Downs, close to Montejinni outstation. It was a good area for an energetic cattleman with ambition; his neighbour's herd of around 170,000 was liberally sprinkled with cleanskins. It was a familiar story, a branding iron and some good stock horses.

In a few years he had industriously branded a sizeable herd, and was so industrious that he became a thorn in the side of Tom Graham, the VRD manager, who decided Bill should move to pastures new. There was no friction: it was all done in a friendly and agreeable atmosphere, which was assisted by the fact that to Bill Braitling it was only a stepping stone. He had plans to get closer to a railhead; Graham merely accelerated those plans slightly.

He took up a few thousand square miles of country that had been Crown Lands, mustered nearly 1000 head of cattle and sold Passchendaele to Graham, who didn't really want it — he already had 13,000 square miles to look after. But there were plenty of enterprising cattlemen who would have leapt into the vacant riding boots of Braitling without hesitation; ready and willing to assist in the branding of Victoria River Downs cleanskins, they only needed a toehold.

When Braitling got to Singleton several months later he had another 250 miles to go, but there was a long dry stage of more than 100 miles in between. Bill Crooks came to the rescue and did a deal that suited them both: Crooks let him run his cattle on one of his wells, and in return, Braitling put another well down.

When the rains came Braitling took his cattle and Bill Crooks' eldest daughter, Doreen, out to his promised land. Close to where the newlyweds established their homestead was a mountain, which he called Mount Doreen. The property became Mt Doreen Station.

I went back to Tennant Creek. In February it rained and the whole country, which had been lying dormant, surged into life, running creeks, overflowing billabongs, waving green grass — it brought a new dimension into our lives. I knew Tennant Creek wasn't for me much longer. I'd told Woodie that I didn't think I'd be making a career of linesman — all I could see was a long stretch of nothing.

A couple of weeks later I said goodbye. I never saw him again: some years later I heard he died in a gun duel somewhere out in the desert to the west. I never heard what it was about and wondered what he was doing out there. The story, as it was told to me, was that he and another man got into an argument and shot it out. They both died.

CHAPTER 11

TRAGEDIES IN THE OUTBACK

I headed north. It was a change to be travelling and not having to worry about dry stages or where the next camp would be. Water and grass were in abundance.

I covered the sixty miles to Banka Banka in two days, spent a couple of nights with the Ambroses and rode on. I camped a night at Powell's Creek, and two and a half days later, rode into Newcastle Waters.

I went up to the homestead intending to get some beef but the manager said they were just about out. He asked which way I was going and when I said across the Murranji Track he told me I'd have no difficulty getting a killer; there were plenty of bush cattle through the bulwaddy and lancewood scrub, all of which was Crown Land.

In the course of the conversation he asked if I'd known Brumby Baker. I said I'd heard of him, why? He then told me he'd perished out in the bulwaddy somewhere and the policeman was auctioning his belongings the following day. Like nearly all of these men, he'd left no will and the local policeman, in his capacity of curator of deceased estates, was selling his horses and gear. I thought I'd have a look and see if there was anything worthwhile. There wouldn't be much competition at the auction and I might pick up a cheap horse.

Baker had died some months previously during the driest month, September. A drover had arrived at a bore that was his last camp and read the signs: a swag that didn't appear to have been slept in for some days, two pack saddles but no riding saddle and, most convincing of all, dingo tracks in the long-cold ashes of his campfire. He rode around and found five horses; one carried a saddle, the others were hobbled and were feeding not far from the bore. He unsaddled the horse and rode into Newcastle Waters and informed the police, who went out with trackers and found the body. Baker had been dead for more than a week.

It was assumed he had ridden out to muster his horses, or perhaps to look for one that had separated from the others. Whatever the reason, he had got lost in the dense scrub. How he had become separated from his horse was a matter for conjecture. It is well known that men become unbalanced when in the last stages of perishing from thirst, but his horse would last longer, knowing exactly where the water was.

Deaths such as Baker's were not uncommon — it was a country of boundless plains and vast distances with no landmarks and, as in this case, heavy scrub. What few watercourses dribbled through the country were nearly always dry. The stock route that strung across from Western Australia to Queensland carried bores, but away from that there were very few roads. Where Baker died was not far off the Murranji Track, which he had been following; to the south were several hundred miles of waterless desert, to the north mostly bulwaddy scrub, and for 200 miles there was no water except in the wet.

I remembered a man named Foley who, because of his vocal powers, was known as Foghorn Foley. After a severe drinking bout at a race meeting of several days' duration he went out to get his horses together. Over the three-day meeting they had wandered a bit further than usual. It would appear he had found some of them and rode out in search of the rest.

At the time he would have undoubtedly have been suffering from the effects of three days' concentrated boozing, an occupation at which he was no mean exponent. He was in an area where it was almost an impossibility to get lost and was riding a horse that knew exactly where the nearest water was: a triangle formed by the Behn River, Stockade Creek and a road. He was familiar with both watercourses and the road, there were waterholes in both creeks (some of them never went dry). The furthest he could have got from water was no more than twenty-five miles.

Almost an impossibility to get lost. Almost. After his drinking session he would dehydrate very quickly, much quicker than normally, but even without the effects of his unrestrained carousing it is unlikely he would have survived. Probably the remarkable part is that he survived as long as he did.

He rode round for at least a day, perhaps longer; his tracks indicated that he travelled in a big circle and at one point was no more than five miles from a waterhole on Stockade Creek. One wonders how the unfortunate horse was feeling at that point.

I didn't hear much of the details leading up to the finding of the body, but assumed someone had come along, noticed the camp and read the signs — not too difficult. If a bushman came to a camp that was deserted and there could be some doubt as to a man's safety, he would take steps to ensure he was not in difficulties.

Foley's tracks were followed without much difficulty; he was found no more than twenty miles from water, lying at the foot of a tree. His horse had died, too. It still had the saddle on, was hobbled and hitched to the tree under which he lay.

Had it been allowed, the horse would have taken him to water as straight as an arrow. Being bred and born in the bush doesn't make a bushman. There is a sense some have; tragically, some think they have it and don't. In addition to this indefinable sense the back up of common sense is necessary — and also sometimes sadly lacking.

Other memories came back to me. Jim Robinson, a bushman bred and born, worked on Alexandria Station — a very big run, something over 10,000 square miles, which was big even by Northern Territory standards. There were three stock camps.

Soudan, an outstation that covered the southeastern area, was where Robinson worked. The head stockman was Jim Fowler, one of the Territory's legendary horsemen. It was Jim who rode the aptly named "Murderer" to a standstill.

Robinson was out at one of the bores. His job was to pump water and keep a huge earth tank full for the two or three thousand head of cattle that were running there; a simple but lonely job. To these itinerant station workers their horses were their life blood, their companions, often descended from horses owned many years previously; no wonder these men were deeply attached to their mounts. Usually a couple of pack horses carried their worldly goods, two or three saddle horses; they wandered around the country as fancy took them, travelling from one station to another, working when it became necessary to replenish the pack bags.

Robinson's horses watered regularly at the bore, wandering in for a drink almost daily, and nearly always at about the same time. One day only three came to the trough. In all probability, partly from concern and perhaps because of the monotony of his job (more likely the latter), Robinson saddled one of the horses after it had finished drinking and rode out in the direction they usually grazed. He never returned.

That afternoon the head stockman, Fowler, arrived with his mustering camp to do some branding and there was no Robinson there to greet him. The story was clear. His riding saddle was gone, the campfire was still smouldering, the tracks of his horse leaving the camp were still fresh.

As time went by, and Robinson hadn't returned, Fowler's concern mounted. By midnight it was clearly serious and before dawn he had water canteens full and on a pack horse, with his best tracker, waited for the first glimmer of dawn when there would be sufficient light to follow the tracks.

They set off as fast as they could and were still able to follow the missing man. They rode round in a sweeping semicircle; there was

114

no difficulty picking out the tracks. After travelling five or six miles they came to the road from the outstation homestead; it wandered from waterhole to waterhole, from bore to bore, finally finishing at the bore where Robinson was camped. There was no other road. It mattered not which way Robinson followed that road — he would have finished up either at his own camp or at another bore.

At that stage he would not have been thirsty but he was clearly puzzled. His tracks indicated he had pulled up and considered what to him was an extraordinary phenomenon. The sun was probably straight overhead and, casting no shadow, he crossed the road and continued south — straight into the desert. The trackers knew then he was lost, though he wouldn't have known it at that time.

Fowler continued to track him. At times Robinson broke into a trot, at times a canter; a sure sign of panic. When it got too dark to follow further, the head stockman reluctantly turned back. He had no option; his horses wouldn't have gone much farther, and Robinson had at least a fifteen-hour start.

His body was never found. Like Foley he need not have died; his horse would have taken him back to water. Animals have instincts — inbuilt senses that act as compasses — that serve them in their migrations and movements. We are given brains: which are not always used to advantage.

Another tragedy that sent shockwaves through the country was that of a young doctor and his wife who died of thirst on the plains of the Barkly Tableland. Dr Straede, not long married, was the resident doctor at the gold mining town of Tennant Creek. Shortly after his appointment a request for medical assistance was received from Rockhampton Downs Station. Mrs Jones, a guest of Mr and Mrs Easey was seriously ill. Would they please send a doctor?

Dr Straede, very much a new chum, made his preparations, which included taking his young wife with him. She, no doubt seeing the whole thing as an exciting adventure, would not have had to apply much pressure.

Padre Arch Grant, who was a friend of the couple, noted in his book *Camel Train & Aeroplane* : "When he received the message he declined offers of help and, though totally inexperienced, set off confidently with his wife and a small dog".

The distance was approximately 100 miles. The road the Straedes followed, although reasonable by the standards of the times, was a dirt bush track that had been cut with a fireplough, a machine used to make fire breaks.

They came to No 3 bore, and here it is important to note that about a mile from the bore the road was completely blotted out by thousands of cattle tracks made by stock walking from their feeding grounds to watering place. They made their own roads, deep pads as they walked behind one another converging on the bore. Though the road was completely blotted out, it created no problem — all roads led to Rome.

Leaving the bore was an entirely different story. The pads fanned out, the road was indistinguishable and anyone, bushman or otherwise, would be unable to identify it. An experienced man would be able to pick it up again, but would need some local knowledge.

What they did was normal under the circumstances — they followed the deepest pads, assuming they would develop into a road. But the pads became fainter and fainter and finally petered out.

They were in tussocky Mitchell grass country — crumbly black soil, badly cracked due to heat and drought, interspersed with gilgai holes that, in the wet season, would be miniature waterholes a few feet across holding water for a day or so. It was February, normally the wettest month of the year, but it hadn't rained and the temperature was 116 degrees in the shade.

When they realised they had lost the road they circled in an attempt to pick it up. It was terribly rough bouncing over the tussocks and potholes. Then the petrol pipe broke.

116

To them the situation probably didn't seem irretrievable. In the search for the road they had twisted and turned a great deal and travelled about twelve miles, not by any means in a straight line. No 3 bore, which they had left earlier, could still be seen shimmering like a disembodied spirit in the mirage. It was eight miles away in a straight line. To these inexperienced people it would have looked a lot closer. There were no trees to impede their view . . . and no shade, either.

We now get to the point where their actions seem inexplicable. The time factors can be constructed with reasonable accuracy. Judging from when they left Tennant Creek, knowing how long it would have taken them to get to No 3 bore, then allowing for their subsequent wanderings while looking for the road, it would have been fairly close to midday.

The sun would have been beating down with relentless intensity. They had water but perhaps didn't realise it. Being a doctor he may have thought it was unfit for human consumption — it was in the radiator of the car.

Whatever they knew or whatever they thought they set off to walk back to No 3 bore across a treeless plain — all of eight miles!

Stumbling over the crumbling black soil, staggering over the broken, cracked ground, the unfortunate city-bred girl, clinging to her husband, they would have been lucky to make one mile an hour. The sun would be rapidly dragging the last drop of moisture from their tortured bodies.

They struggled five agonising miles and died. It would have been an awful death.

George Easey, manager of Rockhampton Downs, was the first to realise something was wrong. Men like Easey don't have to be told how serious that kind of situation is. He swung into action quickly, taking his young son Ron with him who, although only fifteen at the time was an exceptional tracker.

In a letter to me Ron Easey, who today lives at Warwick in Queensland, said:

117

Although only fifteen at the time, because of the horror of the thing no doubt, I still have vivid memories of the whole debacle. It is imprinted on my memory like a red hot brand.

Dad took me because there was no other man available, also I was thoroughly bush wise, useful and a good tracker. We had to follow the car tracks for about twelve miles over difficult country. All Dad's attention was needed to drive our utility. You can well imagine our consternation on seeing a man's and a woman's tracks leaving the car. At the time we did not know the doctor had his wife with him. I can still remember the horrible sinking feeling in my guts.

It was sundown when the car was found and they saw the tracks leading away from the vehicle. As it would soon be dark and quite impossible to track them, George Easey returned to the station to radio the news to the police at Tennant Creek. He returned to wait for daylight and sufficient light to track, realising there would be little hope of finding them alive.

In his letter, Ron goes on to say:

My father very wisely refused to allow me to take part in the final search; heat and red "beef" ants had done awful work on the couple's bodies. We knew when we found the car that there would be little chance of them being alive, hence my not participating to the end.

The real irony was that three miles from the car was another bore, No 7. The windmill wheel could be seen over some trees and would have been noticed by a bushman. The poor beggars were headed back to No 3, eight miles away, which could be seen across a treeless plain.

People not acquainted with the bush — that kind of bush — find it impossible to believe that walking five miles, even in that kind of heat, can kill. But it can, and did. It is a terrible way to die.

I stayed for the sale of Baker's horses and bought a bay mare for five pounds, a solid pack type. I put a halter on her after everything was finalised and took her back to camp. I told her as we walked back that her name was Polly. She just nodded.

CHAPTER 12

OUTSTATIONS OF VICTORIA RIVER DOWNS

F rom Newcastle Waters it was about 120 miles to Montejinni, the Victoria River Downs outstation that would be the next homestead I'd see.

I turned west on to the Murranji Track. After two days the Mitchell grass plains gradually tapered off into forbidding lancewood and bulwaddy scrub; there was no road, but plenty of cattle pads to follow. In the droving season 20,000 head of cattle walked across from the west to Queensland. I didn't envy the drovers watching them at night in that dense scrub. I had heard the expression, "It's so bloody thick a dog couldn't bark in it" — it could have originated here. At Murranji Waterhole, after which the track took its name, I shot a nice fat heifer and salted as much of the meat as I could carry, keeping some of the best cuts fresh.

There were two graves up on the higher side of the waterhole; one fairly fresh, which I took to be Baker's. Neither was marked, and after a few years they would be obliterated by the thousands of travelling stock that watered there. Stark testimony to the rewards of pioneers; there were plenty of similar graves scattered through the country, mostly unmarked, mostly with a story behind them.

In the morning I was preparing to pack up when a mob of horses trotted in from the scrub; they hadn't noticed me as I was partly obscured by my horses. I took them to be brumbies — there were always a few at most watering places — but as they got closer I could see whitish spots on the backs of nearly all of them, which denoted broken horses that had been worked. I counted eight;

they seemed to me to be very run-of-the-mill drovers' horses. There were a couple of old mares with two young foals at foot.

They splashed their way into the water and drank deeply, walked out up the bank and pulled up watching my horses, which were rounded up. As the two mobs stood eyeing each other suspiciously I was able to get a good look. With the exception of one they were very ordinary drovers' hacks; but one, a chestnut, really stood out.

He was about fourteen and a half hands, beautifully put together: clean timber, a good lengthy rein, small head and a kindly eye, strong shoulders, well coupled up and powerful hind-quarters — there was aristocratic blood not far back in his pedigree. I thought whoever lost him would be very sorry. Soon he was close enough for me to see the brand;J2J stood out clearly on the near shoulder. I thought he could be either Queensland or West Australian-bred — the branding act of both states specified two letters and one numeral. (The Northern Territory was three letters, one of which had to be a T. South Australia was two numerals and one letter.) However, nothing was further from my thoughts than the ramifications of the Brands Act.

That chestnut horse had me mesmerised — if I could only get a bridle on him! A few steps at a time, the two mobs closed on each other, whinnying and sniffing: testing the temperature. I picked up my bridle and walked slowly around the mob, getting the strangers used to my presence. They didn't seem concerned about me. I kept moving. Two of them started to get bored with the proceedings and began to walk away, I turned them back. I knew if one took fright and trotted away the rest would follow; I could saddle one of my horses and go after them, but they would be hard to handle in that dense scrub. They would break into a gallop for the sheer hell of it.

Patience was the name of the game. What was that saying? "Softly, softly catchee monkee." It took nearly an hour but finally I got my bridle on him. I thought: What's going to happen now? Would he buck? If I got thrown he would certainly gallop off into

121

the lancewood with his mates, and there was no way I'd get my hands on him again. I'd be stranded without a saddle and bridle. It wasn't worth it, was it? Was it?

I saddled him up, watching his reaction as I tightened the girths, then the surcingle. He grunted as I took up another hole. I led him around for a while; he was a beautiful horse, he'd obviously done a fair bit of work. I disregarded the saying, "never look a gift horse in the mouth" and prised his jaw open. I looked at his teeth: he was rising seven.

A few moments later I mustered up my limited courage and swung into the saddle. He gave a couple of mild pig roots and that was it. I thought "Christ, what a bloody windfall!" He carried on a bit on being separated from his mates, whinnying and fighting the bit to get back to them as they trotted away into the scrub.

I packed up and headed for Montejinni. I wasn't sure how far it was; I hadn't bothered too much with directions. When I asked the Newcastle Waters manager what the track was like, he'd said "You can't go wrong; follow the cattle pads." Distances weren't important — there was plenty of grass and water.

It was late afternoon when suddenly, to my great relief, I broke through the scrub. I was at the Jump Up, so called because of the sharp falling away of the ground. Stretching away into the distance was beautiful savannah country. I was looking across the Victoria River basin; below, a creek wound its way westward. I guessed it rightly to be the Armstrong.

The track down was rough and stony. My horses picked their way carefully, and when they got to the bottom they ate hungrily of the lush growth of Flinders grass. I made camp on the Armstrong. I hobbled my horses out, making sure my new acquisition was hobbled short and that the straps weren't likely to break. I expected him to try and make it back to his mates for a couple of nights; he'd settle down after a while.

The next morning I rode up to Montejinni homestead. The head stockman was Matt Savage — I knew him casually from when I was running the Wave Hill camp. He called to one of his stockmen to unpack my horses and turn them out into the paddock. I saw him eyeing the chestnut horse. I knew he wouldn't be fooled, and said "Nice horse Matt, eh?"

"Christ, yes," he replied, "where'd you pick him up?"

It was obvious to an experienced horseman such as Matt Savage that he didn't belong to my mob; he still had the bloom and sheen of a fresh horse, while mine were looking decidedly weary and travel stained. Despite plenty of feed they were starting to lose condition. I told him how I'd got him and asked if he recognised the brand. He walked around him and scratched his head, "Jay two Jay, eh — never heard or seen it before in my life, I reckon the fellow that lost him would be crying his eyes out. I would if it were me."

"There's no doubt about that," I replied, "I was thinking the same thing. I s'pose I'd better drop word around that I've got him and hope to Christ the owner doesn't turn up."

"You'd be bloody unlucky to strike the owner; there's thousands of cattle and horses go through every year, year after year. You can be sure every drover drops or loses a few horses every trip. I'd say you've got yourself a horse, and a bloody good one at that."

Picking up a strange horse and working it was quite common, and no crime; it was widely practised. There were rules, too, which weren't so widely practised, like telling everyone you came into contact with. . . nearly everyone, anyway. If you were short of horseflesh the advertising bit might be limited.

Over a long stretch of years I have lost a lot of horses; a lot I've never seen again. There have been odd occasions — very rare — when someone has let me know they've picked up a horse of mine, for which I've been grateful.

The horses of Bill Crowson's I took across from Anthony's Lagoon to Newcastle Waters the year before were an example. The chestnut that I picked up at Murranji might have been lost hundreds of miles away. Being Queensland-bred he may have been making his way back, which they very often do, and finally settled for Murranji. There were no fences, except a few paddocks; not enough to stop a horse between West Australia and Queensland.

I left Montejinni the next morning and followed the Armstrong River down. That evening I made camp on a big waterhole. After watching the horses I hobbled them out about 200 yards from my camp.

Walking back, I noticed a wisp of smoke rising further downstream, I guessed it to be nomad blacks and guessed correctly again that when they heard my horse bells they would call on me. I had barely got my fire alight when two gleaming naked hunters appeared, each clutching a few spears.

One of them immediately established a bond of union, "Me savee you", he said "before you boss long Wave Hill number one camp." "Ui," [yes] I replied, then, "How come you savee me?" Knowing full well that just about every blackfellow within a radius of fifty miles would know me — and, of course, just about every other stockman who had been in the district any length of time.

He went on, "One fella stock boy Peter, work long you." He added proudly "Him son belong me."

"Yes," I said, then added quite truthfully, "Peter number one boy, savee ridem buckjumper, savee throwem bullock." He swelled visibly with pride. Then there was a silence I did nothing to break: I waited for the bite, and it was not long coming.

"Boss, me fella hungry, no got tucker, no got tobacco." Their eyes followed me as I walked over to the pack bags and rummaged around inside. I came back with two sticks of tobacco, giving them one each.

"You go spearum barramundi, me give you some fellow tucker."

"Ui," they both said, "no long time me fella come back."

It was an hour to sundown, but I was confident I would have fish before dark. Sure enough, they returned just before the sun went down with five beautiful fish, two of them still alive. I was more than happy to give them some flour, tea and sugar after taking two of the largest fish. I threw them on the coals as they were; when cooked the skin and scales would fall away and they would taste delicious. A billy of black tea and damper and I was overflowing with food and the milk of human kindness. I rolled my swag out on the ground and slept like the proverbial log.

The next morning I stoked up the smouldering campfire and soon had the billy boiling; a quick feed of corned beef and damper as dawn was breaking and, picking up my bridle, I walked out on to the plain for my horses. They hadn't had to walk far to get their fill and looked very content. I quickly unhobbled them and slipping my bridle on a saddle horse, I vaulted on to his back and drove them back to the camp.

I haltered the two pack horses and was busy packing up when my two fishermen friends from the night before appeared with two barramundi. I wasn't surprised; early morning was the best time for spearing fish. I gave them some tobacco, with which they were quite happy, then I quickly gutted the fish, rubbed salt into them and put them in the bag that contained my corned beef supply.

They turned out to be surprisingly good. At my next camp I washed them in the river, boiled them for a few minutes in the camp oven and then threw them on the coals of my campfire. I had never heard of this method of keeping and cooking fish before, but I can recommend it, though I must admit that fish straight off the end of a spear were slightly better.

The next day I reached Pigeon Hole, another outstation of Victoria River Downs, and again I was greeted by the head stockman and my horses were taken over by one of his men. I had got to know Roy Sedetry when I was running the Wave Hill camp. We used to meet on boundary musters where cattle from both places were always well mixed. We went into the house and Roy called out, "Alice, boil 'im billy, make some tea," and a few minutes later a comely young lubra appeared, a huge teapot in one hand and a plate with a big brownie on it. (Brownie is the bushman's version of cake, a concoction of flour, baking powder,

125

whatever dried fruit is available, but usually sultanas — currants as well in a good season, — and of course sugar. Baked in a camp oven or, if at the homestead, an oven it is very good, especially if you haven't tasted real cake for a long time.)

The lubra put a jar of sugar on the table and produced some enamel pannikins and a couple of spoons, all of which I was watching closely. Not because I was particularly interested in her table-setting ability, but because her face was elusively familiar. Then suddenly it came to me in a flash. Six months previously I had received an advice from Roy to say he would be mustering the Camfield, there would be certain to be some Wave Hill cattle there. I took my camp over and met him just below the junction of Cattle Creek. We were camped on a waterhole, each camp a couple of hundred yards apart.

We mustered for four days and I clearly recalled a young stockboy who always rode out with Roy. The stock had been burnt down in a bush fire not long previously and we had to watch the cattle at night; and though they gave us a lot of trouble, fresh and surging all night, Roy's young stockman never did a watch. He seemed a smart horseman, too, with good hands on a horse. I casually mentioned this to Roy one day. He shrugged it off saying that he had something wrong with his eyes, night blind or something he said vaguely. I never thought any more about it. And I remembered he called him Alec.

In the background I could hear a piccaninny squawking. Roy called, "Alice, bring him piccaninny!" A moment later the lubra walked in with a naked, gurgling, half-caste baby boy on her hip, obviously very proud of him. Roy was beaming.

"What do you think of that, Tom?" he asked me, adding, "Our own production."

I couldn't resist a shot at him and said slyly, "What are you going to call him, Roy? Alec?"

He roared with laughter, "Well," he said, "You know that old Territory saying — necessity is the mother of invention and the father of half-castes!"

126

I enjoyed another day with Roy. He was good company, and apart from the mailman once a fortnight in the dry season and once every six weeks in the wet, he didn't have many visitors. During the dry season he would be out mustering most of the time, getting bullocks for the meatworks early in the season; he had the lion's share of branding too. His camp would brand between 8000 and 10,000 calves. Except during the wet he would see his homestead only when he came in for a change of horses, shoe them and replenish his rations; about every six weeks.

I left the following morning, Roy giving me a fresh supply of meat from his butcher's shop. This was a normal procedure; every traveller could call at a station homestead and get an issue of meat. He gave me some mail to deliver to the head station and I went on my way. Two days later I hobbled my horses out just off the Wickham River. I was at Victoria River Downs Station.

It was owned by a British multinational company, Bovril Australian Estates, which was headed by Lord Luke. It came as a surprise to me to learn that though it was the largest property of its kind in the world, the noble earl had never set foot on the place. One would have thought that such property would have generated at least some curiosity — the sheer immensity of it, for one thing. The herd, estimated at about 140,000 (give or take 6000) would be a conversation piece alone in any London club! You could ride 150 miles in a straight line and still be on the property.

I delivered the mail to the manager, Alf Martin, one of the most respected cattlemen in the Territory, who thanked me and asked me if I needed anything in the way of rations. I told him my packs were full, but he said go and see the storekeeper if I needed anything just the same.

He asked which way I was heading and I told him I wasn't sure, but that I was looking for horse breaking. "I can't offer you any myself," he said, "but I believe Harry Shadforth is looking for a breaker." I thanked him and went back to my camp. I didn't know Shadforth but I did know that he was managing Auvergne, one of Duracks' stations further north.

127

I intended leaving the next morning, especially so given the chance of getting some breaking. But when I mustered my horses a bay pack mare was missing. Normally they all stuck together: at the most there would be no more than half a mile between them unless grass was very scarce, which it wasn't. She had a bell on and I didn't anticipate much difficulty finding her. But I was wrong. I guessed she had come on season and had gone off looking for a stallion.

Though my horses were in a paddock, it was a fairly large paddock — probably about 100 square miles, which in open country wouldn't be much of a problem (after all, if it were square, it would only be ten miles by ten miles). But it was scrubby and there were a lot of horses running in it: drovers' horses, station horses and others, which made tracking difficult. There were tracks everywhere.

It was nearly sundown when I found her, hanging her head over the fence whinnying like a bloody banshee. As I expected, she was on season and she had broken her hobbles, too. I was lucky a brumby stallion hadn't heard her or smelt her: he would have smashed the fence down and taken her away, and I'd have been lucky to get her back.

I took her back to my camp, giving her some of my views on mares who went looking for stallions and broke their hobbles — which didn't seem to impress her at all. I put a strong halter on her and tied her up that night; I wasn't going to risk her getting away again. I made sure I got an early start by packing up the night before and shortening the hobbles on my horses so they wouldn't go too far that night. It was 140 miles to Auvergne, and the track headed north through Jasper's Gorge, a narrow rocky pass through which Jasper's Creek ran. I had heard of it; drovers hated it — years before there had been a couple of spearings by blacks and there was no road as such: just a stock route used mainly by Victoria River Downs drovers taking bullocks to the Wyndham meatworks.

Burt Drew would take his donkey team through probably twice a year, to get the Victoria River Downs station supplies, which came round by boat from Darwin. Apart from that it would be used only by the odd traveller such as myself. Motor vehicles were a rarity; there were only three between Katherine and the Western Australian border, 400-odd hundred miles away.

I had no difficulty following the cattle pads, which were deep and plain. Following advice I'd been given at VRD, I camped where Jasper's Creek, running crystal clear, entered the gorge; a good camping spot.

The next day I let my horses pick their way through the gorge. It was easy to understand the drovers' dislike of this pass; it was a most forbidding place, strewn with rocks and boulders. The creek wound from one side to the other, and had to be crossed and recrossed again and again. Sandstone cliffs towered above — it was easy to visualise the spears of wild bush blacks hurtling down.

Glad to break through into open grassland, I went on a few miles and made camp for an hour, boiled the billy and shot a plains turkey. I plucked it, cleaned it and cooked it in a camp oven; when it cooled I packed up and went on.

Just before sundown I got to Skull Creek. George Murray, a drover, was camped there and I pulled off my packs and hobbled out my horses. I was glad to have some company. We had known of each other and he asked me to come over to his camp for a meal; instead I suggested he come to mine and help me out with the turkey I'd shot. We yarned well into the night. He told me he was fairly sure Shadforth had found a breaker, but thought Tom Lawson, the manager of Bullita Station (also one of the Durack stations) wanted a head stockman. I thought I'd better take it: my horses were getting tired and I couldn't wander around the country forever — but I'd have another day's spell first.

In the morning Murray asked about the chestnut horse. I was still making no secret of how I had acquired him. He asked what he was like and especially what sort of a mouth he had: did he pull much? Was he hard to hold? No, I told him, he had a good mouth and was very tractable. Then he came to the point. "Look, Tom," he said, "I've got a horse here that's just about too much for me. He's a bloody good horse — Bradshaw bred — but he's got a mouth as hard as a whore's heart. He wouldn't trouble you much, you're a good horseman, but as you know droving horses have to be quiet. Try him out and see what you think; if you like him I'll swap you. It won't worry me how you got him: I'll take a chance on that."

"Okay, George, let's have a look at him," I said, fully expecting him to try unloading some bloody outlaw on me. He brought up a very nice-looking bay. I looked at his mouth and saw he was six years old. I saddled him, rode out on to some open country and put him into a canter. George was right about his mouth, and he was a bolter, too; he took off with me and went about a mile before I got him in hand again. But I liked him; he had a good smooth gait and walked freely.

Talking to him on the way back to the camp I said, "I'll fix you, you bastard; I'll put a running rein on you." I think he understood, he switched his tail and tossed his head which I understood meant "You try it — it'll take more than that." But he was wrong. A running rein is an extension buckled to the girth then through the bit, giving the rider a tremendous amount of extra purchase on the horse's head.

I had no hesitation doing the deal with Murray. While I was away with the bay he had anticipated the result, and the chestnut, by the time I got back, had a saddle and bridle on. He took him for a ride and when he came back the deal was done.

During the morning another man had arrived to join Murray as a drover's hand. He unpacked and hobbled his horses. His name was Jack Carrol and he was obviously recovering from a heavy drinking session; he looked almost at death's door. Without saying much he rolled his swag out in the shade, lay down with a waterbag beside him and went to sleep, waking up at frequent intervals to take a long drink. Just before sundown he woke, went down to the creek, stripped off and plunged in. When he joined us again he didn't look too bad and announced that he felt almost human.

Listening to the conversation between him and Murray I gathered he'had just parted from a half-caste girl; he'd left her with Matt Wilson, the storekeeper at the Depot a few miles further down the river. He said there'd been a pretty heavy drinking session at the Depot when a boat arrived from Darwin with cargo for the surrounding stations. Tom Lawson, the Bullita manager, had come in to collect his cargo bringing his cook, Peg Leg Wilkins, to give him a hand. Carrol said, "As soon as the boat was unloaded we all got into the rum; it was a pretty solid session." Which I could well believe, recalling the state he was in when he arrived. "One of the deckhands tried to get away with Sally," [I guessed she was the girl friend he'd mentioned earlier.] "So I had to fix him up." I glanced at his shoulders and bruised knuckles and guessed the deckhand was well "fixed up".

"When he came to," Jack continued, "he went over to the boat and came back with a rifle — well, that livened things up a bit. I went to my pack bags and got a revolver, Tom Lawson got a revolver, poor old Peg Leg, Lawson's cook, had nothing — only a waddy." He paused for a while trying to recall what happened next.

"It was about ten o'clock I think. There was a good moon, I got behind a tree, Tom Lawson behind another one, Peg Leg behind the bottle tree, but no one was sure who was behind which tree — we were all pretty drunk.

"There were a good few shots fired. Everybody was shooting at once; it was like the bloody battle of Waterloo. In the end it was Matt Wilson who saved the day — he crept up behind this bloke and hit him over the head with a steel fencing post!"

"Christ! he must have killed him!" said George Murray.

"No," said Carrol, "he didn't hit him that hard, but he bent the fencepost, then old Matt threw his rifle in the river . . . and then Lawson and I threw him in the river!"

"Did anyone get shot?" I asked.

"Well, not really," Carrol replied, "Peg Leg got shot in his wooden leg, but you couldn't count that!"

"What about this bloke," I asked, "did he drown?"

"I don't think so," Carrol replied, "we heard he got out, the river would have freshened him up; and of course there's plenty of crocodiles. He would have known about them, that would have hurried him up!

"You know, he shouldn't have got that gun out, he was a very dislikeable bloke — come from a one-parent family."

"Yes," George Murray agreed, "sounds like he was not only a bastard but a stupid bastard, and that's a lot worse."

CHAPTER 13

DANGERS OF
THE BRONCO YARD

A t daybreak I packed up and headed for Bullita, which Murray said was about forty miles away. He gave me fairly clear instructions on how to pick up the turn-off from the main track. After travelling about four miles, he said, I'd come to a small creek where there was a big fallen gum lying across the road; another half mile and I'd come to a claypan. The turnoff was just past the claypan. I had no trouble.

Bullita was one of five cattle stations owned by that fine old pioneering family, the Duracks. They stretched in an almost unbroken chain from the Victoria River nearly to the sea in Western Australia. One of the finest properties was Argyle, now home to the giant diamond deposits. Tom Lawson did need a head stockman and was pleased to see me; the seasonal muster was about to begin and the horses were being shod. The homestead was on the bank of the East Baines River, which ran through the run. It was forty or fifty feet down to the riverbed and on the flat rocks on each side of the stream crocodiles sunned themselves. They were the harmless fresh water variety, but sometimes had to put up with target practice from the verandah.

After hearing the story of the fracas at the Depot I had been looking forward to meeting Peg Leg Wilkins, Lawson's cook, and hearing his version.

It was pretty well word for word what Carrol had told us: he showed me where the bullet had fractured his wooden leg. He had repaired it by tacking a piece of leather over it, but he said he'd have to try and get someone to make him another one — but, he added, it was hard to find anyone out here who knew anything about making wooden legs.

Two days later we started mustering up the river. The cattle were very wild. The Baines River came out of the sandstone ranges where a tribe of Myall blacks lived and used to come down from the ranges to kill the cattle. We frequently found the remains of a beast that had been speared, the fireplaces around it testifying to their confidence that they were not likely to be disturbed while cutting it up and cooking what they couldn't carry away.

Lawson said he had never seen any; the closest we ever got to them was old campfires and tracks. A previous manager, Jim Crisp, had been speared some years before and was buried on the bank of the Baines; a stockyard built there, had been called Crisp's Yard.

In the muster we got a bullock with a broken spear hanging out of its flank. We yarded it, threw it and cut the spear out; it had a flint head of almost perfect symmetry with razor-like edges. We dressed the wound with Stockholm tar, and I expect the bullock would have recovered completely.

After three weeks' mustering we were back at the station, branded up a hundred or so calves and drafted off some bullocks, which I took up to the Fig Tree paddock, eight or ten miles from the station.

When I got back to the homestead a car was outside, which was a bit sensational. It was none other than Mr Durack himself doing the rounds of his properties. I thought he was a fine-looking man, standing as straight as a gun barrel. His daughter, Mary, has recorded this fine pioneering family in her book, *Kings in Grass Castles*.

I had little opportunity to talk to MP, as he was known. I had my hands full getting ready for the next muster; we expected to be out for some weeks and I was checking the stores and supplies, rations, branding irons and greenhide ropes and testing the pack-bag weights. The next day we left pretty well together; MP drove off to Auvergne, and we mustered across to Bob's Yard, not far from Jasper's Gorge.

We had about 1000 head of cattle together by midday and in the afternoon we drafted off the breeders and the calves that were to be branded. There were also a few big cattle that had escaped the previous muster, which was normal; there was always a goodly percentage on all the big runs.

Bob's Yard was a bronco yard, and for branding purposes had a panel of railings to which the calf was dragged after being lassoed by the rider of the bronco horse. The bronco horse was a chestnut mare I thought was a bit on the light side for the job; when I remarked on this to Lawson he said, "Yes, she is, but she's such a bloody awful hack no one wants to ride her. She works well at this job, though."

The bronco gear was a broad leather breastplate that went around the horse's chest, kept in position with a strap over the saddle and a girth. A greenhide rope about eighteen feet long was buckled on and all was ready.

I started off lassoing the cleanskins, dragging them up bellowing to the bronco panel where they were quickly leg-roped, thrown and branded. Among the cattle was a big cleanskin white cow that must have been missed in at least a couple of previous musters. I tried to rope her a couple of times but missed; she had wide horns and was pretty cunning — it's sometimes difficult to rope a beast with wide horns.

After a while Lawson said, "I'll give you a spell at the roping," so I dismounted and handed over the bronco mare. While he was altering the stirrup leathers to his length I said, "Get that white cow out of the way, Tom; the mare's getting a bit tired." He nodded and rode out among the cattle, but didn't catch her until the very last.

When she felt the rope tighten around her neck she went berserk, plunging, jumping and bellowing. Then suddenly it

135

happened; she had galloped in one direction, and the rope had pulled her up with a jerk and brought her down. She scrambled to her feet and galloped off the opposite way. She was big and strong and I saw the horse stagger: when she came to the end of the rope with a mighty jerk, she galloped off again and this time it was just too much for the horse, which was obviously very tired. This time horse and rider crashed to the ground.

Lawson hit his head on one of the bronco panel posts. The rope had become tangled around his neck, and while the mare was scrambling to her feet I told one of the stockboys to grab her head. Lawson was on the ground, the rope round his neck, a mad cow on one end and a frightened horse on the other! I had a brief vision of his head being sawn off by the greenhide rope, and slashed it quickly with a castrating knife. The manager lay still. At first I thought he had been killed, but then I could see he was still breathing. The rest of the stockmen crowded around. They didn't appear to be unduly concerned; one of them was lighting his pipe with a flaming stick from the branding fire. Between puffs he said, "I think he die finish!" Another said, "No more, he still got wind," referring to the breathing.

I was badly shaken by the events that had so suddenly taken place, but managed to pull myself together. I sent one of the stockmen over to the camp for water — he came back with a billycan full of water and tea leaves. Well, that didn't matter . . . I splashed it over Lawson's head, but nothing happened. I told a couple of men to muster the horses and had Lawson carried over to the camp.

After a while he revived, but didn't know what had happened or where he was; he was semi-delirious. I didn't quite know what to do. I wasn't sure how bad he was, so I decided I'd have to get him back to the station and let all the cattle out of the yard. The white cow that had caused all the trouble galloped out with the rope still around her neck . . . I hoped it'd choke her.

After an hour or so he seemed to have recovered enough to get him on a horse. I got the camp packed up and we left; I had one of the stockmen ride on each side of his horse, and we got to the station late in the afternoon.

I explained to Peg Leg what had happened and asked him to keep an eye on Lawson while I got the camp gear put away and the horses turned out. I still wasn't sure how bad the situation was.

When I got back to the house the cook said he thought Lawson was in a bad way, he'd started drinking kerosene: "He'd just about got through a pannikin full before I spotted it," he said.

"That shouldn't hurt him too much, should it?" I asked.

Peg Leg thought for a while, then said: "I don't think so, it'd probably open his bowels — might even do him some good."

I asked him how long since Lawson had drunk the kerosene and he said about half an hour. I went and had a look at him; he was sitting out on the back verandah talking to himself, but didn't seem to be any the worse for his drink. He had a large lump on the side of his head where he'd hit the tree. It was badly contused, there was some dried blood matted in his hair and from time to time he bled badly.

I thought things over for a while, then said to the cook, "Peg Leg, I'm going to Auvergne and try and catch MP. If I leave now I'll get there before daylight with any luck."

He looked at his watch, "Christ!" he said, "that's eighty-odd miles. Would you have a horse that'd carry you to Auvergne in twelve hours?"

"No, but I reckon on getting a change at the Timber Creek Police Station."

I decided I'd take one of my own horses, one of the Banka Banka colts that I'd got from the Ambroses which had been spelling and was in good condition. Just as the sun was setting I rode away.

I knew that if I couldn't get a fresh horse at Timber Creek I wouldn't get eighty miles out of a grass-fed horse; even the forty miles to Timber Creek would be plenty. If the policeman was away chasing blacks (which occupied more than half his time) I didn't know what I'd do. I thought — and I had a lot of time for thinking — that even if I couldn't get him to a doctor somehow he most likely wouldn't die, unless he got his hands on some kind of poison . . .though at intervals he was bleeding badly.

It was five o'clock by my watch when I rode away. To get the best out of my horse I trotted him for a quarter of an hour and walked him for a quarter. Trotting is a fairly easy gait on a horse, though, hard on the rider: it's by far the most uncomfortable way of riding for any distance, and very tiring, but in this case my comfort was secondary.

At a quarter past twelve I rode up to the Timber Creek Police Station and woke Sandy McNabb. I had ridden forty-one miles since sundown.

I told Sandy what had happened while he was preparing me a meal; he took it all in his stride. I can't think of anything that would surprise a member of the Northern Territory Mounted Police — unless it was nothing happening for any length of time.

He called for one of his trackers, naming a horse and telling the tracker to "get a bloody move on", while saying to me "this fellow will carry you to Auvergne, no trouble". Half an hour later when the tracker returned with a powerful-looking brown horse. I climbed wearily into the saddle, trying not to think of the forty-three miles stretched out in front of me.

I asked my horse to make it as easy as he could for me, which he understood; he had a good gait. I chatted away to him as we rode along, but it was a one-sided conversation.

After a while my old friend the morning star appeared over the horizon, winking at me — trying to give me strength. Except for a few mopokes the bush was silent. It was a long ride and I was tiring badly when I saw the first glimmer of dawn, which had a freshening effect on me. The sun rose in a cloudless sky and not long afterward I saw the most welcome sight I'd seen for a long time — the Auvergne homestead, a car standing outside. My ride hadn't been for nothing.

138

I quickly explained the situation and we were soon on our way back to Bullita, MP's son Reg, not long back from school, drove the car. Tom Lawson was in a bad way. He'd bled a lot, Peg Leg explained, and wouldn't keep a bandage on. Durack had had a very wide experience with every kind of mishap it was possible to imagine, from spearing to fever. He had a look at Lawson, felt his pulse and said he'd live. "I've no idea how bad the concussion might be," he said, "but the bleeding isn't too serious; a man can lose a lot more blood than that before he's in danger."

Tom was semi-conscious when we carried him to the car. Just as he was leaving, MP turned to me and said: "Tom, you take over the management of Bullita; I'll see you in about a month's time."

There was no reason to change anything on Bullita. It had been well run by Lawson. Like most of these places, however, a few more working horses would be very greatly appreciated.

A couple of the yards needed some repair work, one out on Limestone Creek and Crisp's Yard. I knew Lawson intended to try to get a man for the work. I went through the station diary where such things were entered and noted there was an allowance of twenty-five pounds for yard work. It doesn't sound much, but I could get a man for five pounds a week and keep; a good man could do a lot of work in five weeks. I made a mental note to send word in to the Depot the next time I sent in for the mail, which was three days later.

This produced results quicker than I expected. Shortly after, a man rode up to the homestead, announced his name was Jim Nichols and said he was looking for fencing or yard building. I'd never met Nichols before but knew of him. A few years previously he and a man named Renault had set out from Darwin in a small sailing boat. Their intention was to sail down the Western Australian coast; I think Renault was writing a book.

They got as far as Point Blaze and Renault, who had gone ashore for some reason, had been killed by the blacks. I threw out a few leaders about Renault's murder but it was clear Nichols didn't want to talk about it. I got the impression it had affected him very deeply.

I took him out to the Limestone Creek yard, showed him what I wanted done and gave him two of my stockmen to help him. He said it would take about a fortnight. This suited me fine; I was now two men short in the stock camp, but reckoned I'd do a horse muster, brand up some youngsters and probably throw a rope on two or three colts that were ready to break. I could do this easily with the reduced camp.

A fortnight later I went out to Limestone Creek and moved him to Crisp's Yard. After I had shown him what I wanted done we walked over to where Jim Crisp was buried. The grave was almost trampled out of sight by cattle, so as an afterthought I told him to put some rails round it and tidy it up a bit.

When he finished the work I brought him back to the station and paid him off. I would have liked to have kept him on; he was a good man, but I just didn't have the funds. The night before he left, over a bottle of rum, he loosened up quite a lot and told me about the Renault spearing — it had affected him very deeply, and he had obviously formed a strong attachment for the younger man.

He told me he first met Renault, an Australian of French extraction, in Darwin. They became friends, the younger man confiding in Nichols his aspirations — he intended to buy a boat, sail round the west coast and write a book about the pearling industry. He asked Nichols to join him. He readily agreed: He would go with him, perhaps as far as Broome, but first a boat had to be found.

A week later Renault had found what he wanted, a trim, little twenty-five-foot sailing boat. The two men put her up on the beach, cleaned her and painted her. When it was finished they floated her off on a high tide, loaded with provisions, hired a boat boy and left, beating into the southeast trades, idling along, putting into inlets as fancy took them.

They passed the mouth of the Finniss River, rounded Point Blaze and turned into a sheltered inlet. A minor caulking job had to be done: a couple of planks needed attention — a simple job, a matter of waiting for the right tide so the little craft could be beached and safely floated off again. In those latitudes, especially at the time of the spring tides, the rise and fall was more than twenty feet. If beached at the wrong time a boat could lie there for a month or more.

They beached their boat, propping her upright with poles they cut from the mangroves. They rigged a sail for shelter and brought some provisions from the vessel. The caulking job was completed and then they had to wait for a suitable tide.

Renault announced he would walk over to a lagoon not far away and shoot some geese they could see flying around. He cleaned the protective coating from the gun (they rusted quickly in that climate if not cared for), and Nichols said he would walk out to the reef and collect oysters. It was a land of plenty.

He pottered around the reef for perhaps an hour, he couldn't be sure, but at any rate some time later he heard a shot but took no notice, thinking, naturally, it was Renault shooting geese. It was quickly followed by another and, shortly after, their boat boy came running across the reef calling to Nichols that his mate had been shot.

He ran across to the lagoon as fast as he could and found Renault dead with a gaping wound in his chest where the charge had exited; he had been shot in the back.

Nichols was stunned by what had happened. He now had to make his way to Darwin and report the tragedy to the authorities. He and the boat boy built a platform, wrapped the body of his friend in a tarpaulin and put it up off the ground, away from dingos — which would quickly have torn it to pieces.

He sailed back to Darwin and the wheels of officialdom ground slowly into gear. A boat left Darwin for Pt Blaze carrying a coroner and a policeman. It was found that Keith Renault died from a shotgun wound inflicted by persons unknown.

141

Jim Nichols rode away from Bullita the next morning. It was nearly twelve months before I heard of him again. That infallible source of information, the bush telegraph, drummed its message — Jim Nichols had been speared on Mainoru Station, the most remote property in the Northern Territory, where he had been building a yard for Bill Farrar.

Over the next few years there seemed to be a spate of spearings. Few were connected; it was just the way it happened. A lugger was attacked in the Victoria River, then not far away, on the Fitzmaurice River, two men named Stephens and Cook were killed and thrown to the crocodiles.

CHAPTER 14

MANAGING BULLITA STATION

Bullita was not the easiest place to run; it was 2000 square miles, scrubby and rough. Cattle in open country are naturally quieter by nature, the environment contributing to this. An abundance of water ensured the herd ranged over a greater area, while fewer watering points brought the cattle together. No matter how well I thought I'd mustered, cleanskin cattle would always turn up. Spring Creek over toward the western side was always a headache; mustering it involved hard galloping that took its toll of our horses.

The southern boundary was the worst; the river and a number of its tributaries cascaded down from the ranges, levelling off into ravines where there were choice pickings for stock. These places were almost impossible to muster — they were narrow and strewn with boulders, but provided excellent cover for our elusive Aboriginal friends who, though armed with stone-headed spears, were probably the finest hunters in the world, enjoying life to the full — mainly on Bullita beef.

The sheer majesty of these sandstone ranges was breathtaking; when the setting sun reflected the blood-red colouring of those ancient towering cliffs. When it finally settled behind the escarpment, packs of dingos began their mournful serenade, punctuated by the challenging roar of cleanskin bulls, the echoes reverberating and flung back.

Majestic though it may have been, everything was there that a cattleman didn't want — wild Myall blacks, wilder cattle, cleanskin bulls that charged on sight, timber and broken gullies that would bring down the most surefooted horse.

I never wasted any time on the bulls; I carried a Colt .45 strapped to the pommel of my saddle and any that looked ugly I shot without hesitation, noble beasts though many were.

Whichever way you looked at it they weren't a proposition. To persevere took valuable time; with their lethal horns they could kill a horse (a man, too), and if finally you got them into a yard they always gave trouble, slowing the work down. Getting them up to a bronco panel after being roped was particularly hard on a horse, taking two or three times as long as younger cattle. They then had to be leg-roped, thrown, branded, castrated and dehorned; altogether a savage operation they would be lucky to survive . . . frequently they didn't. A year or more later, if they found their way to a meatworks, they might bring a couple of quid; at the best they'd only be second or third rate beef. The men who did all the hard yakka believed in a short cut — shoot the bastards; it was cheaper and easier.

I'd had a hard three-week muster and came back to the station realising that I was a man short, having been moved up to manager I should have had someone to take my place. It was something to which I hadn't given much thought. Horses were a permanent problem, and I'd have difficulty finding a mount for another man.

I put it on one side for the time and sent word to Humbert River Station and Victoria River Downs that I was about to muster the country around Bob's Yard and Jasper's Gorge. There were always VRD bullocks hanging around, lost by drovers, which got as far as the gorge but were reluctant to tackle that forbidding ravine. Humbert River was my closest neighbour; there was always some of its cattle around.

I thought this was a good idea. I'd have some fresh company, and I was starting to talk to myself — not a good sign. Talking to my horses wasn't much better; I couldn't get a decent argument going. Beyond telling them what to do I rarely conversed with my stockmen. We had little in common, no mutual interests except perhaps our horses: most of them were horse lovers and developed an affection for the ones they rode, which was a good thing. That I never got on a conversational footing was probably a fault on my part. There were some like old Charcoal of Wave Hill who were good raconteurs, but they were few and far between.

Frank Spencer, who was head stockman running the Centre Camp at VRD, arrived with his plant and the following day Charlie Schultz rode up to the homestead, his stockman bringing his horses behind. I was hungry for any kind of news. I certainly got some: Spencer told us that the flyer, Kingsford-Smith, was lost somewhere between the Overland Telegraph Line and Western Australia. A big search was on, aeroplanes everywhere, he said, and the day he left VRD one of the planes looking for Smithy was also missing.

The missing aeroplane he said was the *Kookaburra*. There were two airmen in it, they had left Alice Springs a couple of days before he left to come to Bullita. He had pretty well all the details; the two men in the *Kookaburra*, Anderson and Hitchcock, had obviously come to grief between Alice and WA. That was a big stretch of nothing — no water.

The final story is, of course, well known: they died of thirst, which shouldn't have happened either.

Charlie Schultz was an outstanding cattleman and horseman, coming from a family of outstanding men: of him it could have been written:

> *Swaddled in sweat-lined saddle cloth,*
> *Christened in spur-drawn blood.*

He came to Humbert River when he was twenty. A monumental job was dropped into his lap unexpectedly but he handled it with the competence and ability of a much older man.

The history of Humbert River went back a long way; it had not always been a cattle station. Originally it was an Aboriginal reserve of 200 square miles and not very good cattle country. Most

145

of it was grim sandstone ranges; by no means a cattleman's paradise.

The first European to take any interest in it was Brigalow Bill Ward, who obtained an occupational permit for the purpose of running horses. He probably had ideas of expanding into cattle — one corner of the block extended across the Wickham River, giving a small toehold on vastly better country where there were plenty of VRD cleanskins. Whatever ideas he may have had were terminated abruptly together with Brigalow Bill, a couple of shovel spears in his back being an effective medium. Humbert River went back to being a full-time Aboriginal Reserve.

Some time after the First World War, two of the Victoria River Downs head stockmen, Noel Hall and Bill Butler, obtained a grazing licence for which they paid one shilling a square mile per annum. They put some breeders on it and it became Humbert River Station. Though it may not have been good cattle country it rapidly acquired a reputation for being good breeding country; some of the branding tallies were astronomical as told round the campfires, where they lost nothing in the telling. One cattleman was heard to say, "I think their bloody cattledogs are having calves!"

Butler and Hall sold to two drovers: perhaps being head stockman on Victoria River Downs and branding cleanskins on the boundary for themselves may have been regarded as a conflict of interest. The drovers were Billy and Albert Schultz. They took VRD bullocks to the Wyndham meatworks during the droving season and when the rains came filled in their time looking after their cattle with great dedication.

Then wild rumours of a gold strike in Tanami in the desert, 400 miles to the south, filtered through on the bush telegraph. Albert Schultz packed up some horses and rode off to the latest Eldorado. His brother never saw him again. He died of some mysterious disease. There were no doctors — the closest would have been 600 or 700 miles away. In the country if you became ill you either got better or you didn't. Albert didn't.

Billy Schultz carried on taking bullocks to Wyndham meatworks through the droving season and in the wet helped the company in other directions, such as keeping the cleanskins branded up along his boundaries. His only relaxation was the occasional convivial party at the end of the droving season.

Now, a convivial party in that country after the droving season would make a mild saturnalia look like a Salvation Army convention. Schultz, like most men, worked hard and played harder.

After one particularly solid session, when the run was finished Schultz mounted his horse full of enthusiasm and hard liquor, and galloped back to this camp. On the way he hit a coolibah limb hanging across his path at just the right height to connect with his head, knocking him clean out of the saddle. He must have had a fair bit of pace up because it killed him instantly.

The only surviving brother, Charlie, lived in Queensland managing a cattle station in which he was a partner. He came to Humbert sadly to pick up the pieces, bringing his young son, also Charlie, with him. Charles senior had to go back to Queensland and his business interests, leaving the lad a daunting task. I don't know whether he had any misgivings when he left; I think possibly he may have done. But before very long he would have known that they were unfounded.

I saw very little of Charlie Schultz after our muster together with the VRD camp. My next job was to take 500 or 600 bullocks over to Argyle, which was much closer to the meatworks — they would also fatten on the much superior country.

They say the path of true love never runs smooth — well, the path of a cattleman can beat that hollow. Peg Leg, my cook, made a lightning decision to leave and in between going to the Wyndham races, I cursed him up hill and down dale. I couldn't leave the homestead unattended; the bush blacks would make a good job of tidying the place up and I'd be lucky to find the corrugated iron on the roof when I got back.

I immediately packed one of my lads off to the Depot with a letter to Matt Wilson, the storekeeper, asking him to send me a

147

cook of some kind — any kind. It doesn't matter if he can't cook, I wrote: even if he can't boil water without burning it, and, as an afterthought, to tell him, Matt, that the lubras are the sweetest little girls in the Territory — that's how far I was prepared to go to get a cook, at the same time wondering if that was going a bit too far.

At the end of a week, my bullock paddock was just about eaten out and I'd nearly talked Peg Leg into staying when Jack Noble arrived on a bicycle! It must have been the most sensational thing that had ever happened on Bullita; I reckoned it would have been a bigger sensation than the Crisp spearing. My stockboys had never seen a bicycle in their lives. I'm sure they wouldn't have been as impressed if Jack Noble had arrived walking up the river without wetting his ankles. I've mentioned that I thought there were only three motor cars between Katherine and Wyndham in Western Australia, possibly four — but there was only one bike, that was certain . . . and we had it here on Bullita!

The excitement was indescribable, everyone turned out — my stock camp, all hands, their wives, their children, half a dozen stray nomads and all their dogs. One of the dogs sniffed at the front wheel and started to lift a leg. He only got halfway and an outraged lubra gave him a mighty belt with a waddy. I thought she'd broken his back at such sacrilege!

Peg Leg told Noble: "This puts you about three jumps ahead of Jesus Christ!" And riding the machine was obviously some kind of a miracle. Just two wheels: how could anybody sit on that saddle, nothing like a riding saddle, and make it go and stay on and not fall off? They all crowded round the machine and every now and then looked over to where Jack Noble was sitting on the verandah. He was some kind of a devil-devil . . . but a good kind of devil-devil, that was for sure.

I had never met Noble before, though I had heard of him frequently. He had the name of being a good cattleman and I was fascinated when he rode up to the homestead on his iron steed, as

148

he called it. He had the reputation of being a good hoseman, so I asked him how he came to get himself a bike.

He said he'd had a fair sort of a cheque from a droving trip that was burning a hole in his pocket. He came to the Depot with horses and packs and handed his cheque over to Wilson, telling him to let him know when it was cut out. He couldn't have had a more reliable timekeeper. He then settled down to drink it out.

A boat arrived from Darwin, its cargo including a character with a bicycle who was impressed enough with Jack Noble's personality to help him cut his cheque out. At approximately the time Noble's cheque was permanently transferred over to Matt Wilson, my SOS for a cook arrived at the store. Matt gave him the bad news about his cheque and the good news about the cooking job at the same time. Well, all Jack Noble had to do was muster up his horses and get himself to Bullita; a situation with which he was very familiar. But for some reason he had become fascinated with his new friend's bike.

He told me that after giving it a lot of thought he offered to swap his horses and packs, and his saddle (which surprised me) for the bike. The stranger jumped at the offer, of course.

"All my bloody life I've been getting round the country with horses and packs, finding grass for them, finding water for them and just bloody well finding them every morning," said Noble. "I thought a bike was a bloody good idea; it doesn't need grass, it doesn't need water and when I wake up in the morning it's lying beside me."

But I wasn't so sure his enthusiasm for his iron steed was genuine. He hadn't arrived completely unscathed either; he had a shocking wound in his thigh wrapped in a filthy torn shirt. He said he was riding along the track and had a fair bit of pace up when the front wheel struck a big stone and he shot across into a tree that had a short broken branch like a bayonet which drove into his thigh. He fell from the bike and the muscle was torn apart. It was astonishing that he was able to continue, but he said he knew that

149

if he stopped, except to tie it up, he wouldn't have been able to walk, let alone ride. It happened twenty miles back. I reckoned he was one of the toughest blokes I'd ever known.

Jack Noble settled in, Peg Leg Wilkins left and I mustered 400 bullocks from the Fig Tree Paddock and started for Argyle.

It was an uneventful — or almost uneventful — trip of two weeks. I had one bad night when the bullocks rushed. It was about two o'clock in the morning when they jumped. When I leapt out of my swag and grabbed the spare night horse I had no idea what time it was or who was on watch; fortunately the spare night horse that was tied up close by was the best I had, though the stirrups were about four holes too short for me, being the length of the last man on watch.

But it was no time for the finer points of stirrup leathers. I got to the lead and swung them around: when they were steadied down I discovered who was doing the watch. I stayed with them for another half hour, when it was time to call the next man. I went back to my swag and got another half hour's sleep . . . then it was *my* turn to go on watch.

In the morning I put a count on them and was pleased to find we hadn't lost a beast.

I was glad when Argyle came into sight early one morning. Soon after I crossed the boundary I was met by Patsy Durack, MP's nephew, who was the manager. We counted the bullocks: there were three short, which wasn't too bad. One I had dropped because of lameness, the other two had probably sneaked away during someone's watch — anyway, it was all Durack country.

The first surprise I got was when Patsy informed me that Lawson had recovered and, to quote Patsy, "was bellowing on the fence". When I took Bullita over I'd put Lawson completely out of my mind. I remembered asking someone a couple of times but I got vague replies; I wasn't sure whether he was in hospital in Derby or Broome, and in the back of my mind I imagined that he wouldn't be managing a station in the foreseeable future.

It seemed MP was in an awkward position. I gathered I was satisfactory but he couldn't very well refuse to give Lawson his job back; and there was no other suitable job in the company.

MP, Patsy and myself got together in the stockyard. Perched up on the top rail we talked it over. It appeared I was the only one who wasn't worried about my future; although I quite liked Bullita — there was a challenge that appealed to me — but it wasn't sufficiently appealing for me to stay there forever, or even halfway to forever. Perhaps MP could see that; he was a very wise old bird.

CHAPTER 15

BRUMBY RUNNING AT HOOKER'S CREEK

I rode away from Bullita, crossed the divide between the Baines and Victoria River fall and followed the Humbert River until I came to Charlie Schultz's homestead. I spent a couple of nights with Charlie and rode on, crossing the Wickham River and heading southwest until I came to Mt Sandford, an outstation of Victoria River Downs.

Jack Cusack was the head stockman and the camp was as busy as a bunch of bees shoeing horses. It was the end of the mustering season and I was surprised to see all the activity. I said to Jack, "What the hell are you shoeing up for? You're not going out mustering this time of the year, are you?"

"No, no, Alf Martin has bought all Joe Brown's horses; he pegged out last year and Alf bought the estate. He sent Archie Rogers out to muster them but Archie only got half a dozen or so," said Jack.

I knew Archie Rogers was head stockman at the Moolooloo outstation. "Why couldn't Archie muster them?" I asked. "What happened?"

"Well," Jack said, "it seems they're pretty bloody wild, but I can't understand why he didn't get any — he's not that bloody useless, and I think he's got a good camp."

Joe Brown had been a well-known character who took up 100 square miles on Hooker's Creek and settled there with his horses. He was a recluse and a horse lover, who would ride into Hall's Creek a couple of times a year for stores and supplies and go back to his horses. They were well-bred; he always got hold of a good sire for breeding purposes. In his later years it seems he didn't bother with breaking in the youngsters . . . I think he just liked looking at them.

I asked Cusack: "How many are there supposed to be?"

"Well," he said, "that's a bit of a mystery, too: he left no will and all his belongings were advertised in the Government Gazette and the horses were described as '250 more or less, as is where is'. I've heard figures up to 500, but I think that 200 to 300 would be nearer the mark."

"There would have to be some broken-in working horses among them, wouldn't there?" I asked.

"That's right, but Archie got six and heard that someone got in and mustered up the working horses, and took them over to the Kimberleys and sold them. After old Joe died there was no one within fifty miles of the place — he only had a bark hut and he'd been dead two or three weeks when Harry Farquharson got there."

"What did he die of?"

"I dunno," said Jack. "You see, he had a couple of stockboys worked for him for years on and off. We heard he let one go for a walkabout, then the other one heard on the bush wireless that his father had died and of course he took off, I think to Tanami. So Joe was on his own; when the stockboy got back Joe was dead, so he walked into Inverway and told the Farquharsons. Harry said there wasn't much of him left when he got there; the dingoes had just about eaten him up.

"The dogs must have cleaned him up pretty well because Harry got him in one set of pack bags and took him back to Inverway."

The next morning Cusack asked me whether I was in a hurry: "The boss said that if I wanted another man to put one on; I never expected anyone to turn up, but if you'd care to take it on you're more than welcome."

I was in no hurry to go anywhere and liked the idea of going with the Mt Sanford camp on the muster. Jack said he thought it would be more of a brumby-running exercise than just mustering horses.

He had got a few rolls of calico just in case, and as it turned out he was right.

When the shoeing was finished we packed up and left for Hooker's Creek, about 120 miles distant. We cut across through Wave Hill and got to Inverway three days later. Cusack wanted to have a talk with the Farquharsons; they were the only people who knew much about the country.

Harry Farquharson said there were two or three springs and that the horses were "bloody wild". He said there were probably about 300 and they were good horses, a long way above the average brumby. He lent us one of his stockmen who was born down that way and knew the country.

A couple of days later we pulled our packs off, hobbled the horses, making camp on a spring running clear, cool water that gradually tapered off and disappeared in the sandy creek bed a few hundred yards further downstream. There were plenty of horse tracks mixed up with those of emus, kangaroos, goannas, snakes and assorted birdlife.

Early next morning we rode out to have a look-see, and as Jack said, "to see what I've got myself landed with". The first horses we saw galloped away in a cloud of dust. From the brief glimpse we got there was no doubting their quality; they were fine-looking youngsters. The Inverway stockman took us to the other two springs. One wasn't much — there were a good few horses watering there, judging by the tracks — and it looked as though it wouldn't last much longer. The horses that had been there had pawed at the sand, making holes deep enough to enable them to suck at the receding water.

Five or six miles further was another spring with a good supply; it also ran for a little way, then went underground. We saw a lot of horses but they galloped off immediately, intent on putting a lot of ground between us. There wasn't going to be anything easy about this muster and I started to feel some sympathy for Archie Rogers.

We rode back to our camp. Cusack decided we would run them with calico and asked me if I'd done any brumby running this way. I said I hadn't, but had heard about it plenty of times around campfires. It hadn't sounded too difficult, though a lot of work was involved setting it up. Building the yard was the hardest part; stockmen never did like axes, crowbars or shovels — it was thought to be demeaning work.

The next morning he sent two of his stockmen back to Inverway with a couple of pack horses and a letter to the Farquharsons to borrow some yard-building tools; all we had was one axe.

The country was fairly open — some good plains, good firm ground for galloping, enough light timber for cover — but trees suitable for yard-building were scarce, especially long straight timber for rails. I thought whatever horses we got, we were going to earn them with gallons of sweat. But it was interesting and outside the general run of station work.

Picking the site for the yard wasn't easy: the wind was mainly from the north, which had to be considered, and the site for the yard was most important; not too far from suitable timber and not much more than four or five miles from water.

The boys returned from Inverway with three crowbars, four axes and half a coil of fencing wire. We were in business . . . but not without a lot of sweat. When we finished we had a reasonable yard, but because of the shortage of timber not as large as we would have liked. From the end of the wings we ran the calico that had been torn into strips about six inches wide. It seemed there was twenty miles of calico, but it turned out to be only about 500 yards on each wing. We had chosen a good site, it seemed: it was just over a ridge and the horses wouldn't be able to see it until they were just about on it.

The morning after the yard-building we were up before daylight.

With our best horses we rode over to the main spring and waited in the cover of some timber. We were all well keyed-up. Very soon three horses trotted in; an old mare, a young foal at foot and what appeared to be a yearling, probably her previous foal. We didn't bother with them, but they hung around the water and soon eight more strung in, one behind the other. This was more like it. There was a fine stallion and some good-looking youngsters. It looked like a family; the young colts hadn't been chased out by the old fellow, which would happen when they got a bit older.

The head stockman had us spread out over several hundred yards. I was on the right wing, three of the stockboys were in the middle and Jack was on the outside.

The horses plunged their noses into the cool spring water and drank deeply and thirstily. After taking in a huge quantity of water they splashed at it with their forefeet and drank again; they had been perhaps a couple of days without water. We were lying along our horses' necks, camouflaging ourselves as much as possible, and though we were partly obscured by the timber the stallion saw us. He didn't recognise us as horsemen: the slight breeze was blowing crossways and they weren't getting our scent. When they had quenched their thirst they stood around, bloated and satisfied. With that load of water aboard they wouldn't be able to gallop so freely.

Suddenly I heard the pistol-like crack of Cusack's stockwhip, the signal to go. I gave my whip a crack, our stockboys all started to shout at once and the brumbies thundered away in a cloud of dust, the stallion behind rounding his harem up, biting at their rumps to urge them along. When wild horses are startled, the stallion always gallops behind at first, driving them in front of him.

Unexpectedly, they galloped away at an angle, which wasn't what we expected or wanted them to do. They cut across over to my side but though my horse was already into his stride, I feared they were going to beat me. If I didn't get to the lead we would have lost them; once one broke through, all would have followed. The men at the tail had to keep the stragglers up as much as possible, too: if they strung out too much it would become almost impossible to handle them. My horse knew what it was all about — horses always seem to gallop with greater zest when running other horses. I got up to the lead just in time.

We were now approaching the ridge. Provided we kept them going at a fast pace they should be inside the calico wings before they knew it. My horse was covering the ground with great sweeping strides and enjoying it. He was pulling a bit so I knew he had something left for an extra burst. I'd had a good talk to him while we were waiting, but he knew all about it — I was probably boring him because he'd been switching his tail impatiently.

Then suddenly the whole situation changed. Just as we topped the ridge we met another mob of horses trotting in to water. I thought, "Christ! Here's a go, what's going to happen now?" It was an explosion of horses. The mob we met was startled by our sudden appearance and there was almost a head-on collision. The mob we were running was galloping at a hell of a bat and those coming in to water panicked immediately.

Fortunately, everybody grasped the situation and we all swung out wide so as not to crowd them; the main thing was to make plenty of noise and draw the attention of the other horses to us — we were a common enemy. Then they all started to gallop away and though they were now well spread out, they raced away toward the wings.

Soon we were in sight of the calico wings and the two mobs were coming together, making them more controllable. Everybody was yelling at once. It was important, especially at this stage, to make plenty of noise and frighten hell out of them. They were thundering along, ears laid back and — marvellous thought — heading straight for the wings. Soon I could see the strips of calico fluttering in the breeze; we were inside the mouth, we were all coming together now.

The men on either side pulled back. We were all on the tail now urging them along. Suddenly they realised they were trapped.

They propped and started to break back, but there were too many of us. Yelling, whips cracking, we forced them further towards the gate; the leaders propped but weight of numbers forced them closer and closer to captivity. Once a couple got through the gateway the rest followed and in a trice we had the slip-rails in place. They were yarded.

We were all excited with the success of our first run. I'd never seen the stockboys so worked up: they thought it was terrific . . . and, well, so did Jack and I. For a while we couldn't count what we had: they were galloping around the yard in a frenzy. The head stockman quickly placed all of us around the outside of the yard in an attempt to keep them off the rails — it wouldn't have been too difficult for them to smash a few rails down. Eventually they steadied down. We all got back on our horses and rode around the outside to get them used to horsemen. After half an hour of riding and talking to them we were able to count what we had — twenty-three. It was a pretty good haul, but we still had problems.

"We'll go over to the camp and have smoko and work out our next move," said Jack. After giving our saddle horses a drink Jack told one of the boys to get a few greenhide halter shanks and to tie the sliprails securely.

A quarter of an hour later the stockboy came galloping back. Before he reached the camp he was yelling at the top of his voice, "Two fella stallion fight — bigfella fight!"

"Christ!" yelled Jack, "I should have bloody well thought of that!" We both ran across to our mounts. Before we reached the yard we could see a mighty cloud of dust and hear them squealing. A grey stallion was towering over his opponent, who was down on one knee, his other leg broken. The grey fastened on to the other's neck just in front of the wither with a paralysing grip. They were both flecked with blood and foam. The loser was a bay, a fine-looking horse but not good enough that day.

Suddenly the grey released his grip on the bay's neck, spun around and lashed out with both feet at his opponent's head. I heard the crack of splintering bone. Jack was off his horse and running up to the yard with a revolver in his hand. The bay was writhing on the ground trying to get to his feet. Two quick shots and the poor brute was dead. The grey was prancing round the yard, his tail straight out, head held high, shrilling victory.

We were both a bit upset; the mangled wreck on the ground had been a fine horse a few moments before. "I don't see what I could have done, not without shooting one of them," said Jack. I nodded and thought of a few lines by Rudyard Kipling:

> *There is neither border nor breed nor birth*
> *When two strong men come face to face,*
> *Tho' they come from the ends of the earth.*

We put the incident out of our mind, rode back to the camp and worked out what we were going to do next. The yard we had built wasn't that good. Of necessity it was a lightning job; and if we got many more horses they'd kick it down in no time.

We settled around the campfire over a billy of tea.

"Now," said Jack, "we've got twenty-two horses in that yard and we don't know how many we're likely to get in the next run — we'd be flat out getting another fifteen in without getting the bloody yard kicked down, and that's without any more stallion fights. What do you think, Tom?"

"That's about the size of it, I reckon another ten would be straining it and, as you say, without any more mad stallions."

"I reckon we'd better move them out to one of the Inverway stockyards, otherwise we could get into trouble and lose the lot," said Jack. "I think there's a holding yard on a billabong on the head of the Sturt. It would be the closest; I'd reckon about forty miles."

He called up the Inverway boy, who confirmed that a yard on Pelican Hole, on the Sturt, was the closest. He asked him how far. "Little bit long way," he said. Well, that could have been thirty to fifty miles.

159

"Right," said Jack, "we'll use the rest of the day strengthening the yard. And we'd better put some shin tappers on one or two of those colts. That'll steady them up a bit, and a couple of boys can ride around the yard for the rest of the afternoon, getting them used to the look of a man on a horse."

(A shin tapper was a hobble chain buckled to one fetlock, swinging loose. The chain was about eighteen inches long and kept hitting the other leg with a lot of force. No doubt it hurt them badly; they never galloped very far with one of those on.)

We spent most of the afternoon in the yard. The next morning, when the working horses were mustered we drafted off a dozen and took them over. These were coachers to help settle the brumbies. They were taken to the sliprails, which were pulled out. We waited quietly on our horses: gradually they came out, two or three at a time. We talked to them, gently cracking our whips to deter them in case they decided to make a break.

After talking it over we reckoned I'd better go with the horses so a pack, carrying swags and a couple of feeds, was readied. It was sundown when I got to the Pelican Hole yard. I drafted off the coachers, made sure the brumbies were securely yarded and left them. They would probably have to stay in the yard for a couple of days, but they'd be all right. Hungry and thirsty, they'd be a lot quieter. I got back to Hooker's Creek just before sundown. While I was away the head stockman had got another nine — ten, actually, but, he had to shoot another stallion.

The following day we got fifteen more but that night it rained, which put a stop to any more brumby running. Though it wasn't a heavy storm it was enough to put water in gilgai holes and scatter the horses.

We made ready to return to Mt Sanford. Our total was forty-seven horses of varying sizes and value. It wasn't that successful an operation; we came out of it with a little bit of glory — not much — but what had enhanced it for us was Archie Roger's failure.

When we got back to the outstation Jack asked me if I'd care to stay with him, but it didn't appeal; I had my sights set firmly set on horse breaking. A few days later I shook hands and headed west.

The country was in good shape. Storms had run the creeks, cleaning them out and leaving pools of clear sweet water. As the storms increased they would be running freely, gradually building up into raging torrents charging their way to the sea. Unless they were inland rivers such as Sturt's Creek, ending in a lake that for a while would be an inland sea before disappearing into the bowels of the earth to leave a salt marsh. The interior of Australia isn't very well balanced — you could drown or die of thirst in the same place, depending on the time of year.

I headed for Hall's Creek, a tiny township over the Western Australian border about 250 miles to the west. There were no roads but that didn't present any difficulties. Inverway Station was about halfway, and I knew the country that far. I was well stocked with rations, had a good canvas tent fly to sleep under at night, my horses were in good shape and in good condition. They ambled along snatching at the succulent Mitchell and Flinders grass. When I told them where we were going, they made it clear they didn't want to be hurried with all that beautiful grass everywhere.

Four days after leaving Mt Sanford I pulled in to Inverway homestead where, as I anticipated, I was made welcome. Big Harry, as he was known, told one of his stockmen to look after my horses and I took my swag to the house, where he pointed to a greenhide bunk on the verandah. That night we talked into the small hours, going over the tracks of forty years ago: the big drive with the cattle for Glencoe with uncle Bluey Buchanan.

When they took up Inverway it had been a long, hard track with, as Harry said, "a lot of dry stages". They could have sold out to Vesteys, but decided they wanted to stay together on Inverway.

When they first took it up it was Crown Land; they were the original settlers. Their uncle Bluey helped them with breeders and, perhaps, some finance. Harry and Hughie went droving whenever they could, to help fill the tucker bags. Archie stayed to look after the stock, mustering and branding.

They told me of their record-breaking dry stage of 110 miles across the Murranji Track with a thousand Mistake Creek bullocks, before there were any bores on the stock routes.

Mistake Creek is a well-known station on the Territory side of the Western Australian border, and they had been doing Mistake Creek droving for several years. It was their third trip.

They took delivery of the bullocks in June. The country was in pretty good shape. The weather was almost perfect, with cool westerly winds and very cold nights, and until they got to Top Spring, on the head of the Armstrong, they had no trouble. The bullocks, too, were in good shape; they were what's known as stores.

They had one advantage, though not a very encouraging one — they knew from a couple of drovers coming back that they wouldn't get a drink for 1000 bullocks between Top Spring and Newcastle Waters. There were three watering places; Murranji, Yellow Waterhole and The Bucket. The three had enough water for their horses.

When they left Mistake Creek they had no idea they had such a formidable dry stage ahead; it wasn't until they were nearly to Armstrong River that they found out. It was a tremendous decision to have to make.

Of the three waterholes, Murranji was the largest. They thought perhaps the two drovers who had told them the bad news might have been unduly pessimistic, and held the bullocks at Top Spring while Harry rode ahead to make sure. He returned the next day with the gloomy news that the drovers were right.

It was now July; there was a cold wind blowing during the day and the nights were quite bitter. The cattle wouldn't dehydrate much, so they decided to go on. The day they were to leave they held the bullocks back from water until late afternoon, wanting them to be as thirsty as possible to ensure that they would take in a good bellyful before starting.

It was late afternoon when they headed for the Jump Up, a rocky escarpment that fell away from the western edge of the Barkly Tableland to the Victoria River basin. When they got to the top they faced dense lancewood scrub interspersed with thickets of hedgewood, which the cattlemen called bulwaddy. The drovers dreaded it . . . and it ran for nearly seventy miles.

With two men in the lead to keep them steadied, one on each wing to stop them from spreading too wide and two on the tail, they walked them until about ten o'clock when they rounded them up for a rest. They reckoned they had covered sixteen to eighteen miles — another eighty-odd to go.

The next morning they started the bullocks before the first glimmer of "piccaninny daylight". The beasts lumbered sulkily to their feet: they weren't thirsty and would have preferred to rest longer, but Big Harry and Hugh knew they must cover as much ground as possible during the coolest part of the day.

The stages they walked were indeterminate. They had to be governed by how warm it became once the sun rose; but they reckoned they'd travelled a good twenty miles from the last camp when they steadied the leaders at about eleven o'clock.

Their horses had got a good drink at Murranji where they filled the water canteens. There was a cold wind from the west, for which they were grateful: the bullocks were feeding in a desultory way, which indicated that they weren't too thirsty. Just before sundown they moved off again. The sun set and night came quickly, the darkness intensified by the heavy scrub. They passed Yellow Waterhole, making sure they were to windward. Had the cattle smelt the water they would have been unable to hold them; 1000 bullocks — even if not dangerously thirsty — would be too much for six men to control (or 106, for that matter).

They were striding out now. The men with the leaders had to keep them at a reasonable pace — their endurance had to be nursed, for if allowed they would break into a trot and soon exhaust themselves. Through the night they walked, the tension building. Harry rode on the nearside wing, Hughie on the other.

I had ridden the Murranji Track and could understand the drama. That awful lancewood and bulwaddy, and 1000 thirsty bullocks walking through the night, a hair's breadth from disaster. As they rode they talked to the bullocks as only a cattleman can. They talked to their horses, too, and cursed the scrub and the dark and the failing waterholes, and they prayed: perhaps there was a God somewhere.

Daylight came and they were still in that awful scrub. The cattle were walking determinedly, no longer snatching at tussocks of grass. Thirst was beginning to show. Neither was there any lowing, the bullocks' way of talking to each other; they walked silently with nearly a mile between the leaders and the tail. Hugh watched the tail-enders, the weaker ones, anxiously. They might have to cut off fifty and let them into The Bucket and it wasn't much of a hole at best being the smallest of the three.

Now they had to keep the cattle walking. Any advantage gained by resting them would be dissipated by their increasing thirst. As the sun rose higher they slowed the cattle, but they had to keep moving. The day passed all too slowly, and dusk crept on them as they broke through the bulwaddy into open plain country — another twenty-five, perhaps thirty miles to The Bucket. It was now nearly two miles from the tail-enders to the leaders; the only sound was the padding of their hoofs and a low, moaning noise. Cattle sweat through their tongues, but there was no saliva coming from these beast's mouths; nothing but a muted moan.

Harry Farquharson rode ahead of the cattle with the horses. They were in a bad way, too, but at least they had had a good drink at the Yellow Waterhole and at Murranji. Whatever water was in The Bucket, the horses would have to have priority: if there was enough, some of the tail-enders might get a sup. Harry thought some of the weaker bullocks were ready to chuck it in — they would stop simply lie down and die.

There wasn't much water in the creek bed, but more than he had expected. He reckoned fifty or sixty bullocks would get some sort of a drink — enough to sustain them for another day — but he also knew that however many he let in, there would be none left for any of the others. It was not without some danger. If the bullocks got a smell they would trample each other to death, and would turn the waterhole into a morass. None of them would get any water. Also, with only half a drink he would have difficulty getting the bullocks away and on the track again.

As they approached the little creek they swung the leaders away so there would be no chance of their smelling the water. Hugh, with two of his stockboys, cut sixty bullocks off and let them into the water a few at a time. As the last two or three went in there was little more than wet slush, but it was enough to sustain them for another day. Getting them away was not easy; the men had to flog them out with their stockwhips.

The next day they were sure they would get all the cattle to water, but even so it was not over. Harry rode on to Newcastle Waters and came back with the Newcastle head stockman and some of his stockmen. This was a country where men willingly helped others in trouble.

Hour after hour the bullocks plodded with some kind of indefinable faith in the men who were keeping them in the direction of the water. In the late afternoon of the fifth day the leaders smelt the Newcastle Waters lagoon. It was, Harry said, the greatest moment of his life. The bullocks broke into a trot, but it didn't matter now; they were well strung-out and there was no danger of their trampling each other. The poor brutes plunged in and drank and drank and drank — cattle can take in an enormous quantity of water without ill effects.

Four hours later, the last bullock staggered into that waterhole. Every beast had arrived; they hadn't lost one. It was an epic that stands out. It has never been equalled and I believe, never will.

CHAPTER 16

THE BREAKER
FROM THE TERRITORY

I rode away from Inverway as the sun was rising, musing on the three Farquharson brothers and thinking, as I have many times since, of men of their calibre. Frequently I have heard the expression "they don't make 'em like that any more", but expect they do; it's the times they don't make any more. Perhaps fortunately.

I followed Sturt's Creek, a substantial watercourse well worthy of the title of river. In Queensland it took a number of rivers to make Cooper Creek, the channels, in places, spreading over twenty miles. Sturt's Creek needn't feel inferior.

I camped early on a good waterhole, mainly because there were flocks of ducks swimming around, taking off and landing. After getting my camp set up I sat quietly at the foot of a coolibah with my rifle — I knew I'd only get one shot in and I wanted it to be a good one. If I could get enough of them together I might get two or three, but they were the most obstinate ducks I've ever tried to shoot. Suddenly two mobs came together from different directions and I took careful aim. To my astonishment I got three. I stripped and swam in after them. The last one that had been hit was badly knocked about; the lead bullet had mushroomed, but at least it would make a stew.

The next day I arrived at Birrundudu Station, one of Vesteys places (it was all Vestey country for a long way now). It was run by a head stockman and managed from Gordon Downs, just over the border. He hadn't seen a soul for weeks, didn't have a cook and had been talking to himself for the past couple of months.

I had learned at Inverway that his name was Harry McLean; everybody knew who was where and just about their life story. A long, angular man who looked what he was — a good cattleman and horseman.

I mentioned, as casually as I could, my duck-shooting successes, three with one shot, but I quickly found out I was no legend maker. He dismissed it airily, saying, "That's nothing; I shot six once with one shot!" I didn't say what went through my mind, that he mightn't allow a few facts to spoil a good story. I thought I'd better add a couple more to my tally next time I told someone.

It seemed as though I wouldn't have any difficulty getting plenty of horse breaking. Gordon Downs, the next property down the river, had a breaker, but Lower Sturt, Flora Valley, Ord River, Mistake Creek — all Vestey stations — had no one. George Renton had been doing the work but had taken a job running the Lower Sturt camp for Clarry Wilkinson, the manager. Harry Huddleston was the Gordon Downs breaker; after he'd finished there he was going to take bullocks to Wyndham.

I rode on, following the river. I called at Gordon Downs and got some meat; it was another sixty-odd miles to the Lower Sturt and I kept my stages down to about twenty-five miles a day. There were miles of waving Mitchell and Flinders grass and the Sturt channels had an almost unbroken chain of waterholes.

Reflecting, fifty-odd years later, on what was without a doubt an idyllic lifestyle, it is difficult to find anything or anywhere today that is remotely like it. Motor vehicles tearing across bitumen roads day and night, cattle mustered with helicopters, aeroplanes landing almost daily at the homesteads, radiotelephone communications, massive road trains shifting cattle a couple of hundred miles in a day . . . undreamed of in 1930.

I suppose, in many ways, they're a lot better off. I doubt if they are happier. All life is relative — what you don't know about you don't miss. In 1930, with the shocking depression just starting to bite I would have been one of the more fortunate people in a sad world.

167

I had the best mobile home imaginable, seven horses I knew and loved, a riding saddle, two pack saddles carrying all my worldly goods, a swag that contained blankets and a mosquito net. My spare clothing consisted of a couple of pairs of trousers and a couple of shirts all neatly stuffed — well stuffed anyway — into a flour bag that doubled as a pillow. I had a canvas tarpaulin ten feet by twelve and my pack bags, in addition to ample rations — enough for a month — contained a set of billycans that fitted neatly into each other, and a camp oven. I had shoeing gear, spare horseshoes and extra hobbles; hooked on to the pack tree was a light axe for cutting ridge poles when I was setting up camp or cutting firewood. I had a .32 calibre rifle that ensured that no matter what I would never go hungry. I always slept dry and comfortable. The only means of fuel my transport required was grass and though in times of drought demand may exceed supply it was never an insurmountable problem . . . and it was free. Time wasn't important.

And the future ? Well, that was the future, wasn't it? I certainly gave it some occasional thought — not too much, though: it was too far away to worry about anyway. Let nature take its course. In my swag was a modest volume that never failed to sustain me, my old friend Omar Khayyam:

> *Ah — fill the cup, what boots it to repeat*
> *How time is slipping underneath our feet,*
> *Unborn tomorrow — dead yesterday,*
> *Why fret about them if today be sweet?*

I drifted on, following the Sturt, and crossed the border into Western Australia. At the end of February I rode up to Lower Sturt Station homestead. Clarry Wilkinson, the manager, was pleased to see a breaker; there were forty-odd youngsters he was anxious to get into work. I'd met Clarry previously in Katherine and had got to know him fairly well. George Renton, his head stockman, I recalled casually when he was trying to extract a livelihood around the racing circuit with a horse called Warlock and seemed to be fairly affluent. But he said he never made anything much with the horse; his main source of income was from poker, at which he was very adept. Until he met someone who was a little more adept and he lost all his money and the horse, too . . . which he thought might have been a good thing.

The cook was Peddler Palmer. For some reason or other most Palmers were called Peddler; I don't know why — maybe just the alliteration. Anyway, he was a very good cook, his only recreation was boozing, which he carried out with a dedication that put him in world class. If there'd been a division in the Olympic Games for boozing, Peddler could have represented Australia with distinction.

Right then his hide was cracking and Clarry Wilkinson knew he was likely to head for Hall's Creek, the nearest township, at the drop of a hat. With mustering just about to start that was the last thing he wanted. "Bloody cooks!" snorted Clarry.

The colts had to be mustered for me to make a start; that would take a week at least. Clarry had it all worked out. He came to me one morning and said: "How would you feel about a trip to Hall's Creek? You can cut across the desert; it's about forty miles to Ruby Plains and about thirty-five miles from there to the township."

"Any water?" I asked.

"No, not between here and Ruby Plains, There should be water between there and Hall's Creek, though. Do you know anything about camels, Tom?"

"Clarry, you're looking at an expert." I told him about my Tennant Creek experiences.

There were two camels, Potato, a bullock, and a cow called Lulu. They were used in the stock camp to carry the rations and equipment. Several of the stations in the Kimberleys used camels for this purpose; it saved a lot of horseflesh, since they easily carried the equivalent of six or eight pack horse loads and mostly preferred bushes to grass.

They were brought into the stockyard for my inspection and I did my best to impress everyone with my camel-handling competence; I went over the saddles and pronounced everything in order.

The camel boy, Sambo, was delighted with the idea of a trip to Hall's Creek. Early the next morning I "hooshtered" them to their feet watched by what I assumed was an admiring audience, including Peddler who, I felt sure, had tears of gratitude in his eyes.

Feeling a bit like Lawrence of Arabia I headed into the desert on my errand of mercy. The camels were fresh and travelled well. I rode Potato; Sambo, knowing the track, took the lead on Lulu. Early in the afternoon we reached Ruby Plains homestead and sat the camels down at the saddle rail outside the harness room.

Charlie Darcy and Dave Oliver, the owners of the property, were pleased to know I was on my way to the township. They were running short of a few things that I could carry without any trouble. I could pick up their mail and, of course, bring them back some booze, too.

The next day I set off for Hall's Creek happily warbling alternately, *The Sheik of Araby* and *When the Sands of the Desert Grow Cold.* I was really living the part, I particularly liked the line, "At night when you're asleep, into your tent I'll creep". I gave that hell.

Hall's Creek was a bit smaller than a one-horse town but, as I found out, it packed a fairly solid punch when it got wound up. I padded up the main (and only) street, strung along the bank of the creek itself. As I passed the pub one of the patrons sitting on a bench outside yelled through the door into the bar: "Hey, here comes Ali Baba!" But no one came out to have a look, probably didn't believe him. Sambo certainly wouldn't have impressed as one of the Forty Thieves.

170

In 1929 I was horsebreaking at Mt Litchfield Station owned by Vesteys.

Spearing barramundi from paperbark raft lashed together with vines. Some of the wildlife also uses this form of transport.

In December 1937 Jack Gaden was seriously ill. To get an urgent message to the Flying Doctor by Oenpelli pedal radio these boys crossed the river on oil drums and walked 40 miles.

On Jack Hales MV *Maree*. N.T.'s first Federal Member, Harold Nelson, holding rope—you can tell he's important by the tie.

The big lizards! Jack Hales, now gone upmarket with MV *Maroubra*, holds the tail of a massive saltwater croc. At a guess: fourteen footers.

One of Ginger Palmer's trophy's. No, not the one holding the tail.

A rest between shooting of a different kind. Left, Bill Trerize, Fox Movietone cameraman; seated, some extras; right, standing, self trying to look the part. I never did find out what happened to that film on buffalo hunting.

Buffalo camp at Wildman River.

Riding out in the cool of the morning with a powerful horse under me was an exhilarating experience. In this photograph I am on the extreme left, Clary is in the middle and Ring on the right. The packhorses following behind.

The buffalo are sighted, still feeding unsuspectingly. Girths are tightened, cartridge belts checked, rifles loaded. We leave the cover of the timber fringing the plain. Ring and Clary, experienced shooters, follow me as we ride towards them. Our horses are reefing at their bits and dancing around impatiently.

The buffalo gallop away breaking into two mobs. I take a mob of bulls. One cow and calf cut across as I attempt to drop a bull and miss. He will have to be killed later.

The wounded bull must now be killed. I ride towards it at a brisk canter as it charges, turning Trinket in a wide semi-circle drawing it towards me. Trinket fights for her head, she doesn't like enraged wounded bulls. Gradually it closes, its deadly horns almost brushing my horse's tail. Leaning back I fire. It crumples up dead.

Mounted on Trinket I am about to despatch this enormous bull which I brought down at a gallop using the single shot Martini-Enfield carbine, which I am holding. This bull's lethal horns can disembowel a horse with one powerful sweep. Note the heavily caked mud on its hide from continual wallowing, which is why it is known as a water buffalo.

Getting this buffalo was hard riding through heavy scrub and over fallen timber. Horsemanship was always more important than marksmanship, especially in conditions like this. These photographs illustrate the wide variety of country over which I shot: scrub, dense sedge-like grass and open plains and sometimes, early in the season before the country had dried out properly, heavy bog.

It would take two experienced skinners about 15 minutes to skin a bull. Sometimes the hides would be put straight on to a packhorse, but if shot early they would be covered with bushes to be picked up on the way back to our camp.

Shooting on the plains causes the buffalo to retreat to the cover of the ridges, where galloping through the heavy timber was very demanding on man and horse.

Skinning was never a popular job. When buffalo were picked off in a lagoon the skinners would have to work in the water plagued by leeches below and mosquitoes above.

Late in the season with the continual shooting the buffalo would scatter hell west and crooked looking for cover. Then we would have to ride long distances and when the shooting was over and the last hide was finally on the packhorse we would head back to our camp frequently arriving well after dark caked with mud and blood.

We unpacked on the bank of the boulder-strewn and very inhospitable creek, I thought I might take a room at the pub if there was one to be had; it was a long time since I'd slept in a real bed.

Walking into the hotel from the brilliant sunlight, it was a moment or two before I adjusted to the subdued light. Suddenly, with a roar, the very last man I'd have expected to see claimed me — Jack Noble.

I said "I'm not going to believe you rode a bloody bike from Bullita to Hall's Creek!"

He burst out laughing at that and said he hadn't got on with Tom Lawson, snatched his time, rode back to the Depot, took a couple of bad falls on the way and headed straight to Matt Wilson's store. Matt told him the chap he'd swapped his horses with hadn't been able to find them; got lost every time he left a road — and there was only one road.

The last time he'd slept out in the bush, Matt said he'd spent half the night up a tree — howling dingoes frightened ten years' growth out of him. Eventually he found his way back to the Depot in a state of mortal terror. A boat arrived from Darwin and he took a passage on it — couldn't get away fast enough. The packs and riding saddle were stacked in the back of the store. "You may as well take them," Wilson had said. "You won't see him again."

Noble told me: "I threw the bloody bike in the river and went out and found the horses; they hadn't gone far, they were as fat as mud."

Among the men drinking at the bar was Wayson Byers, known from the Gulf of Queensland, where he was bred, right through the Kimberleys. He'd been managing the Lower Sturt as Clarry Wilkinson's immediate predecessor, but his appointment had been suddenly terminated under unusual circumstances.

He'd left the station for some reason or other for a couple of weeks. He was without a cook so when he left there was no one there except the Aborigines, mostly women. Their work was not very demanding: all they had to do was tail out [i.e. to shepherd] the flock of goats and keep the garden watered. The garden, being an important supply of fresh vegetables, was Wayson's pride and joy.

When Byers returned everything was calm and peaceful. His horses were unsaddled, unpacked and turned out; he had been seen approaching. The billy was in the process of being boiled on the kitchen stove, and Wayson Byers himself radiated goodwill. Until he happened to glance at his garden on the bank of the lagoon. It had a somewhat unusual brownish appearance, not the normal lush green of healthy, productive vegetables.

He strode down to the garden. His worst fears were confirmed — everything was very dead. Byers let out a roar like a wounded bull. He lined up all the lubras and questioned them. They all had cast-iron alibis. Two were sick, so they said, very sick; two were minding the goats; two more thought someone else was watering the garden; two swore they *did* water the garden. It was ten o'clock in the morning and just starting to get hot. He made every one strip stark naked, then made them get up on the corrugated iron roof of the harness room — which was very hot and getting hotter. He made them sit on the roof a few feet apart. After they had been sitting in one spot for two or three minutes, he made them move a couple of feet to a fresh, hotter spot. By now it was fairly sizziing. If any were (understandably) reluctant to move, Byers would give them a flick with his stockwhip, at which he was extremely adept.

In the middle of this command performance a car drove up. This event could be confidently classified as a ten million-to-one chance, because in it was a gentleman who was the District Protector of Aborigines with headquarters at Derby, some 400 miles away. His visit would be as unexpected as the Holy Ghost himself. And his astonishment at what was no doubt the most remarkable exhibition of the care and treatment of Aborigines — and females at that — by a licensed employer can easily be imagined.

172

He was, of course, completely unaware of the circumstances that led to this extraordinary display and assumed it was a form of entertainment devised by Wayson Byers for his personal benefit. However, even had he known the finer details, it is doubtful he would have regarded them as extenuating.

Byers' licence to employ Aborigines was cancelled on the spot. Without that very valuable and precious piece of paper, he was automatically and immediately unemployed.

On a ridge behind the hotel was the police station. In places such as Hall's Creek, the pub is unquestionably the heart not only of the community, but of the whole district. I'm not sure how the police station would be classified, but there would be no doubt as to how Sergeant Archibald (Archie to one and all), would stand among the men of the Kimberleys. He was very well thought of by everyone, and if the hotel was the heart of the country Archie had his finger on the pulse.

A powerful great hunk of a man; I was looking forward to unloading my dog scalps on him, bearing in mind that the Western Australian Government paid two pounds for a dog scalp, whereas the reward in the Northern Territory was only five shillings. The big difference was due to the fact that there were a lot more sheep in Western Australia, with its huge sheep stations. In the Northern Territory there were virtually none; it was cattle country. Sheep were a much easier prey, and dingoes would run through a flock and kill just for the joy of killing; they would hunt in packs and do terrible damage, leaving sheep maimed and crippled.

In the course of my peregrinations I had accumulated quite a few scalps — some I had poisoned myself, some I had obtained from the odd stockman. I had twenty-odd scalps. The local police officer was empowered to receive the scalps from any intinerant trapper and to pay him two pounds a scalp. At the end of the transaction his duty was to burn them in front of an independent witness. It was freely rumoured that this procedure was not always carried out; it seemed a few dog scalps could generate a cash flow for quite a long time (good thing for the local economy, I suppose).

The dingoes themselves had no idea their lives were in greater danger in Western Australia than the Territory. There were dog-proof fences to the south but none in the Kimberleys, so it would be reasonable to assume that in their travels some would cross from the Territory to Western Australia under their own power. Some came over in pack bags, in a reduced form of course. I had twenty-two in a reduced form.

Some trappers, gifted with artistic tendencies, could fashion a very good dog scalp from a kangaroo hide and no matter how much care a trapper gave to preparing kangaroo skins for the market there was no way they would bring two pounds. The generosity of the Western Australian Government supported a modestly thriving industry.

I carefully parcelled up my precious currency and made my way to the police station. It was a fairly big house with a verandah, a portion of which was enclosed all around. About 100 yards or so further up the ridge was a horse yard where two blackfellows appeared to be working some horses. I rightly assumed them to be Archie's trackers.

I poked my head cautiously around the office door. An enormous man was sitting at a table littered with files and papers of an official appearance. There was also something of a distinctly unofficial appearance — a bottle of rum standing among the litter.

I ventured a cautious "G'day Sergeant, I've got some dog scalps." He swung around in his chair and fastened a beady eye on the bundle under my arm.

"Ah yes, I've been expecting you; you'd be Tom Cole I s'pose." This was a bit of a surprise, though I suppose it shouldn't have been; but I couldn't quite understand why he'd been expecting me.

"I've got some dog scalps, Sergeant," I repeated timidly.

"Of course you've got some bloody dog scalps, I expected you

174

to have some bloody dog scalps. I'm well aware that you've recently come from the Northern Territory, every bloody ringer who arrives from the Territory lands here with a bundle of scalps and they all died this side of the border. Northern Territory dingoes are the most suicidal dogs in the whole of Australia — they all come over to WA to die; I've been here for six years and I've never yet heard of a dingo dying in the Territory."

"But Sergeant . . ."

"Don't tell me, just throw 'em in the corner there. You can't think up any kind of a story that I have'nt heard a hundred times. How many are there?"

"Twenty-two."

"Okay, I'll write you out a warrant." Which he did immediately: he didn't bother counting them, but I didn't think it would have been a good idea to even suggest there were twenty-two and a half.

I went back to the hotel, cashed my warrant and ordered the liquor for Ruby Plains and the Lower Sturt. I made sure I got Darcy and Oliver's order completed before I settled down to distributing bonhomie and liquid largesse with my hard-earned reward.

At sunrise the next morning Sambo and I padded out of Hall's Creek. None of this *Sheik of Araby* stuff lightened the way . . . I had a head like an oil drum, a mouth like a lavatory (the bucket variety) and guts like a concrete mixer — about twenty dog scalps' worth.

By the time I sighted the Ruby Plains homestead I was back to a reasonable state of health. I had been giving voice in a very subdued way, starting off with *The Dying Stockman* and moving up to Kipling's *Recessional*; some sort of a health barometer I suppose.

That evening and most of the night was a happy and memorable one. The next day was even more memorable. I had the most monumental hangover I have ever experienced in my life, before or since. It went far beyond "Death where is thy sting? Grave where is thy Victory?" I only wanted to die as soon as possible; an unimaginably happy release. I lived, but only just.

It took a couple of days and the combined ministrations of Dave Oliver and Charlie Darcy to get me back into reasonable working order. They were a great couple of blokes and had been partners in Ruby Plains for many years. Dave, tall and spare of build, was quite a bit older than Charlie who was medium height, a wiry frame and reckoned one of the better horsemen in a country of good horsemen. I could have easily stayed there another couple of days, but knew Peddler Palmer would be anxiously scanning the horizon. I left before sunrise and thought that perhaps *Onward Christian Soldiers* would be an appropriate melody to start with. The camels didn't seem to mind..

I rode up to the homestead in the early afternoon. The warmth of the welcome I received more than made up for the suffering I had endured, though I did notice a mild note of reproof from Peddler who said he had expected to see me a day earlier. I immediately took pains to point out that I would not have suffered such a distressing experience had I not so unselfishly taken on the role of Good Samaritan. My eloquence was, of course, completely wasted; no one had ever heard of any Good Samaritans. I should have known any kind of Biblical allusion would be lost.

The young horses were all paddocked and ready for me to start breaking. George Renton, the head stockman, gave me a good offsider. His name was Robinson but everyone called him Crusoe; a happy, cheerful character with a permanent smile that never seemed to leave his face, even when he got bitten by a bad-tempered colt.

I made good time with the colts. After the first week I was getting through eight a week, and a fortnight after I started Renton came into the station to muster fresh horses. While he was shoeing he let me have three of his stockboys to ride youngsters I

176

had in hand. When he left he took twelve colts with him. They weren't really properly finished, but George said: "So long as they'll lead, tie up without pulling away and breaking bridles I'll take 'em; my blokes will knock them into shape."

When I had a batch of colts finished I would take them out to wherever the camp happened to be mustering. I wanted to get them off my hands and start on the next batch as soon as possible; Clarry Wilkinson had got word from Flora Valley that they wanted me over there as soon as I had finished this lot, so I was pushing them through fairly quickly and Renton, so far, wasn't complaining. They weren't a bad lot of youngsters and not much trouble. Crusoe, who I called Robbie, had been bitten and I got kicked a couple of times, once badly. It was my fault — I walked behind a filly I knew to be nervous and highly strung. When horses kick it's usually through fear, rarely deliberate viciousness.

The last batch were finished except for a couple that were reluctant to have their feet picked up. I was working on them when the manager walked over to the yard and hoisted himself up on to the top rail of the round yard. He watched me quietly for a few minutes then said: "This lot look as though they're ready to go out to the stock camp."

"Yes, I'm aiming to take them out tomorrow. Where are they working?"

"They're way down the river toward the southern boundary at Ima-Ima, the Billaluna camp are with them too. It's a boundary muster."

Just then the smoko bell went and we walked over together to the kitchen for morning tea.

"That droving camp that was speared down the Canning — Thompson and Shoesmith were the drovers — they had Billaluna bullocks, didn't they," I asked.

"Yes, that's right. Thompson and Shoesmith were droving partners. They were speared, and all their men too. I expect you've heard the drover who found the bodies was a namesake of yours; Tom Cole. Have you met him? He's known as Old Tom Cole."

"No, Clarry, I think our paths have crossed a number of times but I've never met any of them. There's quite a big family, isn't there?"

"Six or seven, I think: the eldest would be about eighteen or nineteen — Young Tom Cole he's called."

"Yes, I know, I'm The Other Tom Cole," I laughed.

"You'll probably become Tom Cole The Breaker," said Clarry, which turned out to be true.

That night I brought it up again. The Thompson and Shoesmith spearings had always interested me, partly of course because of my namesake being involved. I had heard the story a number of times around campfires and though they were all basically the same, there were enough variations for me to realise that the full story remained to be told.

It was many years later that I eventually ran to earth — in South Australia — one of the younger sons, Sandy Cole. He wrote me a long letter, which I would say, was not easy for him, and which I appreciated. It is one of the most fascinating letters I have ever received in my life.

Dear Tom,
Your letter came as a very pleasant surprise. I have heard so much about you and know many people that you also knew.

My father died at Rockhole Station, which was owned by Ernie Bridge senior, and is about 20 miles south of the New Halls Creek, on the way to Ruby Plains and Billabuna. Ruby Plains was then owned by Charlie Darcy and Dave Oliver and is now owned by Mick Quilty (Tom's son).

I went into partnership with Ginty Gorey, whose father drilled water bores for Vesteys mainly. Ginty Gorey and I traded under Gorey & Cole Drillers, and over the 40 years we drilled thousands of bores all over Australia but mainly in the Territory. We started off with the old mud puncher and finished up with the modern rotary rig. I am now 61 years old and retired in Adelaide.

178

Tom Cole, my father, was buried at Rockhole at his request.
This is the head of the Canning Stock Route; he was the first
man to get through with cattle. When he married my mother
Mabel Bridge, my grandfather Joe Bridge owned Mabel Downs
Station and gave them 500 bullocks for a wedding present, so
Dad thought he would take them through to Willuna in
Western Australia. He put a plant of horses together and took
his brother (or maybe two brothers), two black fellows, a cook
called Jack the Rager and another bloke, and a policeman
called Penny Farthing [Pennefather], and two blue heeler
cattle dogs which saved his life on more than one occasion.
The trip took six months, and the cattle put on condition —
beautiful grazing country most of the way.

He buried Shoesmith and Thompson and a yellow fellow,
three black fellows and another white fellow [at a place that
became known as the Haunting Well, though the name has
since changed] and put fences around their graves. He said
they had been dead for about a fortnight; the stock had
perished, and the blacks had eaten the tucker and cut up all the
saddles. They had also tried to work out how to shoot with the
guns, but by the evidence they shot one of their own, so
fortunately for Dad that happened. Dad said Shoesmith and
Thompson had made one error that cost them their lives by
letting the gins into the camp, and the blacks speared them all.
Dad told me he never allowed them into his camp — never shot
a gin or piccaninny but the bucks that he came in touch with
died with lead poisoning; it was a battle of tactics who got who
first. They carried on and eventually got through. Tom Cole,
my eldest brother, was born while Dad was taking the cattle
through.

Later Dad bought a pub at Day Dawn near Coolgardie but
never did any good, so they came back and took up land out
near Bedford Downs. I was born there, and Dad brought me
into this world. I was a fortnight old when I got into Halls Creek

— poor Mum must have had a rough time. There were eight of us, four girls and four boys: Tom, Ethel, Teeney, Polly, Harry, Kathleen, me and Charlie . . .

Wally Dowling, the bare-footed stockman, took cattle through the Canning many years after Dad's trip. Then the Lannigan brothers took cattle through in 1941. After the cattle prices came good, a meat works was established in Wyndham and the stock route was closed. Now there is a lot of mining activity going on in that area, and roads everywhere.

You are quite right: the watering points were shallow wells along the Canning and they or Canning put whips over each well and the water was up pulled by horse. The blacks on several occasions burnt the whips and filled the wells in with gum suckers.

[Sandy then gave me the news about mutual friends and concluded his letter.] Well, Tom, I am a poor writer but I would be pleased to hear from you again. That information about the Canning drovers is all correct and told to me by my father.

Cheers for now,
Sandy Cole

PS: I am sure my Dad took the cattle down the Canning in 1911.

I rode away from the Lower Sturt and headed for Flora Valley. The manager, George Brown, had the youngsters paddocked close by. He said there were fifty-two. We would muster them tomorrow, put them through the yard and check them against the horse book. I remarked on the number of horses — Flora Valley wasn't as big a station as the Lower Sturt — but he said Margaret River, another Vestey place west of Hall's Creek, would get half of them. The Margaret was bad horse country, so they were supplied mainly from Flora Valley.

The manager, myself and a couple of boys rode out the next morning and yarded them. They were beautiful horses, just about thoroughbred; Flora Valley horses were regarded as the best of all

Vesteys. It was going to be a pleasure handling such beautiful animals.

When we finished drafting them through the yard there were six we decided weren't fit to be broken just then. One was badly lame, another two were sick (I thought they showed signs of the dreaded walkabout disease) and the others weren't well-enough developed. I had forty-six to break, which was quite a mob.

Then he told me Joe Egan, the manager of Ord River Station, had sent word he wanted me over there as soon as I'd finished. After that I had to go to Waterloo. It was starting to pile up a bit, and I was doing some thinking. There was an unwritten law on horse breaking that all breakers tried to shy clear of — didn't want to know about it. The boss, whoever he might be, was entitled to limit a breaker to four a week, maintaining that any more than four couldn't be handled properly. It was rarely invoked, but I thought I'd better sort that one out for a start. If he put that one on me I'd never get to Waterloo this season; I expected there'd be a fairly big mob at the Ord as it was the company's second biggest station.

I found Brown in his office struggling with stock returns or something. I thought I'd better take the bull by the horns, so I said: "George, do you want to put a limit on my breaking?"

"No, I heard from Clarry Wilkinson you did a good job for him. I made it my business to find out."

"Well, I'm pleased to hear that, of course, and I'll do a good job for you, too. But if you had put a limit on me I'd never get much past the Ord."

A couple of days later I was sitting up on the top rail talking to a couple of beautiful colts I had in tackling. They weren't taking much notice of what I was saying: they both had heavy snaffle bits in their mouth, which they didn't like at all. I was telling them how much good it would do them, which reminded me of something similar my mother used to tell me when she gave me a dose of castor oil. In the middle of all this one-sided repartee George Brown came over and perched alongside me. "How are you finding them, Tom?"

181

I flicked my stockwhip at the colts to keep them moving before I answered. "Well, George, I love your horses. If I didn't have to get to the Ord and Waterloo I'd like to spend the rest of the season breaking for you, but I'll have to push them through. At the same time, I don't want to push them through just for the sake of getting away. In the first place, I'm strongly against not doing a proper job on such lovely horses and secondly, I've no doubt you wouldn't put up with it either."

"What I've come over to tell you is that I got word today from Margaret asking how soon they can expect to get their share of the horses, and that they are hard-pushed for horseflesh. I'll send word back suggesting he send someone over to give you a hand. Jack Barry's the manager, he's certain to send at least one — after all, he has to send someone to pick them up."

"That's a bloody good idea, and tell Barry to send an extra set of breaking tackle, too."

Sure enough, a week later two Margaret River stockmen arrived. They had two sets of breaking tackle, and a note to George Brown complaining bitterly. Naturally not the slightest bit of notice was taken.

One of the two Margaret lads was very good and the other was quite useful. I could push the horses through now and make sure they were well handled. Mark Daly was the head stockman, and was satisfied with every batch I took out to his camp. In the meantime Joe Egan was sending over from the Ord wanting to know if the Flora Valley horse breaker had gone into a state of suspended animation — quite a trick letter writer was Joe; some sort of a humorist.

When I finished it was nearly the end of April. I had worked hard. I gave my offsiders a day off every now and then, but worked a full seven-day week. I was getting well paid.

When I turned the last colt over to Daly, I took a couple of days' spell. It was the end of April, and so far I'd done pretty well. I was established now; it didn't take long for word to get around — the breaker from the Territory, a good man with camels, too! I hoped I didn't have too much to live up to.

I threw my packs on and headed for the Ord, about 100 miles distant; three days' comfortable travelling. The second night I camped early at Dingo Spring. It would be an easy day tomorrow to Ord River Station.

My billy was nearly boiled when I heard the sound of horses trotting and the jangling of bells. Looking across the plain I saw a white man riding in the lead of a large mob. I could see pack horses too, the whole cavalcade driven by two or maybe three stockmen; I couldn't be sure, they raised a lot of dust.

The white man rode up to my camp, dismounted, held out a hand and said: "Ted Whelan's the name!"

This shook me somewhat: Ted Whelan! Jim Webb! Victoria River Downs cleanskins! Stan Brown, Fred Martin.

He saw the look on my face and laughed. "I can see you know who I am, or was, whichever way you'd like to look at it."

After they had unpacked and the horses were watered and hobbled out, he joined me and we had a meal together. He told me he was head stockman at Lissadell Station, which was pretty well what I knew already, but that he was leaving. He was taking the horses to a station on the Fitzroy River, outside Derby where walkabout disease was bad. Due to the disease there was always a strong demand for stock horses on the Fitzroy; Lissadell was one of several stations that sold surplus stock to various cattle stations in that area. It was a savage disease which, in its advanced stage, caused the unfortunate beast to walk continuously in circles. It also went blind and consequently walked into trees. There was no known cure. It was also known as the Kimberley horse disease; it was mainly confined to those parts. For some unexplained reason mules were immune.

Ted Whelan and I talked well into the night. He asked me how I thought he would shape if he went back to the Territory. I said I thought it wouldn't be a very good idea. He laughed and said: "Queensland's a bit dicey, too: I'd better watch my footwork or I'll be running out of states."

I didn't ask what had caused his unpopularity in Queensland, but had heard vaguely there'd been some sort of a branding mix-up over a few horses.

He went on to say that when he came back from the Fitzroy he was leaving Lissadell: he had some sort of a deal with Jack Kilfoyle who owned Rosewood Station. I was curious to know what the deal was, especially after he asked me if I was tied up with horse breaking for the rest of the season. "I could do with a mate," he said.

I was definitely committed to the Ord and Waterloo; if I dropped them it would get me a bad name. Also, I was making good money and enjoyed the work. I thought he might tell me what the deal was he had with Kilfoyle, but he didn't — and I knew better than to ask.

The next morning we parted and went our opposite ways. That afternoon I reached Ord River Station.

There were thirty-one youngsters for me, and another twenty-eight at Mistake Creek, an outstation of the Ord. Although Joe Egan was a very good bloke he didn't win any popularity votes from me. I thought he must have gone to a lot of trouble to find the offsider he landed on me — one of the most unfortunate and useless individuals I'd come across. Apart from having a serious speech impediment, for which I tried hard not to blame him, he seemed to be particularly gifted in doing everything wrong. Even the horses didn't like him; he was bitten once and kicked twice in two days. I was especially grateful to the horse that kicked him the second time. He limped up to the manager and said his leg was broken; not only badly broken but "Brokim finish".

Joe came down to the yard and gave me the good news that my offsider was now my ex-offsider. "I'm going to find it hard to find someone to help you, we've got a flu epidemic. I'll get you

184

someone from McIndoe's camp." McIndoe was the head stock-man. The next day Sandy McIndoe rode into the station with a jackeroo, Bill Cousins, who was quite a good lad.

Up until now I'd had an almost dream run: I suppose I couldn't expect it to continue. Young Bill got the flu after a week, then I started to feel distinctly off-colour. I went up to the station store and asked for something for the flu. The storekeeper explained they were expecting something, he didn't know what, but it would come on the next mail run . . . in a fortnight. "I expect it will have run its course by then, but it'll come in handy for the next lot." He went on to say he had plenty of iodine, and as an afterthought, "plenty of Epsom salts".

I said I had enough to give me the shits without any help from him.

Then the head stockman came in to the station; he was muster-ing on the Nicholson River country and because of the flu was short-handed. He had to have 1000 bullocks ready for a Queens-land drover and 500 fats for Wyndham meatworks. The delivery dates were ten days time for the fats and twelve days for the stores.

"How are you going with the colts?" he asked.

"I've got three in tackling, four I'm trying to keep ridden, two tied up which I want to teach leading today and one with a rope round its neck wandering around the yard, no doubt wondering what he's done to deserve it. And I think I've got the flu coming on, too."

Sandy had everything worked out except how to cure the flu, and he ignored that. "I'll tell you what we'll do, Tom," — an opening I was wary of — "let that black horse go you've got roped and I'll give you a hand to finish the rest. I've got one of my best blokes here, we'll get into them and rough them through. I can't afford to be too particular. Come out to my camp and help me out, I'm bloody desperate. Young Cousins can come, too — I'll go over to his quarters and crack the whip, he's been sick long enough."

The head stockman was a good man and by sundown we had the

situation well in hand. The jackeroo, complaining bitterly, was given the job of teaching some of the horses to lead and worked on their feet for shoeing purposes.

The next evening Sandy pronounced them good enough and we took them out to where the stock camp was working on the Nicholson, getting there at midnight.

We mustered in the mornings, drafted in the afternoons and watched the bullocks at night. In eight days we had nearly 2000 head in hand: a big, unwieldy mob. Fortunately, by this time, most of the sick stockmen were back on their feet and on a horse. We had to take the stock to a place down the Ord on the other side, a short day's drive from our last camp. Everyone was glad the delivery was in a couple of days; we were all tired and weary, we had been mustering and drafting from sunup to sundown and doing three to four-hour watches at night.

We steadied the mob and made dinner camp sometime after midday. We were half a mile off the river and the crossing was another half mile downstream. On our left was a fence we had to go through; there was no gate and it was Sandy's intention to open the fence at a strainer post. At this point the river, over hundreds of years of heavy floodings I suppose, had cut into the country. It was a sheer drop of thirty or forty feet to the river bed, which was the reason we had to take them down to where the bank shelved gently to the water's edge.

Sandy, with someone helping him, opened the fence for two or three panels and the mob started to move through; everything was going fine, the river wasn't far away. It was a straight drop to the watercourse swirling and pounding its way over boulders. The horses and packs, which had been trailing along behind, followed through after the last bullock. I sat on my horse watching the horse tailer fasten the fence, to make sure it was secure.

Then suddenly it happened. I heard that dreaded sound, like distant rolling thunder. I swung my horse round and couldn't believe my eyes. There was a tremendous cloud of dust: the entire mob had turned and was galloping toward the river, 500 yards away — with that straight drop of thirty or forty feet to the boulder-strewn bed.

It is impossible to say what made them do it; some kind of panic infected them, a panic that spread quickly through the whole mob. A stampede, or rush, as a cattleman calls it, is fairly frequent at night and is easier to understand when a mob of cattle is laying quietly sleeping and something startles them. But to happen to nearly 2000 head in daylight quietly walking along — I had never heard of it before. I have talked to many cattlemen since, but none had heard of it happening on such a large scale.

The head stockman and three men were riding on that wing when the cattle turned toward the river. They were in danger of being swept over the cliff with the weight of cattle, and had no hope whatever of turning or holding them. A tremendous cloud of dust rose from the hoofs of the panic-stricken mob. Through the dust, like wraiths, I could see McIndoe and the other three men fighting their way with their stockwhips. After a while I saw they would break through, though there was always the danger of a horse falling.

Panting, red dust from head to foot, Sandy joined me. "Christ Almighty, have you ever seen anything like that before? At first I tried to hold them, I had no hope. I looked back thinking that perhaps when the first of them got to the edge they would stop when they saw the drop. They tried to, but the weight of cattle behind them forced them over: there'll be a good few losses."

It was an incredible situation — an entire stock camp sitting on horses watching helplessly as nearly 2000 bullocks galloped over a cliff. We couldn't do much because of the billowing clouds of dust, all except one unfortunate beast that seemed to be lost, galloping and trotting in and out of the dust cloud, bellowing plaintively. Then one of the stockboys cantered over toward the poor bewildered creature and for some extraordinary reason furiously cracked his stockwhip. I couldn't believe my eyes. With a last despairing bleat it disappeared into the swirling cloud of dust.

"Christ Almighty!" said McIndoe, "that's all I need to round my day off!" He put spurs to his horse. "C'mon, let's get down to the river and see how many are still alive before I kill that stupid bastard!"

We all galloped off together towards the crossing and rode up to where the cattle were milling and bellowing. Most of them appeared to be all right, except that they were all in a state of fright. We rode around in under the cliff and eased them across the river towards open ground, then went back to see the extent of the smash. As it turned out the result wasn't anywhere near as bad as we expected. There were two or three obviously dead, several crippled, with broken legs and at least two with broken backs, but the most extraordinary sight of all was a bullock bellowing and struggling in the fork of a tree a good ten feet up. It was a big bullock, but it was a big tree, too; he had no hope of getting out. The head stockman and I gazed open-mouthed at the sight.

"I'd better go and get an axe and cut the tree down," I said. He nodded, his eyes still on the struggling, bellowing beast in the tree.

I cantered down the river to where the camp was unpacking. Charlie the cook looked at me anxiously as I dismounted, "How bad is it?" "Well," I replied, "not as bad as we expected, maybe we'll lose six or eight, which is remarkable when you realise nearly 2000 went over."

I rummaged around in a pack bag and shoved a dozen cartridges in my pocket, picked up a rifle and the axe and went back to the battlefield. The tree was quickly chopped down. After some frantic struggling the poor beast got to his feet and promptly charged us, which was predictable. He fell over, and Sandy cracked his whip a couple of times. The bullock trotted over to the others, shaking his head, obviously in some pain.

We shot two with broken backs and three with broken legs. I rode among the mob to find the bullock we'd cut out of the tree. I could see he was in a lot of pain and said to the head stockman: "Sandy, I think that roan bullock will probably die: we should cut him out, he'd have a better chance of surviving if he goes bush on his own. The others are horning him now." This was normal animal behaviour — a sick or injured beast is usually attacked by the others.

Sandy and I eased him out of the mob quietly and took him up river half a mile or so to let him go. He laid down under a shady tree gratefully; I thought he'd have a good chance of living.

As it turned out, counting the roan bullock we'd lost eleven which, in the circumstances, wasn't too bad.

The cattle were now quietly feeding across the plain. They had settled down fairly well and Sandy and I thought we'd done enough for one day. The next morning we started cleaning them out, starting with the 500 fats for the meatworks. That evening we had two mobs ready, 1350 to go to Queensland and 500 fats for Wyndham meatworks. There was a holding yard nearby into which we put the larger mob.

As we were putting the sliprails up Sandy said to me: "Joe said to watch the 500 fats; they're liable to get bruised — I never mentioned the shortcut they took to the river!"

I stayed in the stock camp for two or three more days and when I left to get back to the breaking I talked him into letting me have an extra man to make up for the time I'd lost.

I finished the Ord colts then went to Mistake Creek. Three weeks later I was on my way to Waterloo, just across the border. I was back in the Northern Territory. July came and I was halfway through the Waterloo youngsters when a letter arrived from Limbunya Station, seventy miles to the east, ". . . when the breaker is finished at Waterloo, would he please come over; we have about forty to break in", it read.

It was getting late in the year for horse breaking. Most places liked to have them finished by the end of July. It was starting to get dry but all this didn't matter to me, and as it turned out, when I got there I was given an extra offsider.

When I finished at Limbunya it was well into September and by then I was faced with a long stretch of no work: the stock camps would soon be closing down. Anyway, I had a pocket full of cheques I had collected, starting from the Lower Sturt, none of which I'd spent. Though they weren't exactly burning a hole in my pocket, the temperature was starting to rise. It was another three months to the start of the wet season and I didn't fancy riding round the country aimlessly with water and grass getting scarce.

Laurie Pumpa was the Limbunya manager. When I'd got everything tidied up, including my cheque, I suggested that as I had it in mind to have a trip to Darwin, could I leave my horses in one of his paddocks for the wet. I could go across to Wave Hill when he went over for the mail and take the mail truck to Katherine. As I anticipated, there was no difficulty arranging this, and a few days later I was once again in the little township on the bank of the Katherine River, waiting for the weekly train to Darwin. I took a room at O'Shea's Hotel and made the acquaintance of sundry cattlemen and drovers.

Jim Webb/Ted Whelan was in the news again in a big way, this time as a reluctant guest of the Western Australian Government. It was a remarkable story and to do it justice I must take it through to its conclusion, which was quite a few years in the future. As it was told to me, there were three men involved: Jack Kilfoyle, who owned Rosewood Station, Ted Whelan and a man named Anderson.

Wyndham meatworks ran a stud herd of Shorthorns for the benefit of local cattlemen. It was the only stud in the district and due to a decline in the cattle market, sales of bulls had come to a standstill. The meatworks stud paddocks were almost overflowing with beautiful purebred Shorthorns.

Jack Kilfoyle decided it was a situation that needed to be remedied and suggested to Ted Whelan that 100 stud bulls delivered to Rosewood would be worth £500. I don't know what the same number of bulls would have cost in a legitimate transaction, but would think that it would not have been less than twenty pounds a head.

In this day £500 doesn't sound much for a deal of this nature, but a stockman's wage was three pounds a week, a head stockman's four, sometimes five, and few station managers would get more than seven. Alf Martin, who was managing the largest station in the world, commanded fourteen pounds a week with very few fringe benefits..

What made the exercise attractive was the apparent ease with which it could be accomplished. There were several paddocks; a breeding paddock, one for weaners and two or three others for the different ages. Because of the dearth of sales very little attention was given to the cattle. They grazed peacefully and undisturbed, and there were several hundred.

As Kilfoyle pointed out, ". . . you could ride into those paddocks almost any time of the day or night, take half the herd and no one would know." Whelan checked all that out and found it was pretty right. A bit much for one man — it was a fortnight's trip to Rosewood, but two men could handle it easily and Kilfoyle said he would give them a hand.

The mantle of offsider fell on a man named Anderson and together they rode into the paddocks one moonlit night. Kilfoyle had said to try to get a mob around four or five years old; youngsters mature enough to start stud duty right away.

Like a few enterprises of a similar nature it unfortunately did not go according to plan. Ted and his mate had no trouble whatever drafting off 100 bulls, beautiful animals, whose quality would have satisfied the most fastidious buyer . . . especially at that price! But that one in a thousand chance, or whatever the odds were supposed to be, bobbed up.

The Wyndham meatworks head stockman was Jim Weaber, a very smart all-round stockman. He spotted the tracks of 100 bulls leaving the paddock and didn't have to be very good at tracking to realise they weren't leaving of their own accord. He also spotted the tracks of two shod horses.

Weaber and Sergeant Flinders followed them to Parry's Creek, about twenty miles from Wyndham. Jack Kilfoyle was admiring his latest acquisition when they rode up. Flinders really spoilt his day.

The trial was brief and the verdict (a foregone conclusion) even briefer — and, under the circumstances, surprisingly light. But then everyone knew everyone and they were known to be good fellows, bloody unlucky too. "Twelve months," said the beak as he gathered up his papers.

Once again I am indebted to Sandy Cole, who at that time was a schoolboy attending the local school, for details of the next few months.

Sergeant Flinders now had three prisoners who were quite different from the usual run-of-the-mill offenders (mainly natives who had indulged in a bit of cattle spearing, tribal fighting, chopping the odd head off, and similar peccadilloes). Kilfoyle was a leading pastoralist of highly respected pioneering stock, the owner of Rosewood Station. Webb (alias Whelan) was recently the competent head stockman of Lissadell Station, though perhaps not quite so highly respected, and Jack Anderson, a bit further down the scale, was just a good fellow.

The three men were introduced to the local lockup and made themselves as comfortable as possible. Kilfoyle took care of additional comforts in his usual competent and generous manner. Arranging for supplies of liquor to be delivered presented no problems whatever: Sergeant Flinders would be the last to cause any difficulties there. After all, his brother Charlie owned the store.

The three men settled down and did their best to adjust them-

192

selves to their new and unaccustomed lifestyle. Whelan had a good mate, Mick Walsh, who had married Ethel Cole, in turn a close friend of the schoolteacher, Mary McIntyre. The two girls shared Mick's sympathy toward the three men in their predicament and expressed their sympathy in a practical manner. They made cakes and biscuits that were delivered enthusiastically by Sandy Cole, Ethel's young brother.

The jail was adjacent to the school; young Sandy and his friends dragged a forty-four gallon drum over to the corrugated iron walls that formed the jail walls and handed over the goodies. Constable Gordon Marshall, Sergeant Flinders' offsider, was also well-disposed to the prisoners and he, too, was able to make a contribution toward easing their monotony. He gave them a key to a little-used gate, requesting that they use it only at night — it wouldn't do if they were seen wandering about during the day. They respected his wishes and limited their excursions to after sundown.

Quite a lot of this time was spent playing cards with the Walshes and Mary McIntyre. Inevitably a strong friendship developed between Ted Whelan and the schoolteacher. Apart from Ted's desire to get on in the world by way of a short cut or two — a propensity it must be admitted he shared with many others — he was a very good type: Miss McIntyre was a very intelligent young lady as well as an excellent pastrycook. Ted Whelan asked her to marry him, and she accepted.

It was now getting close to the time when the three men would have discharged their debt to society. Whelan was giving a good deal of thought to the future and where he and his wife would make their future home. Western Australia didn't appeal, Queensland was bad news (they had long memories there) and there was still a warrant outstanding in the Northern Territory relating to the Victoria River Downs exercise.

I think it was Sergeant Flinders who was the catalyst. Alf Martin, the manager of Victoria River Downs, frequently came to

Wyndham. There was always business at the meatworks where his bullocks were processed and the sergeant freqently had to be consulted regarding stock movements: among other things he was a stock inspector. Martin was well aware of Flinders' star boarders and Ted Whelan's matrimonial plans; that kind of news travelled at approximately the speed of light.

As I heard the story, the Sergeant casually mentioned to Martin the prospective bridegroom's uneasiness regarding the warrant probably outstanding in the Territory.

"Tell him I'll have the warrant lifted, and that it's a wedding present from me." Alf Martin was a good man indeed.

Mr and Mrs Phillip Ward were married, Jack Kilfoyle was best man and Mary's friend Ethel Walsh was matron of honour. Phillip Ward was Ted's right name but he didn't like the name of Phillip and preferred to be called Ted. Jack Kilfoyle very generously gave the young couple a brand new Ford truck for a wedding present. No doubt Jack Anderson was there somewhere enjoying the festivities, but all through the saga I never did hear much about him.

Some years later I heard a story that he was speared by the blacks somewhere down in the Western Australian desert — beyond that I never heard any details.

Ted and his wife packed up and headed for the Northern Territory: it has always had some sort of magnetism. Tennant Creek goldfield had been discovered recently and there were a number of finds of a substantial nature, so the young couple headed for the new field about seven miles from the Telegraph Station.

It was hard country and though there was gold it had a lot of rock mixed up with it. Jack Noble was there, one of the earliest prospectors, and had made a sensational strike on a claim he had pegged and called Nobles Nob. He had sold his mine to a company and bought Joe Kilgarif's pub; he'd come a long way since he rode up to Bullita on a bike!

Jack willingly helped the Wards and his advice was worth following. At Noble's suggestion Ted pegged a claim he called the Blue Moon, five or six miles from the rapidly expanding shanty town.

It was an inhospitable place — a spinifex ridge strewn with boulders — but they rigged a camp, cutting posts and stretching hessian across for walls with boughs thrown on top for shade. A tent fly rigged up served as their bedroom and with antbed and stone Ted built a fireplace.

"I didn't start at the bottom and work my way up," said Ted, "I started at the top and worked by way down. I would never have believed that ground could be so bloody hard. And there's no hotter place on earth than the spinifex ridges of Central Australia."

He had to learn about dynamite, how to place the charges and crimp the detonators on to lengths of fuse. Hauling the exploded rock to the surface with a windlass by hand was a backbreaking job. Heartbreaking too.

He got to the stage where he'd run out of everything; money, tucker, credit and the will to continue. He punched holes into the rock face, rammed the last of his dynamite home, crimped the detonators to the fuses and after lighting up, made his way wearily to the surface.

A few minutes later he heard a series of explosions one after the other and said to his wife: "That's the last shots I'm firing. You can start packing; we're off." She didn't ask where to, it didn't matter. After the dust had settled he went back down the mine shaft and couldn't believe his eyes. As he expressed it to me: "I'd uncovered a bloody jeweller's shop."

It was a very good mine indeed, and there were no shortage of buyers. He sold out for £25,000. This may not seem much of a price today but it must be remembered the price of gold was then £4 pound an ounce. With the proceeds he bought Banka Banka station and became a well-liked pillar of society.

Over the years I have frequently noticed that when men, for some reason or other, change their names they usually stick to the same initial for their surname, as in the case of Webb, Whelan, Ward. I once heard an intriguing story regarding Alec Moray, pastoral inspector for Vesteys when I worked for them at Wave Hill and horse breaking at the various stations. It was said around the campfires that he was really Morant, The Breaker. In the South African war the senior officers were mainly Britishers and it is very easy to believe that very little affection existed between the rugged Australians, with their free and easy ideas of discipline, and the pukka Englishmen.

Morant was some sort of a folk hero, with his poetry on one hand and his breaking and riding ability on the other. From the moment Morant was charged there were tremendous waves of resentment among the Australians directed against the British. If Morant was not smuggled out, plans would have been widely discussed at the least.

Alec Moray was the right age, the right build and complexion. Morant was a lieutenant and Moray was known to have been an officer in the Boer War, but no one could get him to discuss it. The initial of his surname was M, as in Morant. Stranger things than that have happened.

There is an interesting postscript to Jack Kilfoyle. In the early 1950s Rosewood Station became one of the finest properties in the whole of the Northern Territory and East Kimberleys. Jack Kilfoyle was a purist and though I do not know his age when he sold Rosewood to Vesteys, he would have been full of years. It must have been a tremendous wrench, because he was born there. He went to Perth and took up stamp collecting, specialising in Australian stamps with the dedication that he applied to everything. When he died the "Kilfoyle Collection" attracted buyers from all over the world.

CHAPTER 17

BROCK'S CREEK RACES

The train, Leaping Lena, was never late; it always came around midday on Friday, stayed for an hour then battled on to Pine Creek. By then the sun was getting low so it stayed the night. The next day, it tooted and farted its way to Darwin, collapsing at the station at about three in the afternoon. It had every reason to be exhausted — it had struggled up hill and down dale to Birdum and back, a bit over 600 miles, in four days.

Darwin was the biggest town I'd been in for some years. I suppose it was really a city: it was the capital of the Northern Territory and for me another world. The population was about half Chinese, a quarter Japanese (who worked on the pearling luggers), a sprinkling of Malays and Koepangers, who also worked with pearling fleets. The rest were mainly Europeans, a few other odds and sods who had drifted up, got caught up or drifted off again. I think you'd have to throw a few blackfellows in to make it up to a thousand. It was a kaleidoscope of every creed and colour, where east met west and mediocrity stood out.

Buffalo hunters rubbed shoulders with pearlers, goldminers swapped yarns with cattlemen, the Chinese smoked their opium and minded their own business.

There were only two streets of any consequence and on a population basis Cavanagh Street won hands down; all the Chinese lived there. Smith Street was, I suppose, the financial centre — the Wall Street of Darwin — the only banks in the Territory were in Smith Street. There was the Tin Bank, so called because it was built of corrugated iron. Officially it was the ES&A. Opposite was the Stone Bank, built of sandstone blocks; a notice proclaimed it to be the Commonwealth Bank. Further along, next to the Victoria Hotel, was The Comical Bank . . . perhaps it sounded better than Commercial Bank. The Town Hall was in Smith Street, too, which added to its dignity, and the only European store, Jolleys, catered for the racially discriminating, though I heard credit was harder to get there.

A police station, the Post Office and Government House overlooked the wharf, but with all that the place wasn't a hive of activity. What action there was was confined to the three hotels; The Victoria in Smith Street, the Club overlooking an oval, and The Terminus in Cavanagh Street. I struck up a few acquaintances here and there trying to find out how the other half lived. I started off with some flotsam and after a couple of days switched to the jetsam; there didn't seem to be much difference.

The master pearlers were the aristocracy — they did nothing and made a lot of money. The Japanese leased their luggers and engaged the Malays and Koepangers, who made up the crew, sorted the shell and bagged it. The actual diving was done by the Japanese, who were the world's finest. The master pearlers bought the shell from the Japanese at an agreed price.

I was staying at the Victoria Hotel and just as I was getting bored to the point where I couldn't stand it any longer I was rescued by Roy Patullo, the manager of Burnside Station, who wanted a horse breaker. Burnside was one of Vesteys places and he had come to town on business, to return on the train the following day.

I'd seen all of Darwin I wanted to; it was good to get away and breathe some good clean fresh air. Darwin seemed to have a funny smell; all those different breeds, I suppose.

The Burnside Station homestead was at Brock's Creek, which was a railway siding about 100 miles to the south. It had a police

198

station on one side of the line, a pub (which was also a post office) on the other, and behind the pub was Chinatown. There was a very fine old joss house with some marvellous carvings inside, but a nauseating smell of incense, which burned continually. There were two or three Chinese stores, mostly boarded up. Brock's Creek was an abandoned goldfield; the Chinese were left over from its more palmy days.

I saw Brock's Creek in five minutes flat. On the other side of the creek after which it was named was Burnside homestead. The manager and I stopped at the hotel long enough to wash away the accumulated coal dust we had gathered on the journey.

From Burnside I had to go to Mt Litchfield, an outstation about seventy miles to the west. Three days later I was getting the breaking tackle from the saddleroom. The head stockman was George Ritchie. His cook was Boyd Selman, who had been a fighter pilot in the 1914–1918 war in the Royal Flying Corps — something many people doubted. A bit too exotic for those bushmen's taste and also, I suppose, it was a bit hard to reconcile a fighter pilot with a musterer's cook. However, some years later I was able to verify it. He was a good cook, too.

George Ritchie had finished mustering and let me have several of his stockmen, all of whom were keen to display their riding abilities, though it is doubtful their enthusiasm exceeded my gratitude for the additional help. It enabled me to put through fifteen a week and I finished in three weeks. Forty-three head was the final total and for the season I'd broken more than 200 — which any way you look at it was pretty good.

I stayed another week with George Ritchie, just idling. We rode out to a creek about twenty miles from the outstation and camped for a few days. George took a couple of his stockmen who were good at spearing fish and for three days we gorged ourselves on barramundi which I've always maintained are the finest fish to come out of any water. Like any fish, they must be fresh — the ones we were eating were certainly that.

It was a fascinating experience to watch the spearing of the fish. Early morning was the best time, when no ripples disturbed the surface. The men would stand on a limb overhanging the water, waiting motionless with their spears poised. Suddenly they would drive down with tremendous force and speed, rarely missing. And as the shaft weaved its way over the water embedded in a struggling barrumundi they would jump in and retrieve it.

When we got back to Mt Litchfield a letter from the manager was waiting for Ritchie. Among other things, would he ask the horse breaker to come in to Burnside as soon as he's finished and take over Fiery Cross and Charleston?

This was good news indeed. Fiery Cross and Charleston were two racehorses that had come over from Flora Valley. The annual picnic races were due to be run over Christmas. This sounded exciting: not only was I going to be paid for it but when I delivered the last of the colts to Ritchie my other pay stopped automatically. I couldn't get to Burnside quick enough.

Being from Flora Valley they were among the best bred horses in the north; the only place that could compete with the Flora Valley's was Bradshaw's though the Byrnes boys at Tipperary Station, which adjoined Burnside, had some good horses.

Fiery Cross was a fine-looking gelding of about sixteen hands. Charleston proved to be a very deceptive mare: I thought she was a shade long in the back, but she had powerful hindquarters and a good deep chest. They were both low in condition and needed strengthening up. They had walked over from Flora Valley (it was the only way they could get across from the west) and I was very disappointed with them; I thought I would have to nurse them carefully. Before I took over, two of Patullo's favourite boys had been in charge of them and had obviously been galloping the guts out of them. I wasn't too optimistic of the results come Christmas, which was only three weeks away.

The boss wanted to win the Ladies' Bracelet for his wife and he had his heart set on the main race, the Buffalo Mug. I started pouring the feed into them and for the next few days walked and trotted them; after a week they freshened up remarkably well. I increased the work steadily, giving them short bursts on the track half a mile away.

Patullo was getting worked up about them; I think his wife was on his back. Half his luck, I thought; she was an attractive woman and could try my back any time she liked. I had to be satisfied with the odd kind smile and went back to the trackwork. I kept away from the boss as much as I could ... he was getting on my nerves.

The trophies arrived and were on display at the hotel. The Buffalo Mug was quite a remarkable piece made of buffalo horn and silver mounted. Obviously a very large bull horn had been selected, sawn off and polished; they are jet black and take on a beautiful polish. The silver mountings enhanced it handsomely — whoever had the good fortune to win it could be justly proud. It could take its place with distinction among any trophies.

Visitors and horses were beginning to arrive, my charges were starting to improve and I was stretching them out in their trackwork, but I was still pessimistic. The horse was nominated for the Bracelet and the mare was in the Mug. If only I had got hold of them a month earlier I felt sure I could have taken out the main race, which was a mile and a half.

I expressed my doubts to the Byrnes boys, with whom I had become very friendly. Leo, Stan and Harold were top horsemen and the three of them would ride work together. They had a brown horse I thought would be a certainty to take out the Bracelet. Leo was going to be their jockey, and we used to watch each other working our horses. We were talking horses one night over their campfire and all pretty well in agreement on the chances of their brown horse in the Bracelet when, to my surprise, Stan turned to me and said: "You know, Tom, Charleston is the only one we're frightened of in the Mug."

"Well, I think your bay horse and the mare are the best two in that race, but I'm doubtful of our chances of winning. I'd like to have got hold of her a month earlier."

Stan said: "I've been watching her working; she's improved out of sight this last week. I'll say this, you've done a bloody good job on both of them."

This made me feel good, especially from the Byrnes: they weren't the kind of blokes who would bother dishing out bovine fertiliser. But I still thought the Tipperary bay would beat the mare; it looked to be in good solid condition.

George Ritchie was due in from Litchfield and I was depending on him to ride my two horses. I could have ridden them but I was half a stone heavier which, with the race pad, put me half a stone overweight.

The meeting was to start on Christmas Eve. There would be no racing Christmas Day, which naturally was given over to festivities, consisting exclusively of drinking. If there was any other kind of festivity no one knew much about it. Ritchie came in the night before Christmas Eve, headed straight for the hotel and stayed there. I don't mean he took a room there: he didn't bother about going to bed. The next morning Patullo came to me and said George was "too crook" to ride. I said: "Well it's too late for me to try to sweat any weight off; is there anyone else we can get?"

Patullo said there wasn't, ". . . and anyway I'd prefer you rode them. You've been working them and know them, and they know you."

Mrs Patullo, with a dazzling smile, said: "I'm depending on you to win the Ladies' Bracelet for me, Tom."

The place was starting to fill up, tents and flys were springing up like mushrooms. There were several buffalo shooters who considered they had a proprietorial interest in the Buffalo Mug. Harry Hardy claimed to have shot the bull from which it was made; with laudable professional jealousy his brother Fred said he was a bloody liar; Gaden put in a claim and no one believed him, but everybody agreed that it must have come from a big bull. Brock's Creek was running a banker, mostly rum.

Though December was the start of the wet season there hadn't been much rain, just a few welcome showers at night, and the

Horses were always a problem, and although I had about 60 there were always about 30 or so spelling at any one time. Some were lost because there were no fences or paddocks. Their withers would chafe badly from the weight of the hides; some were injured; there was swamp cancer to contend with; I lost two that were taken by crocodiles; and one was bitten by a taipan.

First the hides had to be washed to remove the mud and blood. After draining they were salted with about 25 pounds of coarse salt for each hide. They were then stacked on top of one another for five days and then hung on racks. The complete process took a week to ten days depending on the weather.

In camp there was a growing stack of hides covered with paperbark and others hanging on racks. At the end of the season the hides were taken by dray to a river jetty to be shipped to Darwin. Life became easier when I became the proud owner of a thirty hundred-weight Ford truck. Later I bought a brand new Ford V8 two-ton truck.

The buffalo hunting season finished towards the end of October. I would expect to see Jack Hales' boat in about mid October. The final tally in 1936, counting the help I received from Hazel Gaden, was 1796 hides. I held 500 square miles of country, about 50 head of horses and a Ford motor truck.

Pioneer buffalo hunter Fred Hardy on the verandah of his homestead, Mount Bundy, in the Northern Territory.

In September 1932 five Japanese fishermen were speared at Caledon Bay, Arnhem Land. A police patrol led by Mounted Constable Ted Morey (above right), with Mounted Constables Jack Mahoney (above left), Vic Hall and Stewart McColl and six trackers, was sent to investigate the killing. The chief suspect was Wonggu (pictured with wives and children).

The patrol left from Roper River Police Post, where Morey split his party. Vic Hall and McColl with two trackers left on the Mission boat *Holly*, to rendezvous with Morey and Mahoney (a dedicated photographer) at a prearranged spot. Morey and Mahoney went overland with four trackers, 50-odd horses and 15 packs. They met at the mouth of the Koolatong River.

After the two parties joined up they went to nearby Woodah Island. On that fateful morning Jack Mahoney enthusiastically photographed the entire party. Shown here from left: Mounted Constable Vic Hall, Trackers Pat and Reuben, Stewart McColl, Trackers Laurie, Lock, Dick, Roper Tommy and Ted Morey. That evening McColl was ambushed in the jungle and died by deadly shovel spear.

Photographs courtesy Mrs K. Morey

McColl was buried where he fell but
later reinterred in Darwin. A
Woodah Island native was arrested,
tried and convicted of the murder.
Missionaries appealed to the High
Court successfully on his behalf. He
was released but never reached his
tribal country. What happened to
him has been a matter of speculation.

sting was out of the ground. Like everyone else I had been working my horses with standard horseshoes; racing plates were a luxury no one enjoyed. In the morning I pulled the shoes off my two and trimmed the hoofs; their feet had good walls and only needed trimming lightly. They would race comfortably bare-footed.

There were two races before lunch. Because of the heat the first was at ten o'clock and the second at ten-thirty. The third race was at half past three — the Ladies' Bracelet.

The Brock's Creek Hotel had set up a booth, and not a moment of the five-hour break between the second and third race was wasted. The booth was patronised with a dedication rarely seen outside the Territory. Which was a very good thing, not only for the publican but also for the bookmakers; the former benefiting from the evaporation of body moisture and the latter from an even faster evaporation of good judgment.

I kept away from the bar as much as possible — within reason, that is. As a trainer and rider I had obligations I endeavoured not to lose sight of and I noted that Mrs Patullo was keeping an eye on me: an eye that could hardly be described as motherly — more hawkish. I took a very light meal and as race time approached had a couple of good solid rums to fortify the nervous system.

I weighed out and saddled Fiery Cross with a lot of assistance I could have done without. They wanted to know whether the horse would win. I was very truthful and said it was something I wanted to know, too.

As in all country meetings it was a walk-up start, which is always troublesome; there's usually at least one horse that won't come into line. However, we jumped away fairly well and immediately Leo Byrnes on the Tipperary horse and Fiery Cross and I went straight to the lead. It was a two-horse race. I was beaten by a length, and beaten easily, too; Leo had his horse on the bit when he passed the post. The extra weight my horse was carrying wouldn't have made any difference. I kept out of the boss's wife's way.

The next day, Christmas Day, I gave the mare a light gallop and explained to her that she'd better bloody well win. She promised she would and I felt a lot better. I made my way to the pub, all social activities having been transferred there from the racecourse until Boxing Day when racing would be resumed and I would be in the hot seat again. After a while I felt my confidence returning. I was starting to see the world through very rosy spectacles, declaring Charleston the winner of the Buffalo Mug by two lengths — "at least". The inevitable result of this was someone telling me to put my money where my mouth was, which I did unhesitatingly.

George Ritchie thereupon put fifty pounds on her and declared he would ride her. The barman held the money. The next morning I felt grateful to George Ritchie for his promise to ride Charleston, which turned out to be misplaced gratitude. I heard that he got into a fight, fell over and sprained his wrist; the sprain was from falling over, not fighting, it was emphasised. He was sleeping it off on the bar-room floor.

I found out I had put twenty-five pounds on the mare. I kissed that goodbye as soon as I was told. I asked what odds I had been given, which turned out to be three to one. My informant didn't seem to be surprised that I wasn't familiar with the details of the transaction. Alcoholic amnesia I think it's called. Fairly common.

In the meantime I'd been sweating it out with a minimum of moisture replacement. I let Patullo think that Ritchie was going to ride Charleston, which enabled me to get to the bar without any undue criticism. Of course it didn't take him long to find out the truth, but by that time I had managed to get my body back to a properly balanced condition.

The race, like the Ladies' Bracelet, was at three-thirty. When I weighed out I found I'd lost a pound in weight, which justified the careful attention I'd been giving to my diet.

There were five starters; we did our preliminary down the straight and went to the starting post. I had drawn the three alley, not that it made any difference. After a fair bit of jockeying around

204

we got away. Leo Byrnes and I shared the lead. The mare felt good but was pulling hard: I tried to restrain her, but she had a mouth as hard as the proverbial whore's heart. Leo was inside me and as we went round the first bend Charleston had pulled herself to a half length lead; she was fighting for her head and I started to worry about her pulling herself into the ground. I was a length in front, which increased to two lengths. We were around the back of the track and I was on the rails three lengths in front and travelling well. I looked over my shoulder: Byrnes wasn't making any move on the bay, I was four lengths in front and had stopped worrying. We were approaching the straight when I had another look back, expecting to see Leo starting to make his run. Suddenly I realised I was going to win, the other horse wasn't going to catch me now, Charleston was travelling too well. I turned into the straight, gave her a friendly slap with the whip and cruised past the post an easy winner.

There was great jubilation in the Burnside camp. Patullo thought I was marvellous, Mrs Patullo thought I was marvellous, and I thought I was marvellous. We were celebrating with some awful-tasting sweet wine from the Buffalo Mug, and Patullo said that he'd put ten pounds on her. I confessed that I had twenty-five on her. He immediately turned on me: "Twenty-five pounds! You didn't tell me you were that sure of her. I understood you to say you didn't think she had a chance!"

"To tell you the truth," I said, "I didn't."

"But you put twenty-five pounds on her just the same." He was quite annoyed. Twenty-five pounds was a lot of money for a horse breaker. Mrs Patullo had been listening: "I didn't back her at all, I would have if I'd known you were as confident as that!"

"Yes, but I didn't know I'd backed her. I only found out this morning." Which sounded pretty silly, being a bit apologetic made it sound worse. Somehow or other it seemed as though I'd double-crossed them.

I didn't let it worry me, I was just about out of a job anyway now the races were over. After a few drinks we all got matey again, Patullo brought the Buffalo Mug down to the pub for an hour or so — none of this sickly sweet wine this time. It's surprising the silver wasn't melting by the time he staggered home.

CHAPTER 18

THE PACK-HORSE MAIL TO LIMBUNYA

I stayed around for a couple of days. I had to give some thought to getting back to Limbunya where I'd left my horses, and the wet season was starting to build up. In the meantime I'd got friendly with Harry Hardy, the buffalo shooter, who kept asking me what I thought I'd do after the wet. I said I expected to get back to horse breaking, explaining that my horses and packs were at Limbunya.

After a while he asked me how I'd feel about taking a job in his camp. This certainly appealed to me — buffalo shooting! He said he was making arrangements with a man named Bond who was starting tours to the Northern Territory and particularly wanted to include a buffalo camp in his itinerary. Harry said he would have his hands full looking after the tourists and as the shooting was his mainstay he wanted someone to run his camp. I didn't hesitate; I'd take the job.

The shooting, Hardy explained, would start sometime in May, according to how the wet season fell: if the wet took up early the shooting would start early. The rainfall was around sixty inches and fell between the end of November and March or April. That was a lot of water jammed into such a short space of time, and the country took a few weeks to dry out sufficiently to stand hard galloping — and even then only on the ridges. Later the flood plains would dry.

My horses and gear were at Limbunya, I scratched my head over that one; had it not been for Hardy's offer I would probably have sat the wet season out somewhere down the line, Katherine perhaps; but now I'd have to head out to Wave Hill for a start. From Brock's Creek to Limbunya was about 500 miles, say about 100 to Katherine. That part was easy, I'd get the next train. From Katherine to Wave Hill was 300 miles, and the only way I could get there was with the mailman: he would be using pack horses and swimming rivers. I'd have no trouble getting a lift and I had no doubt I'd work for it. Oh well, let nature take its course

Anyway, I had at least four months, A thousand miles? Easy; but a bit rough here and there.

Leaping Lena pulled into the Brock's Creek siding Wednesday afternoon. I was a seasoned enough traveller by then to qualify for the Saloon Bar so I climbed into the guard's van clutching half a bottle of rum. Len Scott, the guard, a very understanding bloke, said: "I s'pose the pub's out of grog."

We overnighted at Pine Creek as usual and the next day steamed into Katherine. Mailman, Bob McLennan sensibly had taken a holiday; George Fordham was doing the run for him and he was due to leave in a week. I found him at O'Shea's hotel and told him I wanted to get to Wave Hill, which was as far as he went. Naturally he was overjoyed at the prospect of a passenger and asked if I had a riding saddle. Fortunately I had; the prospect of riding 300 miles in one of his worn-out automatic self-emptiers wouldn't have been appealing; I'd have developed piles before I got halfway.

Fordham's enthusiasm at having me for company for 300 miles was, I thought, a bit excessive. I cautiously asked how many packs he thought he'd be taking. He expected about twelve, he said: he wouldn't know until the day before he left, it would depend on how much mail had built up at the Post Office. He went on to say that he had two horse tailers, so there would be four of us, not too bad, four packs per man to put on and take off each day. "How many horses are you taking?" I asked.

"Well," he said, " this is why I'm glad you're coming along, I've been doing some breaking in and I've got half a dozen colts I'd like to take."

It looked as though I was going to work my passage. I didn't mind. In the dry season Fordham was a drover who had a house and a paddock on the bank of the Katherine River. He suggested that I come over and stay with him. Very soon I was in a yard roping young horses; they weren't much, the usual drover's horses and not much trouble.

Four days before we were to leave we started to shoe them. With the youngsters, he was taking thirty-five head, five of which were mules that didn't need shoeing. Thirty was plenty: it was stinking hot and the rain was fairly regular.

On the morning of our departure we mustered the horses, put the packs on and went to the Post Office. From there to the hotel, where there were a couple of packloads of rum (George Fordham's bonus) to be picked up. We rode out to the township just after sunrise.

George and I rode in the lead, his stockmen bringing the horses along behind. He had been fairly accurate in his assessment of the number of packs; there were ten carrying mail, two full of rum and one with odds and ends, orders that had come in from some of the stations. Rations and supplies, billycans and a camp oven, were distributed among several packs, as were spare horseshoes, hobble straps and so on.

It was forty miles to the King River, the first watercourse of any consequence. George said we were sure to have to swim it, which he wasn't looking forward to. It was fast running and without a good bank on the other side. Bob McLennan had lost a horse there a couple of years ago, taken by a crocodile, which I'd heard about. But George said there wasn't much danger when the river was flooding.

We made camp at about half past three in the afternoon, having travelled twenty-five miles. Fordham said he never stopped for a midday camp; it wasn't worth it. "You've either got to unpack or

209

let the horses stand around with the heavy packs on, which isn't fair to them. It's better to get to camp early, they get a good rest and more time to feed."

We had the packs on and were moving just as dawn was breaking. It had rained all night but we'd camped fairly comfortably. We could hear the river some time before we reached the bank. George said it sounded as though we were in for a hard time. We reined our horses up on the river bank at about ten o'clock and Fordham shook his head dismally. "We won't get across today, no hope."

We unpacked and made camp; at any rate we had plenty of time to make ourselves comfortable. George walked down to the water's edge and planted a stick. About every hour we had a look and by sundown we reckoned it had dropped about two inches. Fordham wasn't too happy about that, but it wasn't rising. All we could do was sweat it out.

That night it didn't rain and the river dropped two feet. The situation looked a bit better. The current was slowing: that was the big worry. The depth of water wasn't important, it was the speed of the current. It could be a disaster if the mail and our gear got swept downstream — losing mail was unthinkable. In the early afternoon we carried all our gear, packs, saddles and mailbags down to the water's edge. It was dropping fast now and we dare not wait until tomorrow; it would probably rain tonight and we'd be back where we started.

We crossed the horses first — at a good shelving bank about half a mile down. The four of us swam on the lower side, so that any horse with a tendency to stay in the middle, following the current, was made to swim across by splashing water in its face. When we got to where the bank shelved they all climbed out.

Three of us swam back and started to pack the packs, packbags, saddles and gear into the tent flys. The top was tied like a huge plum pudding and dragged down to the water; it wasn't much trouble, the bank was wet and slippery. It was a queer-looking outfit but it floated well. The three of us swam beside it pushing it across. It wasn't difficult, a few logs swept by but our navigation was plenty good enough to avoid them.

We were very pleased with the result of that voyage, swam back and filled up the other tarpaulin. We reckoned we could have done the crossing with two trips but the two-thirds left was too much for one fly; it wasn't the weight but the bulk that beat us. We floated the last lot over just before sundown and quickly had our camp rigged up. George said it was worth a couple of rums . . . and there were no dissenters. That night it rained heavily; if we'd waited another day we wouldn't have made it.

Our first mail delivery stop was Willeroo Station. We pulled in to the homestead on the afternoon of the sixth day, having come 100 miles. A day's spell was customary and we had bunks at the quarters and a paddock for the horses. There were about one-and-a-half pack horse loads of mail and parcels; with some redistribution Fordham was able to leave two packs and two horses, which he would pick up on the way back.

The next stop was Delamere, run as an outstation of Willeroo. It was thirty miles so we left early and made it in a day — a long stage for heavily loaded packhorses, but better than making camp. We were going to get a bunk and the horses would have a paddock, so it was worth pushing them an extra few miles for another day's spell. Another horse and pack was left at Delamere.

Our next hurdle was Battle Creek, which was running a banker; another day's delay waiting for it to drop to a reasonable level. George wasn't unduly concerned, since the horses got a day's spell. We had it sewn up now; we crossed the horses, split everything into two equal stacks and made two comfortable crossings. After leaving the King we were out of crocodile country, (not that we'd given much thought to that; we were busy getting everything across).

It was now raining most afternoons and nights, though the mornings were usually clear. We aimed to make camp before the rain started and were generally successful. In a week or so general rain would set in and it would rain for days on end. I wanted to get to Limbunya before it got too heavy; I'd probably be stuck there for a few weeks but I didn't mind that, I'd have a roof over my head and plenty of time.

We reached Victoria River Downs right on time, George said; ten days out of Katherine, 200 miles behind us.

I had been finding the trip quite pleasant; the five colts Fordham wanted worked were no trouble, but they were starting to get weary. Freshly broken horses will never stand up to work like a seasoned horse, and though each was only being ridden every third or fourth day they hadn't managed to adapt themselves to travel. They hadn't learned to manage the hobbles like an old stager and therefore didn't do well feeding.

I had been renewing a lot of acquaintances and friendships. There were a lot of men camped on the river, drovers mostly, and I knew quite a few of them. Tom Ronan was one; he later became a very successful author, winning a Commonwealth Literary Prize with his first book, *Vision Splendid*.

Crossing the Wickham River was a piece of cake. There was a big iron punt and with plenty of help from a few of the station hands we went over pulling it across by a big steel cable. The horses were no trouble. All we had to do was show them the water, they walked in and swam strongly.

Our next delivery stop was Pigeon Hole outstation. Roy Sedatree's piccaninny would be growing up into a big lump of a kid I thought, he'd be tall like his father; Roy wasn't called Jabiru for nothing. A couple of days after leaving the Wickham we pulled up at the horse paddock gate. We were down to six packs now, and another one was dropped here.

Again we had the advantage of a paddock and a spell. From here to Wave Hill was sixty miles, Roy said we'd have to swim the Victoria, but he reckoned it wouldn't be too bad.

That night and the next day we went over some old tracks and they couldn't be described as dry stages — we got through a couple of bottles of overproof rum that Roy reckoned would make a rabbit bite a bulldog.

From Pigeon Hole to Wave Hill was three short stages. A stockman from Limbunya was waiting for the mail, three days later I was back to where I started out on my voyage of discovery in September. It was February and the wet season was starting to make itself felt. Laurie Pumpa was quite content to let me put in the next few weeks at his homestead, his cook was a Chinaman whose conversational abilities were limited. We pottered about making greenhide ropes and odd repair jobs on the saddlery, but mostly we did nothing.

The wet eased up gradually, the monsoonal rain cleared, storms took the place of steady general rain, tapering off to occasional showers. But the ground was still wet and boggy and the rivers and creeks were still running strongly. Once the rain stopped the water courses and channels would drop quickly. I pulled my gear out from the saddle room and straightened it out, going over the girths, surcingles, saddle straps, hobbles and all the miscellaneous gear. I started shoeing up, I had plenty of basalt country ahead of me.

My horses were in great fettle; they'd been in a good paddock for six months. I had four good riding horses and three pack horses. Of the saddle horses I'm not sure which was my favourite. A grey mare, Idol, was a fine-looking horse with a smooth gait that made for a comfortable ride; Simon, a bay, one of the horses I got at Banka Banka, was a solid type who never seemed to tire. He was the one I rode when Lawson had his accident at Bullita. Spark, a chestnut, was a good one too, though somewhat highly strung — he'd shy at his own shadow. I had also got fond of the bay I'd traded with George Murray; he'd settled down a lot. I had three pack horses. One was a spare, since I had only two packs — plenty to carry my belongings.

Mid-March I was on my way. I reckoned to cut across through Mt Sanford and from there to the Humbert, to follow the Humbert River up, cross over the divide, pick the Baines River up at Crisp's

Yard, through Bullita to the Depot. I was sufficiently familiar with that country to get to the Depot without any trouble. I estimated it was 200 miles, give or take ten or twenty.

I planned to cross the Victoria River at the Depot. From there I would be in country with which I was completely unfamiliar but I would have no trouble getting directions. I would be heading northwest and couldn't really get into serious difficulties. Water and grass were plentiful. I guessed it was about eighty miles across from the Victoria River to Dorisvale Station, the first homestead I would see after leaving Bradshaws.

I'd have to watch that I didn't stray too far to the north; the blacks weren't by any means friendly and wouldn't hesitate to spear a lone traveller. Cook and Stephens had been speared fairly recently; I believed the police were out hunting the murderers somewhere to the north of where I would be travelling.

I travelled in easy stages. Four days after leaving Limbunya I pulled into Mt Sanford where it was good to see Jack Cusack again. He had another man in the camp, George Shaw, a well-known stockman in the Victoria district who'd been away droving into Queensland for a year and like myself had got caught up in a drought-stricken area somewhere in the Longreach area. He told us about a rough trip he did with 1000 Rocklands bullocks. Rocklands cattle had a bad reputation on the road for rushing. One man had taken a bad fall at night going to the lead of the galloping bullocks and broke an arm. Another night they jumped and a man got caught running to the spare night horse. He was knocked down and a couple of bullocks went over him. He got two or three broken ribs out of it and reckoned he was lucky; it wouldn't take many bullocks galloping on top of a man to kill him. A large bullock would weigh three-quarters of a ton.

Well, we all knew about rushing bullocks and it's always amazed me that more cattlemen aren't killed going to the lead of a mob of rushing bullocks on a pitch-black night, galloping over country that is more often than not strewn with rocks or fallen timber with plenty of holes thrown in to make it interesting.

214

After a day's spell at Mt Sanford I headed off to the Humbert, crossed the Wickham River and found a track I thought would take me to the Humbert. I was right on target but was disappointed when I got to Charlie Schultz's homestead: he was away mustering, so I pressed on, followed the Humbert River up and crossed the divide to meet the East Baines River at the yard where Jim Crisp was buried. I passed the Bullita homestead; no one was there except the cook. All stock camps were on the move now. I made camp at Barrac-Barrac Creek and the next day rode into the Depot.

It was pretty well deserted, Matt Wilson, the storekeeper, was the only one I knew. George Murray had left for the Wickham to lift a mob of bullocks for the meatworks. At the police station I found Sandy McNabb had been transferred and a new policeman named Jack Kennett had replaced him.

Kennett had come out by lugger, which the Administration had chartered from Jack Kepert, a master pearler. The captain and the mate were Japanese, the crew were a couple of Malays and two Aborigines. They turned into the Victoria River, with which they were not familiar, and ran aground on Mosquito Flats, treacherous shifting shoals.

That night they were attacked by blacks and the Japanese mate was killed. Jack Kennett, because of the hot night, was sleeping on deck. It was a full moon and he was lying on his back, his hand thrown across his eyes as a shield from the moon. A blackfellow had struck at his head with a tomahawk and, fortunately for the policeman, had only cut his hand. By this time the alarm was raised, a few shots were fired and the attackers were beaten off.

This had happened a couple of months ago and only a week or so after the lugger's return to Darwin. The captain, in a fit of remorse or perhaps shame — a Japanese trait with which we are not familiar — slashed his throat from ear to ear, and this is by no means a figure of speech. Dr Bruce Kirkland, who had to inspect the body, told me some time later the Captain had almost decapitated himself. These people can be very dedicated.

215

All this was not very encouraging for a solitary traveller about to venture into the tribal territory of these sportsmen, whose instincts were governed by an axiom I once heard expressed as "Never give a sucker an even break."

Jack Kennett didn't think there was too much to worry about. "Tas Fitzer's out there somewhere and he'll be keeping them on the move; they've had a good run lately, they speared Stephens and Cook, and then this Jap and nearly ended my promising career. I would think they'll rest on their laurels if they've got any sense."

The Devil looks after his own, they say, though I would have preferred something a bit more substantial. I thought The Old Fellow might be a slender reed in a pinch. I crossed the Victoria River at the ford as the sun was rising and the same afternoon I unpacked at Bradshaw's homestead. The manager, Harold Cook (no relation to the man speared on the Fitzmaurice) was getting ready for his first bullock muster for the season, shoeing forty or so horses.

They looked as though they'd have no trouble holding their reputation of being among the best horses in the Territory. I asked him about the bay I'd traded George Murray; he got his horse book out and looked it up. It was by a horse called Vengeance, imported from Sydney. When Murray handed the horse over to me he told me that his name was Revenge, which was fitting.

Harold Cook said it was about eighty miles to Dorisvale Station, which confirmed the information I already had. He gave me very clear and concise instructions on the country I would be going through, telling me to follow the Ikybon River up for about twenty-five miles then after leaving the river to travel in a northeasterly direction for another twenty-odd miles, I should then sight two hills called The Twins, which could be seen for a long way. I would have to pass between these hills and keep going northeast. From there I would follow any creek I came to; they all ran into the creek on which Stan Brown's homestead stood.

We discussed the spearings that had kept the mounted police busy: a lugger called the *Ouida* had been attacked in the aptly named Treachery Bay and two men, Bill Tetlow and Herb Watts, had been murdered over on the Daly River. In the lugger attack the captain, a Japanese man named Nagata, had been killed with his own gun. Two other crewmen, Yoshida and Owashi, had been tomahawked to death.

Constable Fitzer was out now looking for two natives named Nemarluk and Narragin. Cook said that before the wet Fred Don and Bill McCann from the Daly River Police Post had caught Widjulli, who had speared Herb Watts. Apparently it had been a hard patrol. They lost one of their saddle horses to a crocodile while crossing the Fitzmaurice, they had run out of rations and had been living off the land for a couple of weeks.

I left Bradshaw's giving quite a lot of thought to the hazards of the next eighty miles. As I was leaving Cook had said: "You'll be all right. They're more likely to be running around in circles down on the coast among the swamps and mangroves, where it's practically impossible for a horse to follow them."

Just the same, I must admit to a certain amount of nervousness. When I made camp I took the bells off the two pack horses, laid my swag out and rigged the mosquito net as I usually did. I doused the fire before I took to my swag where I had no trouble sleeping and dreamed of a very nice girl named Jean I had met at Brock's Creek races.

Some time next afternoon I sighted The Twins and kept going until nearly sundown, camping on a small creek that should take me to Dorisvale Station the next day. It had been a long day; I reckoned I had travelled thirty-five miles, I had kept fairly well on course, and shouldn't be more than twenty-five miles from Dorisvale. I promised my horses a couple of days' spell at Stan Brown's.

I calculated my travelling at four miles an hour — a generally accepted estimate. It usually worked out over a full day to within

217

four or five miles anyway, but I found that if I was in country with which I was not familiar it always seemed longer, and of course in such circumstances one was bound to wander to a certain extent. Anyway I didn't sight Brown's place until late afternoon. Visitors were very rare at Dorisvale, especially from the direction from which I'd come. Stan said he hadn't laid eyes on anyone for a couple of months and was news hungry, but I couldn't tell him much. I asked about the police patrols, he said he thought Don and McCann from the Daly River Police Post were down on the coast somewhere. He'd got the news from some walkabout blackfellows. Nemarluk was right at the top of their wanted list: it was hard country to be riding, with ti-tree scrub and mangrove swamps, and Nemarluk and his mates knew every inch of it.

At this point Stan's erstwhile friend Jim Webb/Ted Whelan — who, as we know, made a substantial contribution to Stan's transfer from Dorisvale to Fanny Bay a couple of years previously — was now known to be if not enjoying the hospitality of the Western Australian Government, certainly committed to it for the best part of twelve months.

Bush wireless was a very high-speed mechanism; Stan was familiar with all the details of Ted Whelan's recent error of judgment and was, of course, in a position to sympathise. I was able to fill in a few details, such as the favourable conditions under which he and his mates were restrained.

We thought that it was unfortunate the wheel of fortune had chosen to spin so unfavourably. All they were trying to do was rectify a balance that was in serious need of rectification to the advantage of the cattle industry.

I told him of my intentions to go buffalo hunting for Hardy and that I was due there in a few weeks. He asked if I'd break in some horses for him if I wanted to fill in some time. He wouldn't be in a position to pay me; he had a fair bit of lost ground to make up. The upshot was that I was once again getting breaking tackle ready.

There were fifteen youngsters Brown wanted broken and though they were, mostly, beautiful-looking horses, they were very bad-tempered. He had got an Adelaide sire that I think had Valais blood, which would account for their temperament. There were two or three average stock horses, but the rest were without doubt the most difficult I've ever thrown a rope on. I could have broken twice as many of almost any other breed; these were just plain bloody stinkers. It wasn't the extra time that I was spending on them that worried me — I had plenty of that — it was just that they were uniformly bad tempered. I got bitten twice; once I was bending down to unhobble a dirty brown horse that grabbed my back, and another time I was bitten on the upper arm. It was excruciatingly painful, and exhausted my vocabulary in ten seconds flat.

Stan, sitting on the top rail, thought it hilarious. I changed his mind about that when I picked my stockwhip up; I was able to reach him as he took off toward the house. He kept out of my way for the rest of the day.

At the end of April I left, crossed the Daly River and reached Pine Creek the next day. Two days later I was at Burrundie, a railway siding two or three miles from Harry Hardy's homestead at the foot of Mt Wells. My buffalo-shooting career was about to start.

CHAPTER 19

BUFFALO SHOOTING ON THE COASTAL PLAINS

T he history of buffalo in the Northern Territory is of more than passing interest, and it can be said with a great deal of truth that they owe their presence there largely to the determination of Captain Maurice Barlow, the first Commandant of Fort Dundas in 1824.

Named for Sir Phillip Dundas, King George IV's First Sea Lord, it is reasonable to reflect on the choice of this site for a garrison — an island twenty-odd miles from the mainland — when the entire northern coastline was available. The reason for a garrison in the first place was due to some uneasiness in London, generated by the aggressive activities of the Dutch who were entrenched in the East Indies.

Several sites on the mainland had been examined but there was some problem finding one with a suitable water supply, which is surprising when one considers the rainfall of sixty to seventy inches. However, it was October and perhaps an exceptionally dry year; there would have been some pressure on the captain to get his garrison together with forty-odd convicts settled in. He would have been aware he was within the hurricane zone.

When the monsoon swung to the southeast he despatched the brig *Lady Nelson* to Timor with orders to bring back a cargo of water buffalo. The *Lady Nelson* never returned. The worthy captain was not unduly dispirited, certainly not sufficiently to abandon his self-imposed task; he engaged a semi-privateer, the

Stedcomb, owned by Captain Barnes, an adventurer of dubious character, whose commission was to deliver fifty buffalo to His Majesty's latest outpost.

With foresight, which may have been dictated by the loss of the *Lady Nelson*, Captain Barnes remained ashore. The *Stedcomb* was never seen again either.

A lesser man could be forgiven for abandoning the undertaking, but the second disaster seems to have strengthened Captain Barlow's resolve. Perhaps, like many before and since, he was not deterred by losses borne by His Majesty's Government twelve thousand miles away.

At any rate the next attempt was more successful, if only marginally so. A French trader in Timor, Monsieur Béchard, agreed to supply fifteen head "trained to the yoke".

The schooner *Isabella*, perhaps not without a measure of uneasiness, sailed for the Dutch dominion. Two months later she returned; of the fifteen animals only three survived the voyage. The Frenchman then contracted to supply 200 head a year but the records are shrouded in the mists of time, and it is doubtful if he made more than two or three voyages. It would appear the total number that reached our shores was approximately forty cows and, obviously, a few bulls.

Fort Dundas proved to be a tragic and costly error and the second commandant, Major Campbell, was transferred lock, stock, barrel and buffalo (or at least some of the latter) to Raffles Bay on the Cobourg Peninsula, but not before the surgeon, Dr Gold, and another man named Green had been speared. Raffles Bay was also relinquished and the next attempt was at Port Essington.

Port Essington had one brief moment of fame — it was into this outpost, on December 17, 1845, that an emaciated Ludwig Leichhardt staggered, long after being given up for dead. He stayed for a month awaiting transport and even then spoke of encountering wild buffalo several days' march from the settlement.

In 1849, after fifteen years of misery and hardships and almost forgotten by their masters, HMS *Meander* arrived to rescue the last of the Empire Builders. It must have been a sad departure, leaving behind the row of graves they knew would soon be claimed by the jungle.

A contemporary described it as the "most hopeless and heroic enterprise in the history of the British Empire", and it would seem that the captain of *Meander* agreed. In an attempt to remove the stain from the history books before he sailed he turned his ship's guns on the abandoned settlement. Fortunately the gunners appear to have been indifferent marksmen — half a dozen of its unusual conical chimneys, the powder magazine and the row of graves escaped destruction and were left for posterity . . . along with a hundred or so buffalo and millions of buffalo flies, which would torment our cattle in the coming years.

The buffalo that wandered off into the hinterland discovered a perfect environment. They worked their way westward and found the coastal plains very much to their liking and, though they were completely flooded in the wet season, when the water drained off lush grasses were uncovered. They grazed and proliferated undisturbed for the next fifty years.

Then a man named E. O. Robinson came on the scene. Not a great deal seems to be known about this customs agent, trader and man of many parts. However, whatever his background, he had done his homework and knew there was a market for buffalo hides.

Robinson got hold of a young man named Joe Cooper and they became partners. They took a lease of Melville Island — the buffalo that had been left there had also multiplied a thousandfold. Cooper, a superb horseman, went over to the island and, to use his own words, "shot it out hair, hide and tail". The buffalo were boxed up on the island and couldn't get away. In five years he shot

222

more than 6000 buffalo, and those years were not without incident.

Over a campfire and a bottle of rum he told me in graphic detail how he acquired a wife — I think acquired is the right word.

He had been speared by a Melville Islander. He took the spear in his right shoulder and managed to break it off but couldn't get it out; those Melville Island spears are vicious weapons, and he was in a bad way. A young island girl and her mother helped him to a canoe and they started to paddle to Darwin. They were fortunately picked up by a coastal vessel, otherwise it is doubtful they would have made it in time.

When he recovered he married the girl, one of those fairytale endings, I suppose. All the romance wore off in later years, of course; when Joe got drunk she used to belt hell out of him.

Professional buffalo shooting was well away by the turn of the century and there were established markets for the hides. Those who gravitated to what was one of the last frontiers of adventure found what was almost a readymade operation. Quite a few attracted by the life found their way down to the coastal plains, but few stayed more than a season; most were entirely unsuited to the life and environment. It was a country that soon sorted out the men from the boys.

Those who did stay were successful — true professionals — and are still remembered. They shot year after year, their tallies from 1000 to 2000 bulls in a season of approximately five months.

Joe Cooper, the grand old man of that fraternity, rightly heads the list. Paddy Cahill of Oenpelli; Jim Moles, killed by a buffalo bull at Cannon Hills; Cecil Freer of Point Stuart; Barney Flynn, speared on Bamboo Creek; Fred Hardy, who went to the happy hunting grounds by way of a fall from a horse; Harry Hardy, his brother; and George Hunter, who wrestled a buffalo bull — he didn't win the contest, but remarkably he wasn't hurt. With the exception of Paddy Cahill and Barney Flynn I knew them all. Their ghosts still ride the plains. When Fred Hardy took the fall that broke his neck it was from a horse he bought from me. As they say, "it was one of those things".

Hardy's place was called Annaburroo, which was a mild corruption of the native word for buffalo; 'annaburra'. He had two separate leases, 400 square miles on the Mary River (the buffalo country) and 500 or 600 bordered by the railway line and running eastward. The Burrundie block was his wet season camp; he ran 1000 or so head of cattle, which he worked between shooting. The two blocks were fifty or sixty miles apart.

He also had a nice plump wife who was a very good cook, and a nice slender daughter, who I was quickly informed, was engaged to a doctor a few miles up the social ladder from me. Any excess enthusiasm I may have displayed was quickly diverted into shoeing horses for the shooting camp. That soon absorbed any interest I may have unwittingly shown. He had a couple of bad-tempered bastards I thought he had saved up for me — one of his stockmen said: "No good bugger true that twofella", which I'd already found out. They were fresh, strong and determined, but I got them shod after a titanic struggle and some appropriate observations on their ancestry.

Hardy was happily planning the tourist side of the coming activities, looking forward to a profitable sideline, doing a lot of travelling back and forth from his house to Burrundie siding where there was a telephone. He never discussed the details with me; all I knew was that they would arrive in a few weeks. They were coming by the "Ghan" (this was the name given to the train that ran between Adelaide and Alice Springs), and Bond would bring them up the road by coach, fifteen head plus Bond and a mechanic.

It was about 800 miles from Alice Springs to Burrundie over a track that, for the first trip for sure, wouldn't be in very good shape. Most of the creek crossings would be washed out from the previous wet season. The Government never did anything to the road — that was up to the travellers. Hardy said Bond had done

224

one trip up and back and didn't anticipate much trouble; his fifteen passengers could do some pushing and pulling if necessary. They'd probably enjoy that — all part of the deal. With any luck Bond would get three trips in. I wondered what Hardy was charging them: I never did find out.

A week later we went out to the buffalo camp at Moon Billabong on the Mary River. We had seven boys, five of whom had wives. Harry and I drove out in his truck with the camp gear, rations and women; the horses had gone out with the stockmen a day earlier. The first day the two of us rode out together for a look-see while the camp was being straightened out. A few miles down the river ceased to be a confined channel and became a huge flood plain. During the wet the entire Mary River catchment emptied itself over several hundred square miles of treeless plains, which became covered with eight to ten feet of water. When the rains ceased the water drained off into salt arms.

When Harry and I reached the edge of the tremendous sea of water, stretching away as far as the eye could see, we reined in our horses and I stared in amazement. I had never seen anything like it in my life: wildfowl were everywhere, swimming, feeding and circling. The din of geese was almost deafening; there must have been millions of them, and scurrying along the water's edge were dozens of half-grown youngsters scuttling for cover.

Buffalo were everywhere, too; hundreds of them. In the shallower water they were feeding on the floating grass, further out I could see large numbers of bulls, cows and calves, swimming about aimlessly I thought. Majestic paperbark trees grew to the water's edge. These trees, as the name implies, had a bark composed of literally thousands of layers of tissue-thin, flimsy covering that was stripped easily from the tree and that made a very effective and rainproof shelter. Hardy's camp, which was being renovated, was covered with the same material. The paperbarks appeared to fringe the entire plain to a depth of a quarter of a mile or so.

Harry's object in riding down to the flood plains was to estimate how long it would be before they dried sufficiently to ride. To my inexperienced eye it looked like a permanent lake. He said it was surprising how quickly it drained off. There had been later rains than usual this season, and consequently they would take longer to dry; he reckoned four or five weeks.

We returned to the camp and spent the rest of the afternoon checking the rifles, oiling them and firing a few shots testing the sights. They were .303 calibre, two were bolt-action Lee Enfield magazine rifles and three were single-shot Martini Enfield carbines. The Lee Enfields were ex-military weapons from the 1914–1918 war, readily obtainable from any army disposal store, as were the Martini Enfields, which were Boer War relics. The Lee Enfields were for foot shooting, while the carbines were for horseback use.

The next morning the real action started. The horses were up at the camp before daylight and nosebags were put on two shooting horses, which steadily munched away while everyone else had their breakfast. While Hardy and I were saddling a shooting horse each, others were tying a length of rope round the neck of the five or six pack horses that would be carrying hides.

We rode out of the camp, Harry and I in the lead with our rifles strapped to a saddle dee, the barrel under the flap. Beside us walked the foot shooter, his rifle over his shoulder. We all carried a cartridge belt round our waists; the pack horses walked behind, driven by the skinners, some of whom were walking.

We rode for the best part of half an hour before anything happened. The timber was dense by any standards; galloping through that stuff wasn't going to be an armchair ride, but I was riding a trained shooting horse and he'd know what it was all about. There were plenty of tracks, mostly fresh. Hardy pulled his rifle out and laid it across the pommel of his saddle in front of him, and I did the same. He told me not to try to shoot for a while. "When we come to buffalo, follow me and watch what I do." I nodded, all tensed up.

226

The foot shooter who was walking ahead of us suddenly gave a low whistle and pointed. It was difficult to see too far ahead in the thick timber and the buffalo were a slate grey colour that merged easily into the shade. As he sighted I saw them, two bulls: one lying in the shade, one standing looking toward us. We reined our horses waiting for the man on foot to get a shot away, but they had seen us and galloped off. Our horses had been reefing at the bit, having seen the buffalo as soon as the foot shooter did, and were dancing around impatiently. Hardy galloped away as soon as it was clear that the foot shooter wasn't going to get a shot. I followed him closely; it wasn't as easy as I had first thought.

My horse, thinking no doubt he had a polished professional aboard, tore off after Harry and left the rest to me — things such as low limbs that could sweep me out of the saddle. The buffalo were going at a fast pace and were taking advantage of the cover. They were faster than I had expected and we had difficulty keeping them in sight. But after the first burst they steadied down quite a lot and Harry started to catch them.

I followed as closely as I could, holding the rifle in my right hand and feeling it getting heavy. In my left I held the reins; I didn't have to guide the horses: all I had to do was watch I didn't get knocked out of the saddle. Harry was closing fast now, the bulls galloping one behind the other. At a brief break in the scrub, Harry drove his horse up on to the first bull and lowered his rifle. His horse jumped to one side as he fired and the bull fell, he was quickly up on to the next one — another shot and it was down. Both had broken backs. It was complete professionalism.

I pulled my horse up at the first buffalo and dismounted beside the crippled beast. Hardy was riding back. As he got off his horse he said with a smile. "Well, there it is Tom; that's all there is to it." We sat on a log side by side waiting for the horses and skinners to arrive. I wouldn't have admitted I couldn't do it for a million quid. I was sure I could, but probably not as quickly as I first thought. I'd done a fair amount of scrub riding in my time running cattle, but this was a different kettle of fish. I had certainly discarded my original belief of riding flank to flank with Hardy dropping buffalo for buffalo.

"I'll be okay in a day or so; I'll soon get the hang of it."

"You should be. As you can see, it's not a matter of marksmanship — its purely horsemanship."

And he was dead right, all you had to do was get through that bloody scrub a bit faster than a buffalo — that's all. I was a good horseman, sure, horse breaker, race rider . . . a couple of days, I thought, a trifle uneasily.

The horses arrived, one carrying a pack had the skinning knives. The bulls were both skinned quickly, their tongues taken to be salted down later. The hides were folded and covered with bushes to be picked up on our way back.

We went on. It was getting close to midday when we came to eight or ten cows with a few calves at foot. Harry pulled up, watching them as they all turned to look at us. "I'll have a look at this lot," he said, "we need a fat cow for beef."

I could see them sniffing the air uneasily and starting to move away as he put his horse into a gallop. He was soon up among them and shot a fat young cow. After the hide was removed the best cuts were taken which, when completed, was less than half the carcass.

The meat was dark red in colour, darker than ordinary meat and the fat was white — more like mutton fat. It was covered with bushes and the hide pulled over it to prevent the crows, hawks and flies getting to it. We took enough with us for a dinner camp and rode down to the edge of the flooded plains for water to boil the billy.

A fire was soon going and the billy boiled while the meat was cooking. There's something satisfying about the smell of grilling meat and the smoke of a campfire. A loaf of Mrs Hardy's bread was produced from a pack and we had a good meal. I thought the meat was excellent, there was nothing rank or gamey about it. If I hadn't known I would have had difficulty telling it from ordinary bullock meat; a little richer, perhaps. While we were having our meal the horses had wandered off feeding along the water's edge. When we had finished they were brought back, one of the horse tailers saying he had seen four bulls walking from the water into the timber, perhaps a quarter of a mile away. "We'll have those. You can have a shot, Tom," said Harry.

We saddled up. I made sure my girth was tight, we swung into the saddles and rode across to cut the tracks. We didn't go far before we found the tracks. The animals were wandering along in a desultory manner, breaking off branches as they went, snatching at grass tussocks, completely oblivious to us. Harry thought they'd be about a mile away. "They won't go far, they're looking for a midday camp in the shade." Now we had the tracks the foot shooter strode away in the lead. We let him get a good distance in front of us before we followed; he was slipping through the forest with all the hunting instincts of his ancestors.

Suddenly he gave a piercing whistle and we stopped. I could see the four bulls; two were lying down. The foot shooter was standing behind a tree sighting his rifle, then a loud report echoed through the forest. One dropped, and the other three galloped away.

In an instant our horses were into their stride — this was the real thing. For a while the bulls stuck together but as we closed they started to split and I took the one directly in front of me. I was managing to negotiate the timber better than I expected and wasn't keeping such a tight rein as I had when I followed Hardy. We cleared a big log, I lay over his neck as we came to a limb, hoping I didn't come to a low limb and a big log together. Hardy started to close on his target and I decided I'd better do the same. My horse was willing enough, but as soon as I decided to get up on to him a bloody great log appeared. Eventually a brief break in the timber gave me the opportunity; I drove my horse on to the bull, the horse swerved as he was supposed to do to avoid being brought down by the falling beast. I fired and down he went; at the same time Harry fired and his dropped, then he raced away after the last one. I was sitting on my horse admiring my first buffalo when he returned.

He dismounted and walked behind the wounded bull examining the spot where I had placed my bullet. "That's right," he approved, "you must make sure the bullet hits just in front of the coupling at an angle and goes down and breaks the back. If you miss the backbone and he doesn't go down you can be in a bit of trouble. You can't have a wounded bull on his feet — too dangerous, they'll kill a horse no sweat.

"If you are having a run, say four or five or more — and on the plains you'll get anything up to twenty — and a bull doesn't go down, don't stop or you'll lose the others. With a bullet in him he won't go far. Come back after you've finished the run and kill him; that's not always easy, but you've got to kill him."

When the skinning was finished we turned back. The sun was starting to swing over to the west; there were hides and the meat to pick up. We had a full load, one hide was plenty for one horse. We threw them on bareback and secured them with rope which each horse carried around its neck. We picked up the beef and the cow hide was put on the pack horse; now every horse had a hide.

We were about two miles from the camp when a solitary bull jumped out from a clump of bushes. "Away you go Tom, he's yours," yelled Harry. Full of confidence I took off but he gave me a hard ride, twisting and turning into every bit of cover. Eventually I got up to him and dropped him with a good clean shot; I was starting to feel like a veteran hunter. Harry rode up and looked approvingly at where my bullet had entered. I shot the bull in the head as the horses trotted up.

One of the women looked after the cooking; nothing fancy, but food wasn't important. (The hygiene might have raised a few eyebrows, but ours wouldn't be among them.) There was plenty of fresh buffalo steak, which was good fuel. We had our evening meal and the last of Mrs Hardy's bread and sat on a log by the campfire, drinking pannikins of black tea and yarning. Harry was all fired up with the tourist experiment. It was going to be a revelation to city folks, especially when they got out on to the plains and saw the teeming wildlife, the buffalo herds and those magnificent sunsets.

We turned in. A hundred or so yards away the throaty beat of a didgeridoo drifted down from some ancient corroboree, a splendid accompaniment to the music of the night; the croaking frogs, night birds calling, whooshing of wings, a million insects and from the lagoon the splash of a barramundi — sometimes the heavier, more sinister splash of a crocodile. In my mosquito net I made sure the edges were tucked in; mosquitoes could find their way through very small openings.

The next day we rode out to a lagoon Hardy wanted to show me. It was a tremendous sheet of water covered in waterlilies and thousands of birds. Geese predominated, and there were several different species of ducks. I saw black duck, whistle duck, Burdekin duck; there were beautiful pigmy geese, tiny things with lovely plumage. There were egrets, spoonbills and storks walking daintily through the shallow water. We rode up to an old camp Harry said would be where I'd be moving to next. He spoke as though he wouldn't be there; I assumed he'd be running his dude ranch setup. The camp was pretty well the same as the one at Moon Billabong, paperbark sheds and lean-tos.

Suddenly one of the skinning boys sung out "Pig!" I looked to where he was pointing, on the other side of the lagoon about a dozen pigs were ambling down to the water. Harry said to the foot shooter, "Go and shoot a young sow, a fat one." He didn't need any second telling and strode off, his rifle over his shoulder.

I lost sight of him after he went into the timber for cover; one of the skinners climbed a tree to get a better view, jabbering information to the others below until Harry told him to shut up. After about a quarter of an hour we heard three shots in rapid succession. All hands immediately raced off to the other side of the billabong and came back with two pigs, a young sow three or four months old and another, larger boar, which Harry said was for themselves; they preferred the stronger meat. In no time they had both pigs butchered and laid out on freshly cut bushes. It was about ten o'clock and there was work to be done. Two boys were left behind and half the pack horses; we took five with us and rode away, planning to have a dinner camp on our return. Unless we struck a big mob of bulls I was to do the shooting, which suited me. We saw three bulls, the foot shooter got one and I got the other two. I was riding with confidence now. They were skinned and tied on to the pack horses; we circled back to the camp without seeing any more. When we arrived, the lads we'd left behind had the billy boiling. There were two delicious cooked salted tongues for Harry and I; the boys were getting into the pork, which had been thrown on the coals.

I shot a bull going home. Four for the day: Harry seemed satisfied. The next day he stayed in the camp, saying he wanted to do some writing. He had a leather satchel in which he carried his diary and writing material. He told me to follow the edge of the paperbarks on the way out and to come around by the lagoon. We got back at sundown with four hides; the foot shooter got two and I shot two.

I now had plenty of confidence. The combination of man and horse is of the utmost importance. It's a relationship impossible to define, that first ride; getting to know each other. Every horse is different, every man is different. I always tried to establish a relationship with my horses as soon as possible, whether they were saddle horses or pack horses, night horses, camp horses or the horses in my camp that my men rode or handled.

When you're riding in tricky situations a lot has to be left to the horse, especially when riding in heavy timber. The country was mainly gently undulating, the timber stringybark, woollybutt and ironwood, the most aptly named of them all. Ironwood lasted longer than forever — it and cypress pine were the only timber white ants wouldn't touch. Cypress had a powerful smell; it made them ill, and they broke their teeth on ironwood so they left that alone. Termites aren't as silly as you'd think.

The ant hills they built were up to ten or twelve feet high. The outer covering was five or six inches thick, the interior was a mass of honeycomb. I've never studied ants closely — too many other things to think about.

The next day I could have done without them. I took off after a couple of buffalo and my horse hit an ant hill; only a small one, perhaps a foot high, but it was enough to bring him down. I wasn't hurt, but of course I lost the buffalo; by the time I had picked myself up and remounted they would have been miles away.

Harry decided he'd better go back to Burrundie. He was anxious to keep in touch with Bond. "You'll be all right," he said. "I expect I'll be away about a week." He cranked up his old truck and disappeared in a cloud of smoke and dust. Five days later he was back. I was throwing half a dozen hides off when he drove up. I rubbed my horse's back down and gave him a nosebag before I walked over to the campfire, where Harry was rolling a smoke. He asked me how many hides I'd got. I said "thirty-two," which I thought was pretty good. He gave a grunt; I'd have thought it was worth at least a couple of grunts and a smile. He seemed to be in a bad mood and got stuck into one of the lubras because the billy wasn't boiling, which was a bit unfair I thought.

He walked over to the truck and came back with a bottle of rum. He took a couple of pannikins and poured two drinks — judging by the smell it was a pretty solid brew. He handed one to me: "You might need a drop of water in it." He still wasn't talking much. I splashed some water into my pannikin and took a mouthful. "Christ!" I said, "that's not rum, that's bloody barbed wire!"

Something was troubling him: I thought it may have been a domestic upset, these married men always seemed to be in strife. I hoped he hadn't beaten his wife, she seemed a happy puddeny type and made good bread, too.

"Tom," he said, "I've got some bad news — that bloody Bond has pulled out of the deal."

This was quite a shock, and I wondered immediately how it was going to affect me.

"I was on the phone to him two or three times," he went on. "He's in Alice Springs. Then yesterday he suddenly said he'd changed his mind about bringing his tourists here."

We had another rum. I sensed some bad news was coming up — bad news for me, I was right.

"The situation now that Bond isn't coming has changed everything; I can't afford to keep you on."

It was a very severe blow to me; with station work it never seemed to matter, there was always plenty of work — stock work, horse breaking. I could get whatever I wanted. But this was different: there couldn't be any great demand for buffalo hunters. Hardy poured another rum; I think he was trying to soften the blow, but it did nothing for my feelings. He was forcing the conversation, saying how sorry he was to have to let me go. At the same time I realised that it was a one-man camp and he didn't need me once the tourist deal fell through. But I had really got wrapped up in it — and in a brief moment it was all over.

The rum was doing more for him than it was for me; all I was getting was more despondent. He poured another and we were more than half-way through the bottle. I noticed it had no label and asked what brand it was. He said it wasn't any brand really.

"A Queensland mate of mine, a sugar planter, makes it. He started off with the idea of running his truck on it, but when he found out how good it was he reckoned it was a pity to put it in his tank. I used to get a barrel off him now and then, this is the last of it. He died last year — got a liking for the stuff and overdid it a bit."

"It's powerful right enough," I said. "I reckon if you put it in a truck it'd blow the cylinder head off."

At the end of the week Hardy took me back to Burrundie, where I mustered my horses and rode away. When I left I knew what I was going to do — I was going buffalo shooting, not straight away, perhaps, but before very much longer. There would be some vacant Crown land out there somewhere. I knew all the country where the main herds were running was taken up, but there would be something along the boundaries of the existing leases that wasn't held by anyone. All I wanted was a toe hold.

I headed south, turning over plans in my mind as I rode along the dusty road beside the railway line. Over the months since I'd come over from the west, in Katherine, Pine Creek, Brock's Creek and Darwin, I had gleaned a lot of information one way and another. It was a new area to me and I always listened to the talk round campfires and in bars. One thing I learned was that buffalo shooters, because of the nature of their work and the climate, were always short of horses. This would be my starting point.

Dick Guild was a battling cattleman I'd met in Katherine. He'd come over from Queensland, taken up some vacant country on the Edith River and was building up a herd of cattle pretty well from scratch. Manbulloo, one of Vesteys properties, was on his boundary, which was handy; there were no fences, and cattle can't read maps. He was keeping his tucker bags full with horse-dealing, which was a pretty hard track with a lot of dry stages. There were plenty of brumby horses there for the taking — if you were good enough. I don't think there is a tougher way of making a quid than running brumbies, especially in that country with its timbered stony ridges.

I followed the Overland Telegraph Line and the railway line, which ran parallel. I reached the Edith River, turned and followed it up until I came to Guild's homestead. A cloud of dust was coming from the stockyard: I could see Guild on one end of a greenhide rope, a squealing brumby stallion on the other.

We shook hands, and he showed some surprise at seeing me. "I thought you were buffalo shooting for Harry Hardy."

"It fell through," I said. He nodded and dropped the subject. "I s'pose you'll stay the night. When you've unpacked, let your horses go in this paddock. I'll let this horse go and I'll be with you."

At the house, he pointed out a bunk made of laced greenhide and told me to throw my swag on it, it was excellent to sleep on. A lubra had the billy boiled and we sat down to a meal. So far he hadn't asked me any questions; it was up to me.

I gave him a brief rundown on why I had left Hardy, then told him what I had in mind. "Dick, I want to buy about twenty head of horses, broken: they needn't be very good as long as they're broken, and I haven't got enough money to pay for them. All I've got is forty-odd quid."

He smiled and thought for a while. "I expect we can do a deal. I can muster about fifteen, maybe sixteen head and they'll cost you four to five pounds a head. If you were paying cash I could let you have them for a bit less, but I can get a fiver cash for any of them from a drover." I knew this was right and realised the offer was very generous.

"Anyway," he went on, "if you can't sell them bring them back, but if what you say is right you shouldn't have much trouble unloading them."

We mustered the paddock and put thirty-odd head through the yard and drafted off sixteen that were broken in — all shapes, sizes and colours.

There were a few details to be attended to: sixteen horses needed sixteen pairs of hobbles. I also wanted someone to help me, since with my own horses I would have twenty-three head, too many for one man to handle. Where I would be going there were no roads most of the way; hobbling them out and mustering them in the morning, particularly mustering them, would take up a lot of valuable travelling time. Dick said we would go into Katherine the next day, there were a few things he wanted and I would have no difficulty picking up a horse tailer.

Three days later I had everything shipshape and had found a likely looking lad who said his name was Tiger.

At the crack of dawn I left Guild's place and headed north. I planned to make the first day a long one, so the horses I had got from Dick Guild would be too tired and too hungry to want to make back, which could be expected the first night away from their home paddock. Once they settled down I could shorten the stages. I wanted them to arrive at their destination, wherever that might be, in good condition.

It was rough and stony travelling, which worried me a little because the Guild horses were all unshod. When I made camp I was on the Mary River. I judged by my watch that I had travelled about thirty miles; there was good grass and I was now on softer country for travelling.

Breakfast before daylight was very rough: corned beef, damper and black tea. After listening to the horse bells clanking in the distance we were on our way, a bridle slung over one shoulder as daylight filtered through the trees. It took the best part of an hour to get the horses together. I got back to the camp first, Tiger arrived driving the rest, with a dead goanna he had treed and killed tied around his neck.

We packed up quickly and were away, following the river flats between the stony ridges and the watercourse, running from large pools to quite big reaches. Clumps of bamboo grew along the bank, magnificent gums were scattered through the flats and sometimes we came to large billabongs left from the old river course, which had changed over thousands of years. Wallabies hopped around feeding on the lush growth of grasses; bird life was everywhere, from brilliant parrots to tiny finches that broke in swarms from bushes. There were other, less pleasant forms of life, too; March flies with a spike-like proboscis I thought would have no trouble going through a pine board. When they hit a man it really hurt; a horse would jump as though struck with a stock-whip.

We rode on down the river and the country changed gradually. We left the ridges and came to broken plains, sparsely grassed and dotted with stunted paperbarks. It was inferior looking country, which I judged would be flooded during the wet season. We were now starting to see buffalo, mostly cows with calves and the odd solitary bull. I camped on a billabong and shot some ducks.

The next day I came to Fred Hardy's buffalo camp. Shooting was in full swing; there was a great stack of hides covered with paperbark, some hanging on racks and others being salted down. I unpacked nearby and Tiger hobbled the horses as I walked over to Hardy's camp. I'd met him previously at the races, and he knew that I'd been briefly with his brother; he knew all about that. It was fairly well known that the brothers were not the best of friends, and it was with what appeared to be a lot of satisfaction that Fred related the real reason the Bond deal had fallen through.

Every now and then, apparently, Harry would think up an additional charge to tack on to the original quotation, one of the reasons I suppose he was doing so much telephoning. He had heard there were a couple of movie cameras being brought along, so he told Bond that he wanted a shilling in the pound for all film rights. Bond cancelled the deal on the spot and when he eventually arrived he was able to take his party to Marrakai Station, one of Vesteys places, for which there was no charge. Under the circumstances I guessed he was glad to get out of it. As it turned out the cameras were home-movie types. Harry Hardy had made a rod for his own back, and serve him right, I thought.

Yarning over the campfire that evening produced some useful information. Fred said he was fairly sure George Hunter was short of horses; he'd seen him at the Adelaide River a month back and they'd discussed the horse problem. Hunter's country was down on the coast, from the Adelaide River to the Mary.

In the morning Hardy looked my horses over and after walking around a bay and a chestnut a couple of times asked what I wanted for them. They were the two best looking Guild horses and I thought for a while about whether I should let them go. Then I said: "Well, Fred, they're the best two in that lot. I've ridden both of them and they are both good and fairly solid; the chestnut's four and the bay's five, and I couldn't let them go under ten quid each."

He had another walk around them. "I'll throw a saddle on them and give them a lap," he said. "If I like them it's a deal."

He caught the bay first, saddled it and rode across the plain, first a canter then a fast gallop. I saw him twisting and turning through a clump of trees, the horse was behaving well. When he came back he said: "He's okay — I'll take him."

He then saddled the chestnut and put it through the same routine; as he dismounted I knew I'd sold them both.

"I'll give you eighteen quid for the two," he offered. I expected that, of course, and shook my head. "Twenty or nothing, Fred; they're the pick of that lot and I won't take anything less."

"Okay, I'll take them." He left his saddle on the chestnut and wrote out a cheque for twenty pounds. He gave me directions on how to get to Hunter's place, said it was a short two-day ride and suggested my next camp would be Wild Boar Lagoon. He reckoned Gaden would be camped there; he'd heard his shots in the early morning when it was cool and they could be heard a long way.

I packed up and left, confident the trip was going to be successful. Hardy's directions were clear; I came to couch grass plains, buffalo were everywhere and now and then we saw skinned carcasses which, judging by the stench, had been shot several days previously. Crows and kite hawks were tearing at them; we frequently saw well-nourished dingoes too.

Wild Boar coame into sight in the early afternoon. As Hardy had predicted, Gaden's camp was there. As I came closer I saw Bond's tour bus parked on one side: there was a kind of marquee and a few tents and some odd people walking around. Tourists are the same everywhere — most of them were plastered with some kind of cream, some had small mosquito nets hanging from their hats and they all looked uncomfortable.

I unpacked and made my way to Gaden's camp, I had met them at the Brock's Creek races, too. Gaden's Christian name was Hazel, which seemed unusual. I believe he had a brother called Gladys, too; perhaps their mother had a longing for daughters . . . a bit tough on boys, I thought, especially bush kids. However, they seemed to live with it all right, I rarely heard it commented on and Hazel was well thought of.

I could see this was a bigger operation than either of the Hardy's. Marrakai was owned by Vestey and Gaden's camp was probably the biggest producer on the coast. It appeared to be well run. There were the usual humpies, with a timber framework covered by paperbark. There were several hundred hides stacked and covered by paperbark, too.

As was customary I had a meal with Gaden, who confirmed what Hardy had told me about Hunter being short of horses. He gave me directions on how to get there, and next morning I set off hoping it would be the last stage of my journey. It was good travelling. The floodplains had dried out, I skirted the paperbarks, sometimes coming to patches of dense jungle-like rainforest and in the afternoon reached George Hunter's homestead on Lake Finniss.

The only sign of life was a flock of goats, most of which had taken up residence on Hunter's verandah and were doing a good job of fertilising it. After a while an old blackfellow and his lubra appeared, rubbing their eyes. They shooed the goats from the verandah and looked questioningly at me. I asked them where Hunter was, they both pointed across the plain and said; "Thataway, close up long saltwater," which of course conveyed nothing to me. I didn't think it was much good asking them how far, nevertheless I gave it a go. "Little bit long way."

It was too late to go looking for him: I'd probably end up getting bushed in the dark. I unpacked and camped.

The next morning Tiger managed to extract reasonably clear directions to Hunter's shooting camp from the goat shepherd. We crossed a black soil plain that had very little in the way of pasture. It was now September and the "dry" was starting to make itself felt. Back on the Marrakai country there was still a good coverage of grass, but closer to the coast I thought it was terrible. Around Lake Finniss there had been reasonable feed for the horses but here the ground was dry, with deep cracks. It was bad travelling; the horses were stumbling badly through no fault of their own. We left the plain, turned into some dense timber and after travelling for an hour came out on another plain stretching away to the hazy distance. We followed the edge of the timber — it looked better here, there was a good covering of couch grass. A few miles further we came to Hunter's camp.

Hunter was a massive man, built like an ox. Looking at him, barefooted and wearing only shorts, I had no trouble believing the story that he had wrestled with a buffalo bull without coming to any harm. In such a contest a draw could be regarded as a mighty achievement. He was surprised to see me; I rightly guessed he didn't get many visitors. When I told him my name he said, "You were shooting for Hardy, weren't you?" Everyone knew almost everything about everybody. I admitted I was and didn't go into any details; he probably knew about that, too. I just explained what had brought me there.

He seemed so pleased I made mental note to add another quid to the price. I told Tiger to unpack and keep the horses rounded up, while Hunter called to a lubra to boil the billy. I joined him at his campfire over a pannikin of tea. He asked me what the price was and allowing for the horse trading part I said nine quid a head. "That sounds too high for me and I've nearly finished for the season," he said, which I thought might be right . . . and, on the other hand, might not.

We walked over to where the horses were rounded up. I explained that the horses branded TGW were those for sale, that being Guild's brand. I didn't intend selling any of my horses. It didn't take him long to make up his mind. "I'd like to buy them, but nine pounds is too high for me."

241

I went into a rigmarole of how little I was making on the deal and asked: "What's your best offer?" He said he wouldn't go higher than eight and after some humming and hahing I accepted. It was time for the midday meal. Over a buffalo steak he asked where I was going from here. I said I thought I would head across through Freer's place and on to the Alligator River, I intended looking for some vacant Crown Lands where I could get a foothold and start buffalo shooting. He nodded and thought for a while. "How would you feel about running my camp for the rest of the season?" he asked. "I haven't been further than Darwin for eight years. I want to get away for a month or so, have a look at Sydney — it's a place I've never seen. There's a boat due in a couple of weeks' time, the *Marella* I think, there won't be another one for a month after that. I need another 300 hides to finish my final contract. If you'd care to take it on and finish the contract I'll either pay you five pounds a week or we'll go fifty-fifty."

"I'll take it on and I'd prefer the fifty-fifty deal," I said without hesitation.

We shook hands. "You take over the rations and cartridges — at a rough guess, the whole lot would come to about fifty quid, you can check it out if you like."

Hunter started getting all steamed up about going away. He had a boat, a former pearling lugger he'd picked up at a sale and done up. It was moored at his jetty in a salt arm close to the Adelaide River. An old New Guinea boy was his captain; Moses, who also used to cart the hides in a dray between trips. A couple of days later the last of the hides were carted down to the boat, Hunter sailed away to Darwin and I was on my own.

It was a good camp; they were mostly Melville Island boys, except a foot shooter, Bamboo Charlie, his lubra (who was the cook), and one other. Counting Tiger there were eleven of us. Bamboo Charlie was a very good shot.

There were plenty of buffalo but they were getting low in condition: the country was being eaten out, the water was drying fast now and the heat was building. When I was in Hardy's camp the buffalo were in good condition, strong and would gallop solidly. Here though there were plenty of young bulls, they wouldn't run far before turning on a horseman. Then they were dangerous. Early in the morning before the heat built up was the best time; they would gallop further and I could usually drop them before they turned. It wasn't difficult to shoot a bull when it was galloping away, I could get up behind it, hit it in the backbone and down it would go. If there were more than four or five in a mob you could depend on the last couple turning. When they turned it got extremely awkward. With their great sweeping horns they could disembowel a horse. They were tremendously powerful — I've had a horse turned completely over, and it frightened hell out of me.

In shooting from a galloping horse there was no marksmanship involved, it was purely horsemanship. As it was necessary to get up on the beast and bring it down as quickly as possible, the horse was galloping very fast. The shooter carried the rifle in his right hand and, of course, the reins in his left. The horse didn't need much guiding, only perhaps if you were among a mob that was splitting up and you were deciding which would be the most advantageous to drop. It was then only a matter of the lightest touch on the reins: after you'd ridden a horse a few times and you got to know each other it became a perfect partnership.

But I always noticed that when I got on someone else's shooting horse he always appeared to be a bit restrained for the first few rides. He would undoubtedly be assessing the rider's ability to keep out of trouble, especially when a bull turned. Once he decided you knew what you were doing, he would gallop much more freely. A shooter would soon get to know when a bull was about to turn and charge. They would slow down and start swinging their heads from side to side, looking back at the approaching horseman. Then they would suddenly prop, turn and charge. I don't really know, but I suppose a big bull would weigh a ton.

243

This was the real test of how much faith the horse had in the rider. When the bull turned, it wasn't always necessarily knocked up. Mostly it had got to the stage where it wasn't going to run away any more, and when it charged it came very fast; the horse didn't need any guiding, I can tell you — it got out of the bull's way as quickly as possible. The next stage wasn't entirely to the horse's liking. It would fight for its head and though it knew its work I think it regarded the task as some form of insanity.

If I were galloping behind a bull I thought was about to turn, I would immediately steady my horse down. I would literally have my hands full. In all probability I would be in the process of reloading after the last shot; in my left hand I would have the reins and the rifle, flicking the breech open to expel the last shell, pulling a fresh cartridge from my belt, slipping it into the breach with the right hand. It was tricky.

When the bull props and turns it usually hesitates for a second before launching itself at its tormentor — sort of taking aim. This is a good thing, allowing the horseman to put some distance between himself and the enraged beast, to get himself settled into what you could call a working distance — about some twenty or thirty yards.

The buffalo, its adrenalin working overtime (I would think a mad buffalo bull has adrenalin in large quantities) would come like a shot out of a gun. I'd be talking to my horse, telling him not to worry: "just leave this part to me, you just watch where you're going, keep out of holes, don't stumble for Christ's sake . . ." He'd be fighting for his head, not at all keen on slowing down with a raging bull, murder in his heart, closing fast. This is when everything had to go right.

As the distance shortened I would be looking back over my shoulder. Closer and closer the bull came, until the horse's flying tail would be brushing its face. Leaning back I would fire into its head.

There were other times when a buffalo wasn't hit properly. If the bullet didn't hit the backbone it wouldn't go down. Then it became important for it to be killed; the skinning men coming along behind on foot could be at risk, though this was unlikely on the plains. They could see a long way and hear every shot, of course — if a bull was hit and didn't go down it was simply a matter of keeping a safe distance until a horseman came back and killed it. When a horseman finished his run he would ride back and have a good look at each buffalo, make sure it was safe and kill any that were wounded and hadn't gone down. The bulls with broken backs would be finished off either by the horseman or the foot shooter, then skinning would proceed.

I had more than ninety shot when I reckoned I should move camp. They were getting further and further away; I was riding long distances and returning to the camp late at night. Before Hunter left he had given me a rough sketch map showing the various camps, an estimate of the distances in between and what water was likely to be there. Waterholes were drying fast now and as far as I could see there weren't many that were permanent though most of them had wells.

To complete Hunter's contract I now had something more than 200 to get. The shooting didn't present any problems; there were plenty of buffalo and I guessed they'd be walking long distances from water looking for feed, which was starting to get scarce. But of course there weren't plenty handy to where I was camped — I had shot and driven them away.

I took a day off from shooting, with a guide and Hunter's map. Wherever I moved to I had to have camp water for washing hides and grass for the horses. A conference with my helpers hadn't yielded much more than "might be" and distances were mostly "little bit long way".

I found the map very difficult to work out. Some of the camps Hunter had marked seemed to be miles inside the Marrakai boundary. Sure, boundaries were very much a give-and-take affair but it appeared Hunter's was more take than give — which was okay if you could get away with it. In a 1000-square-mile property, four or five miles wasn't important. Finally I got it sorted out.

Hunter had marked north where south should have been and vice versa.

I rode off just as the sun was rising with one of the skinners who said he'd been with Hunter "four fella rain"; four or five years I judged.

After riding for about three hours I came to a camp that really impressed me. Buffalo were everywhere, there was a reasonable waterhole — stinking but reasonable — a good well with a windlass and some rough troughing made from hollow logs. I peered over the edge; the water seemed to be about eight feet from the surface, there was a dead snake that hadn't been able to get out. My guide assured me it was "good fella water". I guessed it was — without the snake, though.

The next important thing was grass for the horses — There was none; it had been eaten and trampled out by bufffalo, which effectively put that camp out of bounds. No grass, no horses: they wouldn't have stayed without any feed. A horse is no different from a man or any kind of an engine — no fuel, no go.

The next camp was another five miles, situated in a pocket. I was glad to see a good well-grassed plain; there was a long lagoon surrounded by paperbark trees, but it was completely dry. I rode across it; it was soft underfoot and the moisture had generated a good growth of grass. The camp was the usual collection of bark houses, nearby was a well with a windlass and hollow log troughs. In the distance I could see buffalo, there would be plenty within a radius of five or six miles. This would be my next camp.

Some distance away, sunlight bounced off a large quartz out-crop from which the camp took its name, White Rock.

Moving camp was a laborious two-day job. I sent down to the jetty for Moses and his offsider; they arrived with the dray loaded with a ton of salt and 1000 cartridges. Getting it across to the new camp and back took all day. The next day it was loaded with rations, swags, billycans, camp gear, didgeridoos and spears, plus lots of unidentifiable goods. Trailing along behind were lubras, dogs and half a dozen goats, an invaluable source of milk.

There were plenty of buffalo. I was comfortably averaging twelve or so a day, but they were low in condition and wouldn't gallop far before turning. I could see I would easily complete Hunter's contract so I didn't always take on a bull when it turned; with so many about it wasn't worth it.

The hides were starting to pile up and I could see I'd have the contract completed in another week. Shooting continued uneventfully — more or less, anyway. A skinner named Andy-Andy was kicked by a horse and broke his arm. I was fascinated the way his lubra and another woman splinted it with bark and hessian strips. It appeared to be a clean break between the elbow and wrist. No one seemed unduly concerned, but went about fixing it in a quiet, businesslike manner that impressed me. They cut up strips of bark, ripped up an old flour bag and got the arm straightened to bind the bark in place. Then they padded it with a layer of paperbark, which is almost as soft as cotton wool. His wife explained to me gravely that he wouldn't be able to go out with us for a while. To soften the blow she said he would be able to help with the hides in a day or so. I scratched my head and said, " 'spose he like." I didn't want to appear unco-operative.

The horse that kicked Andy-Andy was a grey called Swanee, a quiet old stager that wouldn't hurt a fly . . . unless it happened to be a bloody March fly drilling into him. It had me slightly puzzled. I was sure Andy hadn't done anything to provoke the horse: he never treated a horse badly, in fact very few of them did. Maybe he got in the way when the old fellow was being hit by a March fly, but there seemed to be something strange about it. I heard a casual remark the next day. I don't think I was supposed to hear; something to do with a Melville Island boy.

I forgot about it — or nearly. The next day I had fourteen bulls down and was doing some skinning with Bamboo Charlie. We were working on a bull some distance from the others so I said to Charlie, more to make conversation than anything, "Time Swanee kickim Andy-Andy — alla same what name? 'Im 'e no cranky bugger that Swanee."

247

"True boss, 'im 'e no cranky bugger that fella Nanto [horse]. Onefella man long Melville Island sing 'im Swanee, make 'im kick 'im."

Ah, I thought, now we're getting to the bottom of it — someone on Melville Island 100 miles or more away. Powerful stuff that sing-sing. "Alla same what name? What for Melville Island man sing 'im Swanee? 'e no like 'im Andy-Andy? Alla same what name?"

Charlie smiled at my ignorance — these white men never seem to understand.

"You no savee, eh? That fella lubra, Alice — 'e no belong Andy, man belong Alice stop long Melville Island, Andy steal 'im before, onefella rain before 'e steal 'im. This fella man 'im 'e strong long sing-sing, 'im 'e sing 'im Swanee make 'im kick 'im."

"I see," I said ... which I didn't, "by 'n by this man sing 'im more?"

"Me no savee," he said, "might be 'e sing 'im crocodile."

"Sing 'im crocodile, eh? Make 'im eat 'im?"

"Me tink 'im he try long crocodile, might be snake."

"Andy-Andy, 'im 'e worrit [worried]?" I asked.

Bamboo Charlie smiled and said "Before 'im 'e worrit, this time 'e get up strongfella sing-sing too. Mefella 'elp 'im. Thisfella boy Tiger belong you — 'im 'e 'elp 'im, Tiger strong long sing-sing."

This was news to me; you generally hear one way or another of their various attributes and different devil-devils, their particular demand for medical purposes. Some were very important men. I always thought Tiger was among the lower echelon, but you never really knew.

"Thisfella Tiger — 'im 'e 'elp 'im Andy-Andy long sing-sing, eh?"

"Ui [yes]."

"I see." I still didn't — not quite, anyway.

"Andy-Andy pay 'im Tiger belong 'elp'im long sing-sing?" (Tiger being from a different tribe — and a long way away at that — he wouldn't be doing it for tribal or kinship reasons.)

248

"No, 'e no pay 'im properly, Tiger 'e sleep long Alice twofella time one week." Greater love hath no man than this, I thought.

I couldn't help thinking it may have been a March fly after all.

I never did find out the final outcome, but guessed there'd be some powerful stuff flying backward and forward between Melville Island and the mainland. The didgeridoos were working overtime. I thought Tiger was starting to look decidedly weary; burning the candle at both ends ... and, the middle too, I expect.

A week later I had Hunter's contract completed. I shot twenty or so extra, which should take care of any rejects. Although I was inexperienced in the marketing side I thought they were a good lot of hides and had kept a close eye on the curing.

Moses, his bosun and another fellow, a deckhand I suppose, carted the last of them to the boat. I moved the camp back to the station headquarters and let the horses go for a spell, keeping two or three and my own in a paddock. I reckoned I'd better go to Darwin. Tiger would keep the horses together. There was the odd storm now and grass was beginning to grow; they wouldn't stray far while they had some decent grazing. The boat was loaded and I boarded her just before the high tide one morning.

Having a proprietorial interest in the hides put me into the world of big business and I thought I'd better find out how it worked, bearing in mind that in the very near future I expected to be shooting for myself. I wasn't sure what the next step was. The only European firm in Darwin, Jolley & Co, was Hunter's agent. I guessed there would be some paperwork to be attended to. Hunter had given me an outline of the terms of his contract; the price was fivepence per pound FOB Darwin. The entire shipment had to average sixty pounds dried weight. I'd weighted a few on an old pair of scales and, allowing for some inaccuracy, reckoned they were well up on the required condition. FOB stood for Free On Board, which meant the seller had to deliver to the ship's side; freight and other charges were the responsibility of the buyer. It all seemed fairly simple.

Sailing to Darwin was a very pleasant experience. We passed the mouth of the Adelaide River, various headlands, slipped between islands, and sailed into Darwin Harbour in the afternoon of the second day, anchoring among an assortment of pearling luggers and other craft.

I had been to Darwin before, but was now seeing it from a different angle. At the wharf a large steamer flying the Burns Philp house flag was busily discharging cargo. Darwin, what I could see of it, was sitting up on a cliff. I thought I recognised some of the buildings; the police station and a row of government offices.

A dinghy was lowered into the water, I was rowed ashore and landed between two careening pearling luggers lying on their sides. I climbed up a fairly steep hill until I came to Cavenagh Street; a crew boy followed behind balancing my swag on his head. I crossed the street and went on until I came to the Victoria Hotel, where I again booked a room — quite a lot of water had flowed under the bridge since my previous visit.

The next morning I called in on Jolley & Co, introducing myself to the manager, Jim Fawcett. He knew of me and my association with Hunter. Arrangements were made to pick up the hides and have them weighed. Jolleys was the agent for the buyers too, in fact it seemed the firm was the agent for just about everything and everyone. I guessed impartiality might be strained here and there.

There was no word from Hunter. Fawcett thought he'd probably be back on the next boat, since he'd just about have run out of money by then. I hoped there'd be some left for me . . . a prophetic thought as it turned out.

There wasn't much for me to do. I wandered back to the hotel and struck up a conversation with some of the occupants of the bar. Most of them seemed to know about me. I got to know a pearler, a drover, a couple of lads from one of the banks and one from the British Australian Telegraph Company.

In the afternoon I went to the Department of Lands to see some maps covering the country between the Mary and South Alligator Rivers and pondered over blank spaces, irregular lines and wandering creeks. A clerk said the maps weren't accurate; none of the area had been surveyed. I thought this might be an advantage.

The occupied country was all leasehold, marked with the names of the lessees; Hunter's name was shown, as were Freer and the two Hardys. I was informed that land could be taken up under a Grazing Licence, which was a kind of occupation permit. The annual rental was one shilling a square mile plus a one pound licence fee.

I made a sudden decision and ruled off a strip of land along Freer's southern boundary measuring twenty miles by five. I solemnly paid a clerk six pounds and he, with equal solemnity, issued an official receipt together with an impressive looking document titled Grazing Licence No 716. According to the preamble I was entitled to graze 100 head of stock per annum. It didn't say what kind of stock, and it didn't say what you couldn't do. I thought I might be able to improve on the stocking conditions.

I walked out into the blazing sunshine wondering what I had done. I'd always wanted independence but didn't realise at the time that this was the day I lost it.

I went to Jolleys store and after a yarn with Jim Fawcett arranged credit for up to 500 pounds.

CHAPTER 20

KAPALGA AND THE CALEDON BAY MASSACRE

I had been making quite a few friends in Darwin, including Evan and Oscar Herbert, sons of the late Judge Herbert. Tall, lean cattlemen, they owned Koolpinyah Station about twenty-five miles out of Darwin. Evan invited me to stay with them until Hunter returned, for which I was grateful.

The homestead, standing on a ridge overlooking a beautiful lagoon, was presided over by their mother and the late judge's sister. The few weeks I spent with them were among the most enjoyable I had experienced for some time and, they were among my best friends for many years.

When Evan was a small boy, his father was serving as a judge in Papua. While in the care of a nurse girl Evan was playing on the beach when he was shot by a native who, presumably, had been the recipient of one of his father's judgments. The bullet lodged in his jaw and he was very fortunate he wasn't killed. The wound never really healed and he suffered continually from severe headaches. Some years later he and I were out riding on Koolpinyah when he suddenly gave a mighty cough and a piece of bullet shot from his mouth. From that moment the headaches left him and the wound healed completely.

The boat was due from Sydney and, anticipating Hunter's return, Evan took me into Darwin in his truck. Early the following morning I was at the wharf as the *Marella* nudged her way to her berth. I could see Hunter at the rail, looking as though he'd been in a good paddock — he must have put on a couple of stone. He waddled down the gangway, grasped my hand and we exchanged greetings. He enquired anxiously how the shooting had turned out.

I told him I had completed the contract with twenty or so over. He was visibly relieved. He said he'd got through a lot more money than he had anticipated and I felt this didn't augur too well for Tom Cole. I was right. When I left him he gave me £40, saying he'd make the balance up as soon as he could.

There was a saying in the bush that was often applied in similar situations "it looks like there's a bit of Kathleen Mavourneen about this" — *Kathleen Mavourneen* being an Irish song with a line that went: "It may be for years and it may be forever!". That's the way it turned out. I was thankful he'd paid for the Guild horses before he went to Sydney, and that I'd forwarded what I owed on the deal.

As soon as the country was dry enough to ride, I took my leave and headed back to Pine Creek. The little mining town was in full throat, most of the decibels coming from the pub. A government-induced mining boom had rejuvenated the country. Largesse was being scattered around in an attempt to get unemployed out of the cities and at the same time give the mining industry a boost.

It seemed you didn't have to be a miner to qualify, but I suppose it helped. The Mines Department was doing a roaring trade issuing Miners Rights at five shillings each. Fortunes were being made and lost, the former by the Collins and Pitt Street "miners" and the latter, in perhaps a more limited way, by the men on the field doing the hard yakka.

One of the first men I ran into was Stan Brown. He had his camp along the creek not far from mine and he hailed me enthusiastically. "I'm looking for someone to give me a haircut — you'll do!"

Haircutting was an almost compulsory qualification for a bushman; there wouldn't have been a professional barber in the whole of the Territory at that time. As an inducement Brown said:

"I've got a bottle of rum at my camp to help us through the ordeal."

To keep his mind from the damage I was probably doing to his hair I gave him a rundown on my previous year's activities. I told him of my experience with Hunter and how I'd taken up some country on the Alligator River.

"I'm sure I can help you," he said, "I haven't forgotten that you broke in some horses for me when I was very hard-up and you didn't ask me for a penny; I appreciated that. Come out to Dorisvale and we'll have a look through my horse paddock."

After the hair massacre we saddled a horse each and rode up to the hotel. The shade tree used to tether horses was cluttered up with two men having a fight: as we dismounted they obligingly moved away. It wasn't a very interesting fight, so we made our way to the bar.

Sheer bedlam ruled inside the hotel; miners seemed to be an entirely different type from the bushmen I was used to. Stan and I made our way over to a corner of the bar where he recognised another cattleman, Jim Hart, who owned Claravale Station. I recalled that he was the son of Matt Hart of Lewin Springs, who was Webb/Whelan's first choice.

We talked mainly about my next venture. In the course of the conversation Hart suggested I call into his place on the way back from Dorisvale; he thought he might be able to help me with the horses too. I was among friends. Stan and I packed up the next day and left for Dorisvale.

It was a good two-day ride to Brown's place and we reached the homestead just before sundown. The next day I had a look at the dray. Stan said I could have it for five pounds. I didn't know much about drays — there didn't seem to be much to know. The iron tyres were a bit loose, but that was easily fixed with a bit of wedging. The harness looked rough and mildewed, but I reckoned I could get it into shape.

We mustered for three days. After putting forty or fifty horses through the yard I took twelve which, with what I already had, brought my plant up to nineteen. Among them was a nuggety creamy horse I intended making into a harness horse, but he had other ideas. I yoked them up early in the morning. The unbroken youngster, though he had been handled and would lead, and seemed fairly tractable, had never been in harness in his life. The other two were fresh and hadn't been worked for some time. Partly to do something useful, and partly to give the horses a load, I thought I'd cart a load of firewood. The creamy horse was giving trouble right from the start but I had him tied back and long reins hooked to his bit.

They took off and in about five minutes flat smashed up the whole outfit. They just bounced from one ironwood tree to another, then to a couple of antbeds . . . and I had no dray. And no horses, either. I have an entry in my diary dated Wednesday June 29: 'Horses bolted with dray and smashed it up. The only part left intact is the wheels and axle'. I sat disconsolately on a log and surveyed the wreckage strewn across the paddock.

I saddled a horse and rounded up the runaways; at least the harness was in surprisingly good shape. The trace chains were broken but I reckoned I could fix them up easily enough. I took off the gear, turned the horses out into the paddock and went back to what was left of my dray — a horse of a different colour, you might say.

I fossicked around in Brown's toolshed and found some yard-building gear; he had pretty well all I needed. I cut bloodwood saplings and shaped a new pair of shafts with an adze. I cut bigger trees and squared them with the adze for crossmembers. Part of the broken frame I threw on a fire to recover iron fittings, and some of the floorboards I was able to use again. I worked for four days and half the nights by the light of a hurricane light. Five days later I recorded: "Mustered horses this morning in readiness for another start".

I really had my hands full. I was on my own — Stan had taken a mob of bullocks to Pine Creek — and apart from the dray I also had nineteen horses, some of which were unbroken. I certainly couldn't manage all that lot on my own. I took all the spare horses to Lewin Springs and paddocked them in Hart's horse paddock. I went back to Dorisvale and took the dray to Pine Creek, which took five days. I then went back to Hart's place and brought the rest of the horses.

Gradually I got myself shipshape. I sold four horses to a Russian who, for some peculiar reason (at least *I* thought it was peculiar) wanted to become a buffalo hunter. After seeing him in action around horses and talking to him I came to the conclusion that it was about the last job on earth he should take on. He ended up getting bushed and nearly died of thirst. Anyway, his money was what I needed. They were four good horses, not my best, but above average.

Jack Sagabiel, a half-caste stockman, joined me, then an ex black tracker Nichol Peter with his wife named Rosie who had a youngster "at foot". Another fellow arrived, a friend of Peter's — Paddy he said his name was — he put himself on the staff without consulting me.

I started a bit of careful horse trading. I'd heard about a miner who had an outlaw of some kind and was looking for someone to unload him on to. I ran him to earth and he happily sent off a boy to bring up the outlaw for my inspection. He turned out to be quite a good sort of a black gelding. I gave the miner three pounds for him, saddled him up and rode him there and then. He didn't buck too bad; he was a bargain. I was curious to know how and why the miner bought him in the first place. The how part was easy — he was drunk. He didn't know why. I bought two more from a Chinese: they weren't much in the way of horseflesh, but they were in good condition and would carry hides.

I was just about ready to go. I had twenty-five pounds left, which wasn't much good to me out on the Alligator River. I put it in an envelope with a note to Dick Guild, asking him to let me have whatever horses he could spare, giving it to Sagabiel with instructions to take it to Guild's place. I knew I could depend on Dick for something. Sagabiel would catch me long before I reached the Alligator — I'd be travelling at a snail's pace with the dray. I should have had more sense, of course.

I left Pine Creek just as the sun was rising. I had a dray loaded with rations and equipment, twenty-three horses, two native horse tailers, a lubra and one piccaninny. The next day I got to the Mary River. The crossing was deep and badly rutted, steep going in and steeper pulling out with heavy cane grass. It took nearly all the next day working on the crossing.

I camped on Gerowie Creek, below Goodparla Station home-stead, the next night. From here the road (such as it was) cut out and I would be travelling through trackless bush. Without the dray it would have been easy, but I guess I'd be cutting down a lot of trees before I got on to the plains.

Sagabiel should catch me up in a few days. I intended leaving him with the dray and riding on ahead to establish a shooting camp and make a start. A week later I got to Jim Jim. The harness horses were buggered; I'd come through a lot of loose sand, so I took a couple of days' spell, hoping to see Sagabiel before I went on. He was well overdue.

Paddy suggested we ride over to what he called the Goose Camp; we'd be sure to find some boys there whom he said had been in buffalo camps. I thought I might as well be idle as doing nothing; Peter said he'd go out and spear some fish.

The Goose Camp turned out to be a huge swamp into which Jim Jim Creek flooded. There weren't that many blacks about, but a lot of humpies — at times it must have been a fairly big camp. It would have been perhaps ten miles or more around the swamp, which still had plenty of water; it was mostly covered with waterlilies so I judged it to be fairly shallow. Geese were there in millions, landing, taking off and just paddling around sticking their heads into the water. The din of their squawking was almost deafening. The most interesting feature was the goose-killing that was going on: I'd never seen anything like it in my life.

The entire lagoon was ringed by huge paperbark trees that were very tall, probably more than a hundred feet in height. Geese were flying in continuously in flocks of anything from ten to twenty, skimming the treetops and planing down to the water. What took my eye immediately were three or four lubras at the foot of the paperbarks. They were hopping around with delight, pouncing on half-crippled geese that thudded to the ground, wringing their necks and flinging them to a pile nearby.

I looked up for the source of this supply of game and to my amazement, standing up in the topmost branches and swaying crazily, were three naked Aborigines, their feet planted on two or three cross-sticks stuck in forks of the branches. Because of the foliage I couldn't see very clearly but as the birds skimmed the treetops the trio let fly with short sticks. They were so close to their targets they didn't have to be exceptional marksmen, but they certainly had to be outstanding acrobats.

We tethered our horses and I walked over to the scene of operations. As far as I could see, none of the birds was killed outright; an odd one or two fell out into the water, and some managing to flap their way to freedom. While the four women were catching geese they also collected any of the throwing sticks that were handy, flinging them toward the foot of a paperbark. The sticks were all pretty well the same length — about a foot and a half. I picked one up and examined it. The bark had been stripped off and a bit of work had gone into shaping them — not much, however: mostly the ends were thick and knobbly.

Very soon the hunters came down from their eyrie; they had run out of ammunition. Jabbering away and grinning hugely they walked around, picking up what few sticks the lubras had missed. They took the sticks to a fallen tree laying half-submerged and lined them up along the log where the water was about ankle-deep. When this was finished to their satisfaction they walked over to me.

I knew what was coming, "Boss, you got tobacco?" I always carried a few sticks in my saddle bag; it was the best currency in

258

that country. "Little bit," I replied cautiously, "no got plenty."

"Mefella 'ungry long tobacco."

"Youfella like work?" They looked a bit disappointed at that, scratching the ground with their toes while giving the matter some thought.

This was the time of the year when game was most plentiful. These white men always seemed to be crazy about working when there was no need for it. Then the stumpy bright-eyed fellow who seemed to be a leader came up with a solution. "By 'n by," he said. "Ui, by 'n by," the other two chorused and then, as though that matter was disposed of satisfactorily, "mefella 'ungry long tobacco."

I could see I wasn't going to get any recruits here, the country was literally a cornucopia.

"Youfella give me one goose, me givem you one stick tobacco." Then the haggling started. The sun was starting to get low so I settled for one goose for two sticks and bought four. Paddy came to some sort of private arrangement and scored a couple for himself. We gutted them there and then, Paddy taking a piece of vine from a tree nearby and tying them by their necks. I slung two over the pommel of my saddle, Paddy carried two in front and two behind and we headed back to our camp. Peter had four barrumundi and Rosie had three turtles, a possum and a fat file snake. I could see the point of those fellows at the Goose Camp — you'd have to be crazy to want to work.

I hung the geese for the night and took one barramundi for the evening meal. Rosie cooked it on the coals while the billy was boiling and I asked her about the snake. It was called a file snake because of its rough, sandpaper skin; they lived mainly in the water and I knew they were regarded as a delicacy by the blacks. Rosie asked if I'd like to try some, describing it as "number one tucker". She went over to their camp and brought back a piece on a large leaf. I was a bit disappointed; the flesh was white and firm and a bit like fish, but nowhere as good as barramundi.

My harness horses were looking very tired and dejected. I tried to cheer them up, telling them we didn't have too much further to go, but it didn't seem to have much effect. They were the ones doing all the work. There had been some hard pulling and I had a good load, most of which was salt for curing hides.

I took another day's spell for the horses' sake and in the morning rode down the river, I wanted to get some idea of the country ahead of me. I soon came to plains that stretched away into the shimmering distance. Over to the east I could see a hazy line of mangroves marking the South Alligator River. After riding for three hours we came to a large lagoon with a huge Leichhardt pine standing at one end.

The plains had the appearance of good level travelling but in reality they were very rough; I could see it was going to be hard on the dray horses. Next morning I got a crack-of-dawn start. It was terribly rough; rougher than I anticipated. The dray got bogged in a gutter and had to be unloaded before it was pulled out. When we got to the Leichhardt, the harness horses were completely done in.

The sensible course was to leave the dray for the time being. I filled the pack bags and, leaving Peter and Rosie headed for Kapalga, reaching it late in the afternoon. Kapalga would be my depot; it was an old buffalo hunter's camp now occupied by Charlie Burns, a peanut planter who had taken up a square mile under a special agricultural lease.

Charlie was a former miner who decided to go into peanuts when the Administration offered encouraging terms and free land. There didn't seem to be any exacting conditions attached to the terms of the leases; as far as I could make out most of the lessees took the opportunity to acquire a home for nothing. In Charlie's case he came to Kapalga to retire. There was the nucleus of a camp which, though extremely dilapidated and built mainly of bark, didn't require much work to make it habitable. I'm quite sure he never had any intention of planting peanuts — as an old Digger from World War I, he was more than happy to call it a day. I found him a very good bloke, and a useful fund of information on the surrounding country, my future neighbours, the blacks and a few other matters.

He was pleased to see me turn up, for he was right out of rations. While there was no way he'd starve in this land of plenty, there were a few items that made life just that much better. He was dying for a good billy of tea, he said, after the preliminaries were done with. He called to a lubra to stoke the smouldering fire and we soon had a billy boiling. I saw that he was smoking and said, "Well, you don't seem to be out of tobacco."

"No fear of that," he replied, "I grow my own."

After we had finished the billy of tea and some roast pork from Charlie's larder, together with damper from mine, he showed me his tobacco curing setup in a lean-to at the back of the kitchen. The smoke from the cooking operations was diverted into his smokehouse and bunches of tobacco leaf hung from rafters. The next process was a little more complicated. The leaf was damped down and rammed into a shallow box, topped by a board held down with large stones. He took the top off. It looked a dank, dark sticky mess to me but when I smelt it it seemed quite pleasant: like a cigar. He told me the recipe consisted of treacle, saltpetre and overproof rum. I could smell the treacle but the smell of overproof rum seemed elusive: I asked him how much rum was in it. I should have known better. He told me he started off with a couple of bottles of OP rum but thought it was a terrible waste to pour it into tobacco — "I drank the rum and breathed on it!"

I had five packs and had to get the rest of my supplies to Kapalga. Charlie was most helpful; he had two packs and unhesitatingly lent them to me. With the exception of a couple of hundredweight of salt, two trips were sufficient to get everything to Kapalga. Charlie offered to bring the salt down within the next couple of days, for which I was grateful.

Burns' assortment of shacks and humpies, though comfortable enough by a bushman's standards, were built mostly from the ubiquitous paperbark. The house he occupied had a corrugated iron roof and was partially enclosed with a mixture of bark and corrugated iron. Kapalga Lagoon was a pleasant stretch of water sprinkled with water lilies. Between the buildings and the lagoon there was a well and I noted with approval a good horseyard, which would come in handy.

The South Alligator River, about a mile away, had a reasonable jetty built of bush timber. August was now beginning and I was anxious to get started. I left Kapalga, taking as much as I could in my packs and headed to a creek Burns had described to me, my cavalacade following along behind. Fortunately Rosie could ride; I found a quiet pony for her and her piccaninny sat on a bundle of paperbark on the pommel.

I made camp on a creek called Flying Fox. In my diary I noted, "Large numbers of buffalo tracks". I shot two the next day but lost several; I was having trouble finding a suitable shooting horse. The next day's entry reads: "The heaviest hides I have ever seen, it was with great difficulty three of us lifted them on the pack horse". The following day I recorded: "Cracker is the best horse for shooting so far". I shot three bulls, and noted that the scrub was very thick; it was hard galloping.

The next day calamity struck. Monday, August 8: "Wounded bull jammed me in the scrub, horned Cracker, his entrails came out". It looked terrible, but I had to give him a chance. I collected two or three halter shanks — strong greenhide ropes — made up a collar rope and dropped him on to his side. His entrails came out further. Peter and Paddy carried water and I washed his guts as best I could. I pulled some twine from a filthy bag then cut a small sharp stick. We managed to get his guts back in. Peter holding them in while I was preparing my makeshift surgical equipment. I gathered the skin together and cut a small hole with a razor sharp skinning knife. I poked the string through the hole, gathering the skin together and tying it. God, he must have been suffering, the poor brute: I was feeling bad about it, too. I put six stitches in before I ran out of string, but it seemed to be holding fairly well. We eased him to his feet and left him. He looked terrible; I bet he was feeling worse.

Two days later he turned up at the camp. The diary entry is very brief. "Cracker turned up at camp this morning, ten miles from where he was horned. I think he will live, altho' very sick". He did live, and of that I am justly proud; animals have tremendous powers of recuperation.

In the meantime, I had been giving a lot of thought to the elusive Jack Sagabiel. My hopes of seeing him trot into my camp one evening driving ten or twelve horses had diminished to vanishing point. My thoughts were dominated by what I would do with the bastard when I caught up with him . . . if ever. Lying awake under my mosquito net in the still and silent watches of the night, I had no difficulty devising suitable retribution.

During the day I had plenty of other matters to occupy my time and thoughts. Not being familiar with the country was a handicap. Where I was camped on Flying Fox Creek wasn't a good area for my horses; feed was sparse and what there was was of poor quality. They were losing condition rapidly.

I also had to find myself another shooting horse after the loss of Cracker. I tried a chestnut horse called Stockings, who soon made it clear he wasn't going to have anything to do with that stupid caper. The next I tried, a bay called Gambler, turned out to be very good after a couple of days. I found that most horses, particularly if they'd done some stockwork, weren't scared of the buffalo. The report of the rifle going off close to their heads must have been frightening.

I always tried to follow the beast exactly behind it if it were possible, which frequently wasn't in timbered country. Following it I reckoned it would be more difficult for the buffalo to judge how close the horseman was, which would have to be some kind of advantage. And I can tell you any kind of advantage was worth having. Frequently, in the timber, I'd find I was up on to the beast and had to wait for a break in the scrub to give me room to swerve as I fired.

At this point the horseman would be up in the stirrups. When he got to the point when he was about to fire he would take his horse to one side; the rifle would be pointing downward, probably at the same angle as the horse's shoulder. While it would be impossible to miss the buffalo (at any rate I imagine it would), it was by no means impossible to miss the backbone.

It was getting toward the end of August and I wasn't doing anywhere near as well as I had expected. I was getting three or four buffalo a day; one day I got eight, which cheered me temporarily. A lot of my time was taken up packing salt, since the dray was still at the Leichhardt.

A dog stiffener turned up — Jim Howarth, who hadn't been very successful in his chosen profession. Since leaving Brock's Creek a couple of months earlier he managed to poison three dingoes. I immediately gave him a job pulling the dray down from up the river: I had to start thinking about getting some hides in to the jetty. The *Maroubra* was due in about a week, "give or take a month", Charlie Burns said. I was getting low on rations and a few other things.

A boy named Spider turned up with a lubra called Curlew and I immediately gave them jobs. Howarth arrived with the dray; the same day I shot ten bulls and the next day, eleven. Howarth told me of a half-caste camped at Kapalga who wanted a job. I knew of Yorky Billy by repute. He was the son of Yorky Mick, an old Yorkshireman who lived anywhere between Pine Creek and Oenpelli. Howarth knew him fairly well and said he was a very good horseman who took a job in a buffalo camp when the fancy struck him — which wasn't very often. Jim said Yorky Billy would be staying with Charlie Burns for a few days and would then come across and talk to me — probably out of curiosity. He was wondering who this "new bloke" was.

The next day Gambler got staked. Galloping through scrub, a sharp stick went into a muscle just below the shoulder, putting him out of action for a while. Again I was lucky; the second horse I tried, a grey mare called Cloud, came good.

Then everything started to fall apart. A bay mare, Pussycat, became sick, Rocket and Bluebell were so low in condition I had to let them go, a mare called Snowy had a premature foal that died, so of course I had to let her go. Another mare, Dolly, one of the harness horses, got bitten by a snake, most probably a taipan. I had seen a couple — there's no more deadly snake in the world — and it killed her. Then poor little Pussycat died. I was getting desperate and badly needed more horses.

Yorky Billy duly arrived, mounted on a good-looking bay mare and driving four horses, two of which carried packs. Trailing along behind on a pony was his current wife. He unpacked and made a camp for himself on the other side of the creek. I called to him to join me in a feed; I had Yorky Billy's immediate future already mapped out for him.

After a meal I had a serious talk with him. Without much persuasion he agreed to run my camp for me while I went to Dick Guild's place for horses. I stayed for another day to give Billy a rundown on various aspects of my camp, the horses and gear. The next morning I left, arriving eight days later at Guild's homestead on the Edith River. Together with three horses I bought from one of his neighbours, I left on my return journey with eleven. All I had to do was get back to my camp, make some money and pay for them. In seven days I was back.

York Billy had done well; there was a large stack of hides at the camp. We rode out on to the plains and shot nine bulls and a big cow. I also noted: "Cloud fell today — must trim her feet". The next day I pulled all her shoes off and shod her.

In October the clouds started to build up and the heat became intense. Storms were about, heralding the approach of the wet season. I had to make sure I wasn't caught. The next week was occupied with carting hides and building paperbark shelters over them. On November 21, the *Maroubra* tied up at the jetty.

Jack Hales had some sensational news. Two pearling luggers,

the *Raf* and the *Myrtle Olga*, had put in to Caledon Bay round the Arnhem Land coast and the entire crews had been speared. Hales said he thought it had happened about the end of September; the news had taken some time to filter through to Darwin. He said six or seven Japs had been killed but it was all pretty garbled. The luggers had been towed back to Darwin.

Caledon Bay, even today, is one of the most remote spots in Australia — or the world, for that matter. This was the real Arnhem Land coast. We discussed it while my hides were being loaded. It was too late in the year for a patrol to go out: it was a long way and not much was known of the country. We reckoned it would be March or April before anything could be done.

There was one man knew all about the spearing of the five Japanese at Caledon Bay, and that was Fred Gray — he was there when it happened. An Englishman of an adventurous nature, he had an old pearling lugger, the *Northam*, and was engaged in trepanging along the Arnhem Land coast. He also took any freight jobs and brought me five tons of salt to Kapalga.

There had been a drop in the mother-of-pearl shell market and quite a few of the pearling luggers had turned their attention to diving for trepang, which had survived the ravages of the depression and was easy to recover, lying in shallow waters. Trepang is the Malay name for bêche de mer — the sea slug, and there was a ready market in China where it was regarded as a delicacy.

Fred Gray was already established when the *Raf* and *Myrtle Olga* anchored in Caledon Bay. There were six Japanese and twelve Aboriginal crew members. They told Gray they were on their way to Groote Eylandt to start trepanging. From their remarks they were certainly impressed with Fred's stock of trepang. Before they left they asked Fred if he had any objection to their fishing in that area in the event of Groote Eylandt proving unsatisfactory. Magnanimously Fred agreed, saying there was more than enough for the three boats.

They left for Groote Eylandt, but returned three days later: their crews had mutinied and refused to go to Groote, claiming they would all be murdered. This was a lot of nonsense; there was a well-established mission on Groote Eylandt and the natives were very friendly. But as later events indicated, they were frightened of any bush blacks.

They made camp close to Gray, setting up their smokehouses and boiling vats alongside his and it was then that Fred realised their fear of the local people was very real. For some reason they beat up a son of Wonggu — a serious mistake, because Wonggu, with a number of wives and lots of children, was the clan leader.

From then on they seemed to compound their mistakes to the point where they were being almost suicidal. In order to discourage the natives from approaching their camp, they fired shots over their heads, which probably triggered off the massacre. The blacks believed they were being deliberately shot at — what else could they be expected to think?

There was a low spring tide on September 17, the morning of the spearing. Fred was out on the reefs, about a mile away but near enough to hear the commotion. He made toward the shore: there were shots and he could see spears being thrown. They were attacking a dinghy and he saw one of the Japs fall into the water, several spears in his body. A larger number of blacks were on board the *Raf* and *Myrtle Olga*, busy unloading the boats' stores into a dinghy. On shore more shots were being fired, there was general pandemonium, another dinghy was being rowed over to the luggers. The occupants called on Fred to join them. His half-caste boy, Ramon Arabino, said the blacks were killing all the Japanese. He could see a hail of spears on the beach; even the women were taking part. This can probably be explained by a particularly stupid action on the part of the Japanese — for some reason they locked some women in their smokehouse.

Wonggu was of the Balamumu clan and their contact with outsiders, whether European or Japanese, was minimal. Fred Gray maintained that the killings were nothing to do with any sexual

267

transgressions, which to me seems doubtful; in any event, confining the women was an extraordinary piece of insanity.

Once the killing started there was no stopping it. One of the Japanese got away, but he was exceptionally lucky. He ran into the bush with a number of Goulburn Island crew boys. After several weeks they turned up at Millingimbi Mission which, in a straight line, is 200 hundred miles away. Though the Jap was carried towards the end, it was a remarkable feat of endurance. They had no supplies of any description and lived off the land.

After the killings, the blacks looted the luggers. Gray was in his dinghy when the massacre began and gathered up his own crew members who were working the reef for trepang. Shots were still being fired and as Fred was fairly sure all the Japanese were dead, he thought he was under attack.

He watched as all the cargo was carried into the bush and everyone disappeared. With Ramon Arabino he rowed over to the luggers. Everything that was edible had been taken. It was nearly sundown when he thought it safe to walk along the beach in case there may have been any survivors. The first body he came to was at the water's edge, and appeared to have floated ashore. Some distance away he found two more. He and his boys dug a large hole into which they put the three bodies and covered them. A fourth which was some distance away they buried alone. By then it was well into the night.

The following morning they found another body, which they buried where they found it. They followed the tracks of the sixth Japanese and the crew boys establishing that they got away. Gray then put a skeleton crew aboard the two luggers and convoyed them to Darwin with the *Northam*.

CHAPTER 21

ANOTHER SPEARING AND MORE MISADVENTURES

T he *Maroubra* sailed with 251 of my buffalo hides, and so ended my first year. When they were weighed they averaged seventy-two pounds, a weight I never bettered in the coming years. I had thirty-one horses, among them two good shooting horses, Gambler and Cloud. I had a hundred square miles of country I intended extending, a fully equipped buffalo-hunting outfit . . . but very little money. I paid off the camp and squared my numerous debts. What was left was not difficult to count: I had five eighths of bugger-all. But I was an established buffalo hunter.

I now had to do some survival planning. The approaching wet season would end somewhere between March and mid-April, but the country wouldn't be dried out sufficiently to ride until June at the earliest. I had seven months in front of me to live on my accumulated fat, as the saying goes. It was a very thin layer.

The swamp country of the coast was no place to stay. I stacked most of my gear in one of Burns' sheds, took three packs, all the horses and headed back to Guild's place. Peter and his family came with me. We got to the Edith River, where Peter and his tribe went on a walkabout, which began and ended at Katherine.

The thought of being idle for the next six or seven months frightened me, and I knew it would be something in the nature of a miracle to get work of almost any kind, except perhaps horse-breaking. Dick Guild had a good paddock and I was welcome to leave some of my horses. I put in a week straightening up my gear and shoeing.

I took five of my best horses and rode away. The first night I camped on Vampire Creek; the next day I reached the Katherine River, eight or nine miles below the township. The river was running strongly and I had to cross it, which meant swimming for sure.

I camped and warned my horses they were going to have to swim tomorrow. I didn't mention crocodiles — it always seemed to me there was very little danger when creeks or rivers were running strongly, what few attacks there were seemed to be in quiet reaches and waterholes.

I looked at the northern sky. It was clear. If there were no rain up the river there was a chance it would drop, but there was no way it would drop low enough to ford. The only advantage would be that the current would slow down. I wrote in my diary: "Katherine River half a mile wide, camped". The next day it dropped three feet and the weather looked good, so I risked another day.

A few hundred yards up the river I had noticed a wisp of smoke; someone was camped there. I didn't give it much thought beyond vaguely wondering who it might be. When I rode past, however, there was no one about: a tent fly was rigged and a campfire smouldered. The next morning I mustered my horses, brought them to the camp then rode down to the river. It had dropped another couple of feet, so I decided not to trust providence any longer: this morning I would cross.

On my way back I rode up to the camp I had looked at yesterday. A half-caste lad of about fourteen or fifteen was busy around his fire, four horses were rounded up. I guessed he was looking after them for someone.

"Who does this camp belong to?"

"Jack Sagabiel."

"Jack Sagabiel?" I whispered, half to myself. "Jack Sagabiel!"

"Ui."

I could hardly believe my good fortune. "There is a God after all," I said to myself. I sat on my horse for a moment or so, deciding what to do next, which caused the half-caste lad some discomfort.

"You savee me?"

He shook his head. After another brief silence I said, "Well, I'm Tom Cole." I let that sink in; I could see my name was enough to throw a scare into him. The story was well known. Dick Guild had spread it around and I believe Sagabiel himself had dropped enough to verify it when he had a few drinks aboard.

I didn't waste any time. I told him to saddle a horse and he put a bridle on the bay mare without any hesitation. "Okay," I said, "we'll take these horses over to my camp."

Before I had gone down to look at the river I had made everything ready to start; it was only a matter of throwing on the packs. We drove all the horses down to the river. With a couple of flicks of my stockwhip they walked in and started to swim. We were soon across and climbing up the bank on the other side. I didn't bother looking back; I expect the boy would have walked into Katherine and told Sagabiel the bad news. I hope he did, anyway. Four horses and a saddle by no means squared the account, but I was lucky to have got that much.

When I got up the bank I rounded up the horses and unhooked the packbags. Some water had got in, but the important items in my rations were well protected with canvas bags. I camped early so the pack saddles and riding saddles could dry: The linings, stuffed with horsehair, were sodden.

I was now able to take stock of my latest acquisition. The bay mare was a good type of stock horse, another bay and a chestnut were quite ordinary and the grey mare was obviously a pack horse. The riding saddle was in good condition . . . I could put it to good use.

When I got to the King, it was running strongly; almost exactly two years ago I had stood on the bank with George Fordham waiting for it to fall. I crossed without any trouble; my horses were becoming accomplished swimmers. Again I camped early and did some drying out. The next creek of any consequence, Limestone, was saddle-flap deep.

It rained all the next day and I camped on Native Cat Creek. On the following day I rode up to Willeroo Station homestead in pouring rain: The wet season had really set in. It was Christmas Eve and I was glad to have a roof over my head.

It poured again on Christmas Day, but it didn't matter. In my forward planning I had endeavoured to take into account every contingency, which included Christmas. I had a few bottles of rum in my packs; I was doubly welcome.

Bill Crowson was the Willeroo manager, having sold his droving plant and settled down to the more sedentary occupation of managing a 4000-square-mile station for Vesteys. There was Jack Ryan, whom I had known for some time, and Harry the cook who had fashioned a plum duff of imposing dimensions. We were gathered on the manager's verandah when Crowson said to Jack Ryan: "Send a boy down to Snowy's camp and tell him to come up for dinner."

Snowy was a well-known bushman I had never met. Ryan said: "You'll like Snowy, Tom; he's a real bloody character. Some of the things he comes out with I could piss myself laughing; he once told me that there was royal blood in his family — he had a cousin who was a queen!"

He arrived soon after with a very attractive lubra who appeared to be about sixteen or seventeen. All eyes followed her as she modestly took herself off to the end of the verandah. Her mammary glands were of majestic proportions. She sat down quietly crooning corroboree songs that sounded quite melodious.

Snowy was certainly entertaining. I guessed he'd had an above average education. His surname was supposed to be Smith; I gathered he'd had an earlier one (not Smith, though) and a wife somewhere, too; not Smith either. Not uncommon. He told us he'd won Daisy, the lubra, in a poker game from a bloke who was known as the Bull Roarer. He said Daisy told him afterwards she had "sung" the cards to make sure Snowy could win. He said he thought he'd take up poker professionally.

He had a racehorse and was still licking his wounds from the last Katherine race meeting. He explained that he was a bloody good horse, though. "He must be; it took eight horses to beat him." There were nine horses in the race.

It was a pleasant day and one I shall always remember. When we went to our bunks the throaty beat of didgeridoos keeping time to a thousand-year-old corroboree wafting across the night breeze from a nearby Aboriginal camp. I hoped they weren't rainmaking.

I had another day's spell. The weather was clearing a bit but I knew that wouldn't last for long. The next day I left for Delamere, another of Vesteys places run as an outstation of Willeroo. It was seventy miles from there to Victoria River Downs. I unpacked on the bank of the Wickham River, half a mile from the station, on New Year's Day.

Two days later I headed for Limbunya where, to my great relief (and no doubt the great relief of my horses), I got some breaking. There were thirty-one youngsters that I made spin out to seven weeks. I had no desire to go chasing around the country any further, and I wasn't losing sight of the three pounds a week in addition to the contract price of twenty-five shillings a head.

The wet season had pretty well run its course when I got my packs out for the return. I unloaded the Sagabiel grey pack horse to a travelling stockman who was heading for the Kimberleys — it was the right direction. I got a mule he told me was a "real bastard to catch". He was right, but I fixed it with a few bags of sand in addition to the fairly heavy pack load. When it got into camp it would walk up to me to get its load off; at night I hobbled it short.

Again I camped on the Wickham River on my way back. Tas Fitzer from the Depot Police Post was there buying horses for yet another patrol into the Fitzmaurice country. The previous year

273

Fred Don and Bill McCann from the Brock's Creek police station had taken a patrol out looking for the elusive Nemarluk who, since the *Ouida* spearings had added two prospectors, Stephens and Cook, to his tally. He was blamed for it, anyway. It was awful country; ti-tree and mangrove swamps. They saw neither hide nor hair of him and to add to their woes one of their pack horses was taken by a crocodile while crossing the river. After eight weeks they ran out of rations and battled back to Brock's Creek with a consolation prize: they had accidentally picked up Marragin, who was supposed to have speared Freddy Brooks. He was discharged for lack of evidence.

Fitzer then went out with Bul Bul, the best tracker in the north, and Nemarluk felt the cold grip of handcuffs. He was duly sentenced to ten years. Some of his fellow countrymen who were brought in as witnesses had no hesitation in testifying against him; though the interpreter these same men asked to go to jail with him, saying they would not expect any pay. (This, however, was refused.) Three months later Nemarluk walked away from a road gang working outside the jail. He was soon back where he started — so were the police. Fitzer was justifiably annoyed, and was getting ready for another expedition.

As soon as I heard he was buying horses I immediately thought of unloading the mule on to him. I found him at the station store getting rations and asked if he'd be interested in a mule, a good one — a good weight carrier, I emphasised. Fitzer had one look at him and wrote me out a government warrant for ten pounds. I was glad to see the back of the bastard.

I left the next day, which was just as well. I heard later the mule was seen galloping through Jasper's Gorge with a tracker hard on its heels. He never did catch up with it: I think he had a fall or his horse went lame or something. A drover picked him up a week or so later. Some time later I ran into one of Tas Fitzer's fellow policemen, Fred Don, who advised me to steer clear of Fitzer for a while. "He'll bloody well murder you over that mule deal. You swore he was a quiet mule, talk about a man smoking at the arse — there were streaks of blue flame coming out of Tas's backside!" It was probably a year or more before I ran into Tas again. We had a drink together and he was quite affable; the subject of mules didn't come up.

At the end of April I was back at Guild's place, gearing up for the shooting season. I knew what it was all about now, what stores and supplies I would need, how to arrange hide contracts and shipping. My shopping list seemed to go on for ever: no sooner would I reckon it was complete than I'd think of something else. Apart from rations there was ten tons of salt, a couple of new rifles, a thousand cartridges, skinning knives, sharpening stones and steels. There was horse feed, horseshoes, horseshoe nails, hobble chains, a side of leather for running repairs to the saddlery. The camp (I calculated about half a dozen men and about the same number of women) had to be clothed. Fortunately the climate leant itself to the bare minimum: mostly bare. Neither last nor least a few bottles of rum to cope with such emergencies as snake bite, being struck by lightning, volcanic eruptions and so forth.

On Friday, train day, I flagged Leaping Lena down at the Edith River bridge and joined Len Scott in the saloon bar. Saturday afternoon the old girl staggered into Darwin. It was Monday before the wheels of industry started to revolve again. I had to talk my way into some credit. The first question Jim Fawcett asked was how much could I put up. Practically nothing, I told him. What about some hides, he said — Jolley's had gone into the buffalo hide market, largely out of self-protection I imagined. I had to be a bit cautious. I said "What price?"

"Fivepence a pound." I knew the market was at fivepence halfpenny. I said, with a modicum of prevarication: "I've already taken a contract at five and three-quarters. How many would you want?"

"At least 200."

I thought to myself, I'll take a contract for 500 at fivepence halfpenny; I might be flat out getting 700, but I expect I could do some juggling around. I had to have the credit anyway, so I might as well resign myself to paying for it. I put my order into the Country Order Department after having satisfied an undertaker-looking bloke that it had Jim Fawcett's approval.

I wandered round to the Sydney hide buyer's agent, who had an office in Cavenagh Street, a box of a place wedged between Fang Chong Loong the tailor and another Chinese store oozing with children. The hide buyer was out; a notice flapping on the door read "Back Later". I walked into the tailor and asked an old fellow who was sweating over a sewing machine if he'd make me a suit — I didn't own one. He couldn't talk for a mouthful of pins and nodded vigorously. I looked at several rolls of light material, picked out something I thought was very nice and asked how much.

"Thlee pound ten. Velly cheap." I asked him how long it would take. "Four o'clock, maybe five o'clock today." By this time he was busy measuring me up "You come back two o'clock something tly him alli?"

I made my way back to the hotel thinking I'd better not let Jim Fawcett see me walking around in a flash new suit; such signs of opulence didn't go very well with my declarations of poverty. At the hotel the barman had a message for me. Would I go down and see Dave Cameron — he was a bit crook. I knew Cameron from way back, an itinerant bush worker, mainly fencing and yard building. The last time I had seen him he was building a stockyard on Wave Hill when I was running the camp. A champion axeman, he could make a Kelly axe sing. He was camped with a half-caste family at Doctor's Gully, a mile or so away. I asked the barman to ring one of the only two taxis in Darwin and found Dave's lodgings without much trouble. He was on a bunk on the verandah, and he was crook right enough. The half-caste family seemed nice people; the man said Dave had been on the grog but thought it was more than that. He looked like he had one foot in the grave; I guessed the other one was in the poorhouse. I got him into the cab and into hospital.

Three days later I got another call, this time from the hospital; would I come and pick up my friend? The hospital had done a good job on him, he looked pretty good all shaved and in clean clothes. After yarning for a while he asked me if I'd give him a job cooking. "I don't want much Tom, I'm drawing the pension. All I'm looking for is a camp, a few clothes to get me by, maybe a quid a week." He looked at me anxiously; he was obviously too old to go back to axes, crowbars and shovels, and I couldn't think of any tougher work than that in the climate.

I thought it was a good idea. Sometimes I would get back to camp at nine or ten o'clock at night after a long ride, not finding buffalo until close to sundown, then skinning and packing them back. I'd be just about done in, stinking with caked blood. The only good part would be a billy of black tea; the rest would be a very rough feed knocked up by a lubra. It didn't take any thinking about. "You're as welcome as the flowers in May, Dave; you can go out to Kapalga on the *Maroubra*. Charlie Burns is there, he'll look after you — I expect he'll be pleased to see the boat, I've no doubt he's out of rations by now."

I explained that I had to get back to Guild's place at Edith River, get my horses together and travel down to the coast. I reckoned it would take something like a fortnight.

I fixed Dave up with a bed at the hotel and we made our way to the bar, where the main topic of conversation was the Arnhem Land spearings, the latest being the confirmation of Trainor and Fagan.

An expedition was being got ready. Ted Morey would be in charge, a very sound decision. He was, I reckon, the most competent horseman and bushman in the entire police force, already something of a legend. Tall, handsome and popular, he had represented Australia in the rough-riding division of the Empire Games at Wembley in England. He won several trophies, including the Rider of the Day award.

The next day I went round to the police station to arrange the various licences and permits. I had to renew my permit to work Aborigines, and a couple for native shooters. Sandy McNabb fixed me up; we were old friends from my Bullita days. He told me Vic Hall was going down to Mataranka to join the patrol. Ted Morey and Jack Mahoney were in Katherine getting horses together. Stewart McColl was the fourth member, he was at the Roper River police post from which the patrol was to start. Two of them were to go by boat from Roper River and two were to travel overland with horses. Hall was selected for the boat trip; he had worked on pearling luggers at Broome and was assumed to have some knowledge of seamanship.

I caught a brief glimpse of Hall, whom I already knew fairly well. While chatting away to Sandy, Superintendent Stretton walked by and gave me a brief "G'day, Tom". He looked like a man with plenty on his plate. Which right then would be no exaggeration — the early 1930s were vintage years for the spearmen of the north. There were murderers footloose in the Daly River swamps, there were murderers roaming the lower reaches of the Victoria River, and there were murderers enjoying life somewhere in the jungle fastnesses of Arnhem Land.

Stretton was one of nine children born at Borroloola, one of the more remote outposts where his father had been sergeant of police. Consequently his knowledge of the Territory and its problems was unparalleled.

From the southern border to the outlying islands of the Arafura Sea was more than 1000 miles; from east to west was 500. A total of 523,000 square miles into which most of Europe could be dropped. Within those borders were vast deserts, impenetrable swamps, tropical jungles, unmapped rivers and awesome ranges. The few roads, such as they were, meandered through the country and were impassable in the wet season, even for horses. Stretton's force numbered thirty-two men with which he administered law and order. Excluding Darwin, he had eighteen police posts, most of which were manned by one mounted constable and a couple of black trackers. Their only means of transport was horse and sometimes they would be on patrol for months at a time. In the wet season they were paralysed by flooded rivers and bog to the eyebrows. Apart from the few stations on the Overland Telegraph Line, none of them had any means of communication: ignorance was most certainly bliss.

I got everything tidied up in Darwin, making a point of having a drink with Jack Hales who owned the *Maroubra*. I told him I wanted Dave Cameron to go out with him and he promised to get him aboard "drunk or sober".

I boarded Leaping Lena on train day and on Thursday was back at the Edith River. I didn't have to wait long at the crossing for Dick Guild to turn up with two or three packs to carry the stores and supplies I had brought with me. Nichol Peter, his wife Rosie and offspring were there with Paddy, a young fellow who Peter said could ride "little bit".

That evening, just after sundown, we could hear the rattle of bells and hobbles. Dick and I walked out on to the verandah: two horsemen were heading a mob of horses, some carrying packs. It only took a moment for us to recognise them as police. Ted Morey, riding tall in the saddle, was easy to distinguish; the other was Jack Mahoney. Driving the spares were a couple of trackers.

Ted Morey came straight to the point. He wanted horses for the Arnhem Land patrol — good solid horses, for saddle work and packs too. Could either of us help him out?

"I don't know, Ted," I said. "You know how it is with buffalo shooters, always short of horses."

"Sure, but there seem to be a lot of horses out in that paddock. We're going out into that bloody Never Never and once we leave the Roper there's nowhere we can get any fresh horses. As a matter of fact, there's nowhere much that we know of even around here except you and Dick."

Dick told Morey: "By the way, Ted, there's a chestnut horse in the paddock that belongs to the police. I sold him to Bob Woods last year; he turned up here a month ago." (Bob Woods was sergeant of police at Katherine.) Dick added: "He'll probably buck a bit." Knowing Dick I guessed that "bit" could be translated into "plenty".

"Could you have him up in the yard in the morning, Dick? I'll have a look at him."

It was before breakfast. I was changing a girth on my saddle when I noticed Morey lugging his saddle down to the yard. I didn't take much notice. Shortly afterwards I could hear a commotion. Looking across to the yard I couldn't see much for a great cloud of dust, but I knew someone was riding a horse and that horse was dishing out plenty. Every now and then I could see a hat; there was a man underneath it and I had no doubt Ted Morey was "having a look" at the chestnut.

Just then the old Condamine bullock bell rang out its summons to breakfast. Morey was the last to sit down, saying to Dick with a half-smile: "You were right about that chestnut bastard, Dick; he could buck a bit. Maybe Bob Woods lost him on purpose. Anyway he'll be all right; Bob won't get him back now."

We all went over to the yard. There were somewhere between thirty and forty horses milling around when we started drafting. One of the first to go through was my grey mare, Cloud. Ted Morey was perched up on the top rail of the drafting yard and yellled out: "I'll take that mare."

"No you bloody well won't," I said, laughing. "That's one of my best shooting horses." He frowned momentarily, then said to Dick: "Look, you fellows draft off the horses you don't want to part with. I know how you feel about good horses and I realise Tom won't want to let a shooting horse go."

That evening we talked of the coming patrol. Ted said two would be going by boat because of the quantity of supplies. By the

280

time the horse party had reached Caledon Bay they would probably, if not out of rations, be perilously short, and then there was the return journey.

Morey said with a smile: "As the fly crows it's not far short of 200 miles from the Roper to Caledon Bay, but we won't be flying like crows or crowing like flies . . . and though I can joke about it now, I don't need to tell you two fellows that it's going to be one bloody tough patrol. That reserve is 30,000-odd square miles, completely uninhabited except for blackfellows; and right now I can do without them. And you can add some of the worst terrain in Australia to that. I wouldn't mind being a crow — just for this trip, anyway.

"The maps aren't reliable and I haven't got a tracker I can really depend on. Big Pat says he knows the country but I've got my doubts about that; I've heard that story too many times. When we get down to the swamps and ti-tree and salt marshes we can really get into trouble."

He told us Vic Hall had been selected for the boat trip, because it was assumed he had some knowledge of boats. Before joining the police he had been working with the pearling fleets out of Broome.

"I think that's right, but they go out for months at a time in the pearling season and he'd have to know a bit about sailing. Anyway that's why he was picked; he'd be the closest we've got to a sailor."

Jack Mahoney said, "Stewart McColl is going with Hall — second mate or something — he might know something about boats. Anyway, they don't have to know that much, there's sure to be mission boat boys and most of the coastal blacks can handle a sail and steer a course. The missionaries will be with them from the Roper to Groote Eylandt and from there it's not that far to where we expect to meet up. All they have to do is dodge from one island to another. I wouldn't reckon they'd be much more than five or six miles from land at any time; half their bloody luck. They'll be sitting on their arses surrounded by those Groote Island half-caste

281

girls eating their bloody heads off while we'll be sweating our way through those stinking swamps."

Groote Eylandt was a mission station selected by the Northern Territory Administration as a kind of depot for half-caste girls. They were supposed to be reared in some sort of ecclesiastical atmosphere and educated to a standard that was fairly limited, though they could recite the Lord's Prayer with precision if not enthusiasm.

The girls themselves were taken from their mothers at a very tender age, probably four or five, provided they could be tracked down. This was one of the duties of the Northern Territory police. The tribe endeavoured to hide them, but it was usually done with relentless efficiency. For some reason or other the boys were segregated from the girls, the former usually being sent to Alice Springs. The mothers rarely saw their children again: a rather specialised form of cruelty.

Morey and Mahoney left the following day and a few days later I packed up and left for my buffalo camp.

It's worthwhile following the Arnhem Land police patrol through to its bitter and tragic end, however. The manner in which the expedition was planned was sound and sensible — for which Ted Morey was entirely responsible. The weak links were Hall and McColl. For example, I don't believe Morey would have selected McColl; he just happened to be at the Roper River Police Post at the time, being Frank Sheridan's junior officer.

What maps were available at that time were mainly the result of compass traverses and "by guess and by God" — none of which could be described as reliable. They also had optimism and Tracker Big Pat as a guide; the dividing line between that lot was very fine indeed.

The patrol followed the Wilton River for approximately 100 miles before turning eastward. Shortly afterward they encountered extremely rough ranges not shown on the map. When they got clear, the country levelled off into open forest. There was a myriad of small streams trickling their way to the sea, but Tracker Pat had no hesitation picking the one that would lead them to their rendezvous.

As it gathered tributaries the stream became a creek and winding its devious way through the forest it increased to substantial proportions, with intermittent pools teeming with wildlife, finally joining a river Big Pat triumphantly proclaimed to be the Walker. When they reached the mouth they were five weeks out of the Roper Police Post at the estuary of the Koolatong River. The Walker River, where they were supposed to meet Hall and McColl, was forty miles to the south — but no one knew that.

After the departure of Morey and Mahoney, Hall and McColl were busy loading their supplies on the mission boat *Holly*, a sturdy former pearling lugger. The plan was for them to go with the missionaries on their boat to Groote Eylandt Mission. From there they were to take a twenty-five foot cutter, load their cargo, sail across to the mainland where they would meet the overland party at the mouth of the Walker.

They sailed from the police post on an afternoon tide, wound their way down the Roper River to the sea and sailed the eighty miles to Groote uneventfully. The two constables stayed at Groote for almost exactly a month; some minor repairs had to be carried out on the cutter *Hope*. In Vic Hall's book *Dreamtime Justice* he refers to it as "a trying month"; he didn't explain what they were trying, though there was a passing mention of the half-caste girls being "well and truly locked up in their dorms at night".

The southeast monsoon was starting to make itself felt when they chugged down the creek to the open sea, heavily loaded but under the lee of the island. They towed a canoe that they used as a means of going ashore; there was no room to sleep on the boat. The next morning they made a dash across to a small island and here they stayed for a whole month.

In the meantime Ted Morey and Jack Mahoney settled down at what they thought was the Walker River, keeping signal fires going day and night. They had run out of rations and were living off the land, eating mainly wallabies. Week after week went by and still no sign of the sea-going party, which was sheltering on what was probably Connexion Island, three or four miles from its first camp at the northern end of Groote Eylandt.

Eventually they set sail and headed for the Walker River. No one can really be blamed for the land party not being there, and anyway Hall and McColl had enough sense to turn to the north where they sighted the smoke signals just before sundown. A joyful reunion took place. Nine weeks had passed since the two parties left the Roper River Police Post, at least half of them wasted by the two constables waiting for suitable weather. One can't help feeling that nothing other than what Hall described as "a perfect calm" would have suited them.

From here there seem to be some imponderables — why did they go to Woodah Island? They were on a patrol to investigate the murders of five Japanese and two Europeans at Caledon Bay, 100 miles to the north of Koolatong River. Hall claimed to have known some of the Woodah natives, mentioning Tuckiar, but there is also another account in which they attempted to round up some natives who managed to elude them.

There are so many different stories, including one imaginative account in a book called *The Self Made Anthropologist*, by one T Wise, in which credulity is strained with a description of the police riding around the island on horses.

Whatever the finer details, the four police and six trackers set sail for Woodah Island in *Hope*. It always seems remarkable to me that not even one tracker was left behind to look after the fifty-odd horses, saddles and gear. It would seem that they didn't intend staying away long.

According to Vic Hall's book they camped on the beach the first night and the next day started to comb the island on foot. They captured some lubras, who were left with McColl and a tracker, Roper Tommy. Morey, Hall and Mahoney went scouting around the island, looking for more natives. They appeared to have no success and camped on a beach that night. McColl and the tracker were on their own some miles away.

It is worth quoting from Vic Hall's book, *Dreamtime Justice*, the final dramatic events in this tragedy:

"'Where blackfella?' he demanded of the shadowy figure. He could just make out the woman's answering gesture and the flash of her teeth. The rhythmic clicking sound came again, dead ahead. Twenty paces in front, Tuckiar crouched with his cousin Merrara at the edge of the trap clearing. He fitted his killing spear to his woomera and edged forward to get throwing clearance for his arm. The trap clearing was made for such a purpose as this. It was the only place where there was room to throw a spear. Behind him Merrara was tapping out his message to the woman who was bringing the white man.

"The signaller paused to listen, the two little hardwood sticks silent. Tuckiar peered across the tiny clearing, reached back, grasped his cousin's arm and whispered. They were coming . . . the little sticks need talk no more. Soon they could hear the rustle of approaching feet in the leaf mould. As Tuckiar took his stance the ten-foot spear quivered along its length.

"Ahead of the woman in front of him McColl saw the light of the little clearing. They must be nearly through the jungle . . . so much the better. He'd had enough of the steamy darkness of this blasted jungle. Better get his gat out though . . . He fished the heavy Webley from its holster and finished the last few paces with it in his hand. As he came into the sunlight the woman jumped aside and threw herself to the ground. McColl saw a black figure for only a fleeting second, and had not quite levelled his pistol when the spear crashed into his chest.

"Outside the jungle, sitting beside the captive women, Roper Tommy heard a new message being tapped out by the two sticks. Listening, he put his face in his hands and wept."

That was Hall's reconstruction of the spearing of McColl. The only people who really knew what happened were Tuckiar, a lubra and perhaps Roper Tommy, and, of course, McColl. When it happened Morey, Mahoney and Hall were on some other part of the island. They found his body early the next morning.

Hall wrote, "Big Pat . . . turned Mac over on to his back and a rush of air came from a gaping wound in his chest". A shallow grave was dug with sticks at the foot of a cedar tree. Vic Hall endeavoured to recite the burial service: "I heard my voice stumbling through the half-remembered words. Stooping, I took a handful of light earth and cast it into the grave. It rustled as it fell on the folded hands of my friend. Big Pat, Roper Tommy, Dick, Reuben and Menikman squatted around the grave and cast in their handfuls of earth. A soft Aboriginal requiem mingled with birdsong in the aisles of the forest".

A couple of days later Morey and Mahoney packed up and left for the Roper River Station, while Hall sailed his lonely way back to the Groote Eylandt Mission to radio the shattering news of McColl's spearing.

When it reached Darwin it registered something like ten on the Richter scale. Never before in the history of the Mounted Police had anything like it happened. The uproar and reactions were predictable. There was talk of a punitive expedition, promptly denied by the Commissioner of Police.

There was a lot more talk of the mission about to be attacked and Hall settled down to garrison duty. The only people who didn't seem to be alarmed were the missionaries. Hall was advised that he would be reinforced as soon as possible.

The newspapers were having a field day. The battle lines were drawn: God-botherers v The Rest. Reinforcements arrived with news of a "Peace Party"! The God-botherers, fearing a wholesale slaughter out in Arnhem Land (perhaps with a certain amount of justification) offered to bring in Tuckiar, to which the Government agreed with alacrity.

To everyone's astonishment they were successful; they had no trouble locating Tuckiar and talking him into accompanying them to Darwin. Perhaps they told him God would look after him. Whatever it was he believed them, and it wasn't much help. He was charged with the murder of Mounted Constable Albert Stewart McColl.

The court case was something of a shambles; what few witnesses there were couldn't speak pidgin, there were no competent interpreters and Tuckiar had no idea what it was all about. This did not deter Judge Wells from directing the jury to bring in a verdict of guilty, which they dutifully did. In sentencing Tuckiar to death, His Honour commented caustically on policemen playing missionaries (referring to the Groote Eylandt garrison) and missionaries playing policemen.

This resulted in another tidal wave of uproar. The southern God-botherers appealed to the High Court of Australia, which wasted no time quashing Judge Wells' verdict with some pungent remarks on the subject of lack of witnesses.

Tuckiar was released from Fanny Bay jail, but never reached his homeland. What happened to him was a matter for speculation.

As for the original reason for the patrol, that got lost somewhere along the way. That Tuckiar speared McColl there seems no doubt. I believe he paid dearly for it. Anyway, eight men died. Probably nine, with Tuckiar.

Wonggu, who was believed the instigator, and who certainly took a prominent part in the Caledon Bay killings, was never brought to justice. No further attempts were made to apprehend him, which always surprised me. After all, seven was a fair tally.

Apart from tribal killings — and they were going on all the time — there were no more disturbances and Wonggu rested on his laurels. I don't think he turned over a new leaf; it's more likely his territory was struck off the visiting list of most travellers.

I had left Guild's place and headed towards the buffalo country long before the tragic events had run their course.

When I rode away I had Peter and Rosie, their youngster and Paddy. At the Mary River crossing I picked up another half-starved fellow who said he was "properly 'ungry", and looked it, too.

I reached Kapalga after riding for ten days. Dave Cameron had settled in with Charlie Burns and the two of them were getting along famously, as I expected. All the rations and cargo had been stacked away. Most of it had been opened and Dave complained that I had forgotten the rum. I hadn't, of course, it was in a case very clearly marked "horseshoes". Dave said rather plaintively, "Didn't you trust us?" I explained that it wasn't so much that I didn't trust them, but I thought that after a couple of bottles of overproof Old Kedge rum they might have lost count. "OK" rum was pretty powerful.

I shod a couple of shooting horses and took the camp out to Flying Fox Creek. It was going to be hard for a start; in the wet season the spear grass grows to a height of six or eight feet, and when the rain stops it falls over and mats up. When it dries out it has to be burnt off. The heat of the grass fire generates a growth of green grass referred to as "burnt feed"; the horses love it. But right then it wouldn't burn; it was too damp underneath. It was a foot or so deep, hiding stumps and logs and it was too easy to have a bad fall. I didn't like it at all. As was usual at this time of year, the buffalo were scattered hell west and crooked.

I found that sneaking round the lagoons was profitable; buffalo sometimes walked into the water to feed on the swamp grasses and waterlily stems. I often picked off one or two. Skinning wasn't the most popular occupation: the water was swarming with leeches and skinners would be scraping them off their legs with the skinning knives. The mosquitos were bad, too, and would continue to be until we could get a decent burn.

So far there was no sign of Yorky Billy, who'd declared he would be shooting for me again when we parted at the end of last season. Charlie had warned me not to depend on him; he'd been through every buffalo camp on the coast at some time or other.

288

His father, Yorky Mick Alderson, had been around the Alligator River country "since before Pontius was a pilot", to quote Charlie Burns. I had met him a couple of times and he spoke of some of the original buffalo hunters, Paddy Cahill and others who had been dead for years before my time. I reckoned his son Billy to be about twenty-two. Mick was the typical prospector, who knew of some mysterious gold deposit he intended working "next year", but it was either too dry to get at or too wet to work.

Then I took a bad fall. Three bulls jumped out of a patch scrub so dense I had to let them run for a while before I could get a break in the forest. The timber opened up, I got up on to the first one and knocked him down. I was just about to close on the others when we came to a small creek with steep banks. The buffalo landed at the bottom, where there was a little water covering a black boggy bottom. The buffalo went down to their guts and floundered out. I knew then I had no hope; it was too late to pull up Dollar. We hit the mud and he went down to his flanks; I shot out of the saddle and landed on the other side. I wasn't hurt up to then. I think Dollar was half-blinded by the mud — he struggled out and as he climbed up the bank he stood on my right thigh. A horse weighs quite a lot.

For a moment I thought my leg was broken, and I suppose it was some kind of a miracle it wasn't. I was partly paralysed and the pain was excruciating. The skinners wouldn't be along for a while; I heard a shot, which would be the foot shooter despatching the bull I'd shot. They would skin it and then follow my tracks, and I didn't expect they would be in any hurry. A crow came along and settled itself on a tree overhead. It peered at me, gave a "kark", and I told it to fuck off. I was nowhere near ready for him.

By the time the skinners arrived I'd dragged myself up the bank and was sitting on a log. Dollar was feeding around not far away. I told one of the boys to find my rifle, which had gone flying when I fell. Then I got Dollar unsaddled and a comfortable pony — one that wasn't so far from the ground. Saddled up, Dollar was about sixteen hands.

When I got back to the camp Dave boiled up a bucket of water, got some towels and applied hot foments. The leg didn't look too good. It was a dirty blue colour and felt as though there was a horseshoe in it.

The next day I sent the camp out foot shooting and occupied myself marking hides with the destination cipher, wishing to hell Yorky Billy would turn up. Two or three horses walked in for a drink at the spring. When they'd had their fill they walked over to where I was sitting on a stack of hides and dribbled some water on me. Suddenly they lifted their heads sharply, pricked their ears and looked up the road from Kapalga. Through the trees I saw a cloud of dust that developed into a horseman riding at the head of a mob of horses. With great relief I identified Yorky Billy.

The first thing Billy asked for was tobacco. Dave got a few sticks of twist from a box — he wouldn't smoke anything else. He threw a couple of sticks across to the two lubras unpacking the horses.

He looked as lean and hungry as a blackfellow's dog and was soon wrapping himself around a feed. Knowing what a good bushman Billy was I asked him if he hadn't been able to shoot himself a feed. He said he'd been up in the ranges working on a tin deposit he'd discovered: it was "real hungry" country, mountainous and rough.

Dave, who had had some mining experience, questioned him about it and seemed quite impressed. After a while Billy called to one of the lubras to bring a bag over. I saw her delve into a pack bag to pull out a small calico bag. Billy poured into the palm of his hand what appeared to be black sand. I had a look at the bag; it was quite heavy for such a small amount.

Billy said it came from Myra Creek, a tributary of the East Alligator, which headed away up in sandstone ranges. He said he got about a hundredweight or so but didn't have any equipment to work it properly. Yorky Mick had taken the tin to Pine Creek from where it would go to Darwin. All tin had to be sold to the

290

Government, which determined what price would be paid for it. At that time it was £200 per ton.

None of this interested me very much; all I was concerned with was getting my camp moving again and getting some hides in. I had just about decided to move the camp and Billy's arrival finalised the decision. It would be a couple of days before I was well enough to ride, and moving camp was a full day's work for all hands except me.

I had in mind to move to Gipsy Spring. It was a good camp with much better grazing for the horses, there were comfortable paperbark sheds that wouldn't require much attention to get in order, clear spring water and it was close to the plains, which would soon be firm enough to gallop over.

I had it in mind to split the camp two ways. Billy could take three or four boys and shoot up one side of the river, and I could take a few and shoot the other side. I sent him off to Kapalga to try to pick up a few more horses; there were at least another six around there somewhere. I gave him one boy to help and he took the young lubra with him, which caused a bit of a disturbance. Mary, the one he'd had for some years, started to abuse both of them, saying some very unpleasant things about her genitals — all very entertaining, but Billy soon put a stop to that with a few cuts from his stockwhip.

I moved to Gipsy Spring and Billy got back next day with four fresh horses, one a mare named Trixie with a pretty little mule foal. I knew there were some wild donkeys around, though I'd never seen any — only their tracks, which are quite distinct, smaller and narrower than those of a horse.

He also brought another lad. Billy said he knew him quite well and he was a good horseback shooter named Ring. He was the son of Hobble Chain, who had achieved some sort of fame in a book called *Buffaloes* written by a man named Carl Warburton: he had shot for a short time over the other side of the South Alligator River just after World War I.

I suppose that the name of Ring was appropriate for a son of Hobble Chain, at the same time wondering how the father had managed to have the name of Hobble Chain bestowed on him. I have frequently noted some of the seemingly ridiculous names inflicted on Aboriginal stockmen and station hands — Quart Pot, Pocket Knife, Snapshot. Looking through some of my diaries a stranger would have difficulty discerning which list was of horses and which was of stockmen, even throwing in a few Paddys and Tommys. Discussing this around the campfire, I once heard a reasonable explanation.

Most of the tribal names were nearly always of five or six syllables — real tongue twisters and practically unpronounceable to the average bushman: one Centralian name, Agnalpulla-alpunsha, had been abbreviated to Punchy. Though a lot of the names to which they were changed appear to be very undignified, I only heard of one objection.

A young fellow walked into the camp looking for a job. Ring brought him to me, mainly I supposed for purposes of interpreting. He was a real Myall bush black, smelling strongly of turtle (it was the turtle season). I asked Ring what his name was and he said he didn't have one. I christened him Snowball, which was the first name I thought of. Later, Ring came to me and said the new recruit didn't like his name, could he be Billy. I readily agreed, I didn't mind what he called himself. I learned later that the objection to the name was based on what they regarded as genital connotations.

I took Ring with me, as I was anxious to see what sort of a shooter he was: I liked the way he approached his horse, gave him a friendly pat and then had a good look at his feet. He saddled him, checking everything before he mounted, adjusted the stirrup leather lengths to his liking and we rode away together. The pack horses followed.

After riding for half an hour we put up a couple of young bulls. Ring looked at me as I nodded: "They're yours; knock 'em down."

He gathered up his reins. Dollar, of course, knew what it was all about and was into his stride immediately. I soon saw by the way he rode through the timber that he was a fearless rider. I had a good man.

The hides were starting to pile up and the creek crossing between Gipsy Spring and Kapalga were starting to dry out. I put Peter in charge of the dray carting hides to the river. Everything was going well. Paddy, who had worked for me last year, arrived; I had two Paddys now, so I told him he was Paddy One — which seemed to please him.

Then an entry in my journal: "Shooting through the scrub, eight bulls one alligator". Which of course was a crocodile. Though no other details are recorded, I clearly recall the incident because of the 'gator, as we called them. We had been working through the scrub and came to a small spring sometime about midday, just right for a dinner camp. One of the skinners said he'd seen a 'gator asleep under a tree not far away and would I shoot it — they wanted the meat. Though I knew they travelled from one hole to another when the water dried, I was surprised this one was so far out on the ridges; it would be at least five miles from a decent waterhole.

At that time I wasn't aware of a market for the hides, but I always shot them, having seen horses and cattle cruelly mauled. It wasn't far away, lying in the shade of a tree. It looked an evil brute. I dismounted and taking my rifle, walked towards it. As I did so several boys called in unison, "Don't walk in front, 'im 'e bite." I had no intention of doing that; I had heard they were likely to take a jump at anyone who walked in front of them. It was safe enough to walk behind, but a good idea to keep clear of the tail. Its eyes were closed but I had no doubt it was well aware of what was going on. I quickly despatched it and they soon set to work skinning the tail portion.

While they were busy at this they told me about a man who had come out on to the Alligator River country some years ago. I gathered he was very much a new chum, and a smartarse as well — not a good combination. I wasn't sure whether he was trying his hand at buffalo shooting or prospecting. Whatever it was, he came across a crocodile in similar circumstances and though his boys warned him he walked in front of it, and in order to establish his stupidity beyond any doubt, picked up a stick and started to poke at its eyes.

The infuriated crocodile leaped at him and seized one of his legs in a vice-like grip. As they told the story, splitting their sides laughing, I could visualise the situation fairly clearly. It would have been sheer pandemonium. The man, whose name was George something, was screaming for help. His boys would have been in a hopeless panic, all yelling at once, telling someone else what to do. To get him free they had to chop the crocodile's head off. When a crocodile gets hold of something in its jaws it won't let go easily, but when it is shot they can be opened without any trouble. I would think the man would have most certainly had a gun with him, but his blacks didn't know how to use it.

We got back to the camp with eight buffalo hides, our pack horses carrying one pack bag full of buffalo meat and a crocodile tail in the other. Although everything was going smoothly I was beginning to give some thought to that perennial problem — horses. Very soon we would be shooting the plains and the tallies would jump. I made sure the shooting horses were looked after, but the others doing the real drudgery of carrying hides were starting to look the worse for wear. They carried the hides bareback, secured with rope; consequently their withers chafed and they had to be turned out until they healed up. There were always ten or fifteen spelling at any one time; some stood up to work better than others, but right through my diaries I note: "so and so sick, so and so lame, another missing, a mare foaled", which was common — there were brumby stallions just about everywhere. There was no such thing as paddocks and when horses were turned out it was in hope they wouldn't stray too far.

The *Maroubra* came and I loaded 250 hides. I got some mail away, including a letter to Dick Guild asking him for horses. I reckon it would take a week or more to reach him.

It was almost exactly a week later that I had an experience I will always remember. Our tallies were dropping off a bit, and I would soon have to move the camp. In the meantime we were still getting enough to make it worthwhile staying a while longer — moving camp was quite an operation.

I had just opened a fresh case of cartridges and the same day I had two misfires. The first time I reloaded and brought the buffalo down, but the second time I didn't have time to get another cartridge into the breech before he beat me into a swamp. That evening when I got back to the camp I put the offending case on one side and opened a fresh one, at the same time remarking to Dave how unusual it was to have such an experience. I found that with the military Mark VI .303 the misfire rate would have been less than one in a thousand. I emptied all the cartridge belts and replaced them with fresh bullets.

In the morning we were away as usual just after sunrise. Because of the scarcity of buffalo, Ring and I split up, riding parallel tracks about half a mile apart. A couple of buffalo jumped out of a thicket and galloped away, one a good young mature bull, the other, which took the lead, was a tremendous old fellow with horns like slip rails.

I was quickly up on the youngster and brought him down, slipped another cartridge into the breech of my rifle and steadied Cloud as we approached a fairly large clump of paperbarks. The bull plunged in, following a well-worn track. As I galloped in, the timber increased in density; it was much further through to the other side than I first thought.

Suddenly, to my astonishment — and, I might say with all honesty, a good deal of fright — the bull came charging back straight at me. It was all so terrifyingly sudden; here was I cantering blithely along, one bull down and another as good as shot. When I first saw the bull it appeared from around a bend and was only a few yards away, its head down and murder in its heart. There was no time to do anything and no way I could do anything. The timber was too thick for Cloud to have jumped to one side to avoid it. I was completely stunned by its sudden appearance. It wasn't supposed to do that sort of thing.

As we met, Cloud reared, the bull's head was straight under me, the mare's legs straddling its neck. I leaned out of the saddle and placed the muzzle of the rifle on its neck just behind the ear and pressed the trigger. There was a dull click — the cartridge misfired. The infuriated bull gave a frightening twist to its head and turned the mare completely over. I was underneath.

She scrambled to her feet, nostrils distended, snorting with fright. I jumped up and grabbed at the reins. I was in some kind of shock but my main concern was for Cloud; those frightful horns! I first took her head in my arms and spoke to her. I was almost afraid to look at her belly, I had seen it before — I would never forget Cracker.

At last I brought myself to look at her chest and stomach. My relief was indescribable; there wasn't a mark or scratch of any kind. It was nothing short of miraculous, there wasn't even an abrasion, though I expected some bruising. I gave her a hug and she nuzzled me under my arm.

I realised what had saved her; the wide sweep of the horns. When the bull had his head beneath her chest they were so wide that they were sticking out each side, and once he tossed her out of his way all he wanted to do was get to hell out of it. He was probably just as frightened as I was, though I doubt it.

What had me puzzled was why he had come galloping back; it was a most extraordinary thing for him to do. The more I thought about it the more I was mystified. Had I been right up on him and he turned, I could have understood it, but he was too far ahead of me to suddenly turn; I was probably fifty yards behind him in dense timber. I picked up my rifle, took the undischarged bullet from the breech and put it in my pocket. Then I followed the track to see if I could find some reason for the bull's sudden reverse. I had walked only fifty or so yards when I came to the explanation. There had, at some time or other, been a freak wind — which was fairly common, though I had never experienced one, only the results. It must have been a miniature cyclone that came tearing through at a million miles an hour but, from what I had seen, took a very narrow path. They would lay the densest timber flat; the cyclone season being the wet season, trees were easily uprooted from the soft ground. Where I stopped was an impenetrable wall of twisted, matted timber. There was no way he could have got through, so he simply turned round and came back. It was as good as a dose of opening medicine.

Cursing my stupidity, I walked back to where Cloud was feeding, undid the reins, mounted and rode back to where the boys were skinning. I examined the bullet I had put in my pocket. I knew perfectly well what had caused the misfire, there was nothing wrong with the cartridge, nor the case I had put on one side; it was my rifle. I was really upset thinking of what could have happened. Had it been the younger bull with the shorter horns, Cloud might have been killed.

The Martini-Enfield carbine, which we all used, was lever action. After firing the shooter flipped down the lever under the stock, which ejected the spent shell. The block dropped, exposing the breech. Another cartridge was slipped into the breech, the lever was brought back into position, closing the breech, and the rifle was automatically cocked ready for firing. The firing pin was actuated by a powerful spring released by trigger pressure.

After about a thousand rounds (though in this case, sooner), the spring was likely to weaken and would not strike the cartridge hard enough to discharge it. It was a simple matter to rectify . . . the block could be taken out easily and the spring adjusted with a screwdriver.

I told the skinners we had finished shooting for the day; they were to come back to the camp when they had finished skinning.

Dick Guild was at the camp with seven fresh horses and two bottles of rum — God bless him.

By October the tally was close to the 700 I had contracted for; I was going to get 800 easily, probably more. It was starting to get hot, the buffalo were falling away in condition and they wouldn't gallop far before charging. There were all the signs of weariness in the camp.

Yorky Mick turned up looking for the "young fellow". I told him he was camped at Mongulla. Yorky had some money for him, the proceeds of the tin, together with a letter from the Mines Department that he showed us. It described the tin as being of very high quality, and that should the deposit be of a substantial nature it could be of considerable significance. Dave Cameron and Yorky Mick started to talk tin . . . I yawned and went to my bunk.

CHAPTER 22

PROSPECTING
IN ARNHEM LAND

A fortnight later I finished shooting; the total was 815. There were storms around now, so I gathered everything up and moved to Kapalga to wait for the boat. Billy brought his camp in and we filled in the time straightening out the jetty, which was pretty flimsy. The toredos, the white ants of the sea, could saw their way through cast iron.

When Billy arrived Dave asked him how big he thought the tin deposit was. All he could say about it was "plenty". Was there much overburden, Dave asked. "Not much, maybe five or six feet; the creek was about fifteen feet wide."

Dave had been a prospector and it doesn't take much to get a prospector wound up. That night, at the campfire, Dave said: "You know, Tom, I really like the sound of that tin show of Billy's. It's new country out there. I don't think anyone has ever done any prospecting before."

"I'm sure that's right," I said. "It's well into Arnhem Land, the blacks out there are real sporting types; they throw the prettiest shovel spear in Arnhem Land. I suppose that's why it's never been prospected much." Actually I didn't know anything about them.

"Do you think there'd be any danger?"

"It depends largely on how you treat them. I'd say you'd have to watch them, once you cross the East Alligator you're in real Myall country, none of them would speak pidgin, except perhaps around the Oenpelli Mission and that's a long way away. What have you got in mind?"

"Well, I've been talking to Billy about it. He wants to go back there, put in a good sluice box and work it properly. What he brought out last year he dug up with one old shovel. He realised he hasn't got the know-how, or the money or enough horses to carry the equipment. I've done a fair bit of prospecting; if you'd like to give it a go I believe it could be a good thing."

"Let me give it some thought. Prospecting is a closed book to me."

We both turned in and I started to think about it. Perhaps it was worth looking at; the wet season was a six-month drain and the idleness never appealed to me. The horses got fat and I got thin, financially. Last wet season I rode 600 or 700 miles, and it was the horse breaking at Limbunya that saved me. I didn't want to go through that again; there was an element of luck getting any kind of work at that time of the year.

The next morning I dragged an old map out and Dave and I pored over it. Yorky Billy couldn't read a map — couldn't read at all. It was old and stained, partly obliterated with creases. We found Myra Falls on what was presumably Myra Creek — it was difficult to see where it started or finished. It wasn't clear whether it was a tributary of the East Alligator or the Liverpool River, but it was well out into Arnhem Land.

I questioned Billy on what the country was like for travelling. He said it was good travelling most of the way. I guessed we would go up the South Alligator from Kapalga, for about forty miles, crossing the river where it was shallow, then across to the East Alligator. We should be on low ridges for about sixty miles to the river crossing, which was a flat, rocky bar. The river poured out of a gorge there; Billy said we would follow it up the other side, it was good travelling. As I understood it it was about six or eight miles through the gorge and, from there a large open plain about five miles across. We would then come to a creek that had to be followed up — I guessed another eight or ten miles. From there, though he didn't say so, was rough going; a couple of days' travelling.

300

I had it worked out at about 150 to 160 miles. It didn't sound too bad. I got the impression he was doing his best to make it sound good. I expected the foothills and the range, probably a divide, would be bloody rough.

"What are the blacks like?" asked Dave.

"They're not too bad; I know most of them."

I had another look at the map. If I took it on, a lot of equipment would be needed and some of it — a lot of it, in fact — would be awkward to carry on pack horses. Picks and shovels would be no problem, but we needed timber for sluice boxes. I got a sheet of paper and started to work out a few things.

Then the *Maroubra* arrived and we were busy loading hides. I was in the wheelhouse checking them as they came aboard; Jack Hales was in a deck chair emptying a bottle of rum with some assistance from me. When I judged he was in a reasonably pliable state I asked him when was his next trip to Cape Don lighthouse.

"About a week; I go back to Darwin from here, unload this lot, then load up for Cape Don."

"Jack, I'm going out to Arnhem Land on a prospecting trip and I'll have to go to Darwin to get stores and supplies, which will be a fair bit. If I came in with you and got all the stores and supplies I need, could you drop me off here on your way to Cape Don?"

"Yes, sure," he said, then as an afterthought, "it'll cost you a case of beer." To which I readily agreed — after all, I'd probably drink half of it.

I got Billy and Dave together. "Are you fellows sure you want to take this on? If you are I'll go into Darwin on the *Maroubra* and get all the gear and stuff we need."

Both of them were full of enthusiasm; I knew Dave would be, but I wanted to be sure of Billy. Without him we wouldn't know where it was, we'd be up that well-known creek without a paddle.

At sundown Jack Gaden and Bill Jennings rode in and I opened another bottle. They were crocodile hunters and weren't much help except with the rum, but they did their best. Tin? They knew a bloke who knew a bloke, or something. As the evening progressed Charlie Burns said he'd like to have a shot at the tin. Burns had been a mad miner in his day too. Miners believe anything — they live in hope and die in despair.

I'll never know how it happened, but the next day everything was worked out. Some time afterward I recalled a quotation: "Those whom the gods would destroy they first make mad."

I told Dave I'd be back in about ten days and boarded the *Maroubra*. Two days later I stepped ashore at Darwin. The ship was unloaded the next day and the day after that Hales' engineer informed him the engine needed some attention. Two days later I had everything tidied up . . . and the *Maroubra* engine was still in pieces. Eventually it was all stuck together again and we sailed. Storms were increasing in severity and it rained nearly every afternoon.

We tied up at Kapalga halfway through November. Dave was at the wharf, looking very gloomy; I soon found out Yorky Billy's young lubra had run away with a Myall blackfellow and he had taken off after her, breathing death and destruction. He told Dave that when he caught up with them he was going to shoot and burn the blackfellow — or maybe burn and shoot him. A story had come through that the eloping couple had gone up into the "stone country". He wasn't likely to be back. This was a devastating blow; without Billy I had no idea where the tin deposit was. I knew it was on Myra Creek, but I had little chance of picking out that creek or any other.

I had several hundred pounds' worth of stores, supplies, gear and equipment. I had spent more than half what I had made buffalo shooting. I cursed Yorky Billy and opened a case of rum.

Charlie Burns said he had a boy named Whalebone who knew where the tin was; he'd worked for Billy. I said I wished I'd never heard of tin, or Yorky Billy either.

The following morning I talked to Whalebone. Yes, he said, he knew where the tin was; yes, plenty tin — full up. How far? Little

302

bit long way. Little bit long way could be anything from fifty miles to 200 . . . I opened another bottle of rum.

Charlie Burns had a waggonette, and after a lot of discussion and head scratching we decided to take it, fully aware that it would be an impossibility to get it any further than the East Alligator because of a gorge that would be difficult enough for pack horses.

I was giving some thought to the first thirty miles up the South Alligator, to the head of the tidal waters — which would be the first suitable crossing. There was a question mark on a couple of creeks in between. I saddled a horse and rode off for a look-see.

The question mark was erased at the first creek crossing; it had flooded for several hundred yards each side. Then Charlie came up with a good idea: "What about floating the waggonette across the river right here?" There were a few old forty-four gallon drums lying around. They were rusty, but we rolled them over, gave them a few belts with an axe and pronounced them seaworthy. It didn't take long to lash them together. With a dugout canoe and a couple of boys providing motor power they were paddled across. It took three trips and nearly all day, but it was worth it.

It was now December 17. We made about ten miles the next day and the day after it rained heavily; the following day the waggonette was bogged. It took half a day to get it out of the morass and the king bolt was bent — we took nearly all the next day to straighten it.

On Christmas Eve we were well and truly bogged again. A wheel collapsed and nine spokes were broken. This was really serious; there were only sixteen spokes in a wheel.

Rain was beating up, we weren't going to move that day even if we had four wheels. Dave got busy and cut limbs from wattle trees, selecting fairly straight lengths with, if possible, a twist in them. After trimming them roughly he gave one of the boys a job dragging them back and forth through a fire to season them. We had a reasonable range of tools, and they were finished off with a

303

tomahawk and shoeing rasp. On New Year's Day the last spoke was finished and I went out and shot a buffalo cow.

For the next fourteen days we cut our way through timber, getting bogged often. A good harness mare, Peggy, dropped dead; then we came to a swamp that effectively and permanently stopped the waggonette. From here everything would have to be packed. We ploughed through the swamp, crossed a creek and made camp.

I could hear the drumming of didgeridoos not far away. Several blacks walked into the camp and asked for tobacco; they seemed quite friendly but I was concerned about the rations and equipment that had been left on the waggonette.

They said the next creek was Majela, and from what I could make out it was running a banker. I took all the packs, went back with Charlie to the waggonette and brought everything over. I had to keep all the stores and equipment with us; there were a lot of blacks about. It took two trips to move to our next camp, which I have down in my diary at Chubba-luka. (Today this is called Jabiluka.)

I reckoned we weren't too far from the East Alligator River; I could hear it roaring ominously. I rode across to have a look. It was running strongly and we would have to swim. Not far from our camp were a group of bush blacks busily engaged in making a canoe. I threw them a couple of sticks of tobacco, a sort of public relations exercise. I said to the only one who said he could speak English; "Youfella likem me 'elpem you?" There was a rapid exchange in their language and a chorus of "Yuis". I returned to our camp and Charlie and I would be canoe-making the next day; with ordinary luck we would be able to get our gear across the river safe and dry.

We finished the canoe in two days, hooked one of the harness horses to it and pulled it down to the river. The next morning I found Whalebone and his lubra had left for greener fields. They had taken the canoe, paddled across the river and left it on the other side. I got the owners together and explained what had happened. they didn't seem to be unduly disturbed. I suggested they swim over and bring it back. They looked at me in astonishment, smiled and said "Bye 'n bye." I stripped off, swam over and brought it back myself.

The next day I got all the gear and rations across and swam the horses. We were now camped on the higher side of the river and should be able to ride up river without any difficulty until we got through the gorge. It rained for the next two days and the river was roaring. Though we had good heavy canvas tent flies, everything was damp and smelling. The sugar was seeping through the bags and the flour was developing a thick, greenish crust on the outside. The blowflies were having a field day.

Though we had lost Whalebone, our guide, there were lots of bush blacks about. Most of them seemed to know where Yorky Billy's tin find was: there wouldn't be much going on they didn't know about.

It was Sunday, January 28. Charlie and I packed up seven horses with about half of our stores and tools and made a start up river. My diary entry reads: "Bad day. Charlie and I started up river with seven packs. Half a mile up carried everything across a deep channel. Further mile made a paperbark raft and swam horses. Afternoon left Charlie and went back to Dave's camp. River still rising".

The next day: "Shifted the rest of the camp up with boys carrying about fifty pounds each. The first bad channel, which had about five and a half feet of water yesterday, has risen. Boys walked under water carrying everything above their heads. God help us if the river rises four feet tonight; she's roaring through these ranges like a locomotive".

January 30 reads: "Packed six boys and seven horses this morning and went about three miles after much trouble unpacking and packing. Swam horses round a rocky point where the gorge meets the main channel. Carried everything through a narrow crevice about a foot wide. Got through the gorge and camped at the junction of the river and a creek that heads in the tin country. This creek is a mile wide here".

January 31: "River still rising, raining on and off all last night. All the tents and flies are leaking, everything damp and mildewed, flour going green. Beef finished. Shot three geese. Two blackfellows brought some fish freshly speared."

We were now through the gorge and what was shown on the map as a plain was a huge sea of water. Charlie was anxious to get up into the hills; we thought it was only about twenty miles or so to the deposit. He reckoned if he could get across to the other side of the flooded plain he would walk up into the hills. I didn't like the idea at all. He would be on his own and very vulnerable. There were blacks camped in little bark humpies and they seemed to come and go, though I must say they all seemed friendly enough. When it rained, they stayed inside and played didgeridoos and sang corroboree songs all day; smoke seeped through the bark and it must have been stifling inside. Their lungs were undoubtedly different from ours.

Charlie made a large paperbark raft and with two boys started off across the plain. I wrote: "I climbed a hill and could see his fly rigged. Later cut a big tree down, about four feet through and started some boys off making a canoe. River rose two feet."

It took eight days to finish the canoe, and I found out a lot about the Arnhem Land shipbuilding industry. Charlie came back and said that after working a few gullies he thought the prospects were good; there was tin in almost every one. We dragged the canoe down to the edge of the water, gave it a push and to my surprise it floated remarkably well and perfectly level.

All I wanted now was a day without rain. With the canoe and lots of paperbark for a raft we reckoned we could cross the floodplain in a couple of trips. We would have to walk through the water and push the raft and canoe, swimming the deeper channels.

Then I found a pack horse dead; it was in good condition, too. It must have been a snake — there were plenty about, driven to the

306

high ground by the floodwaters. I reckoned it was a taipan, because it takes a fair bit to kill a healthy horse. Scarcely a day passed without our killing a couple of snakes; there were death adders and black snakes, both of which were poisonous but not powerful enough to kill a horse.

The next day the weather cleared and I wasted no time loading the fleet, Charlie and I crossed the plain with four boys and had a camp rigged by sundown. The next morning three of our assistants had gone; we still had one young fellow who said the others had gone off to spear some fish and would be back "bye 'n bye". I wasn't unhappy about the prospect of fish, but I was anxious to get back to Dave and get him across before the rain started again. By late afternoon it was clear we weren't going to see them again. They were bush blacks who only joined us for the fun of it — we just ran out of fun.

I got back to Dave's camp comfortably and when I told him that three boys had disappeared in the still watches of the night he surprised me by saying; "Yes I know; they came back here and said you'd sent them back for the gun and cartridges and a tomahawk.

"What did you say to them, Dave?"

"I didn't say anything, I picked up the gun and fired a shot over their heads; at the rate they left here they'd be in Queensland by now."

The next day Whalebone turned up, very apologetic. He explained that he had to go to a corroboree — he was an important musician I understood. Lena had a black eye and was a bit bedraggled; it seemed she had been doing her share of entertaining in an entirely different field.

It was February 24: three months since we left Kapalga. The three of us walked over to where Charlie had done some preliminary prospecting in the creek. He'd sunk a couple of holes to one side of the stream, and they were now partially filled. The creek wasn't running too strongly; I guessed that it wasn't very far to the head.

Charlie explained that the creek bed had to be stripped down,

307

which meant moving a lot of boulders and gravel. I wasn't impressed with this mining racket; we were going to need some labour and I wasn't sure how we were going to manage that.

We went back to the camp to assess our resources. We had quite a lot of tobacco, fortunately: it was important currency. There was some sugar and five-fifty pound sacks of flour, well caked on the outside and with about thirty pounds of weevil-ridden flour inside. We had hops and cream of tartar and bicarbonate of soda, a bit green but it worked all right. There were a few tins of jam and about fifty pounds of salt.

It started to rain again and we stayed in our bark house playing cards. We were, for the first time, fairly comfortable. It was quite roomy; we had bunks and a good firm bark table around which we sat on logs set in a fork. There were blacks coming and going all that time, but during the rain they holed up in humpies.

The weather broke and we started work on the creek. It really came home to me then how crazy we were. The next day some blacks walked in with some buffalo meat on a pole. It was a bit grubby but it hadn't turned; we were right out of meat and I was glad to see it.

There were six in the party, and when I asked them how they got it they said they'd speared it. I knew their shovel spears were deadly weapons — and looked it — and I had heard of them spearing buffalo but was always doubtful. They said they'd found tracks and followed them for a day, coming up with the buffalo half-asleep under a tree just before sundown. They got two spears into it before it galloped away.

They tracked it until dark, camped on its tracks and started again at first light. They caught up with it about mid-day, got two more spears into it and picked one up that had fallen out, which was important — they had to conserve their ammunition. They caught up with it again about mid-afternoon and got another spear into it. This time it didn't gallop away but bailed up, trying to charge its tormentors. They were all behind trees and didn't have

308

much difficulty dodging it. Eventually it went down; it had taken ten spears to kill it and I imagine it had dropped from loss of blood.

We worked on the creek, keeping our number of boys to four. It was a peculiar situation because very few of them worked for more than a couple of days: I always thought it was partly out of curiosity and mostly their need for tobacco. If a couple left, two more would be there to take their place. Personally I thought it was a form of insanity and could never understand the incredible dedication of prospectors. Charlie had a sample of tin, perhaps three or four ounces in a pickle bottle, which he'd recovered earlier. He would fondle it, examine it, hold it up to the light and tell me what good quality tin it was. To me it was black sand, a bit like gunpowder and suprisingly heavy.

There were a lot of blacks about, their humpies strung out down the creek. The leader was a tall, wiry, fierce-looking fellow who could speak very little English — from what I could tell, none beyond the word tobacco. He never moved without a couple of shovel spears and a woomera, which was used to throw the spear with tremendous speed and accuracy.

He had a son, a happy, chubby fellow of about seven or eight who took a great fancy to me and used to follow me around like a dog, chattering away. He had evidently been to a mission school and could recite a few letters of the alphabet. He would often come to our camp at mealtimes and one of us would give him a slice of bread and jam. He said his name was Mulangarri.

Another week and we'd just about got down to where the tin lay. Dave and Charlie scratched around with a shovel and agreed there wasn't much, though there'd probably be some good pockets lower down the creek.

We were out of meat again. There were lots of bronzewing pigeons and I had been keeping the camp going with half a dozen or so a day, but cartridges were getting low. One morning some boys came into the camp and said there were the fresh tracks of a buffalo not far away. I immediately buckled on a cartridge belt, saddled a horse and rode out. Whalebone came with me to drive the spare horses, the fellow who brought the news walked along beside me, and another old fellow came along . . . just for the hell of it I suppose.

We found the tracks of a big bull and followed them until dark. Going by bruised leaves and droppings he wasn't too far ahead; I hoped he'd camp at night. We followed him all next morning and by then we'd got into low-lying country that soon became very boggy. I hobbled the horses, covered the gear with the tent fly and followed him on foot. It got dark, we collected some bark, made a fire and camped.

We were on his tracks at daylight. The bull was taking more time feeding now and we were catching up with him fast. He headed up into a gully and though it was heavily timbered it was narrowing. I felt sure I would have him soon. We had had nothing to eat for a day; the blacks showed me some bushes covered with white berries that they said were "goodfella tucker". I couldn't agree with the "goodfella" part, but they filled a void.

Suddenly one of the boys gave a whistle and pointed. The bull was in sight, feeding along slowly. The scrub was dense and the light was bad; I could barely see his slate-coloured form. As soon as he moved from one bush he get behind another. The grass was long, adding to my difficulties. Then I got a fairly clear view, sighted the rifle and fired. I heard the bullet thump into him and saw him jerk with the impact. Then he galloped away.

I got on his tracks again at daylight, hoping he'd weaken and pull up, but if anything he was improving. I turned back. We'd had nothing to eat since the previous morning except the white berries, and they weren't very sustaining. I got to where we left the horses, packed up and headed for the camp with empty packs. The sun was shining over the west; we were in the foothills about five or six miles from the camp. I was riding in the lead, the horses were strung along behind being driven by Whalebone. Suddenly I heard a commotion. A horse snorted, another started to gallop, the boys were shouting something about a broken leg. Christ, I thought, that's the last bloody straw, a horse with a broken leg. I swung my horse around, they all seemed all right. Whalebone was dismounted, struggling with a big kangaroo he had by the tail. I trotted back: he was grinning from ear to ear.

"Onefella horse kick 'im, broke 'im leg." He said it had bounded through the horses, scaring them. As it went through the mob one horse let fly with a well-aimed kick and smashed its hip. It was quickly killed with a billet of wood. One boy made a fire, I gutted it and took the liver and heart and head.

We thoroughly enjoyed a meal of what seems to be referred to by butchers for some reason, as offal. After nearly a couple of days without anything but berries it tasted delicious.

We had now shovelled our way down to the tin, which lay in pockets. There wasn't much. The rain was starting to ease as March came to an end. On April 2, I wrote: "Working the gully, the wash here is carrying the best tin we've seen so far, rich but small pockets. As we are starving we will be unable to work it right out and nothing will drag me back to this country again".

The weather was taking up and I started to get the saddlery into order; it had taken a beating in our travels. Stitching was breaking away in the pack saddles, but I had saddler's hemp and needles and pulled most of it together. Charlie was cleaning up the tin; there wasn't much, there couldn't have been more than fifty pounds.

On April 10, we packed to leave. About twenty blacks crowded round telling us how sorry they were that we were going. They wanted to know when we would be back. Mulangarri was crying and Dave gave him some stale damper and half a tin of jam the ants had got into — we didn't have much left in the way of rations. A black saddle-horse was very sick and I had to leave him. He looked as though he wouldn't last much longer — if he didn't die of whatever was wrong with him the blacks would spear him and eat him. I asked Charlie to shoot him. And so we left.

I rode in the lead, picking a track through the hills down to level country. The horses were strung along behind, Dave and Charlie with Whalebone and his lubra bringing up the rear. The country was still soft and boggy in patches; we reached the river, which was still running strongly. I had hidden the canoe we had made in February and to my surprise it hadn't been discovered.

We camped on the river and around the campfire that night Charlie told us that riding along that day he was talking to Whalebone, who told him there had been some plans to spear us. Mulangarri's father was the ringleader, which was easy to believe — he certainly looked the part. Whalebone had told him the lad had talked his father out of it; the kid had liked me and wouldn't let him spear us. I suppose he couldn't very well spear Charlie and Dave and leave me.

I asked why Whalebone didn't warn us, but he said that he didn't know about it, which was reasonable. Dave said: "Well, I'm buggered; if I'd known that I'd have given the kid a full tin of jam instead of that tin with the ants in it."

Thinking it over I concluded there might have been some truth in the plans, but at the same time I knew that around their campfires there was a lot of wild talk that was mostly boastful bravado. Nevertheless, there was the odd spearing going on somewhere or other and, after all, McColl was speared only last year, as were the Japanese. There's an old saying, "Somebody up there likes me". A little Aboriginal boy liking me was much better.

The plain, which was flooded in February, had now dried out though it was boggy in places and one or two gutters were still running. We put most of the gear and what little we had left in the way of rations in the canoe, and Charlie and Whalebone paddled it down to the crossing. Dave and I took the horses across the plain and through the gorge in a day. We crossed the saddles and packs in the canoe, swam the horses and camped on the other side. The

312

next day I rode out and shot a buffalo cow, and when I got back to the camp Dave had a couple of big barramundi grilling on the campfire.

Three days later we were at the Jim Jim crossing, out of rations and living entirely off the land. I knew of a mine operating in the foothills about twenty-five miles to the south, so I took a couple of packs and rode over. They were a good lot of blokes and somewhat amazed at the experiences I had been through with Charlie and Dave, though I gave them only a very rough outline of our travels. They filled my packs and though I offered them a letter to Jolleys to replace what I had got, they refused to accept anything.

I rode back to Jim Jim giving some thought to the approaching buffalo-shooting season. I would have to go to Darwin to arrange hide contracts, stores and supplies. Pine Creek was the nearest town, about 100 miles. I told Dave it would be best if he went back to Kapalga with Charlie; I would go to Pine Creek and on to Darwin. I expected I would be able to get a boat out with the stores within a couple of weeks; I hoped I'd be back in three, but no more than four.

I picked out three of the strongest saddle horses, a couple of pack horses and left. I also took a spare saddle, reckoning on getting a horse tailer somewhere along the track.

Looking back, our entire adventure has all the appearances of a continuous exercise in insanity . . . and I suppose it was. Like many other people, when it comes to hindsight I am an Olympic Games gold medallist.

I reached Pine Creek in four days — the day before the train was due, arranged with George Stevens to keep an eye on my horses, sent a message to Dick Guild and boarded Leaping Lena for Darwin. By Monday morning I was with Bill Grant, the hide buyer. The news was shattering. The hide market had collapsed and he was waiting for telegrams. Come back tomorrow, he said,

There was only one place to go after that — the pub. Cecil Freer was in the bar. Freer was an old operator from way back. He had the largest holding of buffalo country, something over 1000 square miles. "The market's going through one of those cycles," he said.

"Maybe it is, Cecil, but whatever kind of a cycle it is the bloody wheels have fallen off; Grant hasn't even got a market."

"I would guess his people will come up with three, maybe three and a half tomorrow. You've been out prospecting, haven't you?"

I nodded. It wasn't my favourite subject.

"I take it you did no good?"

'I did worse than no good," I said morosely, "and the drop in the hide market is just about the last straw."

We chatted for a while, he finished his drink and was about to leave when he said, "Come and see me tomorrow. I might be able to offer you something."

He had a cottage in Mitchell Street and the following morning I was there on the stroke of eight-thirty. Freer was stretched out on the verandah in a squatter's chair and motioned me to one beside him.

He quickly got down to business. "I could offer you a contract for 1000 hides at three and a half, but what I suggest you do is see Grant; he may be able to offer better. If he can't, come back here and we'll talk it over."

I went straight back to Grant's office but he hadn't received any replies. I told him Freer could offer three and a half. "Tom, my advice to you is take it. I don't expect we'll be able to come up with anything better." In business matters it was noticeable everyone was very straightforward.

I had arranged to see Cecil Freer at the hotel in the afternoon; in the meantime my head was working like a tin of worms. I could probably get him to guarantee my account with Jolleys and preserve my meagre capital. Freer had his own boat so I would try to get him to make the contract delivery at his wharf — a little light was seeping through the gloom.

314

I was in the bar waiting when he walked in. I said without any preamble, "I've decided to take up your offer Cecil, and I'm hoping perhaps you'll agree to delivery at your wharf at the Wildman."

Then I went on. "I've taken a hammering on this mad prospecting trip; would you guarantee my account at Jolleys?"

'Yes sure, I'll see Jim Fawcett first thing tomorrow."

'What about the contract: do you want me to sign anything?"

'No, you give me a fair go and I'll give you one." I knew I had no worries.

On May 22, I noted in my diary: "Accepted Freer's offer. Saw Fawcett re rations and five tons of salt".

I returned to Pine Creek and got my horses together. I had no trouble picking up a horse tailer named Spider. There was a letter from Dick Guild asking if I wanted any horses. I wrote back telling him I would be shooting for Freer, probably somewhere down the Wildman, and reckoned I'd be pleased to see some about August. I then left for Kapalga.

I made good time. A mission lugger was tied up at the wharf when I got there, apparently looking for one of the mission's up-and-coming young black Godbotherers. A young fellow — some sort of a Jesus apprentice — was skippering the boat. He told us Jim Moles had been killed by a buffalo bull at Cannon Hills on the East Alligator. I had met Moles a couple of times and he seemed a very competent bushman. He had been buffalo shooting for a season with a half-caste named Jack Cadell, who was very well known as a rough rider.

I started to muster horses. Most of them had been on the prospecting trip and were pretty rough, certainly in no shape to start a buffalo season. A mare called Ladybird had developed a bad swamp cancer, for which there was no cure. This always upset me, she would have to be destroyed. Another horse, Dragon, had died, and a bay, Dynamite, looked ready to chuck it in. I mustered twenty-four that were in good condition, all horses I had left behind when we went to Myra Falls. My shooting horse, Gambler, turned up rolling fat. I hadn't seen him for nearly a year and assumed he had died. I was pleased to see him; he was sure-footed and good in timber.

There were quite a few buffalo camp boys camped at the other end of the Kapalga lagoon, so I wasn't going to have any problems with labour. Among them was a fellow named Singing Man Billy, whom I'd heard of — he was a crack foot-shooter and had been shooting on Marrakai for the past two or three seasons. As his named implied, he was a corroboree singer and because of this always had a following.

I now had to get my camp together and cross to Point Stuart, which was what Freer called his place. It was named after the explorer John McDouall Stuart who crossed Australia from south to north in 1862.

I made a start with thirty-one horses and six packs; the dray could come along later when the country had dried out more. There was nothing much in the way of rations and stores, because all my supplies were coming out on the boat. Four days later I was at Freer's landing. He had a nephew, Max Freer, in charge of things and though he didn't appear to be an experienced bushman, he was very helpful and good company. I got my camp set up on a spring and a day later saddled Gambler and started shooting. It was scrub shooting for a start, which was normal; it was good to get into action again. Everything was going along smoothly and nothing was happening to disturb the even tenor of our way, which was unusual.

The tallies were starting to build up. My diary records on successive days: eight, eight, eleven, ten. Then, "Black mare Mischief got bogged, took half a day to get her out".

She had walked into a buffalo wallow that had a deceptively thin crust covering a bottomless bog. It is impossible to imagine the infuriating difficulty involved in getting her out. The wallow was about eight or ten feet across; a nice fit for a horse. I had ropes that we used to secure the hides on pack horses and I joined two or three together. After a lot of burrowing into filthy black slime I

316

managed to get the rope under her chest. To stop her struggle which was making the situation worse, I put a bag over her head. I had to send back to the camp for axes and shovels. We enlarged the hole, cut poles and eventually levered her out. When it was all over and the mare washed down we were all buggered, horse and all.

Freer's boat, the *Venture*, arrived with some startling news from Darwin. Jack Gaden and Bill Jennings had been crocodile-hunting on the Mary River. They had a boy in the camp named Butcher; it seemed there had been some trouble with him and he had been ordered out of the camp. He had come back during the night, taken a rifle and shot Bill Jennings and two lubras as well as blowing off half Gaden's hand.

We were warned that he was armed and believed to be heading out our way. The message, which was verbal, concluded with, "If you see him, shoot the bastard."

I was very upset to hear of Jennings' murder; I had met him a number of times and liked him. He was a good all-round bushman and horseman, and the last time I saw him was when I was preparing to leave for Myra Falls.

The police wasted no time in getting on Butcher's tracks; he didn't have much chance of getting away. All the blacks were terrified of him, especially when he turned up in a camp with a rifle and a belt full of cartridges. Bill Littlejohn from the Brock's Creek police post arrested him about a week later.

I have an interesting note in my diary: "Letter from Jim Moles saying he branded a colt of Bill Jennings by mistake, if I see him would I please let him know".

Well, it didn't matter now; they were both dead.

CHAPTER 23

CROCODILE HUNTING WITH HARPOON AND GUN

The next time the *Venture* arrived from Darwin there was some mail, a few bills and a letter from Grant the hide buyer asking if I'd be interested in shooting crocodiles. (I noticed he had their name right.) He said his company would pay one shilling and sixpence an inch, measurement taken across the belly. A diagram was enclosed showing the skinning method and a few details on curing.

Gaden and Jennings were the first to take it on commercially and I had heard them talking about it. There were plenty to be had; riding past a waterhole where buffalo carcasses were lying from previous shooting it was a common sight to see crocodiles tearing at them. On our approach they would scuttle quickly into the water.

At that time nothing was known about spotlight shooting at night, which in later years decimated them until protective measures were brought in. Gaden and Jennings' boys got them by spearing, though I had never seen them doing it.

I had only about 200 hides to get to complete Freer's contract; at the rate I was going I would have them in a couple of weeks. I could easily split a few boys off the buffalo camp and start them crocodile hunting.

The enthusiasm the new venture generated was quite surprising; my difficulty was determining who would go. Everyone wanted to go, for which they could hardly be blamed. It was starting to get hot and buffalo hunting was getting wearisome. I knew how they felt — just like I did.

The operation was something they knew all about, and it was something on which I was happy to be guided by my boys; after all, they were among the best hunters in the world. We were camped at Fish Billabong, where we would start, but first I had to get the proper equipment.

Harpoons had to be made. I was able to get a length of half-inch steel rod from Max Freer, who had also become interested in the new operation. I gave Dave Cameron the job of making them. They had to be a foot long with a sharp barbed tip. He heated them in the campfire and belted away at them, eventually coming up with quite an effective product that was lashed to a rope just above the barb and fitted with a long pole in such a way that it was tight enough to stay in place but would come away when plunged into a crocodile's back.

In the meantime the lubras had been busy collecting paperbark for a raft, which they lashed together with vines. We were ready.

It was explained to me by Charlie that we would start at the first crack of dawn — piccaninny daylight. It was essential there was not the slightest breeze to ruffle the surface of the water and the excitement was such on the first morning of our operations that everybody was sitting around the campfire waiting anxiously for dawn to break.

As soon as there was enough light to see, Bamboo Charlie stepped on to his strange craft and poled his way out to the middle. He reversed the harpoon shaft and started thrashing the surface of the water furiously. Very soon a line of bubbles appeared on the surface — something was moving along the muddy bottom. That something was a crocodile! Then the bubbles stopped. Charlie quickly reversed his harpoon and held it poised over the water as the flimsy craft glided over the bubbles. When he got to the spot where the bubbles stopped, he drove the harpoon down in the water with all his strength.

Charlie's thrust was accurate and there was a mighty swirl as the rope snaked out, more than half of it disappearing into the water. He poled his way to the bank and gave the rope to one of the

319

boys waiting excitedly. Willing hands came to his assistance and it became a one-sided tug-of-war.

With a lot of shrieking from men, women and children, a ten-foot crocodile, was dragged to the bank thrashing wildly. I quickly despatched it with a bullet to the head.

The harpoon, which was firmly embedded in its back, was cut out and Charlie, with a great smile of satisfaction, poled out into the middle of the billabong again. Quickly he harpooned another one, a bit smaller than the first but nevertheless a useful size.

By about 10am a breeze sprang up and ruffled the surface of the water to such an extent that the telltale bubbles could not be seen, so we stopped hunting. We had five and they were all skinned, salted down and stacked away in the shade.

I had to get back to finishing Freer's contract and left Singing Man Billy with the crocodile hunters. They got eleven more over the next two days and Charlie said the hole was cleaned out, so I moved them over to another good lagoon a few miles away.

By mid-October I had finished Freer's contract; all the hides were at his jetty and I moved over to join the crocodile hunters. The novelty of the new venture appealed to me as much as the camp, which was enjoying the change of crocodile meat. I tried to eat it but couldn't bring myself to even taste it; it had a most revolting smell and anyway there was no shortage of barramundi, duck and geese.

We were at a waterhole called Alec's Hole but didn't do any good; there were too many waterlilies. The leaves were the size of a large plate and the crocodiles, when they were disturbed, went into them: the bubbles couldn't be seen. From there we went to another hole on the Wildman and got nine. The next hole, two or three miles further down, yielded thirteen. The next was called Alligator Camp and I noted: "Things slowed down a bit, this lagoon not so good for harpooning, too many bullrushes, forty-four skins to date".

The final waterhole was at Ban Yan Point, the last hole on the Wildman. From here to the mangroves, where it was tidal and salt, there was an unbroken plain of several miles where the river made again into a salt arm winding its way to the sea.

Ban Yan Point was quite a big stretch of water, Even so I was surprised at the results. We got twenty-two, which wrapped it up. Storms were about and there was a big plain to get across. But first I had to get a supply of beef: for one thing the salad days of crocodile meat were over for the camp, and I had a yearning to get my teeth into a good juicy buffalo steak. This didn't present any difficulties — I could see buffalo grazing out on the plain a few miles away. I saddled Gambler and with a pack horse to carry the meat I rode out just after sunrise.

As I got closer to the buffalo they sighted me and started to move away. I broke into a canter to close the gap; soon they were galloping and I gave my horse his head. He swept across the plain and cut the distance down rapidly.

I was watching the buffalo when, suddenly, Gambler shied and swerved sharply. It was normal for a horse to do this when galloping across the plains to avoid a buffalo wallow — a fairly frequent hazard. But he had shied so violently that I took a quick look over my shoulder to see what had startled him to such an extent. To my astonishment I caught a glimpse of a fairly big crocodile, obviously dead, lying in the grass. A few more strides I came to another one, and another; they were all dead.

This puzzled me tremendously, but I had to put it out of my mind and get on with the job in hand. I soon caught up with the buffalo and knocked down a young fat cow. The pack horse trotted up a few minutes later driven by one of my lads, and as we took the pack bags off to get the knives out I asked him if he'd seen the dead crocodiles.

"Ui, boss," he replied, "sixfella me lookim."

We butchered the cow, filled the pack bags and rode back to the camp. On the way I did some scouting around. The dead creatures had aroused my curiosity and I counted eleven altogether.

Turning it over in my mind as I rode along, I formed a theory that was undoubtedly the answer. As we moved from waterhole to waterhole down the Wildman the tallies increased; nine, thirteen, twenty-two — nature's survival telepathy began to operate. Alarm bells were rung, the survival instinct went into action, and the crocodiles knew death was abroad. The survivors moved out during the night.

When we got to Banyan Point there would have been a sharp increase in the crocodile population and I have no doubt the newcomers would have been able to convey their fear to their reluctant hosts. All mature animals have their own area and they resent intruders. Couple this with our activities, and problems arise.

So, when I started to hunt Banyan Point another exodus started, but this time it was a long way to go — too far. They would have plodded along during the night and by sunrise they weren't halfway. The sun would have killed them before it reached its zenith.

The crocodile skin total was fifty-two, most of which had gone to Darwin in Freer's boat; some of the Banyan Point skins I had sent by pack horse across to Max. I had eight with me and they would go in some time later.

I moved my camp back to Kapalga. On the way I left half a ton of salt at Gipsy Spring; maybe I would be shooting my own country again next season if the market improved.

CHAPTER 24

TIME BELONG . . .

There were quite a lot of blacks camped around the lagoon, in anticipation of the end of the shooting season. I knew a corroboree had been planned and my lot were looking forward to a week or so's entertainment — which would go on night and day without a break. Sleeping would be intermittent; their stamina was quite remarkable.

It was strictly an all-male show for the first couple of weeks. The women had their own form of entertainment that wasn't quite so strict, and when it started to taper off, the women came into it, mainly as dancers. Then after another week — and a few fights — it would fold up. There was to be another big gathering at Cannon Hills and most of them headed off.

Christmas came and went; the New Year saw the end of the rum. January ran into February, the plains were flooded and the geese were nesting. This was a welcome and remarkable event; welcome because of the surfeit of eggs that would result and remarkable because of the immensity of one of nature's natural phenomena. It was "time belong goose egg".

The Aborigines divide their year into "time belong". After the geese nesting there was a gap — the heavy rain, "time belong 'ungry", then the welcome "time belong burnem grass", clearing the ground of dense matted grass, facilitating travelling and hunting; then the green shoot generated by the burn fattened the kangaroos, it was "time belong kangaroo". As the waterholes dropped and the choice waterlily roots and seeds became more easily available the geese fattened, "time belong goose" arrived, and it was then too that the crocodiles nested — "time belong crocodile egg" . . . and so it went on.

I was invited to participate in a goose-egg expedition, so early one morning I saddled a horse and rode to the edge of a flooded plain about a mile away. There was quite a crowd gathered around three canoes, mostly naked and partly naked men, women and children. I shed my boots, leaving them for my horse to look after, and joined the milling throng who were all talking at once — creating more decibels than the geese, which was quite an accomplishment.

It was suggested I ride in the biggest canoe which, though leaking, had a generous supply of soft paperbark in the bottom. In no way would it make any contribution to keeping me dry but it would at least allow me to get wet more comfortably.

Off we went, gliding through the reeds. It was no distance to the nests and the geese were in their thousands, sitting on nests no more than a few yards apart, flying around and creating an indescribable din with their continual honking. The area covered by this nesting place was probably about 200 acres and right across the tropical north, wherever there were floodplains, there would be millions of magpie geese busy doing what these birds were doing — breeding more geese.

Nearly all the nests carried eggs. An average clutch appeared to be about ten, they were a dull white colour about the size of a domestic duck egg . . . and they were there in thousands. The two smaller canoes were filled quickly; some eggs were left because they were judged to be too close to hatching. I don't know how they could tell, but I had no doubt they were right. Very soon I was surrounded with goose eggs and it was suggested that I get out and walk, not exactly what I had in mind when we started. As I sloshed my way back to dry land I reflected on the fascinating facets of Aboriginal life; getting wet was inconsequential.

For the next week we had goose eggs fried, goose eggs boiled, goose eggs curried. We had them in omelettes and in cakes. One morning I said: "Dave, I think I'm going to lay a bloody goose egg, try to think of something else to cook — please!"

February ran into March and the general rain started to ease. Everything was growing a healthy crop of mildew, so the sun was a welcome sight. I got the breaking gear out and started on four youngsters, two brown colts, a grey filly and a bay. They had all been partially broken in the year before for hide carrying, so it was only a matter of mouthing them, putting a saddle on them and riding them out. Three were very ordinary but I'd had my eye on the bay filly for some time. Her name was Trinket and she looked well above the general run of buffalo camp horses; she had good conformation and seemed to have a good temperament. She came to hand quickly and I promised her I wouldn't put any more buffalo hides on her.

I was giving a lot of thought to the hide market, wondering what the gods had up their sleeves for me this year. Then, one afternoon, Joe Cooper walked into the camp from the jetty. He had brought his boat, the *Maskee*, up the river. He and his son Reuben had a sawmill along the coast where they were cutting cypress pine. He was on his way to Darwin with a load of timber and had run into some bad weather off the mouth of the South Alligator, put into the river and drifted up on the tide. He had a few buckets of turtle eggs they had gathered at Field Island off the mouth of the river: he offered us a bucket, but Dave explained that we had gone off eggs for a while. They were round, soft-shelled, a bit larger than a ping-pong ball perhaps, and I knew that the white never set no matter how long they were cooked.

I got myself a ride to Darwin. We drifted down the river until we got to the open sea when the sails were hoisted. The boat had a kerosene engine but there was no kerosene.

Joe was the first man to shoot buffalo commercially at the turn of the century when he went to Melville Island. He had an inexhaustible fund of stories and I have always regretted I didn't make some notes. He showed me a scar on his shoulder, legacy of the time he had been speared when he was shooting on the island.

The days passed pleasantly; it was between the northern monsoons and the southeasterly weather and there was little wind. It took us five days to reach Darwin.

The hide market had strengthened and fivepence a pound was easily obtainable, even at Jolleys. I took a contract with Jolleys for 300 hides and one with Grant for 500: he also offered me one and sixpence an inch for crocodile skins and said he'd take as many as I could get.

I ordered all my stores and supplies, then saw Jack Hales. His boat wasn't leaving for a couple of weeks so I went out to my old friends Oscar and Evan Herbert at Koolpinyah Station. The time passed pleasantly. I gave them a hand to break in two or three horses and a couple of days' mustering, then went back to Darwin, boarded the *Maroubra* and three days later I was back at Kapalga.

There were lots of blacks around, so I had no trouble putting a team together. I shod three shooting horses, moved out to Flying Fox Creek and started shooting: it was the middle of June. I had a good camp. Ring was probably one of the best horseback shooters on the coast, he liked horses and horses liked him; it always worked both ways. Singing Man Billy was a cracking foot shooter and a good tracker. When we came across tracks in the scrub, Billy could tell how fresh they were and if they were worth following.

One day Ring and I were riding ahead of the pack horses as usual. The timber was fairly heavy but not too bad; Ring was on Dollar and I was riding Gambler. Suddenly a young bull jumped from a patch of grass where it had obviously been asleep. I nodded to Ring, "Knock him down." They were quickly out of sight in the timber and shortly after I heard a shot. Then a few moments later I heard several more in quick succession; he must have run into a mob, I thought, as I put my spurs to Gambler and galloped after him. I followed the tracks he had made when he went after the bull. I came up to where he had dropped it, intending to pass it on one side but suddenly it got to its feet and Gambler swerved sharply. On my right was a stringybark tree, about three feet through, leaning towards me, and although I tried to miss it it fitted me exactly from my ankle to my shoulder.

I was knocked clean out of the saddle, my rifle went flying and I hit the ground in a cloud of dust. I was badly hurt and I had a determined-looking wounded bull very close. There was an excruciating pain in my right knee and my shoulder was nearly as bad. The pain I was in was a secondary consideration; the first law of nature, survival, was working overtime. Somehow I managed to scramble behind the tree that had caused my downfall as the bull charged. He stopped just short of the tree and backed away; I think he was taking aim because he charged again and hit the tree with such tremendous force I felt the concussion. If I could have got my hands on my rifle I could have shot him easily, but I had no idea where it was, and even if I had known it would have been some kind of insanity to have left the safety of the tree. I had no trouble getting my priorities right there. Because of my battered state and the size of the tree there was no way I could have climbed it, and anyway the nearest branch was about fifty feet up. Singing Man Billy or Ring should be along soon to rescue me; they seemed to be taking a long time, or at any rate it seemed like it. I would have thought that with the bullet he had in him and the encounter with the tree the bull should have shown signs of weakening, but to me he still seemed dangerously healthy. Suddenly a shot rang out and he dropped. Billy came running up and asked anxiously if I were all right. I wasn't really, but said yes from sheer relief.

It was a week before I could ride well enough to shoot; for this kind of work it was necessary to be a hundred per cent fit and well. My knee took longest to recover — action in a saddle involved a lot of knee movement and it had copped a solid bash.

As I was out of action for buffalo shooting I thought I may as well turn my convalescence to some advantage. Bamboo Charlie had been at me for some time to know when we were going to start hunting crocodiles, so though it was a bit early I reckoned I may as well set him up on one of the shallower waterholes.

Charlie moved out on to the water as soon as it was light enough to see. He got four, then the wind came up and he couldn't see the bubbles. The next day was perfect and it wasn't long before he had a good one speared. He said that there weren't many left — it wasn't a very big hole and he thought probably three: one, he said, was a big one. He came ashore and asked for a file; he wanted to sharpen the harpoon for the big fellow. He said he'd get him next, speaking with the quiet confidence that goes with the knowledge of bush lore.

He returned to his raft and poled out to the middle. I followed along the bank watching closely. I saw some bubbles rise to the surface but Charlie ignored them and poled his way further along, thrashing the water. Suddenly I saw another line of bubbles clearly and this time Charlie reversed his harpoon. For a few seconds he stood like an ebony statue. Then he drove it with all his strength and as he did so he took a step forward. He had one foot on the coil of rope that was snaking out rapidly as the crocodile took off. I don't know how it happened, but somehow the rope had got around his ankle and tightened. There was a mightly splash as he was jerked off the raft and disappeared; a moment later he surfaced briefly then disappeared again. The rest of the camp was running along the bank, shrieking with laughter, shouting what sounded like encouragement — which could have been directed at the crocodile providing them with such magnificent entertainment. They were all splitting their sides; even old Maudie, Charlie's wife, was laughing as heartily as the rest.

In the meantime the crocodile, which had been effectively harpooned had got to the end of the lagoon and stopped for a moment. Then it swam back to a place where there was a steep bank in an endeavour to find a hiding place.

By the time Charlie had freed himself from the tangle and swam to the bank where I was waiting. He was gasping for breath as I helped him from the water. "You all right old fella?" I asked him as he began to get his breath back. "Ui, me orright, by Cri' boss, me shit plenty!" A statement I had no difficulty believing.

The rope, floating on the surface was quickly recovered and the wildly thrashing crocodile was hauled to the bank, where I soon put a bullet into its skull. I went over to where Charlie was sitting on the bank. I wasn't sure how he felt about continuing so I said to him; "You like go out again Charlie?"

"Ui, me orright, wind belong me 'e come back now."

He went out again and harpooned one more and that was it for that hole. Charlie was now laughing with the rest about his recent adventure: This was a characteristic of Aborigines; once the danger had passed it was never given another thought. It was then that the humorous side surfaced. Bamboo Charlie was a fine old fellow, much respected by the others and was a man of some consequence at corroborees.

It took longer than I expected for my knee to recover; the injury was worse than I thought. It was a relief to get back into the saddle. When I was ready to start again I saddled the bay mare Trinket on whom I'd had my eye for some time. She was a lovely thing, not much over fourteen hands but very strong and with a beautifully smooth gait and, most importantly, a very intelligent head.

I finished shooting at the end of October with 1102 hides. By the time the *Maroubra* arrived and we had loaded them and I had stacked most of my gear away in one of Charlie Burns' sheds, it was halfway through November.

I kept two boys, Clarrie and George; the rest of the camp had decided to go to Field Island at the mouth of the South Alligator River. Field Island was renowned as a place where turtles came to lay their eggs, up to fifty to sixty in one hole. Three canoes appeared from somewhere and they left, all talking at once,

George and Clarrie looked longingly at them as they disappeared round a bend in the river.

Dave Cameron and I and the two horse tailers left Kapala. We had twenty-two horses; I had turned another twenty-odd out down the plain.

I reached Dick Guild's place towards the end of November; the weather was still holding, though there were a few storms about. These weren't the conventional mustering months, but Guild was not a conventional cattleman; he was a battler who, to quote himself, tried to make "every post a winning post". His country covered 500 square miles (at least that's what he paid rent on) and he shared a boundary with Manbulloo Station, which was owned by Vesteys. The Manbulloo stock camp was not nearly as diligent as Guild; mustering during the early storms and heat was not for them. This gave him an advantage in more ways than one — there was no such thing as attending boundary musters and splitting the unbranded cleanskins. A lot of his country was hilly and rough, there was an advantage here, the cattle retreated to the hilly areas when the low-lying parts were boggy and often flooded.

I never knew where his boundaries were . . . nor, I would think, would anyone else. Very little of the country was surveyed and boundaries were largely by guess and by God.

We got three weeks' mustering in before the heavy rains put a stop to our activities. We had been well mounted, but it had been hard riding and our horses would have shared our relief when we put the slip rails up behind a hundred or so bellowing branders and settled in at the homestead.

New Year's Day, 1936, didn't seem any different to any other day except that we were isolated by floodwaters; there certainly wasn't anything special to celebrate. We busied ourselves straightening up the saddlery and replacing some rails in the stockyard when there was a break in the rain.

At the end of February the rain started to ease and it was a relief to see the sun for a couple of consecutive days. By March it was

330

pretty well all over and I renewed my acquaintance with Leaping Lena and headed for Darwin. The hide market was quite strong, I took a contract for 500 at five and three-quarters; I felt sure that if the market didn't rise it wouldn't fall, and I would take another 500 later on in the season.

I got back to Guild's place and we started to muster my horses. When they were all yarded, Nigger and Hawk were missing. At the crack of dawn Clarry and I were riding out after the two truants; I was on Gambler and Clarry was on Cloud. We picked up tracks quickly. It was Hawk and Nigger right enough, and they were with three young brumby stallions that had no doubt been chased out by older stallions.

I had told Clarry we would let them run for a mile or so; the two working horses would probably drop back and we could cut them off easily. I hoped so anyway. But of course it didn't work out that way; the two horses stuck to the youngsters like shit to a blanket. I had told Clarry to ride behind me as a back-up if it came to running them down; Gambler was going well, pulling a bit but I was able to restrain him. I could see neither of the runaways was going to drop back, so I started to force the pace a bit. We were in hilly country and I didn't like it one little bit.

Gambler and Cloud were shod but I could feel my mount starting to tire and guessed Cloud would be feeling the strain, though Clarry was a lot lighter than I. Nigger started to drop back but Hawk was well up with the leaders and galloping strongly. "Here's a bloody fix," I thought. Nigger was chucking it in and started to slow to a canter — I called to Clarry who quickly ranged up alongside me. I told him to take Nigger back and I'd keep after Hawk; there was nothing else I could do.

Gambler was starting to tire and I could see if I didn't get the chestnut soon I wouldn't get him at all. We came thundering down off a ridge and on to some flat country; if I could get up alongside them I could probably cut him out, so I galloped along the side of a ridge skirting the flats. By the feel of Gambler I knew it was a long desperate throw. We started to make ground. My horse was really

331

tired but I felt sure I could cut in and get the chestnut bastard. I was nearly level with them when it happened — Gambler clipped a log, then struck some loose stone and down we came. The horse tried to recover but we were on a sloping hillside and he had no chance. He crashed down again — my right leg was under him both times.

I was badly hurt and in a lot of pain, my shirt and trousers were ripped and I was bleeding badly from my arm and along my leg. But that wasn't the worst of it — I had an excruciating pain in my ankle, which I thought was broken, or at any rate a bit busted up. Gambler trotted down on to the flat and stood there looking back at me. And not too happily either; I could see he had lost some skin from his hip and shoulder. I thought if I could get to him and somehow mount him I could get back to the station, but now I was starting to feel really bad. I thought I was going to vomit. That passed but the pain in my ankle was almost unbearable and I was starting to get stiff, too. The sun was setting and before long it would be if not cold, uncomfortably cool. I was glad to see Gambler had disappeared over a ridge in the direction of the station. He wouldn't be in any hurry but would get there eventually, and someone would find him hanging his head over the slip rails.

I knew what Dick would do; by seven o'clock he would be getting anxious and would question Clarry about where I was when I sent him back with Nigger. By eight he would be sure that I'd had a mishap. There'd be no point in trying to find me in the dark, but he would have horses in the yard long before daylight and would ride with Clarry to where we had parted, then follow my tracks. I estimated I had travelled perhaps a couple of miles from where I had sent Clarry back.

I started to make myself as comfortable as possible for the night, cleared some stones away and broke some bushes off in an effort to make some sort of a bed. I wouldn't be very comfortable, but it would cushion the hard ground. All bushmen carried on their belt a pouch containing a pocket knife, another with a watch and a third with matches. It was now five o'clock; my watch, as was most bushmen's, was set for six o'clock sundown. It divided the day up fairly evenly; sunrise would also be about six. This was the bushman's way of checking time; there was no such thing as radio stations giving out signals.

I started a fire against the log that had been my downfall, it took fairly well after feeding it with some dry grass and twigs and would keep going all night without much replenishing. My ankle was swelling badly and in an endeavour to ease the pain I cut the boot off by slitting down the back and the elastic on the sides. I don't think it really made any difference, but it gave me something to do. I tried not to look at my watch too often; it seemed as though it was going backwards.

I dozed fitfully. One side of me was kept warm by the fire and when it got too uncomfortable I turned over, but that was a painful operation. Eventually the morning star appeared. It was never more welcome. Just before the sun rose I heard the sound of horses cantering over the ridge. It was Dick and Clarry with a spare saddle horse for me. He greeted me with "Couldn't you find a better place to take a fall? What's broken?"

"I don't know, Dick, but my ankle isn't too good."

"Jesus Christ! I'd say it was broken for a start anyway. We'd better get you on to this horse and get you back home. This old fellow," pointing to the spare saddle horse, "is quiet enough. All we have to do is get you on to him."

Between the two of them they managed to lift me on to the horse. Changing my position from laying down to sitting on a horse was agony, but we managed it, or — perhaps it would be more correct to say *they* managed it.

The ride back to the homestead was sheer agony. I couldn't put my foot in the stirrup; it was too painful to take any kind of weight. It took all morning to get back to the house and I was buggered. I felt a bit better after I'd had a feed and a few pannikins of hot tea. Then we talked about what to do next. It was obvious I'd better get to hospital, and the sooner the better. It was twenty-six miles to Katherine, there were several creeks to cross and no road — just a pack horse track. Dick said he'd ride in and get a car of some sort. I said, "Do you think you'll get anyone to take on that track with a car?"

"I'll find someone. Bob McLennan is back from his mail run."

I knew there wasn't much to choose from, I thought that there were only two vehicles in Katherine. But knowing those men I knew I'd be rescued. We slept on it and the next morning Dick got away before sunrise. Just before sundown I heard a car and shortly afterwards Bob McLennan and Dick arrived, smothered in mud from head to foot. Bob was cursing with great fluency but in a fairly good-natured way. When he saw my ankle he said: "You poor bastard, you'll probably have to have it taken off; the last one I saw like that the doctor said, 'It'll have to come off, it's not worth fucking around with'!"

In my diary for Sunday, April 19, I wrote: "Dick got away early this morning to ride to Katherine to get a car to take me to hospital. Arrived back at sundown. Road in shocking state. Hospital 11pm."

On the way in, to cheer me up, they told me there was no doctor in Katherine. When I asked where he was, they said he'd gone to China! And they weren't kidding, either.

Doctor Clyde Fenton was the resident medical officer in Katherine, though right then he wasn't in residence. He had been in the country only two years but was already a legend. He was Australia's only real live Flying Doctor and by that I mean he bought his own aeroplanes, he flew his own aeroplanes, he wrecked his own aeroplanes — at fairly frequent intervals. And he was revered the length and breadth of a country by men who knew all about overwhelming odds. I always regarded it as a privilege to be one of his friends.

His first aircraft, a tiny Gipsy Moth, was wrecked on the vast Victoria River Downs Station. He was attempting to fly to the aid of a woman who had been gored by a bull. It was his first cross-country flight at night but, as he said, "There was a good moon!" He walked fifteen miles to the VRD homestead, eventually got to Katherine and thence by train to Darwin.

The wreck he walked away from on the Victoria River was not even paid for. Nevertheless, he was determined to get another plane somehow. He had demonstrated its usefulness time and time again but, even so, raising the money in those terrible depression years was a monumental task.

Qantas had a Gipsy Moth for sale and the Commonwealth Government was persuaded to put up the required money . . . but only on the condition that it was a loan against Fenton's salary and, further, that he assigned his life insurance policy to boot! One of the remarkable features of this was that he *had* a life insurance policy; he must have sneaked up on some unsuspecting company when they weren't looking.

This plane lasted for quite a long time, though it took a frightful hammering. Of course it got to the stage where even Fenton wouldn't fly it and Qantas got the job of doing an extensive overhaul. It was spread over the floor of the Darwin workshop when a call came through from Roper River Mission. A native boy had been badly burned and medical attention was needed urgently.

What followed was typical of Fenton. First he got in touch with the Australian Inland Mission asking them to fly to the Mission, but they said unfortunately they couldn't; the Roper River airstrip was unlicensed and would void their insurance if they landed there. As Clyde said to me later, this was the disadvantage of insuring one's aeroplane!

There was a Gipsy Moth in Darwin owned by the creditors of a defunct mining company. What happened next could be straight from Gilbert and Sullivan — the Administrator was got out of bed, in a bemused state signed a guarantee on behalf of the Commonwealth Government, and at dawn Fenton flew off to Roper River. When he got back he was informed by the worried manager of

Jolleys that the Commonwealth had repudiated the Administrator's guarantee. The only thing the harried doctor could think of was to offer the one strewn across the Qantas floor as bail for the mining company machine. Fawcett agreed: the poor fellow didn't have much in the way of options.

The situation then was he was still paying for his first plane, VH-UNI, which had crashed at Victoria River Downs, he was also trying to pay Qantas for VH-UIO (which he used ro refer to as IOU), which was now in pieces and guaranteed for VH-UJN.

He also had the Department of Civil Aviation to contend with; it was by no means happy with him landing all over the place in paddocks and on roads, crashing aeroplanes and walking away without official permission. But he was difficult to discipline. A man at Alice Springs with tetanus, a miner at Tennant Creek with a broken leg, a native at Delamere with a shovel spear through his chest — Fenton flew first and got permission later.

Of course it had to happen. Taking off at night from Manbulloo Station he couldn't quite clear a fence and that was the end of UJN. Again he walked away from the wreckage — practice, I suppose.

Then Qantas came up trumps with UIO (or IOU, whichever way you look at it) and said it was ready to fly once more. I suppose it would be difficult to work out who really owned it; perhaps Qantas thought they did and perhaps Jim Fawcett thought he did but as they say, "possession is nine parts of the law" and Clyde Fenton had possession. And anyway, while people were being bitten by death adders and battered by buffalo bulls all they could do was just pray he stayed alive.

Then, a tremendous blow. His sister, married to a Dutch diplomat stationed in China, died suddenly and his mother who was visiting her daughter at the time — and who wasn't in the best of health — was devastated.

Fenton's decision was instantaneous; he would fly to China to comfort his mother. His preparations did not include any time-wasting exercises such as getting permission from DCA. He just

336

left the bureaucrats to enjoy their apoplexy in comfort, but he did enlist the help of a plumber to recover the fuel tank from UJN, which was still at Manbulloo. There was the formidable Timor Sea to cross, 520 miles of it — all water, — and one tank was not enough. He and the plumber must have done a good job, because he got there.

I had problems. It was going to be a few weeks before I was back in the saddle and I had hide contracts on which I couldn't afford to default. Dick Guild was a tower of strength. He got in touch with Jolleys and the hide buyer and found out Hazel Gaden was looking for some shooting. He arranged it all; Gaden contracted to shoot 500, and I reckoned I should be out of hospital by the time he'd got that lot. He put Dave Cameron on a train to join up with Gaden until I got there while I settled down to make the best of my unsolicited comfort. It was a small hospital of six beds, a charge sister, a couple of half-caste trainee nurses and me as the only patient.

But my recovery didn't proceed as well as expected. No one was quite sure if anything was broken; there was no such thing as an X-ray. After a couple of weeks, to my alarm, my foot started to grow crooked. The sister got in touch with Darwin, there were no doctors to spare and I got the impression they weren't going to waste valuable time going all the way to Katherine to look at a buffalo shooter who had a sprained ankle or something. But there was a trained first aid man coming to Katherine next week, he would have a look at it. I resigned myself to an approaching inspection.

When he arrived at my bedside and had a look he seemed quite mystified. I could tell he hadn't seen anything quite like it before, though he wasn't letting on.

He went away and came back with a hammer, a saw and a collection of planks which, according to the stencilling on them, had previously been surrounding bottles of beer. After some preliminary measuring he started to saw and hammer away at the foot of the bed for the next half hour. He then warned me that "this might hurt" and started to pull my foot back into shape, or somewhere near it. There was no "might" about it hurting — it was bloody well excruciating. He strapped it up and left me grinding my teeth, saying he would probably be back in about a week. I began to worry about what sort of a foot I'd end up with. He eventually turned up again and uncovered his handiwork. I had to admit it looked in better shape; in fact it looked a bit like a foot. After some more sawing and hammering he had another go, which was no more pleasant than the previous experience, but I didn't mind as long as he got it back into working order.

When I eventually got away I was walking with difficulty and a bit lopsided. But I reckoned I'd be able to ride a horse, which was all I wanted. I caught the next train and went to Darwin. I had been in hospital seven and a half weeks.

My horses had gone down to Kapalga with Dave Cameron and now I had to arrange another contract for hides and order some more supplies. I had received word that Gaden was close to finishing his contract.

Over the last couple of years my circle of friends in Darwin had been increasing and one of my closest and most interesting mates was Fred Morris. He was born in Pine Creek and had joined the administration at an early age, but he never missed an opportunity to get out in the bush. He was quite a good horseman, having had a pony since he was knee-high to a grasshopper and had had to ride to school. He was also a particularly good bushman and quite capable of looking after himself if need be. But most importantly, he was excellent company.

He had quite a lot of leave coming to him and had already written to me in hospital, saying he hoped to put some of it in in my camp when I'd recovered. Right then his greatest pride and joy was a recently acquired Oldsmobile car, which seemed a massive great brute to me, and I was a bit staggered when he said we would

338

drive out to my camp. But I certainly wasn't going to talk him out of it; as a matter of fact I thought it was a marvellous idea.

We roared out of Darwin on a Sunday afternoon, my diary tells the first part of the journey:

June 14: "Left Darwin after dinner and went to Brocks Creek, 120 miles".

June 15: "Arrived Pine Creek and camped the night".

June 16: "Left Pine Creek this morning with a big load of benzine and spares. Reached Arnhem Land Mine (84 miles). Picked up a boy here from the blacks' camp."

June 17: "Left the mine this morning, got a good early start but only went about twelve miles and hit a stump and broke the stub axle. Sent the boy on to my camp explaining matters and instructions to send horses back. Will probably take him three days to walk down and the horses two days to get back."

June 18: "Sunk a soak in the creek bed for water, got a good supply."

June 19: "Went out hunting this morning for beef, only have about three days' rations. Shot a kangaroo. Went out in the afternoon pigeon shooting, returned to camp and found our messenger back. Announced 'No more savee that one country'!"

I was furious when he said that he didn't know the country, I said: "But before you talk you savee."

"Ui, me talk me think, now me look me no savee."

He stood scratching his head and digging the ground up with his big toe.

Fred said: "If he doesn't stop scratching his head he's going to get bloody splinters in his fingers."

"I suppose we'll have to walk, I can't see any way out of it." Fred nodded: "How do you feel about that? How far do you reckon it is?"

I would think it's about thirty-five miles to Kapalga, and the idea of walking doesn't appeal to me one little bit."

We took a blanket and a mosquito net each, a shotgun and all the cartridges we had, about a dozen. There was very little in the way of rations. I noted, "about enough for a couple of days".

It was a reasonably uneventful walk except the day we nearly succeeded in burning ourselves to death in a bush fire. I don't know why, but I never recorded it in the diary I carried with me — but I have no difficulty remembering it.

By midday the first day we came to the head of the plains. Stretching away into the shimmering distance like a greyish-green sea was a dence cover of heavily matted grass. It was not going to be easy walking for me. I looked at it for a while, then tossed a match into it. With a strong southerly behind it, it roared quickly away, leaving only a thick layer of black ash. We camped for an hour, boiling the billy and waiting for the ground to cool before we made another start.

Though the ground was still hot when we started off, at least we could see where we were going, and of course we were very soon black from head to foot. By sundown we had almost reached the limit of the burnt ground . . . and my endurance, too. We camped on a good waterhole, washed ourselves and freshened up. The fire seemed to have died out, which we hoped wouldn't happen; we thought it would burn through the night and clear the ground.

Our boy, whom we had christened Leichhardt after the explorer, told us there were some ducks further up the waterhole. Fred walked up and soon came back with a brace of fat Burdekin duck, and Leichhardt went off on his own hunting expedition and scored a goanna and a fat snake. There was no way we were going to starve.

The next morning we woke up as stiff as gidgee logs and looked at the prospect of walking through the matted grass. There was probably a half mile of burnt ground before we came to the grass. There were a few wisps of smoke rising but it was heavily dew-laden and it would be some time before it burned.

We got Leichhardt to walk ahead and pick as good a track as possible which, though wandering a bit, did help a lot. Fred was getting sore now; some years before he had been shot in the stomach with a harpoon (a careless fishing companion was to blame) and it was starting to give some trouble.

It was getting towards midday when Leichhardt drew our attention to the smoking grass, now about five miles behind us. "Fire 'e got up." We looked back. Black smoke was billowing along a fairly wide front and flames were beginning to develop. We were well out on the plains, but didn't realise our danger immediately.

Half an hour later the boy said, "Fire get up strong now."

We looked back. "Bloody Hell," said Fred, "we're in real trouble now!" We were in the middle of a plain that was three or four miles wide; to the east was the mangrove-fringed river, to the west, low-timbered ridges. The fire was developing some speed now. The flames were probably twenty feet high and racing toward us. The wind had come up, and of course a fire develops its own wind and becomes a blowtorch.

What unquestionably saved our lives was a small clump of timber about half a mile distant. These clumps were, in reality, quite dense jungle. Some kind of a leftover from perhaps hundreds of years previously, before the surrounding plains had become flooded. We could hear the fire as we tried to run toward the trees. We stumbled and fell, recovered our footing and stumbled on. The fire was roaring now. Our boy had no trouble; he was racing over the ground well ahead of us and after a while I knew we were going to make it . . . but only just. It was a frightening experience. We flung ourselves into the sheltering jungle and a few minutes later the fire lapped the edges. But it was so dense no grass had grown; there was a fairly thick covering of accumulated leaves that burnt along the outskirts in a desultory way.

We were both very frightened and it was some time before Fred got his customary grin working. "I think the fire fixed that ankle, the way you were flying over the ground," he joked.

"Well, I wouldn't exactly call my exhibition flying but it would

341

have fixed it permanently if I'd slowed down; and I can think of better ways of getting it fixed," I said.

We settled down for an hour or so spell to let the ground cool and after a while sent our boy off to see if he could find some water. There were usually buffalo wallows scattered over the plains, and they retained water for some time. Half an hour later he came back with a billycan full of water and ash, but that didn't matter. We made a billy of tea and it tasted none the worse for being fortified with burnt grass.

We made another start in the afternoon and at sundown caught up with a nice waterhole. Fred took the gun and came back with three pygmy geese and a couple of whistler ducks. The pygmy geese were pretty little things, smaller than the ducks and very good eating.

I wanted to reach Kapalga the next day, which would be quite a walk, but we both reckoned it would be better to make an effort and get it over and done with. We got a piccaninny-daylight start and made for the edge of the plains where the timber started. There was a fringe of pandanus along the edge, which was better travelling. The pandanus palm must have been some sort of a nesting area for possums, and they hadn't survived the fire. They were shrivelled and charred, and looked horrible with bared teeth where their mouths had been burned away.

Fred, the humorist, said: "That's what we would have looked like if that patch of scrub hadn't been there."

We reached Kapalga just before sundown, completely buggered. It was the furthest I've ever walked in my life.

The next morning I sent Leichhardt with a letter to Gaden, with instructions to follow the dray's wheel tracks, which were fairly fresh. I threatened Leichhardt with all kinds of dire consequences if he failed to find the buffalo camp, all of which he thought was hilarious, explaining that he was "bigfella 'ungry". I had no idea how far he might have to walk; the camp could be anywhere from the West Alligator, which was ten miles, to the Wildman or further.

After he had gone, Fred and I walked across to the river about a mile away. There were several hundred hides stacked and the jetty was in good order. I guessed he must be close to completing his contract, which suited me. I was looking forward to taking over my camp.

We were out of any sort of rations so we spent the rest of the day getting ourselves a feed. Kapalga billabong was fairly big and there was a good sprinkling of ducks and geese. I took the gun for a start and sat in a clump of cane grass while Fred walked round to the other end with the idea of chasing them across to me, but of course they weren't too co-operative. Few of them showed any great anxiety to get themselves shot, but we succeeded in dropping one good fat goose and three ducks. We had three cartridges left after that effort.

We were lucky. The next day three horses trotted up, driven by Clarry; one carried a pack and the other two saddles. There was a note from Dave in which he said the camp was at Red Lily on the West Alligator. In the pack bags was a fresh loaf of Dave's bread and some corned buffalo meat that never tasted better. We rode into the camp just before sundown. Gaden was there with another man, Arthur McKercher, who had been shooting for him over the last two months. He was a stranger to me, but a good horseman and bushman.

Dave Cameron had a good meal going and after we'd dealt with that Gaden and I settled down for a talk. His contract for 500 hides was nearly complete; he thought another fifty or so. It seemed his method of tallying was a bit haphazard. He said he was going across to Marrakai to shoot for Vesteys, which suited me. I wouldn't have taken over the camp from him after he had helped me out had he not had somewhere to go.

McKercher stayed with me; Gaden couldn't afford him at the price he was getting shooting for Vestey. I soon got back into my stride and in the process found I was the owner of a broken-down truck. Hazel Gaden's brother Jack had left it at Gipsy Spring when the radiator blew up. Jack was crocodile hunting down the

343

Wildman and he'd borrowed a couple of tons of my salt; later Hazel had lent him three horses. Hazel said Jack suggested I keep the truck and we call it all square.

I scratched my head and said; "Will the bloody thing go?"

"Oh, my word, yes. It only wants a radiator, and you could pick one up in Darwin for a tenner."

He got a couple of boys to pour water into the radiator and though it ran out faster than it went in, he started it up and ran it for a couple of minutes. I must admit I was quite impressed.

Well, to cut a long story short, I became the terrified owner of a thirty hundredweight Ford truck, which caused quite a sensation in the camp. Acquiring the knowledge necessary to navigate and maintain it was not without its moments. It had no lights and had probably never had a horn. A log tied behind when going downhill overcame the absence of brakes. I gained an insight into the ramifications of the petrol tank and carburettor when a billycan full of water, liberally laced with tea leaves, found its way into the tank instead of the radiator. Two of my most enthusiastic men, taking it in turns to pump up a tyre, discovered that something like 500 pounds to a square inch created an explosion approximately equal to half a dozen sticks of dynamite.

Then Bert Coombs died of thirst.

A modest rise in the price of buffalo hides usually produced a gaggle of embryo hunters who always seemed to have identical priorities. First on the list was getting lost; falling out with the blacks ran a close second. Bert Coombs ran true to form. He took up an area of country between the South and East Alligator River, gathered a few boys together, including my old friend Bamboo Charlie who, in spite of his declining years, was still a good shot.

He had a few horses and an old utility truck that had died of old age. It was an unusually dry year and waterholes were drying up at an alarming rate, which was a good thing for men of Coombs' limited experience because the buffalo became concentrated on the fewer waters.

He had to get hides to the jetty and to overcome the energy problems he hitched a couple of horses to the truck which, with a load of hides, proved too much for them. However, he solved that by taking the engine out and set off for the river landing, taking Bamboo Charlie and a lad of about fourteen, known as Little Charlie.

The first day they travelled about twelve miles to a lagoon they quite reasonably expected to have water. It was dry and baked hard. That night the horses were tied up, or they would have gone back to where they'd had their last drink. They had two water bags, but they had been drawn on during the day; one was empty, the other half-full. What was left was consumed during the night.

At first light they started off and long before midday were feeling the effects of thirst. Bamboo Charlie tried to talk Coombs into diverting to a spring he knew was still holding out, but with an obstinacy that defies reason Coombs refused. As soon as an opportunity presented itself Bamboo Charlie ran into a thicket of cane grass, calling on the boy to follow him. But Coombs was too quick; he grabbed the boy and held a rifle to his head telling the terrified lad he would shoot him if he attempted to run away. They reached the river . . . it was tidal and salt.

Coombs gave the boy a billycan to fill at the river while he lit a fire. He put the billy on the fire and when it boiled he held a towel over the steam in a fruitless endeavour to obtain fresh water by wringing it out. It was quite hopeless, of course, and while his attention was focused on the exercise Little Charlie slipped away.

The lad walked through the afternoon and into the night. His was an enduring fibre beyond his years. He walked until he came to the spring to which Coombs refused to deviate, and collapsed in the water. Simply and graphically he told me how he lay in the water for hours, drinking and drinking and drinking.

Coombs died, of course. He must have had a deathwish he

345

pursued with fanatical determination. Both Bamboo Charlie and Little Charlie were in my camp almost continuously through the following years.

Considering the trials and tribulations I was so unfairly subjected to, 1936 finished better than I'd expected. Counting Gaden's contract, the final hide tally was 1796.

I now held 500 square miles of country, about fifty head of horses, a motor truck of dubious value and lots of confidence.

A booming hide market greeted the start of 1937. Sevenpence halfpenny a pound meant my hides should average about £2.10s each. If the wet season weren't too heavy and I was able to start shooting by, say, May, I reckoned I could get 1500 hides.

As it turned out, I fired my first shots on April 28. My diary records three bulls.

My poor old truck did its best until one day there was a funny noise and it didn't take long to find out I had a broken piston. By this time I just about knew every nut and bolt personally. I took the sump off and was showered with bits of piston. I took the conrod off and carried on with three pistons for a while, but it was nowhere near as good as when it had four. Eventually I went into Darwin and bought a new Ford V8 two-ton truck, which was a miracle of modern engineering.

November 8. I loaded the last lot of hides on to the *Maroubra*. The final count 1728. I settled in for the wet season and on December 11, a boy woke me up in the middle of the night with a letter from Cowboy Collins who had joined Jack Gaden. It seemed Gaden was seriously ill; could I get a message through to the Flying Doctor? First things first. At the crack of dawn next day I carted a couple of forty-four gallon drums to the river, lashed them together and slid them into the water. I put a couple of boys aboard with a letter to Oenpelli Mission, asking them to get in touch with the Flying Doctor with their pedal radio. I watched them until they reached the other side and disappeared into the mangroves. They had forty-odd miles to walk; I reckoned that with Collins and his boys we could hack an aerodrome out before Fenton arrived.

I then set off for Gaden's camp, about twenty miles away. He was in a bad way right enough; it seemed like appendicitis, so we put him in the back of the truck and started back.

With twenty boys we worked all that afternoon and all night, and by midday the next day reckoned we had a suitable landing (if not taking-off) ground.

My truck had taken a battering. In order to put in a short cut the axe-men would cut nearly through a tree, then I would back into it with the truck, knock it over and drag it to one side. I was under my truck tightening up U-bolts that held the body on when I heard Collins call out, "Jesus Christ! He's here!" I knew who he was talking about, of course.

It was twelve months before I saw Jack Gaden again. Obviously the operation was successful.

January 1. Though there had been storms there was no sign of the monsoonal rains and the country was still firm. I decided to make a dash for Pine Creek. Three days later I reached Goodparla Station. George Stevens, who owned it with his brother Fred, was at the homestead. Since their father died they had lost interest in the cattle stations. In addition to Goodparla, they owned Esmeralda and Dorisvale stations.

George asked me if I wanted a cattle station — he'd sell Goodparla cheap. A cattle station? No, I didn't want a cattle station; I had enough on my hands now. From curiosity I asked what he wanted for it.

"We'll take £400 for it, walk-in-walk-out."

"£400! Are you serious?"

"Yes, I'm serious; we've already sold Dorisvale to Jack Liddy, and George Murray the drover bought Esmeralda."

This certainly gave me something to think about. I knew quite a lot about it, having ridden through it a number of times between Pine Creek and the buffalo country. I knew it was 840 square miles and was supposed to have 5000 to 7000 head of cattle, which I thought was doubtful: I reckoned there were probably 4000.

It was originally taken up and stocked by George Cooke, who

had died a year or so back. He was a good cattleman in his day but the last few years of his life had been devoted to drinking himself to death. He was a dedicated rum drinker until he found that methylated spirits, at a fraction of the price, provided a shortcut. Had he stuck to rum he would probably have hung on for another six months. Goodparla came on the market and George Stevens senior bought it. Shortly afterward, he too crossed the "Great Divide".

I slept on it, or partly slept on it — actually my head was working like a tin of worms. Goodparla Station for £400 seemed ridiculous. I decided to have a good look at it and in the morning we set off on an inspection. After three days I'd seen enough to convince me it was a gift and I put a proposition to him. I explained that though I'd had a good year shooting I'd also had a lot of bad debts and didn't have that much spare cash. The best I could do, was £100 deposit and £100 every quarter. I didn't expect him to take it and anticipated some upward haggling, but to my surprise he did. We sat down under a gum tree and on pages taken from our diaries, exchanged letters. Mine contained the offer and George's the acceptance. No mention was made of any interest, and I had no intention of spoiling a good deal with inconsequential detail.

The next day we rode to Pine Creek; I caught Leaping Lena and early Monday morning arranged for a document to be drawn up. Gerald Piggot, the Director of Lands, was good enough to supervise the wording and his secretary, with whom I had a previous passing acquaintance, typed it out, for which I paid her £1. Her gratitude was so touching I made a mental resolution to take the friendship a few steps further. However, that was nipped in the bud when she — foolishly (I thought) — exchanged vows to "love, honour and obey" some character. This may have been a blessing in disguise: the next time I saw her she measured two axe handles across the backside, had three chins and four children.

I returned to Pine Creek and on January 27 took over Goodparla Station officially.

I wasn't sure what I'd landed myself with, but decided to let nature take its course. At the hotel I got hold of a man to do some yard building, took him out, pegged out a couple of yards and left him to it.

Then it really started to rain, which was normal because it was February. In March I went to Darwin to find out what was happening in the great big outside world. As I anticipated, the buffalo hide market had dropped to something like a normal level. I took a couple of contracts and ordered stores and supplies for the shooting season, which would perhaps go out in May. I returned to Pine Creek and was told the Mary River, halfway between the township and Goodparla, was half a mile wide so I settled down to improve the local publican's income.

I had become something of a curiosity; it was rumoured I'd bought Goodparla Station for something between £500 and £1000 — "He must be out of his bloody mind," they said. Something I was beginning to think myself.

When the river settled down I got myself together and went out to my latest acquisition. Mick Madigan, the yard builder was at the homestead. He'd finished the yards, I paid him for his work and let him loose again.

It was now May. I wrote a letter to Monty O'Sullivan offering him the job of running Goodparla and headed for the buffalo country. Dave Cameron was pleased to see me; I wasn't sure whether it was because he was nearly out of rations or on account of the rum I'd brought. When I told him I'd bought a cattle station his only remark was "what, only one!"

Fred Gray and his lugger, the *Oituli*, turned up with my cargo, explaining that the *Maroubra* was on the slips and that Jack Hales had asked him to drop my load off as he was going that way.

The country was slow drying out. When I did start shooting I found the buffalo were scarce; the heavy shooting of the previous year was noticeable.

By June I had shot more than 400 buffalo and there was no sign of the *Maroubra* so I loaded the truck with hides and went to Darwin. The *Maroubra* was at the wharf and Hales was at the pub; he bought me a drink and said he'd be out in a couple of weeks for sure. Then Fred Hardy walked in and joined us. I was surprised to see him because he'd sold his cattle and buffalo-shooting place to Gregory the pearler and retired to Perth. "What are you doing back in Darwin, Fred?"

"I've come back to get warm, I made the biggest mistake of my life selling Mt Bundey; I bloody nearly froze to death in Perth."

We talked for a while, then an idea started to germinate in my mind.

"I take it you'd like to come back and live here again," I said.

"Yes," he replied, "I certainly would if I had something to come back to. I wouldn't want to live in Darwin doing nothing, though."

I then told him about Goodparla and immediately he became interested. He started to question me, all the important questions — water, fencing, stockyards, what cattle were on the place.

It would have been no good trying to fool an old fox like Fred, and I gave him as accurate a description as I could. I told him there was reputed to be 5000 or 6000 head of cattle, but I thought 3000 would be a fair estimate. I told him I had recently got a couple of stockyards built and that over the last two or three years it had been neglected. The cattle were pretty wild, but not entirely out of hand.

He then asked the important question; what sort of a price did I have on it? I said, "A thousand pounds, walk-in-walk-out," and held my breath waiting for his reply. He took a couple of pulls at his whisky before answering and I was starting to breathe hard.

"I'll think it over. Where can I get hold of you?"

"I'll be here at the pub at ten o'clock." And we parted.

The next morning I was at the pub exactly at ten and Fred joined me shortly after. He didn't waste any time on preliminaries, "I'd like to have an inspection of Goodparla and if comes up to your description I'll probably buy — when could we get away?"

"Give me an hour and we're as good as halfway there."

"No, no," he laughed. "I can't get away before tomorrow morning. What about seven o'clock?"

He was staying with a friend and I was at the house on the stroke of seven. At the buffalo camp we got saddle and pack horses and I picked a couple of boys for the horse tailing. Two days' ride brought us on to the Goodparla country and after four days Hardy was satisfied. He only made one condition; he insisted I deliver thirty head of working horses, which was fair enough. There were only twenty-two in the paddock — I knew there were more running outside the paddock but I didn't intend wasting time looking for them. I sent word to Dick Guild asking him to deliver eight head of good stock horses to Hardy.

Fred went to Darwin and we were to meet again for the delivery date in one month. When everything was finished I went back to my buffalo camp thinking I was a bit of a genius. I'd spent £100 and made £600 profit in a few weeks.

McKercher had been doing fairly well, but the tallies were down on last year, which was to be expected with the heavy shooting of the previous season and my being away from the camp so much I thought we hadn't done too badly; the final count was a few more than 1100.

The camp was paid off but after a week and the inevitable corroboree I was thinking of a horse muster. I had kept George, Clarry and Little Charlie for the wet season, there were some foals to be branded and two or three youngsters ready to break in. There was a family of horses running up the river.

I left at the same time as a group starting their walkabout; a few of my mob and their family with a few "friends" who had turned up for the payoff, which added up to about twenty. I camped at Ingarabba where I had a yard and a house, it wasn't far from where

351

the walkabout blacks would cross the river. Bamboo Charlie, an important man at any corroboree and Maudie, his wife, were among them.

They left to catch the top of the tide; there was no current to sweep them up or down the river. Two or three hours later I was busy drafting horses when several boys came running breathlessly up to the yard calling, "Boss! Boss! Maudie go finish, big fella alligator eat him finish!"

The shock of this only took a second or so to sink in. I was horrified. It only seemed like a few moments ago when they had set off for the river laughing, joking, scolding their dogs, calling to the children to hurry.

Maudie taken by a crocodile — I just couldn't believe it. I quickly saddled a horse and rode across to the river; the plain was partly flooded and I had to leave my horse and walk the last few hundred yards.

I reached the mangroves where they were all grouped together crying and wailing. I picked out a fellow who seemed fairly well in control of himself and asked what happened.

He said they had started to swim and were fairly well strung out. The children were clinging to logs that were being pushed by the men; the women were behind. Maudie and another, sharing a log, were last of all. As far as I could understand Maudie and her companion were only about twenty yards from the bank. The crocodile came up behind and swam over the top of her, grasping her with its forefeet, and dived. She never uttered a sound, a moment later it reappeared briefly with Maudie in its jaws. They never saw her again.

They all came back from the river just before sundown. As I'd expected, they had not sighted the crocodile. In the morning Bamboo Charlie asked for a rifle; he wanted to stay on the river until he saw it and shoot it but I felt sure it wouldn't show up for a day or so. He agreed with me but I think he felt he had some kind of duty to keep watch.

I suggested he go out and shoot a wild pig, there were plenty about, to which he agreed. His shooting licence was still current — not that that would have bothered me. He came back with two, a young sow and an old boar.

They dressed the young pig and I took half. They had a wailing feast that night with half of the young sow and half of the boar. What was left they put in a couple of bags and took it to the river where they hung the meat in the mangroves high enough above the ground to keep it from being taken. It putrefied quickly in the hot sun and in a couple of days was an effective attraction. On the second day they shot a young crocodile about eight feet long, but didn't bother opening it up.

On the fourth day, just before sundown, the maneater appeared. It only took one shot. They opened it up and inside found a quantity of Maudie's bones, which they washed carefully and wrapped in paperbark. Most of that night was spent crying and wailing and in the morning Bamboo Charlie said they were leaving. He asked if I would like to see the bones, but I couldn't bring myself to look at them. She was a dear old thing.

They all left together. Their intention was to cross the river close to the Jim Jim junction where it was shallow and easily crossed. They had been put off swimming for some time.

Intense military activity marked 1939. The sabre-rattling in Europe could be clearly heard — even in Darwin. The army arrived and the RAAF established itself; even the navy gave us a wave as it went past.

The buffalo hide market improved, but didn't reach its 1937 level. The demand was so strong I didn't take any contracts, thinking maybe there would be another rise . . . which turned out to be a mistake.

I had a good camp, I was well established, had a good lot of horses and, as I wouldn't hesitate to tell my fellow hunters, some of the best shooting horses on the coast — Trinket, Dollar, Isobel and Magic. I had a truck which, though starting to look a bit battered, was in good working order. I had all the equipment I needed and 500 square miles of country. The last thing I wanted was a war.

George Stevens joined me; the idea of buffalo shooting appealed to him. He was a good horseman and more than welcome. The camp swung into gear in the middle of May and everything went like a well-oiled piece of machinery. Then I received a letter from Major Jim Thyer, whom I had met previously, asking me to call on him at Larrakeyah Barracks at my earliest convenience. Overflowing with curiosity I presented myself at the barracks where I was welcomed by Jim Thyer and a captain.

Even at that stage the military hierarchy had no illusion about Japan. The coast of northern Australia was swarming with Japanese working the pearling luggers. They were reputed to have better maps and charts than we did — which was easy to believe. The maps of the hinterland were very sketchy and far from accurate. The West Alligator River, I pointed out, was probably about ten miles out.

When I left the barracks I had become MRO 3, which stood for Military Reporting Officer No 3, attached to the Intelligence Section of The 7th Military District. My duties were to report anything of a suspicious nature, with particular attention to Japanese activities. I was given a fictitious name and a box number to forward reports — and we didn't even have a war.

Before I left Darwin I met Sam Rogers, who had a letter of introduction to me from a mutual friend. He was keen to have a look at buffalo hunting and I was glad of his company. He was a good bushman, having had some experience on Queensland cattle stations. He proved more than useful in the camp, fitting in like an old hand — and, as I remarked to him one day, I didn't have to pay him. We became lifelong friends.

On the way back to the camp we pulled in to the Adelaide River Roadhouse, which had sprung up recently and was run by a wild Irishman, Harry Gribbon. The place was seething with activity in

354

preparation for a picnic race meeting. Fred Hardy was there, full of enthusiasm. At the bar he told me he had put the brown Beetaloo horse into feed and was training it for the Adelaide River Cup, which he declared he would win for sure. Fred intended riding the horse himself. He had named the horse Goodparla King.

Once we left Adelaide River, which was on the Overland Telegraph Line, we left our last source of information and news behind. Radio broadcasting had not reached the Northern Territory, and there was no such thing as a radio set in any Darwin stores. But in spite of the lack of news (or perhaps because of it) there was a good deal of anxiety felt by most people. Though the world was just pulling out of a terrible depression we probably didn't realise that the international arms buildup was largely responsible. The coming explosion was inevitable.

I carried on shooting and hoped for the best. I endeavoured to rectify a couple of maps for the army and picked a site for an aerodrome. I got a story about what sounded like an oil dump on Pussycat Island at the mouth of the Adelaide River, which I reported but which turned out to be a few drums of fuel oil jettisoned by a trawler in difficulties.

We were getting close to 1000 hides and salt was becoming low, so I loaded the truck and made a dash for Darwin. I got to Adelaide River a week after the picnic race meeting . . . and six days after Fred Hardy was buried. Goodparla King fell in the Adelaide River Cup, and Fred was thrown directly into the path of several horses. He suffered severe head injuries and never regained consciousness.

I was terribly shocked. I had known him for nearly ten years and had liked him; he was a good man to deal with and as straight as a gun barrel. I had sold him the horse that had fallen and I couldn't help feeling that in an indirect way I had made a contribution to his death. I realised I was in no way to blame, but the thought remained with me that if only it had been a different horse. I suppose it was one of those things.

I went on to Darwin in a subdued mood. There was no good

355

news; the buffalo hide market had dropped substantially and I regretted I had not taken a contract. Germany had invaded Poland. I loaded up with salt and headed back.

I reached Adelaide River; it was September 3. That night a group of us was huddled round a radio some surveyors had brought into Harry Gribbon's. We listened to the Prime Minister, Robert Menzies, announce: "Fellow Australians, it is my melancholy duty to inform you that we are at war with Germany."

Shortly afterwards, I shot my last buffalo.

It was forty-five years before I saw Arnhem Land again. I drove out from Darwin to the South Alligator River in four and a half hours, meeting ore trucks hurtling over a bitumen road. I drove down to the river, now spanned by a massive concrete bridge at almost the same spot where Maudie was taken by a crocodile. I called at a ranger station at the place where my homestead used to be. Walking around I picked up a few exploded .303 calibre shell cases. Only the ghosts were there.

The Northern Territory

The Canning Stock Route
between Halls Creek and Wiluna

Leaseholdings in the buffalo country east of Darwin

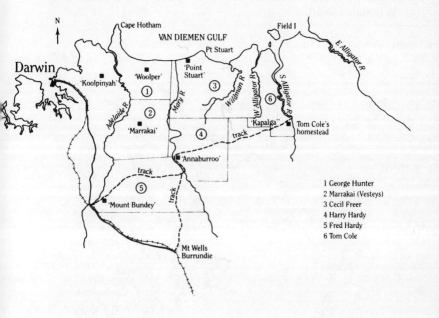

N

Cape Hotham

VAN DIEMEN GULF

Field I

Pt Stuart

E. Alligator R.

Darwin

'Koolpinyah'   'Woolper'   'Point Stuart'

①

'Point
Stuart'

③

Mary R.

Wildman R.

W. Alligator R.

S. Alligator R.

⑥

Adelaide R.

②

'Marrakai'

④

track   'Kapalga'   Tom Cole's homestead

'Annaburroo'

track   ⑤

track

'Mount Bundey'

Mt Wells
Burrundie

1 George Hunter
2 Marrakai (Vesteys)
3 Cecil Freer
4 Harry Hardy
5 Fred Hardy
6 Tom Cole

Arnhem Land

Japanese fishermen were speared at Caledon Bay in September 1932. Mounted Constable Stewart McColl was murdered on Woodah Island.

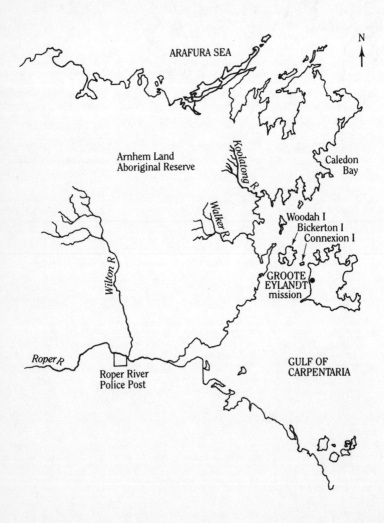

ARAFURA SEA

N

Arnhem Land
Aboriginal Reserve

Koolatong R

Caledon
Bay

Walker R

Woodah I
Bickerton I
Connexion I

Wilton R

GROOTE
EYLANDT
mission

Roper R

Roper River
Police Post

GULF OF
CARPENTARIA